WRONG ORDER

ALICE LI

This book is a work of fiction. Any references to historical events, real people, or real places are used fictitiously. Other names, characters, places, and events are products of the author's imagination, and any resemblance to actual events, places, names, or persons, is entirely coincidental.

Illustrated characters by Esther J Kim
Cover Design by Sarah Kil Creative Studio
Distributed by Simon & Schuster

ISBN: 978-1-998672-36-3
Ebook: 978-1-998672-37-0

FIC027340 - Romance/Billionaires
FIC027020 - Romance/Contemporary
FIC054000 - Asian American

#WrongOrder

Follow Rising Action on our socials!
Twitter: @RAPubCollective
Instagram: @risingactionpublishingco
Tiktok: @risingactionpublishingco

To Elizabeth

Thank you for being the first person to hear this idea, and for giving it a title. Without you, this would still be labeled FINAL in my files.

And to Nilda

Thank you for setting off my writing journey. You did so much more than you'll ever know, and none of this would've been possible without you.

WRONG ORDER

One

Sophie

Joseph's was a dump.

The floors were permanently stained two shades too dark, the windows smudged, and mixed-up orders ran amok.

But being fast and cheap in New York City overrode the fact the place served mediocre coffee akin to brown dishwater. And since it sat only a few blocks from Sophie's job, it counted her amongst its hodge-podge of regulars.

As the assistant to Marilyn Covey, the CEO of a boutique PR firm in Manhattan, Sophie was expected to attend almost every meeting her boss did. The company only had five employees besides them, although Marilyn had growth plans.

Sophie certainly didn't have time to wait around for her correct order. But she was gunning for a promotion, and that sure as hell wasn't happening without caffeine in her system.

Checking her phone for the time, she pursed her lips.

There was a nine o'clock briefing she needed to get to on the Shasta campaign, but Marilyn would understand if Sophie ran a few minutes late.

Hopefully.

Low pop music filtered through Sophie's earbuds and she gritted her teeth, sidestepping a Wet Floor sign.

Their current account director was stepping into retirement next month, and Sophie determined that when she took the position at Covey, the first thing she was going to do was convince Marilyn to build in a ten-minute leeway period for meetings.

The barista called her name and set a cup amongst the crowd of others squatting on the counter beside the dinged espresso machine. "Sorry about that."

"Don't worry about it."

She reached for the cup, and the rose-gold bracelet her mom had gifted her slid down her wrist.

"This was the bracelet I bought when I first moved to the U.S," her mom had confessed as she slipped the accessory on Sophie's wrist. "I was somewhere new and strange, and yes, your grandparents were with me, but I was still scared. But this bracelet ... whenever I saw it on myself, it was a reminder to stay brave. And later with your father ... I needed it again. But now, it's a reminder for you."

She had kissed Sophie's cheeks and continued, "Never back down, XiǎoDān."

And look at me now.

Rearing for a huge promotion after only five years.

Sophie reached for the iced coffee, but before she swooped up the drink, a large hand closed around it. The condensation on the plastic cup formed water droplets that ran over long fingers.

"What–hey! That's mine." She whipped her head toward the person who took her coffee and marched straight into a hurricane.

Something close to recognition seared through her, but that couldn't be right. Maybe she just recognized the type of aura emanating from him.

Power, bright and alarming, rolled off broad shoulders. It was hard to put her finger on it, but he wore a distinct elegance that screamed of generational wealth.

The man pulled his earbud from his ear and took his phone from his pocket before saying something in German. Frowning, he hit a button. "Sorry, what did you say?"

Sophie bristled. She didn't care how much money he had; he was still being a dick. "I said that's my coffee. They had to remake it."

He raised a dark brow and glanced at the cup in the dim light. "Your name's Sofa?"

Glaring at the man, she tipped her chin up. "*Sophie.*"

She met his gaze despite his impressive height and sucked in a breath.

Dark brown eyes lay under a pair of shockingly perfect, sculpted eyebrows, and his black hair, slicked up with pomade, lent an even more polished countenance. His face narrowed to a point at his chin, but he boasted a strong jawline and high cheekbones, which rounded out his look.

Full lips quirked. "Well. It says otherwise here."

Sophie sighed, crossing her arms, and a flash caught her eye.

A shining, silver Rolex glinted against the man's inky black designer suit.

Her gaze traveled to where his sleeves cuffed at his elbows, revealing a gorgeous tattoo that snaked over veiny forearms.

A large compass lay under a bouquet of roses, formed from playing cards. Waves and climbing vines filled the spaces in between, ducking around his wrist and elbow. Anything higher than the roses disappeared into the cuff of his suit jacket, leaving no uncertainty behind it was a full sleeve.

He shifted, and the dark tips poking out from his shirt collar, connecting to something unseen, pulled with the movement.

She cleared her throat, looking away. If she met him before, she certainly didn't remember when or where.

"I ... look," she stammered. "Just give me my coffee."

The man glanced at the murky, brown, iced contraption in his hand before brandishing the cup at her. "Right. Well. Here's your coffee, Sofa."

Sparks of unwarranted tension sizzled in the air, flashing in her vision.

Her lip curled, but she took the drink from him. She didn't have time to argue.

Muttering a thanks, she turned on her heel and strode toward the entrance.

She felt his eyes on her, a heavy weight that didn't seem to lessen with the distance, but she didn't dare turn around.

"You're sure it wasn't a celebrity?" Chloe asked.

Sophie grabbed her plastic cup of iced coffee from the wrought iron table. "Why would he be a celebrity?"

She fanned herself with her hand.

Mid-August in Manhattan always brought boiling breezes, sunny, melting days, and a cloying scent of rotting garbage. Altogether, she wanted to claw her skin off and get a Rhinoplasty.

The cold drink was a welcome relief, though Sophie was the type only to drink iced coffee, year-round.

"You said he was hot and rich, which I know doesn't equal celebrity, but still." Her friend re-propped her cane against the table.

"Uh, no," Sophie corrected. "I said he was well-off. I mean, he had on a designer suit, for God's sake!"

"So what if he did?" Chloe asked. "That doesn't imply well-off. He could've picked it up for ten bucks at a thrift store. Also, New York City gets its fair share of oddities. You know, I saw a woman wearing a fur coat on the subway the other day, like one of those, 'I just murdered my husband for his life insurance policy' coats. And it's August!"

Sophie chuckled. "Okay, fair point. However, he also wore a Rolex. I mean, come on."

Chloe sipped her iced matcha latte. "Maybe he's really committing to the bit."

"Chloe."

"Alright, alright. I'll admit that's not something someone

would wear at a place like Joseph's."

"Thank you!"

Her dark eyes widened. "Oh, my God, you don't think it was part of a bet, do you? You know, to make him seem more down to Earth? Because you said you'd never seen him there before, right?"

Sophie sighed and set down her coffee only to reach back and readjust her long, dark ponytail with damp hands.

Summer days under the blazing sun were when she hated having black hair.

"Or maybe– and hear me out: he just likes it."

"Who in their right mind "just likes" Joseph's?" Chloe demanded. "Especially when they could afford whatever coffee they wanted?"

Unlike Sophie, Chloe's hair was down in a dark cloud around her shoulders. She didn't even seem to be breaking a sweat.

Sophie adjusted her shirt, smoothing it out so no wrinkles covered the cute, cartoon cat. "Okay, true."

Maybe Chloe was right, and that man *was* doing it for the paparazzi.

But Joseph's occasionally had rats, and she didn't think even a

D-Lister would stoop that low.

"Did you get his name?" Chloe chewed on her straw and angled her body toward Sophie. "You should look him up."

"I didn't," Sophie responded. "I don't know, I feel like I've seen him before, but ..."

Was he one of Covey's previous clients?

She rarely forgot anyone who entered their offices, but the possibility wasn't zero.

"Whatever. I'm sure it'll come to me," she said. "Oh, we had this case that came through the other day. I can't go into details, but it's pretty big. And it's making me think Marilyn is definitely going to promote me."

Chloe scoffed. "Uh, duh? It's about time she saw your potential. You've been working for Covey since you moved here, and you've been fantastic at it. I mean, who *willingly* puts in so much overtime, or goes in early?"

Sophie shrugged. "I just want to make sure she gets the materials she needs on time."

"Exactly, *and* you've got a pretty good relationship with your coworkers." Chloe shook her head. "But is Marilyn promoting you? No. You work too damn much to keep going unappreciated like that."

"Chlo," Sophie muttered. "You know why I work so much."

"I know." Chloe sighed and gave a wry smile. "I still can't believe you've been like this since before I even met you."

Sophie snorted and chewed on her dilapidated straw. *Believe me, I don't want to be.*

But what choice did she have?

Her dad walked out on their family when she was far too young, and her mom nearly broke herself trying to glue things back together.

It wasn't Sophie's job to fix things, but she couldn't help trying.

She didn't just deserve the account director position; she *earned* it.

With all her hard work, making account director should've been a piece of cake. But Marilyn posed an unforeseen obstacle.

Sophie walked into Joseph's on Monday to find the usual short line and the familiar smell of burnt coffee beans in the air.

She pulled out her phone while she waited to order, the memory of her last visit flooding her mind. Today, she prayed she could get in and out of Joseph's without any weird encounters with strangers stealing her coffee, even if that particular stranger had been easy on the eyes.

She dipped her attention to the group chat with her friends.

It wasn't even eight thirty in the morning yet, but sixteen unread messages from Oliver and Chloe, exclusively in Korean, sat in their group chat.

"I'll do a medium coffee, no cream, one sugar, and a blueberry muffin."

Her head lurched up, and she glanced at the glass display case. *There was only one left before, please let them have restocked ... NO.*

She groaned under her breath. She already ran late again, and she'd run out of her good mascara that morning, after having only finished one eye. And now, the only person separating her from the register had taken the last blueberry muffin.

Fucking great.

Pocketing her phone, she ordered her usual and moved to the pickup area.

"Here."

A hand extended a paper bag, the starchy brown material emanating a magnetic smell.

Tilting her chin further up, she met the piercing gaze of the man from Friday.

Again, the feeling she'd seen him somewhere before rushed through the gate that slammed inside her.

Her gaze flicked between him and the bag. "I'm sorry?"

"Here," he repeated. "Take the muffin, I don't want it."

Her eyes narrowed as she cautiously retrieved the bag from his grasp. As she did, she caught the glimmer of a limited edition Patek Phillipe watch poking out from under his blazer sleeve.

Why did this guy own so many damn watches?

Do the rich need a reason to do anything? She peered into the bag and beheld a blueberry muffin. "I ... what?"

He shrugged. "It was going to be my breakfast, but I'm not as hungry as I thought. I heard you ordering one on Friday, so ... here. Think of it as an olive branch for taking your coffee."

He remembered that? More importantly, when had he even heard her order? He'd had an earbud in, right?

But her heart stumbled, sending her crashing straight into a brick wall.

She'd had exes who couldn't even remember her damn birthday, but a stranger in a second-rate coffee shop recalled her order from a random Friday?

Was this some scheme? Was she about to get kidnapped? Was the muffin a signal to someone else? Once she accepted it, was a white van going to pull up in front of the coffee shop?

Her therapist's voice in her head reminded her that it was a little much.

But Sophie heard too many horror stories to keep her mind from wandering there, not to mention the trust issues she harbored.

She mentally saluted the man who had abandoned his family. *Thanks, Dad.*

"Look, I understand your hesitation," he said. "But the muffin's not going to eat itself."

He has a point ... and if he's not going to eat it ...

Taking a deep breath, she closed her hand around the bag, the paper rustling with her touch. "Um ... thanks."

He nodded.

She stood there, not sure what else to say. What *did* you say to someone who gave up their breakfast for you?

"James."

She was going to get whiplash from the number of times she looked up at him suddenly. "What?"

His gaze sketched down to her, lingering for a second too long before focusing ahead of him again. "My name. It's James."

She struggled to find the right words. "I ... okay."

He raised his voice slightly to be heard over the rattle of the coffee grinder. "I thought it'd be polite, since I know your name."

He smiled slightly and *fuck.* A brief tilting of the lips shouldn't have been so attractive.

But on his full lips, it was.

Oh, God, what was wrong with her? Why was this stranger who took her coffee and called her a sofa, making her weak in the knees?

Did you learn nothing from your exes?! Or did turning twenty-eight do something to your brain?

She swallowed. "Uh, okay. Is it just James, or do you have a last name?"

He considered for a moment. "Tian."

"Oh, like the shipping company?"

A small smile touched his lips. "Same spelling, but I'm not associated with them. What about you? Last name?"

"Huang."

She didn't consider it wrong to give him her last name. After all, there were probably hundreds of Huangs in Manhattan alone, and she was willing to bet more than a handful of those were Sophies.

Besides, he didn't strike her as a psychotic killer.

Chloe's voice popped into her head. '*Hey, remember when we watched* American Psycho*?*'

James plucked a cup from the counter and extended it to her. "Your coffee, Sophie Huang."

She reached for the cup. "Thanks."

His fingers brushed hers, and she couldn't help it–her breath hitched. It was a miracle she didn't drop the coffee entirely.

Warmth seeped into her fingers, and she frowned.

"Hang on, this isn't mine," she said. "Did they mess it up again?"

She swore she ordered an iced coffee.

"No, they didn't mess it up. Rotate it."

Twisting the blue and white cup, she inspected the name scrawled at the top.

'James'

Her gaze lifted. "This is–you can't give me your coffee *and* your muffin."

That was way too much. He just met her. Who was he to willingly hand over his entire breakfast?

But you're taking it.

He lifted a shoulder. "I just did."

She sighed. "Okay, well. How do you know I'll even–"

She cut off as his order drifted back to her. *'I'll do a medium coffee, no cream, and one sugar.'*

Aside from the hot coffee, that was *her* order.

He tilted his head. "Did I get it?"

Clearing her throat, she clutched the cup. "Right, well. Uh. Do you have the time?"

He hitched up the sleeve of his blazer to check his glimmering watch.

"Eight-twenty."

"Shit," she muttered.

She started to turn on her heel, but stopped and raised the cup towards him. "Thanks for the coffee, James Tian."

Now that she had his full name, she knew it sounded familiar, but still couldn't place why.

Making a mental note to Google him later, she rushed out the door.

Two

Sophie

Sophie tacked onto the end of the fast-moving line inside Joseph's, brushing strands of hair out of her face.

Hitting her phone's home screen, she winced. She needed to get out of her apartment earlier.

One of the men in front of her turned to say something to his companion, and she started as James's side profile hit her.

Cheeks burning, she ran through options of what to say in her head.

'Hey!'–No, that's too generic–Oh, maybe, 'Thanks for the muffin?'–Wait, is opening without a greeting too rude? Maybe it's better not to say anything?

James's friend ran a hand through his dark brown hair, mussing the artfully styled strands. "... You did that? Why?"

James sighed. "I don't–"

"Wait, is that why your stomach was growling throughout the morning meeting?" The other man's Spanish accent soaked his words.

"How do you know that was me?"

He raised a brow. "Really? I swear, Gemma was a second away from kicking you out. Anyway, you never give me your muffins. Why? I thought you loved me. *Give me your muffins.*"

"Oh, fuck off. Also–" James caught Sophie's gaze. "Oh. Hi."

"Uh, hi." Immediately, she lowered the hand she'd lifted

in a wave. "Um ... thanks again for yesterday."

"Sure thing," he said.

Their gazes lingered on each other before the other man cleared his throat.

Sophie tore her gaze away. "Oh, hi, I don't believe we've met."

Redirecting her attention, she was hit with a pair of dark brown eyes, cheekbones, and a jawline that could cut glass ... and a startling sense of familiarity.

The man threw on a dazzling smile and stuck out his hand, his sleeve contrasting against his tanned, pale skin. "Philip Solano Castillo. But I go by Philip Solano."

At his name, something floated through Sophie's head—an article or headline. But the answers remained out of reach, taunting her.

Hm. Curiouser and curiouser.

Work bogged her down before she could look James up the day before, and now with Philip ... she made another note of it.

"Next!"

Philip's awkward smile fell away from her as he turned.

They moved to the pickup area, and she placed her order, taking two pastry bags from the barista.

Walking over to James, she extended one. "Here."

He appraised the bag with a raised brow. "Sorry?"

The sparse LEDs embedded into Joseph's ceiling glared down on her, transforming into a million blinding spotlights. "It's a blueberry muffin."

The corners of Philip's mouth twitched. "Your favorite, cabrón."

Sophie frowned. "I'm sorry, did you just call him a bastard?"

"It's an affectionate nickname," James explained. "Kind of an inside joke we have. It's a long story. Anyway, thanks for this,"—he took the bag, his fingers brushing hers—"you didn't have to."

Sparks danced unbidden up her arm, and she shivered.

"Well, *you* didn't have to give me your breakfast."

"You looked like you were in a rush."

"Yes, but your stomach suffered."

He shrugged. "Worth it."

Philip cleared his throat loudly.

James shot his friend a glance. "Remind me why you're here, Pip?"

Philip narrowed his eyes. "Ay, cabrón de corazón negro. What did I say about calling me that in public?"

"Hm. Is that any way to talk to someone who bought you coffee, and got you a job at my company?" James mused.

Sophie's smile faded. *'My company?'*

"Uh ... I'm sorry," she started, suspicion lingering in her gut. "Where exactly do you two w–"

The barista called Philip's name, and he went up to get the drinks. Frowning, he waved the barista over.

"Oh, looks like they got it wrong," she said. "Hope work doesn't start soon."

"We've got some time." James's hand moved in her peripheral vision to rub the back of his neck. "Question is, do you?"

"Been paying attention to my work schedule?"

"I've been told I'm observant." He shrugged.

"How'd they say it? That can be a con," she deadpanned.

He threw her a pointed look, and her lips twitched.

"If anything, it's a skill in my line of work."

"Right, what is that exactly?"

"Are you free Friday?"

Damn, that was smooth. She scoffed, crossing her arms. "I'm off at six," she said.

A full smile soared on his lips, softening the hard planes of his expression. "Perfect. I'll tell you at dinner."

"Bold of you to assume I'll agree."

He nodded, feigning nonchalance. "Do you? If you don't, we obviously don't have–"

"I never said no," she interjected.

Another delicious smile spread across his lips. "Okay,

then."

Her lungs tied themselves in a knot. "Okay." *What just happened?*

She never took a risk like that. Not since the party when she was a freshman in college, and she'd let loose for just a second, and everything fell apart.

But a slight frown, one he couldn't quite hide, marred his forehead. Almost like he was scared she would take it all back, and it was strangely endearing.

"So, Friday. Six-thirty work?" he continued as if nothing was wrong.

"Only if you're paying," she threw back.

He grinned. "Fair enough."

Clicking out of the computer window, Sophie pulled up the spreadsheet she kept of open campaigns and navigated to the box with 'Shasta' in it.

Shasta Spa and Resorts was the latest conglomerate to seek out Covey for help with its image maintenance.

She enjoyed working with Marilyn on the campaign, and both she and the client complimented Sophie endlessly.

Deep down, I know I did well. But ...

Imposter syndrome was a bitch.

She sighed and leaned back in her chair, picking at the well-worn white leather. A nervous tic she tried to shake time and again.

But as long as her brain whispered doubts into her ear, a hole threatened in her chair.

Shooting off an IM to Marilyn that she had filed the last paper associated with the campaign, Sophie eagerly waited for her response.

Marilyn replied a few seconds later.

Perfect. Meet me in my office.

Oh, God, this was it. This was the reckoning Sophie waited five years for.

Calm down. But it was a moot point as she jolted back from her desk. She swore as she knocked her knee against the underside. After hustling down the short hall, she knocked on Marilyn's door a moment later.

"Come in."

Sophie entered the large, bespoke office as her boss typed away at her computer.

Marilyn eyed Sophie over the rim of her wire-frame glasses and smiled.

At nearly fifty, crow's feet crinkled at the corner of her cornflower eyes, and gray streaks played through her honey-blonde hair.

She motioned to one of the chairs in front of her organized desk. "Ah, Sophie. Sit down."

Sophie fought back the tide of exhilarating nausea in her gut.

Could Marilyn see the anxious trepidation coursing through Sophie's veins? The subtle shaking?

To keep from vibrating too much, Sophie focused on Marilyn's coral-painted lips.

"Thank you so much for all your help on the Shasta case. You were wonderful. I've seen how hard you've worked since joining, and this case was no exception," Marilyn started. "I know you've been wanting a promotion, but unfortunately, I can't offer you that right now. I'm sorry not to have better news."

Sophie's smile faded as Marilyn continued, the ringing in her ears reverberating through her skull.

Dread replaced her excitement. "I'm sorry?"

Failure. You're a failure.

"I'm not saying no," Marilyn rose and adjusted an already perfectly angled picture of her husband and children. "But you know, besides Shasta, we only have one other big client on our roster so far. Right now, I need help with managing the paperwork for that more than I need a new account director."

"But I ... I can help you with that *as* the account director." Sophie's heart pounded and she gripped her bracelet. "The fact that we even have another big client is a sign Covey is growing."

She picked at her skirt, searching futilely for a loose thread.

"No, as account director, you would have your own cases to deal with." Marilyn's mouth tugged into a straight line. "I could give you some of the paperwork, but your attention would be divided, and that's not where I need your head right now. As you said, Covey is growing, and the meeting tomorrow with this company could bolster a lot of potential clients. You never know when you'll need PR help."

Sophie forced her face to remain neutral. "Alright."

Marilyn's expression softened. "I'm sorry, Sophie. But remember, I'm not saying no."

Ice licked Sophie's stomach as she nodded before excusing herself. Buzzing filled her ears as she stood outside Marilyn's office.

'I'm not saying no.'

Sophie dug her nails into her palms and took a shaky breath. Not for the first time, she swallowed her anger.

Shutting her office door, she leaned against the wood.

Deep breaths.

Promotions were hard to achieve in any industry, but especially in the PR world.

Forcing her eyes open, Sophie stalked over to her desk and sat, lacing her fingers under her chin.

'I'm not saying no.'

I still have a chance.

She just had to make sure her performance on the upcoming case was one of the best she'd given yet.

She'd always tested well as a child, and this was just another test in the grand scheme of things. There was no way she'd fail.

Three
Sophie

The stapled packets of papers hit the gleaming table of the conference room with a hearty smack.

Marilyn liked to have things ready for whatever clientele she met with, and it was part of Sophie's duties to make that possible.

Memories of her mother dragging herself into the kitchen after a twelve-hour shift at their local hospital, the same hospital she'd clawed her way up, were riveted into Sophie's mind.

Her mom didn't need to work as hard anymore, but it didn't matter.

I need to push myself harder if I don't want her exhaustion to go to waste.

Sophie finished distributing the pamphlets and adjusted the water bottles in the center of the table, turning them so the logos faced outward.

Marilyn bustled in, a cloud of floral perfume following in her wake. She tossed her honey-blonde hair behind her shoulder as she settled into the chair at the head of the table. "What time will the client be here again?"

Sophie ignored the fact that since Marilyn was the boss, *she* should know. "They should be here any minute."

Note to self: Have Chlo shoot me if I get like that.

Sophie walked around the table again, adjusting the packets, gazing at the swirling logo and neat text covering the front page.

'REPRESENTATION REGARDING LA BELLE EPO-

QUE GROUP'

Their current clientele was a family-run French wine importer, headed by the father, with both his sons holding shares and seats of power.

Success hit hard, and the family held a spot on the Forbes Billionaires List. But that didn't mean they were above further improving their image.

"Speak of the devil," she murmured as three men followed Covey's receptionist into the room.

"Thank you for meeting with us," the oldest man said, a French accent heavily curling his English.

"Thank *you* for coming in, Mr. DuBois," Marilyn replied. "This is Sophie Huang, my executive assistant. She'll be working alongside me on your campaign."

"François, please," Mr. DuBois inclined his head toward the other two men. "My sons, Antoine and Lucien."

"Tony and Luc," Antoine corrected, no accent to be heard in his words. "Our full names can be a mouthful."

All the men wore matching expressions of nervous anticipation for the meeting, although Tony's leaned more uptight.

On the other hand, Luc stared at the table with determination, like he was dead set on making his father proud.

The familiar expression curled Sophie's gut, and she gripped her pen tighter.

Luc shifted, and sunlight dappled his light brown complexion, slanting across a cutting jaw.

Her gaze met Luc's, who examined her with a frown on his face.

His dark eyes flicked to hers, and he reached for the pen she had placed next to the packet earlier, scribbling something down.

Setting the pen down, he cleared his throat, tapping the top of the paper.

But Sophie ignored him and zoned in on the relay zooming between Marilyn and François.

The meeting ended with Marilyn, François, and Tony standing by the door, talking about some of the processes Covey would utilize.

As Sophie started collecting the pens, someone cleared their throat.

"Ms. Huang, do you have a moment?"

She met the warm, brown eyes of Lucien DuBois and nodded, not pausing in her movements. Why was he talking to her instead of with Marilyn when Sophie wasn't the one overseeing his case?

"I couldn't help but notice your coffee cup," he started.

She paused briefly. *This* was what he wanted to talk about? "Oh, yes. What about it?"

He motioned to the logo on her empty cup. "My friend goes to that shop. He just discovered it a few days ago."

She hummed as a sneaking suspicion crept into her chest. "Really? That's a coincidence. Why does he go there? They're not exactly known for their stellar drinks."

Luc snorted. "He says it gets the job done as well as any other coffee."

"Okay, but he knows it's not good, right?"

"So we've tried to tell him," Luc mused. "Anyway, I was going to ask you for your thoughts on their coffee, but I guess you answered my question."

Sophie frowned as the nagging in her chest grew. "Right, well, while I have you. I'm sorry for how out of the blue this is, and maybe it's just the preparation I've been doing, but I swear I've seen your company name be–"

"Lucien, allons-y!" François interrupted.

"Oui, papa." Luc glanced at Sophie again. "Thanks for meeting with us; it was beneficial. The friend that I mentioned, he's currently looking for some new members for his PR team, and–"

"Are you trying to poach me right now?" Sophie asked. *So*

this *was his objective*?

He chuckled. "No, but I'll point him to Covey for any services he may need in the meantime. After all, you never know when you'll need external help. Anyway, have a good day."

He shook her hand, then peeled away to join his father and brother by the door. The three shook Marilyn's hand, then took their leave.

As the door closed behind them, Marilyn eyed her assistant. "What did Luc want to talk to you about?"

Sophie shrugged. "Nothing important. What did you tell François?"

Marilyn smiled ruefully. "Deflecting the situation. I've taught you well."

Sophie snorted as she shuffled the crowd of pens from one hand to the other. *But not enough to give me the promotion.*

"I know what you're thinking right now." Marilyn stopped in front of her office, tapping the toe of one of her no-nonsense wedges. "And you need to stop. Sophie, *I'm not saying no.* Just not yet."

"I know, I know." Sophie shook her head and resisted the urge to squeeze the pens. "If you need me, I'll be getting some work done in my office."

Marilyn nodded before disappearing into her own office.

Sophie scooted down the hall and shut her door. She sighed, rolling her neck. On top of that, a knot formed between her shoulder blades.

But she sat at her desk and pulled up the document she'd been reading.

Chloe flipped the sizzling meat with a pair of tongs. "Okay, explain to me how you met *three* hot guys in one day."

Sophie and her friends decided to meet up for dinner at a Korean BBQ place Oliver discovered in K-Town. Apparently, it boasted the closest Samgyupsal Gu to his mom's.

Taylor gestured to Sophie with his beer bottle. "Also, are we absolutely sure Luc wasn't flirting with you?"

She shook her head and took a shot of Soju. "I didn't get that feeling, and he brought up his friend. When has a guy *ever* done that if he wants to ask you out?"

"Sophie, really? Plenty of guys do." Oliver stuck a piece of grilled pork belly in his mouth.

She shrugged. "Okay, whatever. But even if he did ask me out, I would've turned him down. I'm already going on a date with James on Friday."

"You're *what*?!" Chloe dropped her meat in the sauce she dipped it in. "Oh, my God, Soph. What did we say about telling us things?"

Sophie winced as sauce splattered on her.

It was a habit that chased her since she was young–keeping quiet equated to low maintenance.

Even though her mom always made time for Sophie and her brother, Sophie wasn't about to add to her mom's load by telling her easily solvable problems.

"Sorry, but yeah, he asked me this morning." She poured herself more Soju and downed it.

"Don't you think that's a bit fast?" Oliver asked. "I mean, you *just* met him last Friday."

"Of course, I thought of that," she said. "But you and Taylor met on an app and went on a date after four lines of conversation, and look how well that turned out."

"Okay, but that's a rare case."

Chloe snipped the tongs. "Hey, if Sophie wants to go on this date, then let her."

"Okay, okay," Oliver acquiesced, though there was no exasperation in his tone. "Oh, right, speaking of Friday. Babe, did you buy the tickets?"

Taylor nodded enthusiastically.

As the two started talking, Chloe turned to Sophie. "So, James asked you out. Where are you going?"

Sophie opened her mouth before shutting it again.

Chloe blinked. "Oh my God, you don't know? Okay, text him and–"

Sophie cleared her throat.

Chloe's eyes quickly examined her. "Did you forget to get his number?"

Sophie flushed. "I'll ask him tomorrow!"

"Sorry, I couldn't help but overhear. You forgot to get his number?" Oliver cut in.

Sophie nodded, the fragrant smoke from the grilling meat sending her into a coughing fit.

It hadn't entirely been her fault she forgot, but embarrassment spiked in her gut anyway.

"You *do* want to go out with him, right?" Taylor asked.

She nodded, not hesitating in her answer.

Perhaps she was approaching things differently than with her exes, but there was no doubt she *wanted* to date James.

"Okay, at least tell me you Googled him," Chloe said. "Just to make sure he's not a serial killer or something."

Taylor whipped out his phone. "On it."

But Sophie shook her head. "No, I want to be the one to do it. I just haven't had time, but I promise I will."

They left the restaurant an hour later, with full bellies and a few takeout boxes in hand.

Taylor and Oliver split off and piled into a taxi for their apartment in SoHo.

The two women meandered down the muggy streets near K-Town, Chloe's arm thrown around Sophie's shoulders.

Sirens blared, and the moon hung low through a mist of smog.

Compared to the crystal-clear nights Sophie grew up with in Connecticut, it was terrible. But if someone offered her the chance to go back, she would never take it.

Nothing ever changed in her hometown, whereas in New

York City, everything was in constant flux. The positivity of it depended on the day, but that was what was exciting.

Someone cuffing her shoulder brought her out of her thoughts, and they rounded the corner, almost walking straight into the side of someone coming out of a small store.

"Oh, my–Wait. Sophie, right?"

Sophie blinked at the man she'd narrowly avoided. It took her a moment, but then recognition slammed down.

He looked a bit different–maybe it was the fact he lost the blazer–but all in all, there was no mistaking Lucien DuBois.

She took a step back, dragging Chloe with her. "Hi."

Her friend smiled and cleared her throat.

Sophie snapped out of her shock to introduce the two.

"Ah, so you're the shareholder," Chloe said.

"In the flesh," Luc said.

Sophie's brows raised at the mild curiosity tracing Chloe's face. "What are you doing here?"

Luc cleared his throat and adjusted the sleeves of his shirt. "This shop sells the Soju I like. Sometimes, you're not in the mood for a Bordeaux."

She smiled. "Right, but don't you have ... I don't know, people for this or something?"

He laughed. "I mean, yeah. But it's better if I do it."

Sophie cleared her throat. "Right, well, we shouldn't keep you. I bet you're busy."

"Actually, I'm not. I'm just meeting my friends for a bit, but I don't think one of them is even back yet." He nodded toward a car parked by the nearby curb. "So yeah, I have some time. Do you two need a ride?"

Sophie bit back her sigh. Of course, he owned a car in the city, and of course, it was a BMW.

"Yes," Sophie said at the same time Chloe blurted a hearty refusal.

Luc laughed awkwardly. "Uh ..."

Sophie flashed a smile as Chloe latched onto her arm.

'*What* are *you doing?!*' Chloe demanded silently with her eyes.

'Scoring us a ride home. You really want to take the subway?' Sophie retorted with a flick of her brows. *'Besides, I trust him. He won't kidnap us.'*

'Famous last words.'

Luc cleared his throat into the silence. "So ..."

She blew a breath out of her nose and smiled. "Sure."

Chloe's nose wrinkled. "If I get kidnapped, I'm writing you out of my will."

"How are you going to do that if you're kidnapped?" Sophie mused.

"I'll get Oliver to do it."

"Pretty sure that's not how that works," she said.

Chloe pulled open the back door of Luc's car. "Okay, well, whatever. I'll sort out the kinks later. Gonna have a fuck ton of time to think about it when I'm kidnapped."

Sophie handed Chloe her cane, then sidled in after her. "Luc's not going to kidnap us."

"Sophie, you've met the man once!" Chloe retorted. "Forgive me if I don't think that's the most hopeful statement."

"Look, I know it's a risky move, but did you want to walk instead?"

"If it means keeping my life, yes. This is so unlike you." She peered close. "You look a little red. I think the Soju got to you."

Sophie rolled her eyes. "I feel fine."

"Keep telling yourself that."

She huffed and settled back against the leather seat.

The inside of the car was as unsurprising as the outside. It definitely fell into the category of what she expected for a company shareholder and board member.

But she hadn't foreseen how ... cluttered it was.

Two coffee cups filled the cup holder by the front seats,

papers littered the floor, and a plastic bag sat on the passenger seat, filled with crumpled napkins and tissues.

"Sorry for the mess." Luc hopped into the driver's seat and turned on the car. Immediately, a French song blasted from the speakers, and he laughed awkwardly, turning off the audio. "Sorry. Uh, where to?"

Sophie hesitated. *Oh, God. I didn't think this through.*

Rattling off the number of the next street over, she ignored the triumphant look Chloe shot.

Settling back in the seat, Sophie looked out the window, breathing in the distinctive "New Car" smell.

They stopped at a traffic light, the slice of red illuminating a coffee cup from Joseph's, and the name scrawled atop it.

She blanched, her stomach twisting as the pieces clicked into place.

"What's wrong?" Chloe muttered.

Sophie sucked in a breath and ignored her. "Um ... Luc. What did you say your friend's name was again? The one who's looking for some new PR help?"

He idled at another red light. "Hm? Oh, it's James. James Tian."

Four

James

James reclined in the leather armchair in his dad's living room.

His finger clenched around his glass of Macallan, the amber liquid distorted through the crystal.

He hated the monthly family dinners he was obligated to attend at his dad's mansion in Montauk.

The large windows and soaring ceilings only served as a cruel reminder of the years he spent virtually trapped there after his mom packed her bags and left.

He got out as fast as he could when he was eighteen. But every month like clockwork, he endured the sneers and malice his dad threw for the sake of happier moments when laughter and smiles spilled from the airy halls as easily as breathing.

The cavernous corridors still held the memory of James's mother. And it was the last place he might catch the hem of her pants, or the ends of her hair, disappearing around a corner.

He took a sip of the whisky, relishing the liquor's burn.

"So, James, I heard through the grapevine that you met with Declan Geller this morning." His dad's eyes flashed. "Considering all I've done for you over the years, I'd have thought you'd think twice before stealing my clients."

James frowned. "Excuse me?"

"I know your company is doing well, now," his dad continued, as if he hadn't heard his youngest son. "But it's only a matter of time before that business fritters away. It would do you some good to take a page from Adam's book. At least your brother isn't wasting his time."

"Dad," Adam interjected, but didn't continue. Instead, a flash of guilt coated his expression before it disappeared, replaced by stone-cold indifference.

James's jaw clenched—he didn't know why he expected anything more.

The conversation from last month's dinner floated back.

"What's so hard?" James had demanded. "Why do you *never* say anything?!"

Adam turned away. "It's ... complicated."

James's eyes flashed. "Then, uncomplicate it. You're almost thirty-five. When are you going to stop letting Dad shove you around?"

Adam whirled. "I don't let Dad shove me aro—"

"Yes, you do!" James shouted. "Those arranged dates, where you live, hell, even *your fucking job*—"

"And you're only two years younger than me!" Adam sneered. "So grow up, Jamie, and face the fact you're not much better than me."

"Excuse me?!"

"Why do you think you got as far as you did with your art company?" He wrung the silver Cartier ring on his index finger. "Sure, you only cater to the wealthy. But if it wasn't for our last name, do you think you would've gotten clients so fast?"

James balked.

He wasn't blind to the fact that his success was because every businessperson worth their salt knew Tian Corporation was one of the largest shipping companies in the U.S. But that didn't discount the fact that he spent months cultivating Lotus into a multi-billion-dollar company. That didn't dissolve all the blood, sweat, and tears, or who he really worked his ass off for.

"Maybe I don't say anything because I can't." Agitation had painted Adam's features for a moment before fading behind apathy. "But that doesn't mean I don't care."

James drained the rest of his whisky as movement shifted in his peripheral vision, and he glanced at the door.

Mrs. Le hovered just outside the door to the sitting room.

His father's elderly housekeeper shot James a worried glance, but he shook his head subtly.

Normally, his dad was more restrained at family dinners, but finding out about Geller ...

To say Charles Tian was unhappy would be to put a positive spin on the situation.

James pulled out his phone, zoning in on the words Luc texted him.

You won't believe who I just met

James tuned out his dad completely.

Who?

Remember how I said there was that woman with the Joseph's cup at my meeting this morning? I just gave her and her friend a ride to their place

The cute one? What was her name again? I don't think you mentioned

Her friend was cuter. But don't encourage me. You already asked her out this morning

James's fingers froze over his keyboard.

The chances were a million and one, but somehow, Luc seized them all.

Luc sent another message.

She told me after she saw your coffee cup in my car you slob

A small smile graced James's lips as he tapped in a response.

It's your car. It's not my fault you don't clean it

"What are you smiling about?"

The smile slid off James's face as he looked at his dad.

He sneered at his son, contempt painting an ugly portrait. "Is it your little art business?"

James didn't tell his dad that his "little art business" closed a multimillion-dollar deal that morning, or that they were on the verge of another exorbitant deal with Marco Russo, one of the city's wealthiest residents.

"Nothing." Rising from his seat, he adjusted his shirt. "Is dinner ready?"

James examined his fork, thinking of the different ways he could kill himself with it.

His dad talked around a mouthful of steak about the losses Tian Corporation sustained that month. "It's ridiculous! We'll need to–James, are you listening?"

James speared a piece of asparagus. "I thought you didn't want me anywhere near the company anymore."

His dad squinted. "No, I don't. But you still need to listen to me."

The words aimed to hurt, but James hardly cared, and the guilt fell short.

"Word of advice, Jamie," his brother said. "As COO, I've learned you always need to have your head in the game. That means being present for everything. Even if you don't think it's important, it is."

James frowned. *Does he not think I know that?*

But before he could say something to that condescending son-of-a-bitch, his dad cut in.

"As a soon-to-be CEO, Adam, I expected you to catch the significant drops in productivity this quarter, especially since most of it was in Boston. And yet ..."

A bright red flush coated his brother's cheeks, and James smirked.

Even his father's favorite son wasn't immune to Charles Tian's criticisms.

"Anyhow, James," his dad said. "Aside from Geller, how *is* Lotus doing? A for-sale sign isn't in the future, is it?"

Heated fury flooded James's chest. "It's going well. Really well, actually."

His dad raised a brow. "Enlighten us."

Dammit.

James hadn't thought his dad would start questioning him, but he should've expected it.

Everything was a game, and every dinner was another move across the chessboard.

Ever since his dad lost his queen, he paid even more attention to his pawns.

"Well, I ... we sold two paintings," James began. "At face value, for four million. Each."

His dad raised a brow. "Would I know the buyer?"

"You might." James gritted his teeth. "It's George Delacroix."

Adam choked on his wine, covering his spluttering mouth with his napkin. "Shit, Jamie."

And ... Check.

George Delacroix was one of the most prominent figures in the business world. He owned fifteen different law firms in New York alone, half of which were in Manhattan. He was also a long-time investor in Tian Corporation, and James took advantage of having heard he wanted to decorate his new business.

"First Declan, now George," his dad lamented. "You're really determined to steal my investors out from under me, aren't you?"

James stabbed a bite of steak. "It's not stealing, it's business."

For the first time in a long time, his dad's face looked

mildly impressed.

James wasn't delusional–Charles Tian might've included his youngest in talks of Tian Corporation. Still, the tidbit of news starring Delacroix wasn't enough to get his dad to come around completely. James doubted anything ever would.

Backing into one of the parking spaces in the garage under his building, he got out of his car.

The elevator slid open into the foyer of his penthouse, and he slipped off his shoes, glimpsing Philip's already next to the shoe rack.

"Hey. Did the game start?" James called.

He made his way to the living room and sat on the couch, taking off his tie and undoing another button on his shirt.

Philip emerged from behind the kitchen island with an armful of snacks. "No. By the way, you're out of barbeque chips."

He grabbed two beers from the fridge. "How was dinner?"

James opened his beer and took a sip, flicking on the TV to ESPN. "Same-old, same-old. Where's Luc? He's late."

Philip didn't reply, and James looked over.

The former stared at his phone, his brows furrowed, and his tongue poking

into his cheek.

James reached for a bag of chips. "What is it?"

"Hm? Oh, it's Mariana. Last night, I said something I shouldn't have, and she hasn't responded to any messages until now." Philip frowned. "I'm going to go call her."

He moved off the couch and disappeared into James's office, shutting the door.

James's phone vibrated, but he ignored it and reached for his beer.

It was probably another news alert or notification from his C-Suite group chat. He had been getting them all night, but after dinner, he didn't have the energy to look.

The elevator pinged, and Luc rounded the corner.

"I brought alcohol." He brandished the paper bag he held in the air and removed a few Soju bottles.

He sat, running a hand through his short, cropped dark hair. "Where's Pip?"

James grabbed the chip bag he'd opened. "Calling Mariana."

He explained the situation to Luc, who grimaced. "Man, that guy better not fuck this up. He's so lucky to have her."

James nodded.

Philip had always been an amazing boyfriend to the few men and women he'd dated, but he wasn't devoid of mistakes, and it'd be a shame for him to lose Mariana.

"By the way, Sophie asked me to give you this." Luc passed his phone over.

A page lay open on the Notes app with a phone number and a smiley face typed after it.

Oh, God. I didn't even realize ...

He sent the number to himself, then tossed the phone back to Luc. "Thanks."

Opening a new message, he typed in a text,

Hey. It's James

The blue bubble floated in the empty thread before he clicked his phone off.

There was no use in staring at the device like a sap. It wouldn't make her respond any faster, and yet ... something made him unlock his phone again. He stared at the message, waiting for a reply.

"You should see your face." Luc rolled his eyes, a small smile adorning his lips. "Avoir un coup de foudre, non?"

James chuckled and flipped Luc off.

But ... yes, he was right. James had been walking on air since first laying eyes on Sophie, and every time they crossed paths, it just got better.

Exquisite curves, dark eyes framed with midnight lashes,

cheekbones, and a jawline that cut you and left you begging for more. Her raven hair flowed in loose waves past her shoulders, her full lips parted ever so slightly, and ... shit.

"Hey."

James jumped as the voice launched him from his thoughts.

Philip lingered at the edge of the carpet, eyes a bit too wide.

"Uh ... have you looked at the group chat, or any news reports?"

James hesitated. "No ... why?"

"I ... You should see for yourself."

He swallowed, swiping open his news app.

But before the first headline loaded, his phone pulsed.

Hey. Sorry I didn't get your number

Don't worry about it

James replied, resisting the urge to check the fifteen other message notifications. He told himself to leave it there and not come off as too desperate. But he couldn't stop himself.

So for Friday, I'd recommend a nice outfit for dinner. The place I had in mind is pretty upscale.

Damn, you really foiled my sweats plan

The corners of his mouth kicked up.

I'll pick you up. What's your address?

His phone shook with an incoming call, and he frowned.

His executive assistant's contact slid down from the top of the screen. But she never called after hours unless ...

He stood. "Uh. I'll be back."

Luc frowned. "Everything okay?"

James shrugged. "Yeah, I think. I–one sec."

He strode toward his office, shutting the door. Taking a seat at his desk, he put the phone on speaker.

"Jackie?" he asked. "What happened?"

"Sorry to bother you at home, but ... have you seen any of the headlines from the past few hours?" Her words bumped into each other in her rush to get them out.

"Philip asked the same thing, and the answer's still no. I've been busy. What happened?"

She didn't deign to answer. "Is he there with you?"

"Yes, but wh–"

"Get him on the line while I rope in the others."

James blanched and shouted for Philip.

A second later, Philip poked his head in the office, brow raised. "You're missing the game, cabrón."

James swallowed. "I don't think that matters right now."

He might not understand what was going on, but urgency limned Jackie's words.

Philip frowned. "What's wrong?"

James gestured at his phone. "Jackie wants to talk to us."

"Ay." Philip crossed his arms. "So, it moved past rumors?"

James gaped. "What are you talking about?"

"Unfortunately," Jackie murmured. "Um ... I guess I'll do a roll call. Obviously, James and Philip. What about Camilla?"

"Here. Honestly, Jackie, how many times do I need to tell you? It's Cami," his CIO corrected through a lilting Portuguese accent.

"Yes, sorry," Jackie said. "Do we have Gemma?"

"Present," his COO said.

"Perfect." Jackie cleared her throat. "Let's discuss the new developments."

"*What* new developments?!" he demanded.

"Oh, sweetie. You haven't seen them?" Cami asked.

"Obviously not! I had to get to my dad's today, you know that."

For Christ's sake, the dinners weren't exactly a secret.

James left early on those days every month, putting Gemma in charge.

"Stop, you two. The point is that yes, there has been a *significant* development," Gemma clipped. "Delacroix is done."

James stilled, and hoarfrost crept over his skin, scuttling up his bones. "What do you mean he's done?"

"I mean, he got hacked; his emails, phone records—everything got out to the press, and he was arrested for tax evasion." Irritation burned his COO's syllables.

James hung his head back. "Are you fucking with me right now?"

Given the caliber of Lotus's clients, he was sure plenty of them committed crimes associated with high society. But the difference was that none of them was stupid enough to be caught, and it was something he'd taken for granted.

"What's worse is the bastard had been getting threats for it," she said. "Meaning he knew he might go down."

"Me cago en todo lo que se menea," Philip muttered. "So that check we got from him this morning—"

Gemma sighed. "It bounced."

James's shoulders stiffened and his heart backflipped.

No, that wasn't right, it *couldn't* be. There was no way a check from George fucking Delacroix would *bounce*.

And yet ...

James clenched the arms of his chair, his blood rushing in his ears. He pinched the bridge of his nose between his fingers, then jammed on his reading glasses. "Tax evasion, you said?"

Part of him didn't want to believe Gemma, even though he knew in his gut she was right. Still, he held his breath as he threw open his laptop and Googled George Delacroix.

James shoved a hand in his hair. "You've got to be kidding me."

'Delacroix Loses Everything After Crimes Revealed'

James gusted air through his teeth. "How did *no one* notice anything was wrong? Wait, hang on, are we—"

"We're fine," Cami said. "We're not complicit, but there is the issue of something else."

A dark feeling plummeted in his stomach. "What is it?"

"Uh ... well ..." Jackie started.

James rubbed his chest. He couldn't take any more bad news at the moment. "Jackie."

Whatever she was about to drop, he could take it. He steeled himself enough. He hoped.

"It's ... the Russo deal," she said.

James was positive that if your heart could stop while you kept on living, it was happening to him right then. "What about it?"

Philip's eyes widened. "Ay, la madre que te parió."

James stared at his best friend. What the hell had he figured out that James hadn't?

"I–that is–okay. Russo backed out," Jackie finished.

A cheer erupted from the living room. The door muffled it, but it was enough to remind James that a celebration occurred while his world shattered.

Someone tied weights to his feet and tossed him in the ocean, smiling like a psycho as he sank from view.

"Backed out?" The high-pitched, panicked voice that came out of him was foreign to his ears. "I ... we were supposed to close with him tomorrow! What changed his mind?"

Philip's accent sharpened. "What do you think? It was the Delacroix scandal."

A ten-car pileup screeched into James's heart.

"Are you kidding me?! Russo can't possibly think that it was *our* fault!" James opened a new tab on his laptop and navigated to Gmail.

I'm going to email him and make him see he's making a huge mistake.

All James wanted was to unwind over a basketball game with his friends, not run damage control. But here he was, work overtaking his personal life yet again.

"Of course, he knows it wasn't our fault. But he doesn't want to be associated with us," Gemma said. "Neither do too many of our other clients. They're already pulling their business."

"Especially our European clients," Cami chimed.

James exited out of the email, yanked his glasses off, and pressed his palms to his eyes.

As much as it pained him to admit it, what Russo did made sense.

It would be corporate suicide to enter into a deal with the company a disgraced businessman had done business with, especially so soon after everything went down.

"Okay, well, we still have a few clients, right?" James asked. "Philip, what do the numbers look like this quarter?"

Philip's lips tugged into a thin line. "Last I checked, we are fine. But if we do not do something ..."

James filled the rest in in his head. *We stand to lose everything.*

He resisted the urge to rest his head on his desk and instead settled for tipping it back against the headrest.

Losing Delacroix *and* Geller ... it was like James was seven years old again and staring at his mother walk out the door.

Lotus had been an attempt to follow in her footsteps–that it was more than possible to turn your back on a prestigious last name and succeed. It worked wonders.

But everything he fought about with his dad for all those years, all those voices of doubt ... he couldn't let them come to fruition.

A knock fractured the stretched silence, and Luc poked his head in. "Hey, you guys coming? I'm getting lone–God, who died?"

"Uh ...we will be out in a second," Philip said.

Luc raised his brow at the loss of contractions. "Should I ask?"

James sighed. "I'll explain later."

Luc frowned but nodded and receded through the doorway.

"Right, well, what about our PR team?" James asked.

He was in the midst of hiring new members for Lotus's

small PR team after a few old ones had been let go for not doing their job properly. But whoever was left could handle things.

They have to.

"And what do you think they can do about it?" Cami snapped in Portuguese.

He startled.

Cami said things firmly or pointedly, but she never *snapped.*

"Excuse me?" he asked.

"Who is going to believe the PR team of a company Delacroix trusted?" she continued, switching back to English. "Russo will not, I can tell you that right now."

Jackie's nervous titters radiated through the receiver.

James's eyes bugged. *I know it has to be some coping mechanism, but now is* not *the time to be laughing.*

"Gemma, I bet this isn't how you saw your last month with us going." Jackie laughed again. "Are you sure you want to leave? You still have a month to change your mind."

"Unfortunately, I have to go," Gemma replied. "My parents aren't getting younger, and my mom's hip has been acting up."

"Yes, Gem, we're going to miss you." James turned his chair and faced the darkening city. "But right now, we need to figure out what we're going to do."

"Easy. We need an outside team," Cami said.

"Good, you two are awake."

James winced as Luc's voice filtered into his pounding head.

Sitting up, James gripped his head and looked at Philip, who mirrored him perfectly on the opposite end of the couch.

"Shut up, please," Philip muttered.

James groaned, pressing his palms to his eyes. Flashes of

the night before played out in the darkness.

The news about Delacroix had no doubt crept into mainstream media by now.

Finishing the beer and Soju with his friends, and cracking into the bottle of whisky James had in his apartment. Well, at least James and Philip had. Judging by the fact Luc wasn't nursing a massive hangover, he'd refrained.

"I know we all have high alcohol tolerances, and you two were upset, but you two really tested God last night," Luc continued. "Christ, we're not in our twenties anymore. You're lucky I was here."

"Sí, gracias," Philip said. "What happened?"

Luc gestured at the rug, and James glanced down.

Next to a few crumpled beer cans was a spot that'd been scrubbed down, a dark splotch in place of ... whatever was there.

James groaned and flopped back on the couch, shutting his eyes. "Thanks."

"What are friends for?" Luc said. "Just so you know, I already called Gem and told her you guys wouldn't be in until late, but she said you already put out the order last night that everyone had the day off today."

James hummed, bobbing his head. There was no point in having people go into work, not with the mess they were dealing with.

"Cabrón, have you found someone yet?" Philip asked. "PR wise? Like Cami said, we can't–"

His lungs let loose a choked cough and he covered his mouth, going absolutely still.

"Don't you dare give me a new rug stain," James warned.

Philip's throat worked as he swallowed hard, before darting from the couch and stumbling down the hall to the bathroom.

James squeezed his eyes shut in thought.

Plenty of resources danced at his fingertips on where he could find a PR firm. Hell, he could even use the team of a different company.

But a wedge deep inside prevented him from doing any of that. He didn't need anyone else knowing about his fuckup.

Something dawned on him.

"Didn't you just meet with a PR firm yesterday? What was the name?" he asked.

"Covey LLC. I think they're going to do a good job for us," Luc said. "But Sophie works there, and she's pretty high up."

That's right.

If Sophie was somehow on Lotus's case, then their date on Friday was off.

But ... he was desperate.

"Give me their email."

James's phone buzzed next to him, and he tore his gaze away from his email to look at the screen.

It was a text from Sophie.

Crap, I forgot to respond.

Must've missed you this morning. Also you never texted back last night. Did I offend you or something?

He dragged his hands away from his laptop.

No sorry something came up with work and I got distracted. I took today off to deal with it

Her reply was instantaneous.

Oh well nbd. I hope everything goes ok

For a second, he debated telling her about his dilemma. It would help to get a fresh pair of eyes on the matter.

No, are you crazy?! You're going to her *company for help.*

Thanks
Looking forward to Friday

Diving back into his task, he copied the email address Luc gave him into the recipient box. Laying his problems down in the body and sending the email off, he glanced at his phone.

Sophie hadn't responded, and his mind spiraled. Was she busy or pissed off at him? Was it the wrong move to brush her unspoken question off so bluntly?

He was terrible at saying the right thing. His last few girlfriends made sure to tell him that when they'd broken up. He was always too blunt or too detailed, or worse, he got attached too quickly or not enough.

His phone pulsed at the same time his inbox let forth a pinging sound, and he looked toward his laptop. He had a reply from Covey.

Well, that was fast.

His eyes skimmed the text and hooked on the signature under the short message.

'Sophie Huang; Executive Assistant to Marilyn Covey'

His jaw slackened. *There's no way that's the* same *Sophie Huang, is there?*

Luc said the PR firm wasn't big, and Sophie was high up, but ...

No, it's just a coincidence. Unless it's not, and–

James shook his head. That wasn't his primary focus–what mattered was that he had a meeting with Marilyn Covey tomorrow afternoon.

Five

James

James lurched forward as the Uber driver slammed on the brakes.

Quick as a whip, Philip grabbed his shoulder, pulling him back. "Ay, this is why you use your seatbelt, cabrón."

James nodded his thanks and pressed his phone back to his ear. "Repeat that, Jackie?"

"How did you get a meeting so fast?"

The driver blared the horn and yelled a swear word out the window.

James sighed–rush hour was never fun. "I said it was urgent."

Jackie's keyboard clacked on the other end of the line. "Right, but usually that means nothing to a PR firm."

He shrugged. "Then I guess they looked us up."

Although confidence lined his words, nausea punched through his gut.

Adam was right, and James hated it.

His father's name was what got him recognized and opportunities handed to him on a silver platter. One of the reasons he'd started Lotus was to make a name for himself, and although it floundered, people still chose to recognize Tian.

The irony wasn't lost on him.

"Anyway, I'll keep you and the others updated." He hung up, pocketing his phone.

The Uber arrived down the street from their destination, and he and Philip got out.

Philip dusted off his shirt, swerving to avoid a woman carrying a sloshing soda. "If we didn't have to worry about parking, I'd have driven us."

The corner of James's mouth kicked up. "Thanks, but I'd rather not get on your motorcycle."

Philip clucked his tongue. "In my car, cabrón."

James snorted as he pulled the glass doors of the squat building open, ushering them into a modernized lobby.

Following in the footsteps of half the other buildings in Manhattan, the office housing Covey LLC featured stylish lighting and a small indoor garden bisecting the neat space.

Trendy chairs dotted shiny floors in front of a security desk, and reclining on one, with his nose buried in his phone, was Luc.

Philip grinned and sauntered over. "Hey. What are you doing here? Didn't you meet with Covey two days ago?"

"Hey." Luc pocketed his phone. "Damn, you two got a meeting already?"

"Well, smaller companies mean smaller turnaround times, right?" Philip shrugged. "But my question still stands. What are you doing here?"

"Yeah, did you mess up already?" James teased.

"Funny," Luc said. "Marilyn wanted to go over a few more things regarding brand awareness. My dad couldn't make it, and Tony's out of state for a few days, so he sent me."

"He trusts you with that?" Philip asked.

Luc rolled his eyes. "I'm on the board, you know."

"That was a mistake," James muttered.

"*Excuse you.*" Luc tried kicking him in the shin.

James laughed, stepping back. "Sorry, sorry. You're very competent."

"Damn right. Anyway." Luc cleared his throat. "I'm assuming since you're here, you're trying to figure things out."

Philip nodded. "You said this place was good, right?"

"That's the impression I got. Oh, James, remember Sophie works here."

"Oh, right." Philip adopted a skeptical look. "Well, it's fine ... as long as she's not on our case."

James's jaw clenched. *Ironic how my personal life is threatening my work for once ... no, stop it. You don't know that the Sophie Huang on the email is the same Sophie Huang you met. Two people can have the same name at the same company. So don't lose out on this opportunity just because of a maybe.*

James's pocket buzzed, and he withdrew his phone. It was Sophie.

Because I just got asked. Favorite dessert?

I don't think I have a favorite one. Not really a dessert person

EXCUSE ME?!

He smiled.

Kidding, I have a huge sweet tooth

Oh, thank God. I thought I was going to have to drop you now

A snort slid from his lips.

Glad not to disappoint

Luc cleared his throat. "Is that Sophie?"

The trickle of sunshine leaking from James's chest exploded into a glittering solar storm. "Possibly."

"Figured. You should see the smile on your face," Luc teased. "Anyway, when is your meeting?"

James checked his watch and flinched. "In ten minutes. We should head up. You coming with?"

His friend shook his head. "Just finished mine."

The three said their goodbyes, and James and Philip hopped into the elevator.

"So ... do I have to confiscate your phone?" Philip asked.

"What?"

The elevator arrived on the fourth floor, and the two stepped out. As James waited to check in with reception, he caught flashes of movement in a room down the hall.

Large, clear windows splashed sunshine onto a rounded conference table, already dotted with a few packets and pens. A slender hand, tipped with navy nails, adjusted the water bottles grouped in the center, a bracelet flashing on their wrist.

Paranoia assaulted his nerves as he stared at the bracelet. *Is that the same one Sophie wears, or...?*

Philip shook his head as they took seats in the waiting room. "I haven't said anything until now, but seriously? We have a meeting about how you might potentially lose your company, and you're busy texting a girl?"

"I'm not going to lose anything." James frowned. "You said it yourself–our finances are fine."

"Sure, but what happens when those run out?" Philip demanded. "If we walk away from this meeting empty-handed, we're still going to lose it all. Look, I'm not trying to be insensitive, but don't be cocky about this. Your relationship with your father isn't good enough to afford that, and yes, we know people. But that's only going to take us so far. "

James frowned and looked away. "I know."

"Do you?" Philip challenged. "You used to do anything for this company. But now? This isn't like you, cabrón."

James pursed his lips.

His friend was right, this *wasn't* like him.

A few weeks ago, he let almost nothing distract him from his work, and that was nothing compared to when he first started Lotus.

Would you really want to lose what you started for Mom?

No, but ... last week, he discovered Joseph's. Sophie walked into his life, and everything changed for the better.

And I know Mom would want that for me.

"Pip, you know the lengths I went to for this company–

the lengths I'll *still* go to. But I need this too, alright? Besides, how many times have you texted Mariana on company time?" James rarely pulled rank, but quite frankly, Philip was being an asshole. "You don't get to judge."

Philip grumbled something in Spanish, staring at nothing.

James sighed, understanding completely why Philip reacted like this.

He was CFO, which meant the problems with Delacroix were something he blamed himself for, even if it wasn't his fault.

And James hadn't helped matters either, when he asked multiple times since the news broke why Philip hadn't caught this.

Cursing his insensitivity, James cleared his throat and sought to lighten the mood. "I overheard you and Luc. If you're going to Seoul, I'll text you a picture of these skincare things to bring back. My cousin raved about them, and I'm curious."

An affectionate expression brushed Philip's face. "Alright, but why don't you just come with us?"

"Can't," James said. "Got some work to do."

"So do I, but I'm still going. Besides, you can do it on the jet. I promise we'll leave you alone."

He shook his head. "No, it's fine. You guys just go and–oh. Last time, I got stationary at that shop in Hongdae? Bring some back, too. I'm almost out."

A wide smile lifted his friend's mouth. "The one with the corgi butts?"

James flushed brilliantly. "I ... look. They're cute dogs, and they waddle aroun–"

Someone cleared their throat, and he looked up at the receptionist. "We're ready. You can follow me."

"Do you think he heard us?" James muttered in Italian to Philip.

"Sì," the receptionist responded.

Philip launched into a heavy coughing fit in a poor attempt at hiding his laughter, and James elbowed his gut.

They entered the small conference room, and James noticed several things at once.

A large screen set up at the end of the conference table bore a slide with Lotus's logo, and 'LOTUS ART IMAGE MAINTENANCE' scrawled across the pale background.

Packets with identical words lay in front of four chairs, sleek pens resting beside them.

Three of the chairs were empty–one wasn't. Sitting in it with her nose buried in a packet and flipping a pen between her fingers was Sophie.

James's stomach plummeted seven stories, and he stumbled into Philip's back.

Philip looked up from his phone. "Ay, cabrón, watch–Oh, Christ."

Her gaze snapped up and widened, volleying between them. "You've got to be kidding me."

Alarm bells resounded in James's ears. *Stupid–I* told *you it was the same person!*

"Sorry, do you know them?" Apprehension filled the receptionist's expression.

Sophie's gaze darted to him. "I ... um ... no, not really. Um, I've got it, Nico, thanks for showing them in."

Nico narrowed his eyes but nodded and left.

Sophie's shoulders tensed as she stood. "Someone start t–"

A blonde woman bustled in, balancing too many items in her arms. "Hello, hello. Nice to meet you. I'm Marilyn Covey."

A black hole sucked all the air from the room, and James worked on autopilot as he fell into emptiness.

Could *nothing* in his life go right?

The next thing he knew, he sat in the chair next to Marilyn's, smoothing his fingers over a corner of his packet.

"As I said in the email, the situation is urgent." He avoided looking at Sophie across from him. If he did, he'd combust. But his peripheral vision told a different story for her.

"We need to find out why that check bounced, but in the meantime, we can't have people thinking they can't trust us. This scandal is big, but it isn't the end of the world, and they can still bring their business to us. With our own PR team out of the picture, Covey's help with building up our image would be invaluable."

Marilyn nodded, chewing on the inside of her cheek, and linked her fingers together. "What do your quarterly projections look like?"

He gestured to Philip, who'd been sneaking glances at Sophie since they sat. "I'll let my CFO handle that."

His friend blinked and cleared his throat. "Um. Right, so. Based on our data, we're financially alright for the time being. But if we don't have clients coming in ... well, you can do the math."

Marilyn chuckled hollowly. "And I'm assuming that's less than ideal."

"Yes." He cracked a smile. "If you turn to page two, you'll see some charts I put together with last quarter's information."

Papers rustled as she bent her head toward the figures.

Finally leveling his gaze on Sophie, James's attention skittered over the substantial frown marring her forehead.

Fix it.

It wasn't the most professional thing in the world, but he grabbed a pen, the lithe body weighing heavily.

Bringing pen to paper, he scrawled a sentence at the top of his pamphlet, taking a moment to figure out the upside-down letters.

After the meeting, meet me on the staircase.

Six

Sophie

"I should've put two and two together," Sophie said.

Crossing her arms, she leaned against the wall as James pushed into the stairwell.

Light bags hung under his eyes, and his hair was a little disheveled, but he still charmed her in his button-down and dress pants. Since the meeting ended, he'd cuffed his sleeves once again at the elbows, showing off that devastating tattoo and a brilliant Piaget watch.

"And I almost did," she continued, pushing aside the aching in her heart. "When I saw your cup in Luc's car, I should've realized you were the same person as the email. Also, not associated with the shipping company, hm?"

"Surprise." James winced. "To be honest, when I saw your email signoff, I was scared it was you, but I convinced myself otherwise."

Because, like me, you didn't want it to be.

Pushing off the wall, her heels clacked the short distance to the railing. White-knuckling the cool metal, she closed her eyes. Her heart beat a mile a minute, and the back of her neck broke out in a cold sweat. She didn't trust her legs to bear her full weight.

So stupid of me not to take that extra step. Who else would it be?

How had she messed up like this?

After the revelation the other night, she finally looked him up, and a floodgate slammed open, refusing to close.

Statistics and article headlines bombarded her from every

direction, and everything from the fine watches to the Amex Black Card he flashed at Joseph's made sense.

However, when the email arrived, the 'urgent' label turned it into a rush job. She hadn't even noticed the same names.

"So," she began. "What does this mean for tomorrow?"

Don't say what I think you–

"Simple. Tomorrow's off."

There it is.

Turning, she leaned back against the rail, stretching her arms out behind her and bracing them on the metal. She cocked her head. "Do you really want that?"

His gaze found hers, and the severity of longing resting there cast her into a wall of fire so hot she dissolved before she reached it.

"No," he admitted. "But we can't. You know we can't."

She dipped her chin. She might not be overseeing his campaign herself, but she did work closely with Marilyn.

While her boss wasn't one to be swayed, the public didn't know that, and Sophie was Marilyn's close confidant.

Whether Sophie wanted it to be or not, James's campaign was within the realm of her responsibility. If it got out that she was dating him, neither of them needed to point out the significant conflicts of interest or the scandal that was sure to follow.

'*Was anything you reported on James Tian or his company true?*' phantom reporters demanded of Marilyn. '*Did you know Sophie Huang would be the Devil on your shoulder, so to speak?*'

Sophie swallowed hard. But, no ... they weren't dead in the water before they started. She wouldn't let them be.

A gust of air coasted through her lips. "Then what if we didn't date?"

His brow furrowed. "Come again?"

Stepping out on the ledge in her stomach, she flirted with precariousness. "We don't date, but we do something else?"

The words crept forward into the silence ticking between them, but the last thing she wanted was to stuff them back in her mouth.

"I still don't think I understand."

"Look, I don't want to let you go, and it's the same for you, right? But reversed?" she asked.

"Yes."

"Alright, then we don't have to let each other be the ones that got away."

Trepidation fluttered in her chest and her lungs knotted themselves. "It's like I said. We don't date, we just ... do other things."

He cleared his throat and tugged at his collar, exposing those dark tendrils. "Are you asking me to be fuck-buddies?"

She flushed. Well, when he put it like *that* ...

"I mean, we can't exactly be Friends-With-Benefits, can we?" she reasoned.

"We can if we become friends. But I thought we were already friendly enough." A smile tugged his lips. "I mean, you *did* take my breakfast."

Scarlett heated her cheeks again. "You *offered.* Besides, if you didn't want me to say yes, would you have even tried in the first place?"

He tilted his head. "I guess not."

"Exactly." She pursed her lips. "We have a no-strings-attached situation. We hang out as friends, but that's it. No dates. And aside from close, close friends, no one finds out about it, got it?"

His shoulders tilted up. "But how would we keep people from finding out?"

Sophie cleared everything from her head, telling her she couldn't do it. She *could* and she *would.* "We be very careful."

He snorted. "Thanks for the guarantee."

She offered a small curtsy, the consequences of one misstep floating on a silver platter before her.

Whispers and gossip always did the most harm. The reputation she worked so hard to build for herself would swirl down the drain, not to mention their efforts at a positive endorsement for Lotus would become an unfair smear campaign.

And yet ... no fear filled her stomach as she stepped up to the edge of the cliffside.

His fingers tapped on his biceps, drawing her attention once again to the striking black ink and flitting her mind to dangerous places.

A breath escaped her and she wet her lips. “So?”

His gaze flicked to her tongue, and something snapped into place in his brown eyes. “Good thing I like complicated.”

“Good.” She smiled ruefully. Consternation skipped alongside her heartbeat, but contentment danced down her limbs.

“So, how about coming over later tonight?” He cocked his head. “I can grab some snacks.”

“Someone’s eager,” she teased.

“There’s no pressure to do anything,” he clarified. “I’m never going to do that to you. But I do want to spend time with you *as a friend*.”

After a moment, she nodded. “Okay, text me details. If you’ll excuse me.”

Wiping her palms on the folds of her dark green skirt, she moved toward the door, nerves shaking.

James caught her wrist as she passed, and her breath hitched.

“For what it’s worth, I’m sorry I didn’t tell you.” His cologne—a woodsy, midnight scent—summoned images of fresh rain and shadows twisting at twilight. “I’ll see you later?”

She nodded, not loosening her wrist from his grasp.

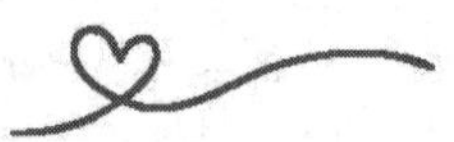

“I don’t get it. Why didn’t you guys stick to your original plan?” Oliver asked. “No one has to find out.”

“Because as a client of Marilyn’s, he would have to come in for meetings with us,” Sophie explained.

“Tell us something we don’t know, Soph,” Chloe deadpanned.

Sophie rolled her eyes with affection. "You know what I mean. If we decide to date, things will be that much harder. Anyone will be able to tell, and that's a risk we can't take."

Chloe frowned. "Won't that still be the case if it's physical, though? I don't know about you, but I personally don't think I can look at someone the same after I've seen them naked."

Sophie snorted as her phone buzzed in her pocket. "Sure, but if we keep it physical, that's all it's going to be. There won't be any feelings involved."

"There are always feelings involved," Oliver countered. "Whether that's now or later."

He had a point, but even though Sophie tried to cover all their bases, it was impossible. All they could do was pray for the best.

Pulling out her phone, she bit back the smile threatening to mold to her lips as she read the text.

James had sent her his address, along with a movie trailer and a brief message.

"What is it?" Oliver asked.

She showed her screen, and his eyebrows shot into his hairline. "A movie? Don't you think that sounds too much like a date?"

She pushed her carton of fries toward him. "We're friends, Ol."

He accepted the food with a pained expression and exchanged looks with Chloe.

Sophie frowned. "What?"

Chloe shook her head. "Nothing, it's just ... I get what Ol's worried about. What if James isn't on the same page as you? What if he's looking for something more than you want to give?"

Sophie shook her head. "Trust me, I made it clear this morning that *isn't* what we're doing."

She had, hadn't she?

But now that she thought about it, that phrase never *actually* left her mouth. What if–

No. She wasn't going to go down that path. Even if she

hadn't definitively said it, James *knew* what their boundaries were.

She slurped the rest of her soda. "Where is this coming from, anyway? Ol, I know you have a little sister, but that doesn't mean you need to play 'protective older brother.'"

"I'm *not*, asshole." Oliver ate a fry, chewing and talking around the food. "I'm playing the friend who doesn't want to see your heart broken."

She crumpled her burger wrapper into a tight ball. "Well, thanks, but I can handle my own decisions."

He held his hands up in defense. "Hey, don't shoot the messenger. All I'm saying is we all need people who aren't afraid to call out our bad decisions."

"Park Baek-Hyun," Chloe warned.

Sophie raised a brow. "You think I'm making a bad decision?"

Oliver winced. "Honestly, Soph? It depends on how you play it, and it starts with what James thinks of your whole arrangement."

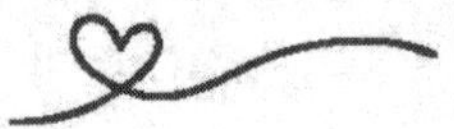

She tipped her head up to take in the full scope of the building.

It had taken her twenty minutes by subway to get to the address James texted her, and she gaped at the sleek, glass building before her.

He warned her in advance that it would be a lot, but that was an understatement.

The building shouldn't have surprised her, given his career and family's money. Still, she couldn't help but gawk at the lit mahogany walls and towering ceilings as she checked in with security and headed toward the elevators.

Pressing the button for the top floor, she stepped out when the doors slid open.

James padded through an archway, barefoot, his hair flopping across his forehead, any remnants of gel gone. A damp black T-shirt clung to his muscles, stretching across broad shoulders, and revealing the tendrils on his neck as the tips of flames.

Her breath spiraled out in a dizzying loop.

James, in a suit, exuded majesty. But James, in casual wear, blazed with resplendence.

"Hi." Droplets of water swung from his hair.

"Hey." Her gaze snagged on his sleeve tattoo. "Um, the elevator stops in your apartment."

A grin tugged at his lips. "Yup, that's kind of how a penthouse works."

"Right ..."

"Uh ... so Philip knows about you coming over." James checked his phone. "He should be coming over to drop something off, so don't be surprised if he pops in at some point."

Sophie took off her shoes. "Breaking our terms already?"

"What? We could tell close friends."

She grinned at his expression. "I'm teasing."

He leaned against the doorway. "If it makes you feel any better, I didn't tell Luc."

"Was that because you haven't seen him yet?"

"Maybe ..."

She laughed and glanced around the foyer, resisting the urge to hang her mouth open. Moving into the living room, she took in the tall ceilings and ample room. The entire place she shared with Chloe in Chinatown could easily fit in there, and there would still be space to move around.

Her eyes caught on a cracked door. "Is that a home office?"

"It used to be a half-bath," he supplied. "But I converted it."

"Can you do that?"

His silence was answer enough. When you had enough power and money, you didn't need rules.

She cleared her throat, stopping in front of one of the

floor-to-ceiling windows in the living room. "I can't believe you live here."

Well, no, that's a lie.

Covey got its fair share of wealthy clients, but there was a difference between being in the presence of money and *this*.

But James didn't display any of the cocky behavior she usually observed in wealthy men.

He sat on the couch, his reflection reclining against the cushions. "To tell you the truth, I don't. I just get paid to answer the door in my pajamas."

She turned. "Oh, I see. Reasonable wages, I hope."

"Very," he quipped. "Like what you see?"

She tilted her head. "I can't tell if that's a come-on or not."

He laughed and motioned toward the glasses and pitcher sitting beside a bowl of popcorn and a few bags of chips. "I wasn't sure what drinks you liked outside of coffee, so ... I hope you're okay with water. If not, I can run and go get some so–"

The elevator dinged, and a moment later, Philip and a woman filed into the room, talking amongst themselves.

With her perfect posture, delicately arched brows, and fine light jewelry, she was nothing less than a portrait of elegance.

"James, I–" she stopped short and brushed an ebony gaze over Sophie. "Oh. Hello."

Sophie cocked her head. "Hi."

"Gemma Adeyemi, Lotus's COO." She extended her hand, a pearlescent bracelet shining against her rich, umber skin. She offered a close-lipped smile. As she moved her chin upward, her smart updo showcased the cut of her jaw. "I didn't know James had a girlfriend. He doesn't like to talk about his personal life with us that much, though I'm surprised Philip didn't mention it."

Sophie snorted and shook Gemma's hand, the other woman's grip soft but sure. "Nice to meet you, but I'm not James's girlfriend. More of a friend."

Gemma raised a brow. "I see. Well, in that case, I didn't

know James had friends outside of us, Philip, and Lucien."

"Excuse me?" James snapped.

The others laughed, and Gemma checked her phone. Her lips pressed together. "I've gotta get going. James, can I talk to you for a moment?"

He nodded and followed Gemma into the foyer, leaving Philip and Sophie behind.

"Is everything okay?" Sophie asked.

"Yes." Philip raked a hand through his hair, his short-sleeved tee shifting to reveal a tattoo of interwoven flowers winding down his bicep. "Gem was still at the office when I went to pick up some stuff. She was rechecking the system, trying to see if there was anything we missed."

"Oh." Sophie crossed her arms. "And did she?"

Philip tilted his head, setting down the papers he held onto the kitchen counter. "No, unfortunately. Whoever did this covered their ass completely. But she wanted to tell James in person what she did."

"Oh?"

"Gem's leaving at the end of next month, and I guess she doesn't want to go in the middle of a crisis. She managed to convince one of our clients to come back." Admiration filled his expression. "She said she told them this entire thing was temporary and at the end of it, they'd still be in need of our services."

Sophie nodded. "Yeah, that makes sense. Why leave now and lose their spot in line when they're just going to come back later? But how...?"

Philip snagged a glass from the coffee table and filled it with water. "Hey, I'm not going to question the semantics. I'm just glad it happened."

"James said at the initial meeting with Marilyn, you all had access to the filing system, right?" Sophie groaned. "God, this would be so much easier if that weren't the case."

"Tell me about it."

She slid back onto the couch, resting against a pillow as her mind kicked into overdrive.

The timing of it all was a little too convenient, and wasn't it part of Philip's job to question the semantics? Not to mention, James would enquire about how it happened.

What if Gemma was lying to James's face right now? What if Philip was?

Sophie's attention shifted as he excused himself from the room.

He wouldn't, would he?

Lotus was his best friend's company—one he'd been a part of from the very beginning.

'I've known Philip for twenty-six years,' James's voice floated in her mind. *'It's unfortunate, but he became Lotus's CFO by being let down by the wrong people and giving up too much.'*

No, there was no way. Not unless something bigger was going on, and this was the only twisted solution.

She startled as the others walked back into the room.

"Well, I should go," Gemma announced. "It was great to meet you, Sophie. James, I'll let you know if I find anything else."

Philip clapped James on the shoulder. "I left the papers on the counter, cabrón. I'm going to use your bathroom."

"Your apartment is only a few floors up!"

"Sure, but your bathroom is nicer."

"What does that even mean?!"

"Upstairs? I thought you had the penthouse," Sophie remarked.

"I have *a* penthouse here," James corrected. "There are three."

"Three," she repeated faintly. "How does that work?"

"Pip's is a little more set back than mine," James explained. "And his balcony also faces a different way."

"Oh, right of course," she deadpanned. "How is it, having your best friend live so close?"

James sat beside her on the couch. "Eventful, and as you can see, I might as well start charging him rent."

She laughed. "He um ... he filled me in before. I'm sorry."

"Thanks."

"I get it if you don't want to hang out tonight." She clenched a bottle of water. "It's a lot."

"Thanks, but having someone else here is exactly what I need." He rubbed his neck, the ends of his flames tattoo pulling with the motion. "Get my mind off things. Did you look at that trailer?"

Grabbing a bag of chips, she ripped it open. "Yeah, it looked interesting. Put it on."

The issue weighed heavily on her mind, but she brushed it aside. If James didn't want to discuss it yet, they wouldn't.

Sighing, she stuck a chip in her mouth. Christ, how did she end up in this situation?

You put yourself here, remember?

She really hated herself sometimes.

Time fluttered and sent them through nearly half of the movie. The snacks lay decimated on the coffee table, with a few stray popcorn kernels scattered across the rug.

The hairs on the back of her neck stood on end as James shifted, spiraling awareness to how close he was into her brain.

There was a slight gap between them, and his arm was slung over the back of the couch. But he might as well have been hugging her.

He cleared his throat and as he shifted, the hem of his shirt tugged up, exposing a strip of skin.

Her breath stuck and she stared, fixated on the puffs of his steady breaths.

Why are you acting like you've never seen a man's shirt rise up? She blew a breath out of her lips. *Well...not his.*

An explosion triggered in the movie, and she jumped, launching herself straight into his side.

"If you wanted to hold me, you could've just asked." His lips twitched.

Her cheeks flushed. "Sorry."

"Don't be. And you know, I don't bite." He smirked. "Unless you ask me to first."

Her blood burned, and her gaze fluttered to his lips. "Has anyone ever taken you up on that?"

"Once or twice." He grinned, his gaze bouncing quickly to her mouth before returning to her eyes. "What about you? Would you take me up on that?"

"Well, I never was afraid of a little pain." Goosebumps raised on her skin and her breathing shallowed.

Friends. Just *friends.*

The mantra thumped in time to her heart, but it was quickly being obscured in the haze.

And if I don't find it again tonight, that's fine by me.

Her gaze flashed down to his bare skin again. Her bumping into him had driven the shirt up an inch higher, and she cleared her throat. "What's that?"

He followed her gaze, and his cheeks flushed burgundy. "Oh, sorry. Here, let me just–"

"No." She caught his wrist. With her free hand, she hovered the tips of her fingers above the black ink soaking his side in a thin oval. "What is that?"

In the dimmed living room, she now discerned tiny feathers amid the ink.

"How many tattoos do you have?"

He hesitated before using his free hand to tug his shirt up enough to expose the entire tattoo.

A giant feather narrowed to a point down his ribs, the tip pointing straight toward a sharp V-Cut that disappeared into his pajama pants.

She swallowed, ignoring the shadows of carved abs teasing the area where his shirt met his stomach.

"Five," he said.

"I see." She extended her hand toward his skin but stopped herself. *Just friends.*

"It's fine." He met her gaze.

She swallowed and traced her touch across more of his

skin, escaping the boundaries of the feather, and arcing onto his stomach, beneath his shirt.

She outlined those defined abs and stilled her hand, splaying it hot across his skin.

He shuddered, his eyes fluttering into hooded half-moons. "Sophie."

She swallowed, curling her touch ever so slightly.

Her entire life, she'd been shoved aside, and she never minded it. She adjusted to putting on a brave face and lying about being fine.

After all, it was necessary.

But if she and James were doing this ... they couldn't hide from each other.

"Why'd you agree?" she asked.

"Why'd you ask?" he returned.

"Because I've always played things safe." She rubbed the hem of his shirt between her fingers. "And for once, I wanted to do something out of control."

His breathing shallowed. "And I'm a risk?"

"The biggest, but ..." She paused, finding his gaze again.

"Sophie," he murmured, his hands covering hers. "Am I a risk you want to take?"

She tilted her head, the last time she'd laid it all on the line screeching through her mind in a blaze of warning lights.

What if...

No.

There was no sign James would do that, and things had already gone differently than planned.

She took a deep breath. "Yes."

He nodded and cast his shirt away.

She sucked in a breath. "Oh, my God."

His sleeve tattoo didn't end at his shoulder. Instead, it turned into a massive clock, swirling ink onto his pec. The clock curved upwards into those twisting flames, thin tendrils winding against his nape.

Her gaze moved to his right side, locking onto the small stamp of Roman Numerals on his collarbone, and that pitch-black feather on the side of his ribs.

"Like what you see?"

"I more than like it." Running her hands down his chest, her nails scoured those defined abs.

He groaned, pulling her into his lap. His lips found hers in a frantic and searching way, like he didn't know when he'd next see her.

In a way, I guess he doesn't.

His teeth nipped her, and he sucked her bottom lip into his mouth, but delicious

gentleness contoured everything. Beneath her shirt, his hands held onto her waist, touch sweeping her skin.

"Your hands have calluses." She lifted her arms for him to remove her blouse. "I didn't expect that for someone who sits behind a desk."

"I go to the gym a lot. Now,"–he tapped the waistband of her jeans–"you going to take these off for me?"

A pleasant aching thrummed between her legs, heat pulsating low in her stomach. Leaning forward, she took his bottom lip between her teeth and tugged gently. "Take me to your room first."

His laugh caressed her skin, and she wrapped her legs around his waist as he carried her to his room. Her lips molded to his again, her hands running through his hair and pressing his head closer to her.

He kicked the door shut, stamping out the blare of the abandoned movie, and pinned her to the wall with his body.

In the sudden quiet, she became much more aware of what they were about to dive into. But she didn't care; she was too overwhelmed by him to worry about the consequences.

She rolled her hips against him, eyes widening as his erection pressed against her thigh. *Oh, my God.*

She moved her hips again, a desperate sound escaping her.

"More," she breathed.

"Well, I guess that answers whether you're sure about a no-strings thing," he groaned. Mouthing along her jaw and nipping along the arch of her neck, his tongue darted out to soothe the bite as he undid her jeans.

Need roared into an inferno under her skin, burning her alive. She dropped her bra to the ground, followed soon after by her underwear and the rest of his clothes.

"Jesus," he breathed. "Sophie, you're pe–"

"Don't," she interrupted.

They couldn't afford to drop compliments.

Still, she didn't hold herself back from running her eyes appreciatively over him.

"Come here," she whispered.

He stepped forward, entangling his hands in her hair. "Still want me to bite you?"

"Always." She pulled him into another deep kiss, craving his taste all over.

One of his hands wrapped around the base of her throat, fingers squeezing as his other hand slipped between her legs.

She sighed in content, pressing her hips toward his touch. "God, yes, keep doing that."

He kissed her shoulder while rubbing circles against her clit, before pushing a finger into her. Adding another, he pumped them in and out as his mouth found hers again.

Her breathing quickened as she sighed against his lips.

His hand left her neck, palming her breast instead, and his fingers sped up.

Groaning, her head tipped back against the wall, and she canted her hips toward his hand.

"There's a good girl," he muttered. "Fuck my hand, just like that."

He toyed with her nipples, tugging and rolling them between his fingers, all while his other hand didn't slow.

Gasping, her head fell forward onto his shoulder, creeping closer and closer to the edge inside.

His head dipped, lips puckering over her nipple.

She tripped over the cliff. Back arching, a flurry of gasps slipped through her lips as her thighs shook.

He caught her around her waist. "You good?"

She nodded, sucking in deep breaths. Tilting her head, she asked, “Is that all you got?”

“Careful what you wish for.” He grinned as he carried her to his bed, dropping her to his mattress.

“Do you know how badly I wanted to ask you out when I first saw you?” Falling to his knees, he smoothed his hands down her body, and his lips traced down her stomach.

“So, why’d you wait?”

“You looked like you were going to kill me that first day.” He mouthed at her hip. “And I knew there was no way you’d say yes.”

She chuckled, the laughter rolling into a groan as his hand squeezed her breast. “You took my coffee. You were lucky I left well enough alone.”

“You really would’ve yelled at me?”

She tilted her head. “Do you want me to?”

“In a way.” He hummed and kissed her thigh. Offering a wicked grin, he slung her legs over his shoulders. “Let’s start by seeing how responsive you can be for me.”

His tongue spread and twirled across her clit, and there was something gentle yet treacherous about the way he licked her.

Gasping, she grabbed at the sheets as she craned her neck to look at him.

His mouth worked as he met her gaze, holding it briefly before tearing away. Slipping his touch to her calves, he widened her legs.

God, the things he did ... she melted into his mattress. Her fingers ran through his hair, holding him to her.

Whispered encouragement floated from her lips as pleasure overwhelmed her.

A moment later, she cried out, crashing over the edge again.

“Such a good girl, letting me hear you.” He kissed her thigh.

Deep breaths inflated her lungs as she stretched out. “God, you’re spoiling me. I haven’t even touched you yet.”

"You don't have to tonight, if you don't want to." His gaze carved down her body. "I can just focus on you."

She snorted. "Nice try."

Catching her breath, she sat up. Her gaze flicked below his hips, and she met his eyes. "Get on the bed."

Bracing her weight on her knees, she gripped his cock and took the head in her mouth.

A tortured groan slipped from his lips, and he roped his fingers into her hair, tugging. "Good God."

She hummed and continued her movements, her tongue swirling around and snaking up to his tip.

Taking more of him into her mouth, she relished the whimpers coming out of him, the noises only adding to the pressure between her legs.

He groaned, his breath coming in labored pants. "That's it. Relax your throat."

Her teeth gave the lightest of scrapes, and he jerked, fingers tightening in her hair.

"*Fuck*," he grunted.

Pulling his cock from her mouth, she peered up at him. "Did I hurt you?"

Most men didn't like it when you got your teeth involved. God knew her ex didn't. But there was something about James that had made her want to try.

"No. It felt amazing." He panted and smoothed his hand down her spine. "Do it again."

She grinned and flicked her tongue against his tip, surrounding his cock with her mouth. Scouring her teeth down his shaft, he unraveled before her eyes.

Racing to the bathroom, she locked the door behind her.

She didn't regret what happened; far from it. In terms of the bedroom, all her exes paled in comparison.

And on top of that ... James had asked if she was alright

with him being into the rougher side, which spoke volumes. Not to mention his constant check-ins to see if she was alright.

But the fact of the matter was, she couldn't stay here. That leaned too ... intimate for what this was.

Blowing out a breath, she pressed her frizzy hair down in the mirror. She had donned the clothes she had worn before and adjusted them, trying to make herself as presentable as possible.

"Fuck," she muttered. *What the hell do I do?*

The easy solution lay before her: sneak out. But that was ... extremely rude.

Still, what other choice is there?

Another deep breath snuck past her lips as she steeled herself and left the bathroom.

Grabbing her purse from the hall table, she crept to the elevator and slipped her shoes on.

She could only pray James slept, succumbing to the exhaustion of the day after making sure she was cleaned up and taken care of.

A chuckle made her freeze. "Well, this is flattering."

She turned, guilt flooding her like she had just been caught sneaking out past her curfew.

James leaned against the wall opposite her, clad in pajama pants with his arms crossed across his bare chest. He grinned and clucked his tongue. "Shame. I must've not done my job right if you can still walk."

"I'd say that's more embarrassing for you than me." She swallowed, desire skittering over her skin and collecting between her legs. "And there's always next time."

His eyes flashed, roaming down her body. "Or you can stay, and we can take care of that right now,"—he winked—"time efficiency and all."

Clearing her throat, she strutted over to him and ran a finger down his jaw.

"Sounds tempting." She smirked. "But unlucky for you, I'm leaving."

Taking a staggering breath, he arched a brow. "It's almost one in the morning."

"I know."

But I can't stay here. I won't.

The practical part of her screamed it wasn't worth it. This was Manhattan, and the train ride alone took twenty minutes, not to mention the time she needed to spend walking.

But if it meant potentially giving her heart to him, she didn't care.

He heaved a sigh. "I have a guest room."

"I said no," she argued.

Stifling silence rained down as scales tipped back and forth in his eyes. His collage of tattoos stirred with every breath.

She lifted her chin in silent challenge.

"Alright, then," he accepted. "But hold on."

Disappearing into his room, he emerged a moment later. Zipping up a sweatshirt, he grabbed a set of keys from the hall table.

"What are you doing?" she asked.

He arched a brow. "Giving you a ride home."

Her tongue weighed a ton in her mouth.

In the grand scheme of things, James driving her home meant nothing. But given everything between them ... it was too much, too soon.

She frowned, shaking her head.

He blew a breath out. "Sophie, if you stay in the guest room, I promise you won't even see me in the morning. Just think of this as spending the night at a friend's house."

"*No*."

Panic and irritation seared her lungs.

Christ, did he not understand how a Friends-With-Benefits arrangement worked?

God, were Chlo and Ol right?

He narrowed his eyes. "Okay, fine. Then just ... wait a minute."

Wandering into the living room, he lifted his phone to his

ear and spoke in rapid Italian after a moment.

A chill filled Sophie's stomach as he hung up. "What did you just do?"

He stalked back into the foyer. "Well, you've got another thing coming if you think I'm letting you take a ride-share this late alone. The private car service line was busy when I called before, and since you don't want me driving you, I called someone."

"I got that." She crossed her arms. "But *who* did you call?"

"Give it a minute." He crossed to the fridge. "Do you want some water while you wait?"

She scoffed and pursed her lips. *This is ridiculous.* "Thanks, but I'll see you tomorrow." Spinning toward the elevator, she reached for the button just as it slid open.

Blinking, she stared at Philip.

"I called Pip," James said. "He's got a really messed-up sleep schedule."

Philip waved, running a hand through his hair and scuffing it up even more.

Irritation burned her lungs. "I don't need an escort."

James frowned. "Sophie, you are *not* crossing the city alone at one a.m. It's either me or Pip; take your pick."

She huffed. "Fine."

It would be awkward with Philip in the car, but it was preferable to the subway or James.

James nodded curtly. "Pip, take my car."

"Just over there." Philip gestured to a navy Mercedes glimmering in the dim parking garage.

The car's headlights flashed, and the alarm chirped as they approached.

He settled into the driver's seat. "Aside from the monthly dinners he has to go to at his dad's, James barely drives this thing. It's a damn shame because this baby deserves better than to sit in a garage all day."

Closing the passenger side door, she buckled herself in. *Then why ... oh.*

Parking was like trying to find water in a desert in Manhattan, and car break-ins were more frequent than desired. Like other wealthy New Yorkers, James must've owned the car for ease.

"Thanks for driving me. I know this is awkward," she said as the engine rumbled to life.

Philip shrugged. "It's no problem. Besides, I'm sure it's better than James driving you or staying overnight."

"Definitely ... I really would've been fine taking an Uber or something."

Philip snorted. "Ay, James can be stupid, but he's not *that* stupid. That was a fight you weren't going to win."

Silence cascaded like a waterfall as they left the garage, and Philip turned onto a mostly empty street.

He tapped his fingers on the wheel. "So. You and James."

They came to a halt at a red light.

"There is no me and James." She looked out the window. A few people littered the sidewalks, and empty cabs idled by the curb. She turned her attention to Philip as they resumed moving. "There is *no* me and James. Got it?"

There couldn't be. Not as long as she worked at Covey and held his company partially in her hands.

There could only be hangouts that led to potential hookups. Nothing more, nothing less.

"Loud and clear." Philip grinned and kept his eyes fixed on the road.

"Anyway, why does James call you Pip?" she asked.

Philip sighed and muttered something. With her rudimentary Spanish, she managed to put together a prayer.

She sniggered. "What, is it embarrassing?"

"No, it's just–my grandma used to call me, 'Mi querida feliz,'" he said.

"'My darling happiness?'"

He tilted his head. "You know Spanish?"

"The basics," she said.

"I see." He nodded. "Well, one time, James overheard her, decided to nickname me Pip, and it just stuck."

She nodded, swallowing the information he gave her.

Of course, James is a family friend.

Now that she looked Philip up, she knew those were his family's banking branches that dotted the streets of European cities.

But Wikipedia hadn't listed him as the current sitting chair of the company. Instead, his sister was.

Sophie hadn't been able to find any information on him at all except for the fact that he resided in America.

Why was Philip working for James instead of his own family? What happened that made it that way?

She frowned, ready to probe deeper when she noticed the look dancing across his face.

There was a story, but one he wasn't ready to give.

"Uh–" she began. But before she could say anything more, the car jerked.

Sophie seized the grab handle. "Shit!"

"Me cago en la cabeza!" Philip slammed the brakes to avoid hitting a jaywalker. Blasting the horn, he muttered a few angry words in Spanish.

"Are you okay?" he asked as they started moving again.

"Yeah, I don't think James should let you drive his car," Sophie quipped.

Philip laughed. "You should've been there when my boyfriend at the time first saw my motorcycle."

"What, did he freak out?" Sophie asked. "I wouldn't be surprised. Those things are death traps, especially in this city."

"That's exactly what my little sister said," Philip remarked. "Her name's Catalina. I think you'd like her."

Sophie stared out the window. "When was the last time you saw her?"

Philip quieted before slipping into a turning lane. "In person? A month ago."

Sophie pursed her lips, suspicion brewing. "And ... when was the last time you saw her at home?"

A funny look settled into his expression. "Um ... fourteen years ago." Pulling to a stop at a light, he scrutinized her sharply. "Did James say something?"

She shook her head, the engine suddenly too loud. "Never mind. Forget I said anything."

The light turned, and the city moved again outside her window.

In the reflection, her rosy cheeks flickered in and out of view.

"I am sorry for snapping; it is just a long story," Philip said, his accent coming through stronger than ever. "But yes, it has been fourteen years."

He said fourteen years with the same air as someone announcing the death of a loved one. If his end goal had been to get her mind off the subject, he failed magnificently.

"Oh." She winced at touching a nerve. Her eyes skirted to the digital clock–how had only ten minutes gone by?

"Anyway, I um ... I don't think I've ever seen James so excited," Philip continued, changing the subject. "When you agreed to a date the other day, I mean. He didn't admit it, but he didn't try to hide it, either." He grinned. "Once he got your number, he was constantly checking his phone and looking at it like ... like no hay color."

She frowned. "There's no color?"

Philip laughed. "He was looking at his phone like there was no competition." Something in his eyes flickered. "He had a million other things on his plate, and yet, the only thing on his mind was *you*."

Warmth trickled into her lungs and pooled there. "I wish everything had turned out differently."

Philip shrugged. "It is what it is." He stopped at a red light and rubbed his jaw. "Sophie ..."

She frowned at the hesitation on his face. "What is it?"

"I trust you, and while I don't think you started dating James because of other stuff, as his friend, I need to make sure you–"

"That I didn't start this to use him?" she cut in.

He flushed, nodding.

She should've been angry at Philip's blunt question, but nothing but admiration filled her senses. Connections meant everything, especially for the rich, and there was nothing better than the ones that came through marriage.

In her quick search, she'd noticed James hadn't escaped that, either.

His romantic history was marked by sightings with socialites and dates with heiresses, and it only made sense for Sophie to want him for the same reasons they did.

But none of that mattered to her.

"I didn't," she said. "Like I told him, I couldn't place who you two were when I met you. Yes, I figured he had money, but that had nothing to do with why I accepted his offer."

"Okay," Philip murmured and smiled. "Good. I'm sorry for that, I just needed to–"

"I get it," she said. "I would do the same thing if I were in your position."

"It just happened more than I wish." He clenched his jaw and pulled the car in front of her building. "Do you want me to walk you to the door?"

She shook her head. "Thanks for the ride."

"Anytime. Have a good night."

She darted out, the neon glow from the noodle shop under her apartment stinging her eyes as she fumbled for her keys in her bag. Looking behind her shoulder, she pushed the door in.

He idled by the curb, his gaze trained on her.

Only when she waved and closed the door did the engine rumble away.

Leaning against the metal, she started up the narrow, darkened stairwell. Each gust of air she sucked in stifled her lungs.

James, striding into that conference room, had sent everything tumbling into a burning, twisted mess.

But things turned out better than she thought.

Heading up to her apartment, she quietly set her things down and slipped off her shoes. Gingerly, she crept toward the bathroom and made it a few feet before Chloe rushed out of her room.

She waved her cane frantically. “You’re home!”

“You’re awake? Don’t you have work in like, five hours?” Sophie asked.

Chloe headed toward the couch. “Yeah, but you just had your first ... I don’t know what to call it. I’d be a shitty friend if I didn’t wait up for you.”

Sophie snorted. “Thanks for looking out for me.”

Chloe waved away the sentiment. “Of course, Soph, always. But why didn’t you text me so I knew you weren’t dead?”

“Sorry, I left my phone on the hall table.”

“It’s fine,” she said. “Just give me details now.”

Sophie laced her fingers around her knee and leaned back on the couch, starting with James’s apartment.

“I bet this place pales in comparison,” Chloe exclaimed.

Sophie nodded, even though she wouldn’t trade their apartment for the world.

At least three mysterious stains dotted the vicinity, but there were so many memories attached to them, it didn’t matter. The smell of cooking food from downstairs adhered to the walls, but as far as she was concerned, that was part of the charm.

Chloe grinned. “What was the sex like?”

Sophie was grateful that it was dark around them. She wasn’t embarrassed, at least not really. But now that the moment stared her in the face, something blocked the words on her tongue, and she wasn’t exactly sure what that was.

“It was amazing, but he’s more ... possessive than I thought, and I didn’t think I’d be as into it as I was.” Her cheeks flushed. “Fuck, what’s wrong with me? I mean, I shouldn’t like that, right?”

“There’s absolutely nothing wrong,” Chloe exclaimed.

"As long as he didn't hurt you, and you didn't feel forced to do anything. You didn't, right?"

Sophie shook her head. She didn't doubt that if she told him to stop, he would've, and if she wanted to leave or change her mind, he would've let her, no questions asked.

Her phone buzzed in her pocket, and she pulled it out.

Did you get back ok? I'm assuming you are bc Pip just texted me. Also, he said to give you Lina's number

He pasted in a contact beneath.

She liked the message and tapped in a reply.

Yeah. Thanks for the ride

His answer mimicked her words earlier.

I can't tell if that's a come-on or not

She snorted.

Chloe cleared her throat and arched her neck to see the screen. "Is that him? He's already texting you? He's not coming off as desperate, is he?"

Sophie shook her head, smiling. She appreciated her friend caring about her, but there was no need to worry.

To Sophie, it was clear.

If James wanted something more or for her to be the one standing next to him, that wasn't possible.

She woke hours later to her phone buzzing furiously. Pushing aside the soreness that rocked her lower half, she squinted at the screen and groaned.

"What?" she snapped into the receiver.

"Hi to you too, Pee Pee." Her younger brother's voice flooded the room.

It's a Saturday morning, what's he doing up?

She checked the time on her phone and sighed. She slept later than she thought. Sighing, she flopped back on her pillow. "What do you want, Noah?"

Silence, punctuated by the closing of cabinets, ruled the other end of the line.

Annoyance crept into her throat. "Noah?"

"Mom wants you home this weekend." He crunched down on something. "So be home."

"What? What if I had plans?"

"Do you?"

"I mean, no."

Not unless getting drunk with her friends and singing "Uptown Girl" too loudly was part of the plan.

"That's what I thought," her brother chirped.

"Shut up."

"Be nice, you're on speaker," he said.

"XiǎoDān, it's been too long since your last visit," her mom reasoned, entering the conversation. "I miss seeing you."

Sophie closed her eyes. "We FaceTimed two days ago, Mom."

Plus, her last trip home was a month ago, but bringing that up wouldn't help anything.

"Aiyah, in person, XiǎoDān."

"Fine, fine, I'll come up," she caved. "I have to go now. See you Saturday."

She hung up and groaned, climbing out of bed.

Guilt riddled her stomach.

Her trips would be much longer than just the weekend if it weren't for her job, but if she got that promotion, it would make up for all that lost time.

All they had to do was be careful.

Yawning, she shuffled toward the bathroom only to be met with a locked door.

The door swung open and Oliver blinked. "Oh. Look who's finally up."

She flipped him off. "What are you even doing here?"

He shrugged. "I needed to borrow your stepladder. Speak of the devil ..."

Chloe came out of the kitchen carrying said stepladder before setting it down. She turned to grab something else, using the wall for support instead of her cane.

"Leave her alone, will you?" she admonished. "You'd be tired, too, if you were getting fucked all night."

"On the contrary, when Taylor and I–"

"*TMI!*" Chloe stuffed one of the apple slices on the plate she held into Oliver's mouth.

Sophie snorted and took the plate from her friend. "Thanks for that."

She put them on the coffee table before disappearing into the bathroom. When she came out, her friends were sprawled out on the sofa, laughing amongst themselves.

Oliver picked up an apple slice. "Soph, do you have a picture of the guy from yesterday?"

"Google him. James Tian," Sophie grabbed an apple and went to sit next to Oliver.

"Excuse me?" He huffed a laugh.

"Just do it."

His keyboard clicked and he choked on the fruit. "O-Oh, that's why you said to Google him. I thought you were joking."

"Let me see." Chloe took the phone, reading aloud from the screen. "James Tian is the executive chairman of Lotus Art Consultation. At thirty-three, he's amongst the youngest people over thirty to hold a spot on the Forbes Billionaires List, with a net worth of" –she gasped–"...Sophie?"

Oliver looked faint. "It says he's the youngest son of the owner of Tian Corporation. As in the private shipping company?"

Sophie picked up an apple slice and played with it. "Yeah."

"How are you acting so nonchalant about this?" Chloe squawked.

"It doesn't matter to me," Sophie said. "So, he has money. He's still a person."

Someone still capable of shattering her just like that asshole had when she gave him a chance at that party.

"You made it sound like he was well-off," Chloe spluttered. "But this isn't I-Own-Multiple-Vacation-Homes rich, this is I-Own-A-Private-Island rich."

"I think the real question here is what does James want?" Oliver asked. Like, is he using you for publicity?" Oliver frowned. "No, wait, you guys aren't going public with it. Maybe–"

"*Maybe* he doesn't have a hidden agenda," Sophie shook her head. "But if you guys want peace of mind, I'm asking him to grab dinner Monday downstairs."

Chloe and Oliver exchanged a look. "We'll be there."

Seven

James

Staring at his computer screen, James's eyebrows knit together.

In the dimmed light of his office, the screen hurt his eyes. He sighed and went to open the blinds, rubbing his temples between his fingers.

The big question was why hadn't Delacroix told them he was in danger of losing his money? Why keep a deal that would cost him millions when he sank into deep water?

And most of all, who knew all that and scheduled him in regardless?

Not for the first time, James wished their technology made it easy to see where the order came from, but alas ...

He sighed and returned to his desk, caught in the middle of a heated email chain with the head of the bank that handled their checks.

The bastard wasn't giving him anything useful.

James reread the sentences.

Unfortunately, we are unable to disclose that information, even to you. Discretion, and all that, you know how it is.

"You can shove your discretion up your ass," he muttered. Removing his glasses, he rested his head on his desk.

This is what I was afraid of.

And now he was on the receiving end of some corporate copout instead of an honest answer.

He groaned, considering sending an email to his friend who usually helped him get his hands on information. But even if he did, without a name besides Delacroix's, Raymond wouldn't be able to find anything they didn't already know.

God, James needed a break.

His phone buzzed on the desk next to him and he reached blindly for it. "Hello?"

"So, I guess things finally blew up." His dad's tone iced over everything it touched.

"Please, let's not pretend you weren't rooting for this."

"You're my son, why would I want to see you fail?" his dad asked. "After all, we have to keep up our family's penchant for success, don't we?"

James scoffed. "Whatever you have to tell yourself. What do you want?"

"Careful, James," his dad said. "I'm still your father."

That stopped a long time ago.

"George's demise isn't good news for my company, either," he continued. "Since he was one of my top shareholders, losing his money was a big hit we honestly weren't prepared for. So, here's what I want to do." A computer mouse clicked in the background. "I need to find out what happened to George, and from what I understand, you're in a similar position."

"You want to work together," James surmised.

"It would be beneficial to both of us, yes."

Laughter bubbled in his stomach and threatened to spill forth from his mouth.

This was ridiculous–was his dad even hearing himself?

"No, it wouldn't," James said. "We have two very different goals and I'm currently handling my problem on my own. I suggest you do the same."

"I think you forget sometimes you wouldn't be where you are without me," his dad replied.

Correction: Without Mom.

"My point still stands," James said.

"Fine. But don't say I didn't ask."

His dad hung up and James sighed, pinching the bridge of his nose.

He doubted his dad even cared about Delacroix at all. Tian Corporation was large enough that the money was insignificant.

But his dad cared how people saw him, maybe even too much. Perhaps the situation with Delacroix hadn't completely unaffected him, but it certainly wasn't as pressing as he made it seem.

James's phone pulsed in his hand, and he glanced at the new text from Sophie.

Do you wanna grab dinner tonight?

He typed in a response, his fingers flying across the screen.

Ok. Did you have somewhere in mind?
Do you need me to pick you up?

He didn't like to drive his car around when he could help it, but for this, he'd make an exception.

God, Friday night ... his lips pressed to satin when he kissed her, and fucking her was a trip to heaven itself.

How do you feel about noodles?

I love them

Perfect. There's a noodle place under
my apartment. Meet me at 7?

He liked the message and scrapped the plans he had to stay in the office until late. He had a meeting with a shareholder at five-thirty, but he could push it to tomorrow.

His jaw clenched and he played with a pen.

Christ, he wasn't *supposed* to need more than their arrangement–he understood that. Seeing her tonight and every time in the future would only plunge him deeper into the ether.

But even though every bone in his body screamed otherwise, she was too addictive to stay away from.

Argh.

He needed a distraction.

Wandering out of his office, he moved down the hall, turning the corner, and knocking on Cami's door frame.

"Hey. Heard anything?" James asked.

Unlike usual, no chatter littered the halls.

The team that made up Lotus was pretty small, but save for him, Jackie, and the rest of the C-Suite, he gave everyone else PTO until they figured out the mess with Delacroix.

Cami set down the spoonful of yogurt she'd been about to eat. She'd opened her mouth to speak when her phone rang. She glanced at it and held up a finger.

James leaned against the door frame, his arms crossed, as Cami spoke in rapid-fire Portuguese.

When she hung up, she played with the device. "So that was Max."

James started. "The one who–"

Cami ate a mouthful of yogurt. "Mmhmm."

Cami's friend's boyfriend worked under Delacroix, and after James mentioned Lotus to Delacroix at a party, they brought it up again to Delacroix's assistant.

"Did Max give us anything we don't already know?" James left the unspoken question hanging.

Why would his boyfriend give our name to a man who faced financial trouble?

Cami picked up on James's concern and crossed her arms. "He didn't backstab us, so you can drop that thought now. His boyfriend just told him that the night before the news broke, there was a rumor Delacroix was done for." She frowned. "They thought it was a joke, but obviously, it wasn't."

The information hit James like a tidal wave, and he was overcome with the need to launch his fist at the wall.

"And why didn't he tell us this sooner?" he asked, keeping his voice level.

His friend eyed him, her gaze flashing down to his curled hands.

"Don't do anything stupid, James," Cami warned. "At the end of the day, it's not their fault."

James sighed. He knew that, of course. But he needed to be mad at someone about this, and Josh and Max had kept the information to themselves for days.

"Look, the point is, it happened." Cami tossed the empty yogurt container in her trash. "There's nothing we can do. Josh is out of a job, and they're busy looking for a new one. Do you know how many places would be willing to hire you when your last employer is a criminal? Not many."

James gritted his teeth.

Soothing thoughts. He had to think soothing, calming thoughts.

That was what his therapist said. That was what got him through family dinners.

"Well," he said. "If they can't find one, tell them to come here. We can find somewhere for them."

"Yeah?"

"Yeah. Also, you have yogurt on your face."

He walked out of Cami's office and retraced his steps toward his.

It didn't matter who told Josh about Delacroix. It was the person who *started* it that they needed to find.

That was the root of the problems. Once they found it, they could figure out who let Delacroix blow Lotus up.

People yelling in different dialects of Mandarin assaulted his ears the second he opened the Uber's door.

He rarely went to Chinatown, since everything he needed was closer to him. But as he passed roasting meats, fluffy, steamed buns, and plump, gleaming produce, he made up his mind to go more often.

Turning the corner, he reached the address Sophie had sent and caught the door as someone was leaving.

The shop wasn't large by any means, and nearly all the booths were full, but he quickly found Sophie.

She shifted, and his mouth went dry. Her simple jeans and blouse pairing might as well have been a bodycon dress.

The red material of her top sent his mind spiraling to a deeper, darker place. One where, instead of the fabric being molded to her skin, it was his hands. His lips memorized every inch of her.

"Hey," he managed. "You look nice."

"Hey! Thanks." She slid a menu toward him with the tips of her fingers. "Um. I'm going to use the bathroom."

Getting out from her side of the booth, she turned.

He nearly blacked out right then and there.

If he thought the blouse was gracious on her curves, it was *nothing* compared to what the jeans did for her ass.

Swallowing, he brought his attention to the few workers kneading bundles of dough behind a large windowpane. Another pair of employees pulled the dough into logs, before slicing them into fresh noodles.

In the back of the workstation, another narrow window looked into the kitchen. Great, big clouds of steam funneled upwards, obscuring the chef's faces.

He cleared his throat and pulled his glasses from the inside pocket of his blazer. Grabbing a tissue, he wiped off a smudge and settled them on his nose. He focused on the menu in his hand, cataloging the different options.

"Have I ever told you how much I like those on you?" She sat again, wiping her hands on those damn jeans.

He cleared his throat and examined the menu again. "You've seen me in them once."

"And it wasn't nearly enough," she replied. "Why do you need reading glasses anyway? Aren't you a bit young for them?"

He shrugged, pushing up the wire-rimmed frames. "Side effect of having to look at small details in art for so many years."

Taking off the glasses, a slight smirk wiped over his face as a flicker of disappointment flashed in her eyes.

The server came over with a pad of paper, pencil twirling

in his fingers.

"Ready to order?" he asked in Mandarin.

Sophie delivered her request in the language, then waited for James to respond.

"Right. I will do fifteen," he said, the smooth tones rolling off his tongue.

The server nodded and wrote down the order as he snuck glances at Sophie over the top of the pad.

James's eyes narrowed and he cleared his throat loudly.

"Could you get me some more water?" He inserted a small bite into his tone and waited until his water came before excusing himself to the bathroom.

On his way back, he made a pit stop at the counter. Looking back at the table, he frowned at the attractive guy engrossed in conversation with Sophie.

A punch rocked through his gut, unfounded worries coating his mind, and his heart plummeted as she laughed.

Hang on...

Her facial expressions and body language suggested she knew him well. Another woman joined them and James cracked a smile.

His heart squeezed as they left the table. Why were her friends acting like this was a date when he could never get that far with Sophie?

As he walked back to the table, the obvious solution crossed his mind: fire Covey and everything would be okay. He and Sophie could date without any obstacles.

But ... Covey was *good*, based on what he heard and read. It would do more harm than good to eliminate them.

He slid back into the booth. "Hey, sorry. How's your food?"

"Good," she said. "What about you? I know it's a far cry from what you're probably used to, but..."

"I like it," he said. These were some of the best noodles he tasted, and he had soba at Tsuta.

A smile danced in her eyes, spreading across her lips. Glancing down, she slid a fatty piece of char siu into her mouth and rooted around in the noodles.

"Dammit," she muttered. "They never give enough."

"Here." He put the piece of pork floating in his own bowl into hers. Maybe it was the lighting, but he swore her cheeks were rosier.

"Thanks."

Conversation flowed easily once more between them, and it was like they'd been friends for years. There wasn't a chance for an awkward silence to develop.

Birthdays were revealed, fears and favorites exchanged, and before he knew it, the server took their empty dishes away.

For the first time, a strained deafness fell.

She cleared her throat and drummed her fingers on the table. "So, um ... how do you want to split the bill?"

Tension coiled in his chest. Friends would've split it, but ...

He squared his shoulders and looked her dead in the eye. "I took care of it."

"What? Why?" She frowned. "The owner also owns the entire building, so I get a discount."

A smile played on his lips. "When you're with me, you don't pay."

"Friends don't do that."

She was right, but he couldn't help the puff of laughter that blew from his lips. "Friends don't typically see each other naked, either, sweetheart."

She snorted. "Did you just call me sweetheart?"

"Are we going to pretend you didn't like it?'

A rueful smile touched her lips. "Touché. But I refuse to believe you, Philip, and Luc haven't seen each other naked."

"We haven't."

"Luc told me about Cabo."

"Luc is a goddamn liar," James drawled, though he was sure even astronauts in space detected the nervous twinge to his words. "Believe nothing he says."

Her rich, tinkling laughter filled the air, and, God dammit, if it was possible to be addicted to a sound, this was it.

"Okay, well, thanks. I need to stop by the bathroom again," she said.

His phone buzzed incessantly, and he pulled it out, looking at the screen. The call came from an unknown number, but something in his gut told him to answer anyway. "Hello?"

"JAMES, HOOOOOOOOOOOOOOLLAAAA!"

He winced away from the receiver as the voice wailed into the phone. "Lina? Whose phone is this?"

She laughed merrily and continued in Spanish, "The phone is my friend's. Ay, guess what? I'm in Boston, cariño!"

"What?!" He pinched the bridge of his nose. Part of him wanted to call Philip and tell him that his sister was across the world on a random Monday. But ... if James were in her shoes, the last thing she'd want was her big brother stepping in.

He expelled a long breath from his nose. A solution lay at the forefront of his mind, but he'd rather eat glass.

Then again, if he didn't want to leave Lina hanging, what choice did he have? "Lina–"

"Everything's fine, cariño!"

"Like hell everything's fine," he snapped. "You know you're slurring your words, right?"

"Well, you don't need to be mean about it." She sniffed. "You know what? I don't need this. I should've known I'd get the same reaction from you as my brother. I'm going to hang up now, by–"

"Wait, I'm sorry," James cut in. "Where are you right now?"

"This restaurant in the Seaport, I think," Lina said after a moment. "Nicole says it's really good, don't you, querida?"

He rustled up all the Nicoles he knew in the area and relief flooded him after a moment.

"Wait, Nicole Amato?" he asked. "Are you there with Nicole Amato?"

If Lina said yes, he could use the information to his advantage.

Nicole Amato started Amato Cosmetics at twenty-six and, within five years, had achieved the title of self-made millionaire. She always traveled with at least one security guard.

"Sí."

His heart leapt. "Give the phone to Nicole."

"Ella está en el baño." Lina giggled. "She's been in there for a while."

He sighed as his patience began to wear thin. "Alright, can you tell me where you are?"

"I told you."

"No, the name."

"Ohhhhh," she dragged out before giving the name of the restaurant.

"Okay, stay there," he said. "I'm going to se–"

A shriek of laughter and a beeping whizzed across his hearing, and he looked at his phone.

"Fuck," he muttered.

"Everything okay?" Sophie peered down with wide eyes.

Holy–When did she get back?! James sighed, steeling himself. "Yeah, just one second. Excuse me for a second, I need to make a call."

Exiting the booth, he headed for a semi-quiet corner. He pulled up his brother's contact information and pressed the call option.

He typically avoided contacting Adam at all costs, but James loved Lina as if she were his sister.

"Hello?" Adam answered.

"Hi," James said. "You remember Lina, right? Well, she's drunk, and I can't be there. So I don't need you to be an asshole about this, and–"

"Wha–slow down. Hang on."

He scowled as the background noise on Adam's end muffled. James tapped his foot, scanning the restaurant as he waited.

Sophie talked to the same man and woman again and she briefly met his gaze before tearing her attention away.

"Alright, what's going on?" Adam asked, the sound on his

end rushing back.

"You remember Philip has a younger sister, right?"

"Sure."

James sighed and muttered a swear. "Okay, well, tell me you at least remember her name."

"Of course. ... Emily."

"*Catalina*," he snapped. "I swear to God, I–no, I'm not doing this today. The gist is that she's in America and drunk. I'm worried she'll hurt herself, and I'm not in a spot where I can go help her, so..."

"You need me to save your ass?" Adam asked. "Well, I have to admit, I'm flattered."

James rolled his eyes. Leave it to his brother to sound cocky about something like this.

Honestly, is his therapist helping him?

"Can you not be an ass right now? She's at Aqua, that new bar in the Seaport with Nicole Amato."

"Catalina's an adult." Boredom suffused Adam's tone. "I'm sure she'll be just fine."

"Adam, just do it," James ordered.

Adam hummed. "While I have you, I need you to do something for me. There might be some videos of me tonight at Oak and Ivy. If anything pops up anywhere, I need you to get them taken down. Now is not a good time for me to be in the news in a negative way."

"Right, because your Daddy's favorite."

"Do me a favor and never say that again."

"The truth hurts, doesn't it?"

"Fuck off."

"Why can't you do this yourself?" James asked. "I know you have resources."

Every good businessperson did.

"Yes," Adam said. "But yours are faster."

"Fine," James said, rolling his eyes. "I'll take it as payment for this."

"Wait, what? I didn't agr–"

He ended the call and slipped his cell back in his pocket,

heading back for the booth.

Sophie tilted her head. "Are you sure everything's okay? You look upset."

He nodded, tugging at his neck. "It's Lina. She's in Boston and hit the bottle a little too hard tonight."

"Lina is Philip's sister, right? Is she going to be okay?" Sophie rose.

"Yeah, I have my brother on it."

I really hope that was a good idea.

James didn't know why Lina suddenly decided to take a trip to America, but he'd bet good money the last thing she needed was Adam being a dick.

"Oh, right, I forgot he lives there."

James paused. "How do you know where my brother lives?"

"Wikipedia."

James grinned and shook his head as he held open the door for her, a gust of smoky air rustling past.

"Thanks for dinner," she said. "I ... guess I'll see you tomorrow at Joseph's?"

He resisted the urge to purse his lips. She didn't think the night was over, did she? He certainly didn't want it to be.

"Actually, I was wondering if you wanted to get dessert," he said.

Pushing open the door to her building, she flicked a switch on the wall and soft, golden light drowned them. "Oh, um ... sure. Let me drop something off and then we can go. Where were you thinking? Oh! Have you been to Little Cupcake Bakeshop? It's a little bit of a hike, but if you're up for amazing–"

"Mmm, I was thinking somewhere closer." His gaze flicked upward.

She followed his gaze toward the stairs, and a delicate, pink blush settled across her cheeks. "I see."

He stepped towards her.

She had resprayed the perfume she usually wore, and the scent was even more addictive. Vanilla and coconut blended seamlessly, winding their way around him.

He caged her in between his arms, pressing his body against hers.

"Do you know what those jeans have been doing to me, sweetheart?" he murmured, his lips skimming down her jaw and neck.

She shuddered, and he groaned as she pressed a hand against the bulge between his legs.

"Hopefully, what I wanted them to," she said. "Also, stop calling me 'sweetheart.'"

His hand inched down to her ass. "Alright, then what do you want me to call you?" His lips spread into a smile. "Dumpling? Muffin? Cookie?"

"Why are they all foods?" She leaned forward, pausing an inch from his lips. "We'll workshop it."

He sat on her bed and slung his shirt back on, fishing his tie from where he'd flung it after undoing it from Sophie's wrists.

"How are you going to get home?" she asked.

"Subway," he replied.

She crossed her arms and frowned. "What do you mean the subway? You wouldn't let *me* take the subway at one a.m."

"Fine. Then I'll take a taxi."

"Again, you wouldn't let me take a taxi or ride-share." She leaned against the wall in the living room. "You know, if we really wanted to make this a full-circle moment, you could sleep on the couch."

Snorting, he pulled up the number of the private car service on his phone. "Nope."

Whatever happened, things couldn't end with him staying the night. That was too much. If he wound up sleeping on the couch, he would explode.

"I know, I was joking," she clarified.

But the hesitancy in her words boomed.

He spun to face her. "I'll call a private car and wait downstairs for it."

She nodded, eyes tracking across his features like she attempted to memorize him.

"Then get home safe," she murmured.

For a moment, he wished that despite his protests, she would reach out for him anyway. But that wasn't going to happen.

She was someone who had their priorities straight. She wouldn't let a leak sink the whole damn ship, and it was time he took a page from her book.

James's grip tightened around the second coffee cup as he leaned against the wall outside Joseph's.

Philip stood next to him, arms crossed.

"You didn't tell me who that coffee is for," his friend said. "Unless it's for you, too? Are you really tired?"

James didn't deign to answer.

In the silence that followed, Philip's gaze lingered on him. "Mierda. Do you have her coffee order memorized? Ay, cabrón, you're in too deep."

James knew all too well that he and Sophie couldn't be anything substantial. They were resigned to strings of meaningless sex. Anything more could only happen if they wanted to lose everything and more in the future.

And maybe it was too much but ... if he could save her at least ten minutes in the morning, he would.

"Good morning," Philip called.

Sophie jogged up the sidewalk, and a small smile graced James's lips.

He left her that morning with her hair a mess, her lips swollen, and her legs wobbly. But now, she looked remarkably well put together for someone who had only gotten five hours of sleep.

He held out the second coffee to her and she blinked.

"It's iced." Her fingers closed around the cup. "Um ... thanks. But you're not giving me your breakfast again, are you?"

Snorting, he resisted the urge to touch her. "Only if you want it. Just got your coffee for you. You don't like hot coffee, do you, darling?"

Since he started going to Joseph's, she always ordered an iced coffee. The last time he bought her coffee, he forgot to ask for it iced, and he hadn't missed the flicker of disappointment in her expression.

He wouldn't be the cause of that again.

"'Darling?'" Philip asked. "Cabrón, you've known her for a little over a week."

"He's trying to find a nickname for me," Sophie explained. "But you're right. A nickname after little over a week is too soon."

"Yeah, true." James shrugged. "I can go back to just your name."

"It's fine," she said after a moment. Her eyes twinkled with sparks of thanks and ... something else. "But we're not going with 'darling.'"

Eight

Sophie

Sophie rested her forehead against the door of her office and squeezed her eyes shut.

Why did he do that?

She turned, glaring across the crowded office at the offending object sitting on her desk.

The coffee sweated a visible ring on the wooden surface of her desk, the water creeping toward the framed photos of her family and friends.

Maybe buying her coffee was meant as a friendly gesture. Maybe James was waiting for her to pay him back but hadn't said anything.

Grabbing her phone from her desk, she fired off a text to him, asking how much she owed him for the coffee. Clicking her phone off, she forced herself to sit. She had work to do, after all.

Losing herself in emails, she moved on autopilot, bouncing from one to the next, and categorizing the most important cases into a spreadsheet. None of them were urgent, but she highlighted the first few and forwarded their emails to Marilyn.

Sophie clicked open the calendar to see when she could start slotting in appointments, and her phone lit up in her peripheral vision.

James: Don't worry about it. It's on me

She groaned and set her phone down again, resting her

head in her hands.

He had to mean that platonically. But judging by the way he looked at her on the street before, she didn't think it was, and that thought scared her more than anything.

Her phone buzzed again with another text from him.

I can get away for lunch. Is your break also at 1? Can I come over?

She stared at the screen.

What was wrong with him? How could he move on like that? When he didn't say anything more, she tapped in a response.

I don't think that's a good idea

The three bubbles indicating he was typing popped up and lingered.

She set her phone down. A watched pot never boiled, after all. Still, her foot tapped until her phone pulsed with another message from him.

Why? It's not like we're going to do anything. If people see us, they see us

She raised her brow. *Does he really not care what people will think? Should* I *not care what people will think*?

But no ... she had to. She didn't have the luxury he did of letting things blow over and starting anew down the line.

Maybe if he came over and people saw, they would assume that she and James were friends, eating lunch together.

But if Marilyn saw, there'd be so many more questions.

Did they have a prior history? Why was one of her most prominent clients eating lunch with her assistant?

It's not going to be like Brian. James isn't going to spite you if you turn him down.

Sophie's forehead wrinkled as her mind volleyed back and forth like a ping-pong ball, and she swallowed down her worries. It was fine; it was worth the risk.

Throwing everything to the wind, she typed in her response.

Fine

Great. What do you want?

Anything is good with me. Whatever you're craving

She clicked off her phone and dove back into work, opening up the virtual calendar on her computer. All too soon, her alarm blasted for her lunch break, and a knock sounded at her door.

She stood from her chair to reach for a stack of files across her desk, knocking over the tiny succulent. "Come in."

"Hey, I—you *are* on lunch right now, right?" James carried a large brown takeout bag emitting a heavenly scent. His gaze lingered on the files before settling on her face.

She nodded and sat down in her chair again, taking them with her.

"Sorry, I didn't realize it was already one. Make yourself comfortable. What did you bring?" She smoothed her hair and set the files on the floor with a thump, along with some papers to clear some room for him.

He set the bag down and rummaged through it. "I was craving a burger, and I didn't know what you'd like, so ... we have options. What do you want?"

She blinked and craned her neck to try to look in the bag.

Had he ordered every kind of sandwich on the menu?!

See? He's being thoughtful. Not like Brian at all.

Pointing to a random burger, she accepted it. Nodding her thanks, she unwrapped the food, took a big bite, and stifled a moan.

"Is it that good?" The tips of his lips quirked. "This burger place is great, but damn."

"I mean, yeah, it's good," she said. "But it's also the first solid food I've had all day, so it's extra good."

A frown replaced his smile, slotting across his brows. "You haven't eaten all day?"

She shrugged and took another bite of her burger, talking around the food. "I usually skip breakfast and eat a little something later in the morning. But today threw me off. Thanks to *someone*, I slept through my alarm."

He chuckled. "Sorry. If it helps, you seemed very put together for someone who slept through their alarm."

She rolled her eyes. "Thanks? But what, you're telling me you wake up to your alarm every morning?"

He shrugged, biting his burger. "No. But I work with Philip. He takes advantage of living so close and having a fob to my floor. So, he'll come over and literally sit on me, screaming until I wake up."

She barked out a laugh and choked on her food. Sputtering, she grabbed her water bottle. "Well, that's one way to wake up."

"I really should take that key away," James murmured.

"Don't bother." She waved her burger. "I'll just get security to give him another."

"And where do you get that clearance?" James grinned. "Unless this is your way of saying you want to be my girlfriend and move in."

Some water went down the wrong pipe and she pounded her chest. "Who said anything about that? I was going to lie and say I was your cousin or something."

"Please don't."

She snickered. "Alright, alright. Anyway, tell me more about you. There's only so much you can learn from Wikipedia."

"Dinner wasn't enough for you?"

"Tell me more."

He pulled a water bottle from the bag and took a sip. "Okay. But for every answer I give you, you have to give me one back."

She stuck her hand out. "Deal. I hope I'm not signing away too much, Mr. Tian."

He grinned devilishly, and a shiver ran through her body. He took her hand and shook it, his fingers branding their touch into her skin. "Never, Ms. Huang."

Sophie's daily routine consisted of her working while she ate, her keyboard cover falling victim to spilled food more than once.

But that day, she boasted no desire to pick up a pen as she learned more about James.

"Give me three things you haven't told me before," she said.

"Three things I haven't told you?" He blew out a breath. "I'm allergic to cats. I took piano lessons until I was seventeen, and I know ten–No, eleven–languages."

"Eleven?!" she squawked.

"Yes. Most of those were taught to me when I was a kid, and then I picked up the rest later," he admitted. "When I was seven, my dad became business associates with Philip's dad, and my brother and I spent summers in Spain with Philip's family. That's where we perfected our Spanish, but everything else was a combination of trips and tutors."

"E-Eleven," Sophie stammered. "That's insane."

"If it helps, my brother knows twelve."

"In what world would that help?" She waved her crumpled burger wrapper. "Sorry to disappoint you, Duolingo. But the best I can offer you is my knowledge in English, Mandarin, and a little Spanish."

He snorted. "I um ... I also used learning languages as a distraction."

"For?"

"Mainly my family being assholes, but also because of uh ..." he looked at the ceiling, then back down, "Arranged dates."

The search results she'd rustled up came screeching back,

and a visceral gnawing started up in Sophie's stomach. "I see ... I'm assuming nothing came of those arrangements."

"No," he admitted. "And once I turned eighteen, my dad realized I wouldn't listen to him about that anymore."

She hummed. "I see."

"What about you?" He drained his water and lifted an eyebrow. "You owe me answers."

She tapped her foot under the desk. Her gaze slipped to the clock on her computer. It was nearly twenty minutes past, but when she opened her mouth, her answers to his questions slid out.

She was allergic to bananas, she had taken violin lessons until her freshman year of college, and her favorite flower was a violet.

He cleared his throat. "Any romantic history?"

She frowned. "That's a little forward, isn't it?"

"I gave you mine."

"Fine." She pressed her lips tight. "There were two guys. The first one, we started talking at a party freshman year of college and ... things escalated. I dated him for a brief time and I shouldn't have."

"I see." Something flared in James's eyes.

"It is what it is." She cleared her throat and shook her head. "It was a long time ago."

Never mind that the moment she spilled her guts to Chloe ten years ago was still crystal clear in Sophie's mind.

"Ugh, you know that guy I've been seeing?" She had flopped on Chloe's bed a few weeks after the start of the semester.

"Brian Ngyuen?" Chloe had tugged her bottom lip between her teeth as she finished applying a second coat of nail polish.

"Yup." Sophie confirmed. "I never told you but... he's my TA."

Chloe gasped, flapping her hands to dry her nail polish faster. "Girl!"

"Shut up, I don't want to hear it." Sophie mimed pinching

a mouth shut with her fingers. "This is why I didn't tell you. Anyway, the point is it's over between us."

Chloe's eyes flared and she twisted. "He broke it off?"

"I did. I mean, it's just not a good idea to keep this up, you know? I don't need him swaying my grades, and then that getting out."

"Okay, but what if it doesn't?" she reasoned.

"Yeah, but it's always a possibility." Sophie huffed a breath and shoved her hand through her hair. "Anyway, you know how that dick reacted? He got upset about it."

Chloe gasped. "Is he going to go to someone higher up with proof?"

"I don't think so. He knows he's going to get in as much trouble as me if he does, and he definitely cares about covering his ass." Sophie had shrugged.

Maybe I should've waited until after the semester. At least then, he wouldn't have had the chance to fail me on purpose and ruin my GPA on top *of saying that I had a threesome with these frat guys.* She gritted her teeth.

It was why she always played it safe–kept her toes in line because she experienced the consequences firsthand.

Until now.

This time around, the stakes were infinitely higher, but the rush to her system was ... different.

Worth it.

James took a deep breath. "And the second guy?"

"Alex Clarkson." Her eyes glazed over.

The guy after Brian, who was supposed to fix everything, but made them infinitely worse.

The whole relationship lasted far too long, and she hated herself for it.

Even when he got rotten and manipulative, she stuck with him. She needed that validation. Craved the idea that someone wanted her around, and she had someone there, too.

Alex was an undeniable part of her past, but she still did her best not to think of him. Plus, he had no part in her plans now.

She stared at her desk, her hands fisted under the surface. "I'm sorry. That's a lot to dump on you."

James's foot hit the takeout bag, rustling filling the air. "It's okay. I–"

A knock pounded on her door and a second later, the receptionist poked his head in.

"Hey, Sophie, I wanted to–" he broke off, eyes narrowing at James. "Hey, wait, weren't you just here the other day? So, you do know Sophie, then?"

Sophie's eyes widened. Anxiety clawed its way to her heart, spiking her pulse. A tidal wave of what type of assumptions Nico made jumped to fill her mind.

"He's a friend," she hastened. "And he was just leaving, right, James?"

"Um ... yes." James picked up the bag. "Sorry to hold you up. I'll see you tomorrow morning?"

She nodded. "Thanks for lunch."

"No problem." He hesitated in his steps. "Oh, Sophie ..."

Pausing by her door frame, he white knuckled the wood. "If you're not going to eat breakfast, don't skip your snack." He seemingly ignored Nico's gaze boring into him. "Please."

Nico cleared his throat, staring behind his shoulder at James's retreating figure. "So, you didn't know him, huh?"

Sophie sighed. "At that point, not really. I just bumped into him a few times."

He asked me out and I accepted. But then he became Marilyn's client and we couldn't date because my dating him could impact the things I tell her about him. Which could subsequently unconsciously influence the news she puts out, and she sees nothing wrong with it because she doesn't realize it. And instead of letting each other go, we're now caught in a frantic dance of God knows what. But semantics.

"I see. Was that why you got his campaign to Marilyn so fast?" Nico asked. "I remember you mentioning it, and Marilyn saying to book him in."

Oh, God. Sophie shook her head rapidly.

Even though Nico was her work best friend, if this was his reaction, she couldn't blurt that out to him.

"No, of course not," she said. "You know he owns a big company, which means it's good business for us. Listen, I really need to get a move on these emails. So ..."

Nico raised his hands in submission. "Alright, I can take a hint. I won't tell Marilyn about you two knowing each other, but ... you sure he's just a friend?"

"Of course."

Nico rose. "Your smile said otherwise."

"Shut up."

She rested her head in her hands after the door closed. *I take it back. Is it really worth it if my heart's going to leap out of my chest?!*

She groaned.

If she were caught this time, things would be much bigger than disciplinary action.

Sophie shifted her weight between her feet and readjusted her grip on the metal subway pole. The train rushed toward its next destination, traveling over elevated tracks and zooming past lit buildings.

She pulled out her phone, opening the thread between her and James.

> Hey, I forgot that I'm going home this week end so I won't be around. Take a rain check on that game you suggested?

Her phone buzzed with an incoming call, and she pressed the device to her ear. "Hey, Chlo. What's up?"

"Hey. I was thinking movie and pizza tonight? You cool with that?" Chloe asked.

"Oh, my God, that sounds heavenly. Yes, a thousand times yes."

The train pulled into Sophie's station and she hurried out of the subway. God, she couldn't wait to get home.

The emails had kept coming that afternoon, and her fingers had flown across her keyboard. By the time she finished cataloging things in her spreadsheet, it was time for her to clock out. Too tired to work overtime, she hustled out of the office.

"I can pick up the pizza," she said. "It's on my way back."

"Cool, thanks. Get two pies," Chloe said. "I invited Ol and Taylor, too."

"Sounds good. I'll see you in a bit." Sophie hung up as her phone vibrated again. She switched to the new message from James as she walked.

How are you getting there? Driving?

The bus, rich guy

She snorted, pausing at the end of the sidewalk.

Taking the train wasn't preferential whenever she went home, but since she hadn't driven since moving, she didn't want to risk it. Plus, renting a car was expensive.

What time are you leaving? I can drive you

She froze in the middle of the sidewalk, people streaming around her.

What?

She couldn't ask him to give up his Saturday like that, and assuming he was driving her back, too, he'd spend two days driving to Connecticut.

It's fine, I'll just go myself. Besides, you're giving up really good seats

No big deal, I can get them again. My friend owns the team. And I can drive you home Sunday too

I'm staying overnight. That means you'd be stuck in CT all weekend

It's fine, I've got friends in Greenwich. I can go visit them

K so you'd stay there?

Upon entering the pizza shop, the scent of melting cheese and baking garlic knots greeted her nose.

Her phone pulsed.

My friend just said their house is undergoing renovations, but I can still stop by. I just can't stay overnight there

She paused, frowning at her screen.

Was he implying he was going to stay with her? *In her home?*

The image of James sitting on her couch while her brother and mom bombarded him with embarrassing stories trailed through her mind, and then the logistics hit.

Since they'd only had one paycheck to live off of growing up, her childhood home wasn't big.

Once she and Noah got steady jobs, they tried to convince their mom to move, but she refused. So, the condo remained, along with its three bedrooms, two of which were occupied.

If James stayed, he'd either crash with Noah or with her, and she'd bet a year's salary that showing up with him would give her family the wrong idea.

She paled. She couldn't have that, she *definitely* couldn't have that. Her phone buzzed again.

As if he'd read her mind, a solution lay splashed out on the screen.

I doubt you'd want me staying at your place, so I can just get a hotel room for the night. Don't worry princess

Her lips twitched.

WE'RE NOT DOING PRINCESS

Worth a shot

"He's what?!" Chloe demanded.

"Driving me home," Sophie repeated. "He offered to this weekend."

Taylor snorted and bit into his slice of pizza. "Oh, this guy's got it bad for you if he's already pulling boyfriend stunts."

"He's not my–"

"Um, yes, he is," Oliver interrupted. "Correct me if I'm wrong, but he paid for dinner without telling you. He brought you lunch today, bought you coffee, not to mention *has your coffee order memorized.* Oh, right, and there's the small fact that you two have hooked up twice over the course of four days!"

"We're Friends-With-Benefits!" she protested. "The things James is doing are kinda built into the definition!"

Taylor chewed on his pizza. "Sure, but they're also moving into boyfriend territory, and you know it."

She groaned. She tried not to dwell on it, but the truth of the matter was, she failed to find any flaw in their logic.

For the past few days, it lingered, dredging up her deepest fears in the middle of the night.

Things might be going in the wrong order for them, but ... her heart leaped.

"Okay, so he's driving me. So what? Friends send each other places all the time," she reasoned.

Chloe snorted. "Sophie, I love you, but you're grasping at straws here."

"She's right," Oliver chimed in. "And doesn't this mean he has to stay overnight?"

Chloe slapped his arm. "Oh, my God, yeah! I was hoping there wouldn't be a catch, but he really does want this to be something it's not, doesn't he?"

Her eyes were saucers, and Sophie could practically see the alarm bells ringing.

"It's fine, calm down!" Sophie said, even though her heart raced. "He said he'll get a hotel room."

Despite what her friends might think, James wouldn't try anything she didn't want him to. Unlike Brian, James thought about the long-term consequences not just for himself, but for her, too. When you put those stakes on a scale ... a clear winner shone through.

The next day, she stumbled into her office, chin dipped as she read a stack of papers.

As she neared her desk, the scent of melted butter and grilled meat hit her straight in the face.

Glancing at the bag sitting on the surface, she took in a swanky-looking name emblazoned on the side. The swoopy letters took a minute to register, but she finally placed the posh restaurant not far from where she worked.

She had passed by it plenty of times, the façade of the building rubbing in her face the fact that she could never afford it.

She backtracked to her door. "Nico, what's this? Was this a thank-you gift or something?"

Nico hurried to the doorway and peeked inside the office. "No, *that* would be a delivery for you from James Tian. He dropped it off himself."

Sophie raised a brow.

He'd what? Did he have time to hand-deliver takeout when he had a company to run?

"From the way he was hanging around, I think he was trying to catch you before he left." A conspiratorial grin dashed across Nico's lips.

She sighed. "I told you the other day, we're just friends."

Although now that her friends came after her with their

arguments, her head spun.

Nico rolled his eyes. “Okay, okay. By the way, he told me to tell you not to worry about paying him back, and to enjoy lunch. You know, as a *friend*,” he teased as he hustled back to his desk, shaking his head.

“Nico, I swear to God!” Sophie nudged her door shut with her hip.

The grilled meat called her name again, and her stomach rumbled in response.

Peeking inside the bag, she took out the shiny takeout container. A sticky note clung for dear life to the plastic cover studded with condensation. Slanted handwriting scratched across the surface.

‘Just in case you missed your snack again’

A text from James came in the next morning while she slurped down her iced coffee.

Outside. Want me to hit the buzzer?

Her eyes widened. She hadn’t given a specific time, but damn, it was *early*. The only reason she was up was because she had some last-minute packing.

Thudding downstairs to let him in, her attention caught on the reusable bag by his feet, the tops of a tea box and a basket poking out from it.

He picked up the bag as he ambled in. “Hey.”

She stepped aside before he crashed into her, but he brushed close enough that his cologne curled up her nose.

“Am I too early, pookie?” he asked.

She shook her head, shutting the door. “I’m going to kill you.”

He grinned, the bag thumping as he crossed his arms. “So, it’s a no to pookie? Are you sure, because I think it’s—”

“*James*.”

He chuckled. "Alright, alright, sorry."

"What's in the bag?" she huffed.

"Gifts for your family. Don't worry, it's nothing too expensive. Just some tea and a gift basket."

"Do me a favor and define 'not too expensive.'"

Dealing with a billionaire, especially one coming from generational wealth, meant you could never be too careful.

Chuckling, he put the bag down again before pulling out his phone and showing her the most recent transaction on his wallet app. "Satisfied?"

She rolled her eyes and nodded. "Did you eat yet?"

She barely heard his response as they entered her apartment, her mind kicking into hyperspeed.

He's in my apartment in the morning! But it doesn't mean anything, remember?

His steps faltered behind her, and she glanced at him.

He stared at Oliver and Taylor, both of whom lay across her couch, snoring.

"Why are there two unconscious guys in your living room?" James asked.

She laughed. "That'd be Oliver and his boyfriend. The four of us had a movie night yesterday and they crashed here."

"Oh..."

James sat on the armchair, twiddling his thumbs. He peered around the apartment like it was his first time seeing it.

In a way, she supposed it was, since the other times, they'd been too busy ripping each other's clothes off.

"Oh, right, um ... I wanted to talk to you before we left." She figured now was as good a time as any to bring up the lunches. It was better than figuring that out when they were trapped in a car for a few hours. "Okay, well. First, I wanted to say thanks for the lunches. How much do I owe you for them?"

"Nothing," he said. "Like I told Nico the first time, they're on me."

"That's too much," she protested. "At least let me pay you back a little."

He frowned, shaking his head. "Why am I accepting your money? You need to eat, and I'm just making sure that happens."

She grimaced as she wet a sponge and squeezed some dish soap onto it. Lathering down her cup and plate, she rinsed the bubbles away beneath the tap. "Alright, thanks. But you need to stop."

"Do you not like the food?"

She shook her head frantically. "I'm not ungrateful for the food, but someone's going to see, and then they're going to ask too many questions. Or worse, Marilyn finds out herself."

Sophie stuck the dishes in the drying rack. Drying her hands on the tea towel hanging off the oven, she turned and leaned against the counter. "I don't know about you, but I personally don't want to tell my boss about what we've been doing."

"You're right," he said after a moment. "I didn't even think of that, I was just ... anyway, I'm sorry, I'll stop. But take this."

Drawing out his wallet, he slid out a credit card, handing it to her.

She gaped at the sleek black card in her hand, the plastic sinking a million pounds into her fingers. "What–"

"To buy your own lunch," he explained. "You need to eat a good one, you understand me? I don't want you to go hungry again. While you're at it, buy whatever else you want with that."

No, no, no.

Why was he so concerned? He wasn't her boyfriend; he *shouldn't* care.

But a part of her that grew rapidly enough to frighten her loved that he did.

"This is too much, I can't accept this." She bristled. "First the lunches, now this. Do you think that I can't take care of myself or something?"

"Not at all." He still held the card aloft between them. "But I'm not playing around when it comes to you, Sophie. So, take the card. There are no strings attached to it, and you don't need to worry about paying me back for any expenses. I'll get another card, but this one's yours now."

"James–"

"Sophie." His eyes gleamed. "Let me take care of you."

She tilted her head, observing him.

Philip's words in the car came roaring back. '*That was a fight you weren't going to win.*'

"Alright." She accepted the card, sliding it into her pocket.

They made it out of the city, talking about unimportant things like the weather. Yet somehow, it wasn't boring, and before she knew it, an hour flew by.

Pulling her laptop and a bag of Starbursts out of her backpack, she popped one in her mouth and clicked open a PDF reader. She had downloaded some documents that Marilyn wanted looked over before she left and now was as good a time as any.

"What are you doing?"

James's voice cut across the space between them, but she didn't look up from her screen.

She scrolled with the trackpad. "Just some reading. Want some candy?"

He held his hand out, sticking the candy she offered in his mouth. "For fun?"

"For..." she trailed off, then went with the honest answer. "For work."

"Sophie."

Something about the way he said her name made her look at him.

A small, amused smile played on his lips. "I'm a CEO,

and I don't work this much."

He stuck his hand out for another Starburst.

"Well, unlike you, I don't have millions in my bank account," she shot back. "And I don't work *that* much."

Understatement.

It was a Saturday, and she was going home for the weekend. She needed to take a break, she knew that, but ...

"I just ... I want to get promoted, that's all." Her laptop warmed her lap. "Our account director is retiring and I'm more than ready to step into his place. I was supposed to, well, I wanted to, with our last big case, but ... it didn't happen. The spot's still open, so..."

The Starbust turned to a flavorless wax lump in her mouth.

James's brows rose. "Account director already? How long have you been there?"

Sophie shrugged. "Five years, but I've learned a lot under Marilyn and the vice president. I also learned a lot about the company itself in that time. Plus, my degrees are in business and communications, and I worked internships in those fields."

James let out a whistle. "Damn, okay."

She eyed him. "You don't think it's possible?"

She was more than qualified. So why did the prospect of him doubting her sting so much?

He blew out a breath and changed lanes. "Do you want the truth?"

"Of course."

He was silent, as if trying to parse the words that would hurt the least.

She frowned. "James, I can take it."

"Alright," he acquiesced. "I think it's ambitious and a big leap. I mean, five years, Sophie? Really? But–"

She bristled. "Fine, forget I asked."

"Let me finish." He smirked and took the next exit. "I think based on what you've told me, if there's anyone who can do it, it's you."

Her heart beat resounded in her ears. Glowing warmth from more than just the laptop flooded her. "You're just saying that."

"No, I think you can," he replied. "Really. I'm just impressed, that's all. If I was in your shoes, I don't think *I* could do it."

She snorted. "But you did. You had shares in Tian Corporation, right? And I don't know, maybe you still do. Also, you were set to take over a seat on the board. Why would you leave all that when you didn't know the outcome?"

That gamble turned out well, but what if it hadn't?

"See? You'd give Wikipedia a run for its money." Merging into a turning lane, he waited for the light to change. "You can more than handle this promotion."

"James."

Silence met her, sticking to her skin like wet clothes.

She pressed her lips into a thin line and winced.

Some things were better left to the unknown, and it looked like his family history was one of them.

His fingers tapped frantically on the wheel, and he came to a stop at another red light. "You probably know my mom left when I was younger."

She stared at him. "Um ... yeah, I saw something online about that."

He sighed. "Well, my dad took it pretty hard. He got angry. He still *is* angry. But at that time, it was worse, and my brother wasn't happy, either. You can guess what teenage hormones and a burning anger at your mom led to." He shrugged. "My whole life, people said I looked like a carbon copy of my mom. So naturally, my dad couldn't stand to look at me after she left. And when he did, he yelled at me. A lot. He said a lot of things, and Adam did too." He stopped talking for a moment as they turned onto a highway. "Never laid a hand on me, though."

"Well, thank God for small blessings," she whispered. Her heart sank and settled into her stomach. "But ... why art?"

"My mom liked art." He shrugged again. "And I don't

know, it just felt right."

The muscles in his arm tensed, and a subtle shift caused his sleeve tattoo to ripple.

The desperate gleam in James's eyes that day in the conference room slotted into place.

He lorded over a billion-dollar company, and he might've played off the issue as simply a money thing, but it was so much bigger than that.

One wrong move and he'd lose the legacy he started for his mother.

"Why'd you agree, then?" she asked. "To all this, I mean. You never told me."

"Sophie." He glanced at her. "Are we really going to pretend you don't know?"

She blinked. "I–"

"The stakes are high for both of us." His knuckles whitened as he gripped the wheel. "And despite all of that, if you were willing to stick your neck out, then isn't it only right for me to, as well?"

She sucked in a breath as her heart softened.

Throughout her entire life, she had been accustomed to being stuck as an afterthought. Certainly not someone who warranted the risk of losing something near and dear to their heart.

But now...

Unsure of what else to do, she grabbed his hand. Her thumb swished slowly against the side of his hand.

"Thank you," she whispered.

"For?"

She was quiet for a moment. "I told you about my dad, right?"

The deadbeat who left his wife with two kids under ten.

James nodded and his jaw tightened.

"Well, my dad was always running," she began. "When he left, I saw how it hurt my mom, and I ... should've taken something away from that. But I didn't and I don't know why. Every guy I've dated before has done the same thing–

ran when things got tough. They didn't want to deal with me, not if it meant they could cover their own asses. So ... thank you." She smiled. "For not running."

They rode in silence for a few minutes before he asked, "If you could go back and change things so that your dad never left, would you?"

"No," she replied, that exact question having crossed her mind numerous times. "Would you change your mom leaving?"

He was silent for a moment before giving her his answer. "No."

Nine

James

James's phone buzzed in the divider between seats, and he glanced at the screen. Hitting the right options, he put Jackie's call on speakerphone.

"Yeah, Jackie?" He came to a stop at a red light.

"Hi!" his assistant chirped. "Sorry to bother you on the weekend, but I heard back from the people you had me contact yesterday? A month ago, they hired a new employee who had been recently laid off by Cross. When he first got there, he was telling anyone who'd listen how terrible Cross was."

James's brow furrowed as Sophie motioned for him to continue straight.

Cross Law was the head of Delacroix's conglomerate of law firms, and everyone in the business realm heard about the budget cuts they made a few months ago.

"So that's our guy," he surmised. "Do you have a name?"

"Unfortunately not." Dejection lined Jackie's voice. "Because of the nature of the information he possesses, he's being protected by an NDA."

James scowled. Damn security protocols. They were hardly a deterrent, but a pain in his ass, nevertheless. "Okay, well, is there any way we can get that info regardless?"

He didn't care what he had to do or pay. He was sure this was the person they were looking for.

Jackie sighed. "Yes, and I can speed things up by talking to connections I have, but it'll still take some wiggling and time."

"Of course," he said.

"You owe me, James," she teased.

He chuckled. "Keep me updated."

"Will do. Have a good weekend."

The call ended and in the corner of his eye, Sophie's brows furrowed. "So, I'm guessing that was your assistant you mentioned?"

"Yes," he confirmed and parsed out the trepidation in Sophie's tone. A small smile played on his lips. "Don't tell me you're jealous."

"No. I was just wondering, that's all."

"Alright, whatever you say," he quipped. "You just didn't sound too happy."

He navigated through the streets of a residential area until he reached an

intersection. They slowed, turning into a condominium complex, and rolled past the buildings.

"That's not it at all," she protested.

A lazy grin settled onto his face. "I know, I know."

The GPS announced their destination, and he pulled into a parking space, killing the engine. Rolling his shoulders, he caught the sour look still on her face.

"Sophie, I'm sorry, I was joking," he said. "Look, Jackie is a forty-five-year-old woman with three kids and is happily married. I think we're fine, cupcake."

"I ... we're not doing cupcake," she spluttered.

He lifted his hands in surrender, then unbuckled and got out of the car. A rush of cool air hit his face as he headed for the trunk.

Vanilla and coconut carried on the breeze and he turned.

"Thanks for the ride," Sophie said. "I can take my things in if you want to go."

He made no move to hand her bag over. "Anytime. But I can give you a hand. My friend texted, and something came up, so I've got time to kill now."

She nodded and gestured for him to follow her toward a

set of buildings.

"Look ...why don't you just stay for a bit?" she suggested and stopped short outside her house.

He nearly crashed into her as his heart rate ricocheted. "I thought you didn't want me to."

"I mean, my mom knows a friend is driving me. She told me she already prepared some fruit and snacks for you, so since your plans fell through, you might as well." Sophie shrugged.

He swallowed and nodded. "Okay, then."

Her body heat radiated against him on the narrow doorstep, and even though his heels hung off the edge of the stoop, he didn't dare move. If he did, he risked bumping into her when he was already in danger of imploding.

Confusion invaded the crevices of his brain as she knocked on the door.

What changed her mind? And she still wanted him to get a hotel room for the night, right?

"Sophie," he started. "About tonight–"

A man swung the door open. "Pee-pee!" His eyes caught on James, and he raised his brows. "And ... friend."

"Ah, you must be Noah," James said, snapping into business mode. "I'd shake your hand, but as you can see ..."

He shifted to keep his balance as he wobbled, grip tightening on the bags.

Sophie grabbed his bicep to keep him from falling backward and his heart flew into his throat, a strangled yelp threatening to flow past his lips.

If she was trying to stabilize him, her touch wasn't helping.

"Didn't Mom tell you my friend was driving me?" she asked Noah. "This is James. Where's Mom?"

"Kitchen," Noah responded. He stepped aside to let them in as he sized up James, eyes narrowing.

"Cool." Sophie took off her shoes. "I'll be right back. Play nice!"

James had half a mind to run after her as she disappeared

into an adjoining room, but a throat clear caught his attention, and a chill worked down his spine.

Noah sized him up, curiosity rounding his eyes. "You're a friend, huh?"

James cleared his throat. "Yes. Uh ... just a friend."

"Really?" Noah's brow raised. "A friend who was willing to give up his Saturday and drive two hours into the Connecticut suburbs?"

"Uh ...yes. So why do you call her Pee-Pee?" James asked. He sent a silent apology to Sophie, but he needed a change of subject.

"Oh, because she has a small bladder," Noah said, jumping on the chance to embarrass his sister. "You should've seen that one road trip we went on–"

The kitchen door swung open, and a woman who looked like Sophie hurried out, a plate of orange slices in her hands.

"You must be James!" The woman smiled and set the oranges down on the coffee table. "Thank you for giving my daughter a ride home. Sit down, you must be tired. All that driving and I know Sophie's chatty."

"Wow, thanks, Mom." Sophie placed the teapot she held on the table. "For the record, I didn't talk *that* much. And I compensated him with candy."

"It was no trouble at all, Mrs. Huang. I was headed out this way," James said and took a seat. "Thank you for preparing this. You really didn't have to. Oh, I brought some things for you." He gestured to the gift basket on the table. "I hope you like them."

Sophie's mom's eyes widened. "Oh, my, thank you! And please, call me Lisa. So, how long have you been friends with Sophie?"

"Only about a month," James lied.

"Which is why I didn't say anything when I saw you guys last time," Sophie added.

"Aiyah, I suppose it doesn't matter," Lisa said. "A two-hour drive is exhausting at any point in friendship."

The conversation spiraled into James's plans for the rest

of the afternoon, and when he tried to excuse himself, Lisa jumped in.

"Why don't you stay for dinner?" she suggested. "Since you have the time."

Unease tightened its vise around his throat, squeezing until black spotted his vision. Given the deepening feelings he and Sophie had for each other, his staying for dinner layered trouble onto his shoulders.

"Uh ... thank you," he started. "But I don't want to cause you any trouble."

"No trouble at all!" Lisa waved her hands. "I already started preparing food."

James glanced at Sophie, sitting next to him on the couch.

An alarmed expression coated her features, but she cracked a smile. "Yes, why don't you stay?"

He blinked before sense settled into his brain.

The more they pushed against this, the more suspicious Lisa would become.

"Alright, then," he agreed. "But please, let me help. It's the least I can do."

"You can cook?" Sophie asked.

"It's not just takeout all the time."

Rising, he didn't get a step in as Lisa's voice stopped him. "No, no, you sit. You're our guest, I can't–"

"Yes, you can," Sophie interrupted. She rose and pushed James towards the kitchen. "If he's staying for dinner, he needs to pull his weight."

He snorted, pressing past the swinging door. "I mean, she's right."

Her mom laughed. "Alright. Also, I wanted to ask you if you were planning on spending the night in Greenwich."

James pulled a chair out at the dining table. "Oh ... um, yes, I was."

"But your plans with your friends fell through, right?" she continued. "And I'm assuming your lodgings, too. So why don't you stay here tonight? There's no need to waste money on a hotel room."

Jitters crawled up James's limbs as he locked eyes with Sophie. His heartbeat faded into turbulence, shaking his very core. "Oh, I um–"

"Don't push it," Sophie murmured. "We don't have more than three beds."

Taking that into consideration, he swallowed, pushing past the nails lining his throat. "I couldn't. Thank you, but I can't trouble you even more."

Lisa waved away his protests. "Nonsense, you won't take up any room at all! You can stay in my son's room with him tonight."

"Mom, please," Sophie said in Mandarin. "Do not force it."

James focused on the bean sprout he pinched, hurricane-force winds whirling through his mind as he tried to think of a good excuse.

"Um ... I have an early morning meeting tomorrow," he said in Mandarin. "It is virtual, but it really would be easier if I stayed somewhere else tonight. Thank you for the offer."

"You have a meeting on a Sunday?" Lisa asked.

"The client is in Osaka."

She nodded. "I see. Still, it is fine if you stay. I can ask Noah to sleep downstairs tonight, so you do not have to worry about waking anyone in the morning."

Knowing there was no getting out of this, James nodded, relenting. Ignoring the daggers Sophie threw at him, he thanked her mom and refocused on the bean sprouts.

His lungs wrung themselves dry, and his leg drummed up a storm beneath the table.

"Mom, you should go sit." Sophie rose and took the cleaver from her mom's hands. "We've got it in here."

"But he's our guest!" Lisa protested, frowning. "I can't–"

"Again, yes, you can. You already told me the menu, so just go," Sophie said. She chased her mom out of the kitchen before she could protest too much. Turning around, she shook her head. "She's stubborn."

"I'm sorry about staying. I really don't ... I can go," he

said.

"No, it's fine. Besides, you'll be in a separate room."

"James, I wanted to ask you something before Sophie gets back from the bathroom," Lisa said in Mandarin. She took up residence in Sophie's abandoned seat and laced her fingers, taking a deep breath. "Are you really just friends with my daughter?"

His eyes widened for a moment, then he sighed, slumping forward. "No ... it's complicated."

"I thought so. Not with the way you look at each other." Lisa paused for a moment. "James ... did you know my daughter only comes home every month for a few days? Do you know why she's aiming for a promotion after only five years at her job?"

He shook his head, drumming his fingers on the table. He had a suspicion, but ...

"It's because her father left, and all her life, she's seen *me* work hard to make her and Noah happy." Lisa's face softened.

James pursed his lips and nodded.

If he ever got his hands on that asshole ...

"She might deny it, but I know she wasn't happy growing up." Lisa sighed. "Which is why she worked herself to the bone in school to get the best experience and education for herself."

"I see."

"And ... she won't talk about it, but something happened her first year of college." Lisa wrung her hands and stared out the window. "It made her focus on school *that* much more, but it also made her different."

"Different how?" He frowned.

"Just small things I noticed when she came home for

breaks." Lisa adopted a faraway look. "She wasn't going out as much anymore, and when she did, she always came home early. On top of that, she said there was no one she was interested in, which I knew had to be a lie because ... well. I'm going to be transparent about it and tell you that Sophie was the type to rarely be single. So, for her to say that ... I know I should've been happy as her mother, but it worried me."

James was quiet and fiddled with a bean sprout.

"All this to say, it doesn't matter how much money you have, or where you can take her. Given her experiences, Sophie is never going to change the fact that she works too hard, or that she wants to be seen for *her* accomplishments."

James hadn't packed a pajama shirt. In his defense, he expected to spend the night in a hotel, alone. But he should've had more foresight to realize before he was out of the shower.

It shouldn't have mattered. Plenty of people slept shirtless, regardless of their surroundings. And yet ...

It's too strange here.

He stood in the small bathroom Sophie and Noah shared, unsure if he should risk darting down the short hall.

Steam curled around him as he ran a hand through his damp hair, and he settled on a decision. It would be damaging, but what else could he do?

Sighing, he grabbed his phone and texted Sophie.

> Can you bring me one of your brother's shirts?

She replied after a moment.

> Excuse me?

> I didn't pack a shirt ok? And I doubt I'd fit any of yours

Well not with that attitude you can't

Sophie

Sitting on the closed toilet lid, he shoved a hand through his hair again and blew a breath from his lips. God, this was embarrassing.

A knock rattled the bathroom door and he cracked it open.

"Here, put this on." Sophie handed him a bunched cloth through the opening. "I don't see what the big deal is. I've seen you without a shirt before."

He slipped the shirt over his head and pulled the door open the rest of the way. "Yes, but it feels ... weird here."

Sophie snorted and crossed her arms. "I promise you; my mom won't care."

"What about your brother?"

Sophie cocked her head. "Alright, maybe."

James hummed as he clocked the terry cloth pajamas she wore, and his mouth dried out.

This was why he hadn't wanted to stay overnight. He wanted to carry her to her room, rip the matching set off her, and spend a good, long while worshipping her body.

She cleared her throat. "What was wrong with your shirt from earlier?"

He snapped out of his stupor. "It's dirty, and the one I have for tomorrow is out of the question."

The client tomorrow was the one Gemma managed to coax back, but he doubted they would agree to anything if his shirt was wrinkled as all hell.

"Right, and in case that shirt doesn't get them tomorrow, you have a great backup option." Sophie's lips twitched as she nodded at the shirt she gave him, featuring a gigantic rubber duck. Sunglasses dominated its face and a speech bubble leading from its mouth declared, "Life Is Sublime!".

"Why does your brother have this?" James asked.

"He saw it in a gift shop when we were on a family vacation and thought it was funny." She rolled her eyes.

"Well, everyone does love ducks." James grinned and followed her to her room. "By the way, what's your Wi-Fi password?"

She scrunched her nose and moved to sit on her bed. "I know you said the client is in Japan, but why call a work meeting on a Sunday morning?"

He passed her his laptop, shrugging. "It was the only day the client could do a meeting. And you're one to talk, Ms. I-Read-Work-Documents-For-Fun."

She stuck her tongue out at him and typed in the password. "I have my reasons, you know."

Sitting on the edge of her bed, he didn't dare inch too close to her as he took his laptop back. "Oh?"

"Yes." She cleared her throat and pulled her legs up to her chest. "My mom was always working. And I wanted to change that. Correction, I *want* to change that. And you being here ..."

He swallowed hard as her unspoken words shot barbs into his chest.

It jeopardizes that.

In his peripheral vision, her chest rose and fell with rapidity as her eyes widened.

"Pumpkin, we're in different rooms," he pointed out.

She shook her head. "First off, don't call me pumpkin. Second, I know we're in separate rooms, but ... that doesn't matter."

He swallowed. "I know."

Dismay and anger consumed his heart. This entire thing would've been a little easier if he'd been firmer and put his foot down about going to a hotel. Hell, he should've left during the afternoon.

Sophie shook her head. "It is what it is."

"I guess," he acquiesced. "Just don't make me make you regret those words."

Once the syllables rolled off his tongue, he tensed. *Fuck.*

Mentally slapping himself, he shot her an apologetic look. "Jesus, sorry. I didn't mean it like that."

She snorted. "It's okay. But out of curiosity,"–her cheeks turned vermillion as she shifted–"how?"

He cleared his throat, considering all the lines that would be crossed if they had sex that night. Yet the next thing he knew, he plopped his laptop on her blankets and stepped between her legs. Caging her body in his arms, he leaned forward while she bent back. "You really want me to answer that?"

Her breath caught and her tongue darted out to wet her lips. "I asked, didn't I?"

His gaze flicked to her tongue, just as her core gave out, and he cushioned the back of her head with his palm as they fell onto her mattress.

He hovered over her, gaze catching on a lock of her hair.

"If you want, you can always boss me around," he murmured. Pressing a kiss to her neck, his lips lingered against her skin. Her breathing quickened, but he ignored it as he kissed her again, dragging his mouth down to where her shoulder met her neck. "And you can always tell me the shots I need to call. But if you ever change your mind," he smoothed his lips to her collarbone, "all you have to do is ask."

He backed away, dragging his gaze down her body.

Her chest rose and fell rapidly as she peered up at him. "James–"

"Night, Sophie." He walked into the hall, shutting her door behind him.

In their situation, she had the royal flush. One word from her and Lotus wouldn't be represented by Covey LLC. any longer. They would be over, too.

But he hadn't been joking around. If she asked, he'd gladly fall to his knees for her.

It neared one in the morning and James sat upright in bed, staring at the rolling darkness. Heaviness dragged at his eyelids, but they refused to slip shut for long, keeping sleep at bay.

Blowing a long breath out between his lips, he rubbed the blankets between his fingers and slid his eyes shut again.

A muffled choking sound passed through the wall, and his eyes snapped open.

The gasping came again and he gulped, lifting himself from the bed. Immediately, cool air swarmed his skin, raising pebbles. He tripped over something and staggered into the wall, looking over his shoulder at the discarded shirt on the floor.

Creeping toward the door, he exited into the hall and lingered outside Sophie's.

Sniffling traveled through the wood, muted but omnipresent, and he inched the door open.

"Sophie?" he whispered, sticking his head in. e floor.

A dark mass huddled in the middle of her bed, shaking a little, but otherwise still.

"Are you awake right now?" he hissed.

No response.

Glancing behind him, he stepped into the room and carefully shut the door. Everything blurred into a mess of pale moonlight and shadow as he crossed the small space to her bed.

He peered at her. "Sophie?"

Her eyes remained firmly closed, but she *sobbed*, every sniffle and choked hiccup a dagger to his heart.

"Sophie." He shook her shoulder. Nothing happened and he shook her a bit harder, cold sweeping his entire body. "*Sophie.*"

She sniveled, rolling away into a fetal position.

To hell with staying quiet, she was *fully weeping in her sleep.*

He had to wake her up.

He climbed onto the bed and jostled her insistently. "Sophie!"

Her eyes finally opened, and she sat up, looking around wildly.

"Where ... where'd he go?" she stuttered. Sucking in breath after breath, her hands gripped the blanket.

James placed a hand on her back. "Where's who?"

Her shirt had rucked up, and a cold sweat slicked her skin, but she might as well have been holding a blowtorch to his hand.

"Are you okay?" His heart raced in the silence around them.

She whimpered slightly, and although her breathing settled from rapid jumps to a plummeting monotone, he drew her into his chest.

"It's okay," he mumbled into her hair. "It was just a dream. You're okay."

"I'm so sorry, this doesn't normally happen," she murmured.

"It's fine, I've got you." He pressed kisses to the top of her head. "It's okay."

She curled further into him, and he did his best to forget how she acted like it was as natural as breathing.

"Are you okay?" He wouldn't rest easy until she said 'yes.'

"I was dreaming about my dad," she muttered after what felt like ages. "And the day he came back. I just turned seven, and Noah turned five a few months before, so I thought Dad came back for our birthdays. But ... it wasn't for us, like I thought. Mom told us years later that it was because he needed money. I was downstairs, and I heard someone in the kitchen. So, I went to look, and ... he was sitting at the table."

Her face morphed into something lost in memory, and her eyes welled with tears again.

Brushing his thumbs to her cheeks, he wiped away whatever fell.

"I was so happy," she whispered. "But then, Mom came

in and started yelling, and she made me go away. And that's when things changed."

"Changed?"

"In reality, both Noah and I hid in Mom's room, and we stayed in ignorance until a few years later. But in the dream, it was like Noah didn't exist, and I stayed outside the kitchen." Sophie's breath shook. "Suddenly, the yells stopped, so I went in and ... both Mom and Dad were gone. I was all alone, and scared, and ..."

"Jesus," James muttered, holding her tighter.

She quieted, scratching a finger down her blanket. "This isn't the first time I've had this dream. But it is the first time where it made me remember that we never mattered to my dad." She shrugged. "We were just a get-rich-quick scheme that didn't pan out, so he tossed us."

James's jaw clenched.

She sniffled again and swiped violently at her eyes with her palms. "I'm really sorry again; I promise I don't usually cry at night."

A boulder fell onto his heart.

She shouldn't have felt the need to apologize to him for something as simple as *feeling.*

Wrapping his arms tighter around her, he buried his nose into her hair. Every inhale brought with it the scent of her shampoo.

"Don't," he whispered. "Don't apologize for this. You *never* apologize for this."

She sniffed and murmured something unintelligible into his shoulder.

Her lips grazing against his skin sent a shudder down his spine. "What was that?"

"Stay with me, please?" Pulling back, her eyes gleamed in the dark. "Don't leave, too."

He swore the crack of his heart was audible.

Why would she think she needs to ask unless... He swallowed hard as realization tumbled through him. *Unless she's been left too many times.*

Someone who was never really alone but might as well have been.

And don't I know what that feels like.

Lying back, his arm went around her waist, and he tugged her back against him.

"James," she mumbled.

He glanced at the top of her head, trying not to think about where they touched. "Yeah?"

Her hands covered his arm. "Thank you."

A soft sigh reached his ears and he pried his eyes open to hazy sunlight.

Craning his neck, he glimpsed the time on the digital clock sitting sentinel on Sophie's nightstand. *Fuck.*

If he wanted to make it, he needed to hurry. But there was a small problem.

During the night, Sophie somehow ended up on her stomach. Her head rested on his chest, her cheek against his bare skin, and she held him like a teddy bear.

He tried not to think too much about how he held her, too, one of his arms wrapped around her waist, his hand resting against her mid-back.

Oh, and great. He slipped his eyes shut in resignation as his hard dick pressed against her hip.

With some effort, he withdrew his hand from her back.

"Sophie," he whispered, then repeated her name a bit louder.

He had to get up if he wanted to make the meeting.

The client, Fukada Technologies, had just opened a New York office and was seeking art pieces to decorate it.

Unfortunately, the lead decorator was located in Japan, which set the meeting at six a.m.

She didn't budge and instead let out a sigh that sent blood rushing straight to his cock. She pressed closer to him, and he held back a groan as she shifted against him, wiggling her perfect, rounded ass in the air.

For a moment, he contemplated giving up trying to extricate himself. But no, this meeting was too important for him to miss.

Aside from Gemma somehow getting them back, landing a deal with Fukada would show other potential buyers that Lotus was still a trustworthy business partner–that they could dig themselves out of the trenches.

This was precisely the type of promotion Marilyn wanted.

She had been contacting him biweekly since that first fateful meeting, suggesting new promotional strategies and articles to put out.

He took all of them save for one: leaking a false rumor to a tabloid that he was in a relationship.

According to her, if people were interested in him, they would inevitably want to find out more about him, but he'd drawn the line.

He glanced at Sophie, asleep in his arms. An increase in attention meant nothing if he dragged her down to do it.

"Sophie," he insisted again. Christ, if she moved anymore, he was going to lose it.

She grumbled and rolled onto her back.

"What time is it?" she mumbled. Her eyes screwed shut, and her brow scrunched.

"Too early, but I have my meeting in half an hour." He smiled as her nose crinkled adorably. "I just wanted to tell you so you don't flip when you wake up. Go back to sleep."

She moaned, draping her arm over her eyes. "Okay, go."

Her shirt rose with the movement, baring her stomach, and James's heart dipped.

Deep breaths.

He shifted off the bed, but a hand tethered his wrist. Glancing behind him, he started.

Her hair was a mess, and her clothes wrinkled, but all he could focus on was the fact that early morning sunshine filtered in, making her look like a fallen angel.

Rising onto her knees, she leaned into him. "Thanks for staying."

His breath stopped as she pressed a kiss to his cheek, her lips lingering a second too long.

Dropping back down, she snuggled into her blankets.

He stood frozen at the edge of the bed, white-hot longing shooting through him.

He had had a few one-night stands since breaking up with his ex, but they were all flings with girls who were more interested in his last name than him.

But with Sophie ...

His heart pounded stronger for her than it had for any of his exes, and it scared him.

It scared him shitless.

She didn't want anything serious between them and he understood her reasoning behind that. But every day, he waded deeper into her, and he had no intention of turning around before the water submerged his head.

Forcing himself to lift from the bed, he quickly went through the motions of getting dressed and taking a freezing shower.

Satisfied he looked presentable, he ambled back into Noah's room, firing up his laptop.

The hour flew by as he negotiated and talked up Lotus, the smooth Japanese syllables flowing off his tongue.

At the end of the call, he hung up with high hopes.

The preliminary meeting had gone far better than he expected, given Fukada's previous skepticism. The decorator wound up setting a secondary meeting, and James foresaw a hefty check.

Someone knocked on the door and Sophie appeared, damp hair fanning out behind her shoulders.

A mid-thigh length pastel sundress adhered to her curves, and his heart squeezed.

"Damn, you really do know Japanese," she remarked. "And here I thought maybe you were lying."

He tilted his head, pushing back from the desk. "Why

would I be lying?"

"I don't know, I guess I was just trying to make up something to wrap my head around the fact you know eleven languages. Like ten was any less mind-boggling." She shrugged. "Was this one of the ones you learned for fun?"

Snickering, he followed her out and down the stairs. "No. As I'm sure you're aware, Tian Corporation conducts a significant amount of business in East Asia. My dad wanted my brother and me to be well-versed in whatever business environment we were in over there."

He fell into silence to avoid saying something that would make him look like a pompous ass.

Wandering into the kitchen, she stuck some bread in the toaster, chuckling to herself.

"What?" he asked. Maybe he hadn't made the right choice not to say anything.

"Nothing, I ... it's just damn impressive. How did you not get overwhelmed learning all of them?"

He shrugged. "I didn't learn them all at once, but I also have an easy time with languages."

"So hypothetically, if I were to ask you to speak a language in a sexy context, would you?" she mused.

"What did you have in mind?" he asked, switching to Italian.

"That better have been hot, or we're going to have a problem."

Stepping up to her, he rested his hands on either side of her body. Bending so his mouth was level with her ear, he murmured, "I meant what I said last night, by the way."

She went perfectly still. "About asking?"

He nodded. "Wherever and whenever, Sophie."

Although that wasn't quite true, and his heart wrenched.

"Consider this me asking." She smiled like she saw the truth, too. "You know, I really should see Lotus's offices. For research purposes."

"I have to go pick up some papers," he murmured, sliding his hand down her curves. "So, a pitstop wouldn't be unwarranted. I can give you a ... private tour."

She sucked in a breath. "I see. And if I–"

His phone buzzed in his pocket, and he resisted the urge to throw it across the room.

Sophie pressed her hips against him. "You should get that."

He groaned. "They can wait."

The buzzing ceased, then started right back up again, and he sighed. He stepped back, answering his phone. "Hello?"

"Mec, I've decided. Can you ask Sophie for her friend's number? The one I saw her with last time." Luc sounded far too energetic for the morning.

"Ask her yourself." James tapped Sophie's shoulder and passed her the phone.

Pulling the toast from the toaster, he set the plate of them on the table, along with the jam jar Sophie handed him.

"You are?" she asked.

He glanced over his shoulder and tilted his head. "Put it on speaker."

She waved him off and hummed. "Alright ... just be careful how you do it. Chloe doesn't have the best trust in the people she's dated, and she's been hurt one too many times."

She rattled off a string of numbers, rapping her nails on the counter.

He frowned, mouth opening to ask questions. But she mimed a mouth pinching and he shut up.

"Right, I gotta go. Good luck," she said before hanging up and passing the phone back. "Did Luc tell you beforehand that he was planning on asking Chloe out?"

"This morning was the first time I heard," James said. "Listen, it'll be fine. Luc's a good guy, and–"

"That's what Chloe thought about her last ex, too," Sophie interrupted. "And he cheated on her."

James's eyes widened, his hand curling into a fist. He wasn't exactly the poster child for "the perfect person", but as far as he was concerned, there was a special place in Hell for cheaters.

"But from what I've seen after getting to know Luc more these past weeks, I can tell he'd rather walk into traffic." A smile touched Sophie's lips and she crossed her arms.

James chuckled. "You got that right. Luc's ... had his own trials and tribulations with cheating. I don't think you have anything to worry about."

James's phone buzzed in his hand, and he glanced down, swiping open the text from Jackie.

Got the name of the guy who used to work at Cross. Damien Torrence.

James schooled himself.

That was quick

Yes, well, I have my ways.

He snorted.

Thanks

Anytime. And remember, don't do anything rash.

James gritted his teeth. Like hell, he wouldn't.

This was his company, the one he built from the ground up. He was lucky that they generated so much revenue so quickly and carved out a place for themselves. It provided a stable place for employees like Jackie and their other team members.

But Torrence obviously hadn't thought much about that when he leaked the news about his former boss to the government.

"Sorry, I need to make a call," he said.

Striding back upstairs to Noah's room, he shut the door behind him, dialing the number of a friend who worked at a different security company than Torrence's.

James could only blame his pride for holding him back from contacting his friend. He hadn't wanted to get anyone else outside of Lotus involved, but now he had no choice.

"Hello?" his friend greeted.

"Hey, it's me," James said. "Sorry to bother you on a Sunday, but I need a favor."

Ten

Sophie

The banister threatened to crack under James's whitened knuckles as he came back downstairs, his cheeks blotchy.

"What happened?" Sophie asked.

He cleared his throat. "Nothing, really."

"James–"

A door opened down the hall and Noah emerged, hair damp from a shower. He yawned widely. "Morning."

She greeted him and narrowed her eyes at James.

Something swam in the recesses of his expression, but he turned away to talk about basketball with Noah.

For the rest of the morning, she kept a careful eye on James, though he cracked jokes and made conversation like nothing was wrong.

Maybe that's the case. Maybe he just heard something about the meeting he had this morning.

But on their way to the car, his mask had slipped. It was only for a second, but it was enough to confirm new worry and irritation.

The bag of oranges her mom gave them bumped into her

ankle as James made a turn onto the highway.

"So, Chloe and Luc, huh?" he asked.

She shrugged. "Maybe."

Luc had asked for Chloe's number, yes, but he wouldn't get anywhere unless he played his cards right.

James hummed. "What do you think? You know, as her best friend?"

"Obviously, I'll be happy for her whatever she chooses. Chlo definitely thought he was cute," Sophie said.

"Maybe she needs to go for an eye exam," James muttered.

Sophie laughed as she glanced at him, debating whether she should ask about the furrow in his brow or not. What if he wasn't going to open up to her about it? She didn't have the kind of relationship with him that would warrant her to know.

His gaze met hers for a second. "What is it?"

Sighing, she steeled herself. "What was that call you made this morning? After you got that text."

"It was work," he said after a moment. "There've been developments in the problem that I came to Covey about."

She frowned and worried her lip. "Oh. Then we need to call Marilyn."

Pulling out her phone, Sophie swiped open the appropriate application and stopped.

It would be odd if she knew before Marilyn.

Sure, James could've called Sophie, but why? Marilyn was handling his case, not her. It would surely rouse Marilyn's suspicions that something was going on.

Sophie put her phone away before glancing at James, who wore a stream of identical thoughts on his face.

She frowned. "How are we—"

"It's fine. I've got it handled," he interjected.

"Okay, but you still need to tell Marilyn."

"And I will tomorrow." He flicked his gaze toward Sophie. "But for now, I've got someone working on it."

He left it there, but unease ate away at Sophie's innards.

Why do I feel like he's not going to tell Marilyn anything?

Sophie squinted at his side profile and snapped into business mode. "James, do I need to remind you that by signing that contract with us, you agreed to let us help you?" She frowned. "That includes all past, present, and future events regarding the issue."

"I know," he said. "But the thing is, this could lead nowhere, and since I already have eyes on it, we should let *them* handle it for now."

She sighed, considering the point he made. "Fine."

They drove in silence for some time before they hit traffic.

Glancing at him as they inched forward, she changed the subject. "Uh ... so what does the tattoo on your collarbone mean again?"

His lips twitched. "What if I told you I just think Roman numerals are cool?"

She grinned. "Do you?"

"Well, they do look cooler than regular numbers."

She laughed. "I'll give you that. Seriously, what does it mean?"

His expression pinched, and something cracked inside of her.

He wasn't going to tell her, and why would he? Last night had been a fluke, after all. There wasn't any more profound connection between them just because they had shared the same bed.

Yet, he hadn't left, and the look he bestowed upon her that morning left her stomach tying itself into intricate knots and releasing a typhoon of butterflies.

"It's the day my mom left."

His voice caught her off guard, and she jumped.

"I ... I see," Sophie said.

She stared out the window as they changed lanes. "Oh, about last night ... thank you for staying. You didn't have to."

"I wanted to," he said and glanced at her. "On top of that, you were upset. What kind of person would I be if I left you like that?"

Little glowing pockets burst and fizzled in her chest, and her cheeks heated. Her foot tapped incessantly, and she zoned in on her shoe.

"I don't know why I need it," she admitted quietly. Dipping her head, she fiddled with her bracelet.

"Need what?" he asked.

She sniffed and reached into the bag. Pulling out an orange, she played with it. "Someone to be there when something like last night happens. Like I said, it wasn't the first time."

When she was younger and she had nightmares, her mom's room was always there. That or she'd hunker in Noah's room, listening to him tell her fairy tales and silly stories until she laughed the tears away. Regardless, she was never alone, and maybe she'd grown too accustomed to that.

She dug her nail into the orange peel, unleashing the citrusy aroma. Clearing her throat, she shook her head. "I shouldn't need that, but thank you."

She could take care of herself. Had done that for years and she wasn't about to start being needy now.

The car lurched and she grabbed onto the safety handle as they slowed magnificently.

James stared at her, ignoring the honks behind them. "Sophie, *what*?! In what world is that being needy?" He shook his head before pulling to a stop in the emergency lane. Tossing his emergency lights on, he twisted to face her. "Look, I *know* what you're thinking. Believe me, I know."

She dropped the orange. "How?"

"Because I have them, too." He took the discarded orange and peeled it. "But you're not being high maintenance or bothering anyone by asking for comfort. If anything, that's the least you can do."

He handed the fruit to her and flicked on his blinker, checking the coast was clear before merging back onto the road.

She stared at the orange. "James ..."

"Sophie," he murmured. "It's okay. I said it before, and

I'll say it again. Just let me be there for you."

Brisk, autumn wind whipped, and she hugged herself, cursing the fact she didn't wear a cardigan.

"Wait." James shrugged out of his sweatshirt.

An extra layer cloaked her shoulders along with a fresh wave of cologne, as he bundled the fabric around her.

"Thanks." The too-long sleeves hid her hands. "But you don't need to give me this. It's only a few blocks."

"And it's a few blocks where you won't be cold." He took up a steady pace beside her, keeping his hands in his pockets.

She nodded and curled her hands inside the sleeve, her heart warming.

As they approached the appropriate building, she eased out of the warm fabric. "Thanks. But we don't need anyone wondering why I'm wearing your clothes once we go in."

"Dante?" James gestured to the hulking security guard. "He won't care. But alright."

He held onto the sweatshirt as he knocked on the door.

Dante let them in and she followed James through the quiet lobby, their steps ricocheting against the shined floor.

The elevator shot them to the top floor, with glass double doors protecting an empty reception desk, and a large logo on the wall behind.

She expected Lotus's offices to be much bigger than they actually were, though she should've foreseen the small size considering the entire staff comprised of fifteen people.

Past the doors, he paused outside the door at the corner of the resulting hallway.

"Like I said, I have some papers to pick up." He opened the door. "You can either wait out here or come in."

"What happened to the private tour? Or was that it?" She raised a brow. "If so, you're a terrible tour guide."

His lips pulled up. "Well. Good thing I'm not in that business then."

Ambling into his office, she shut the door after her. "You're not? Then why did the tour office assign you as my guide?"

He clucked his tongue. "I think they thought you'd enjoy the view."

"Narcissist."

He grinned. "Yet you're not denying I look nice."

"No, I'm not." Her lips curved up and she took a seat in his desk chair. Spinning the chair with her toes, her breath flew from her lungs.

Her office at Covey fit a desk and a few other things, but strained to accommodate her squat bookshelf and sparse filing cabinets.

On the other hand, James's desk was parked in front of a wall of windows, which drowned the room in sunlight. Extensive wall space on either side allowed for large bookcases and a few chairs. Across from his desk, two panes of the paneled walls turned to mirrors, the space between them eaten up by filing cabinets.

"Enjoying the view?" He stilled the chair from behind, his lips gracing the shell of her ear.

"Yes." The sunlight entering the glass blinded her, but she didn't care. "It's amazing."

"I think so, too."

She turned her head and inhaled sharply.

He looked right at her, a soft expression in his eyes.

Clearing her throat, she turned the chair again from his loose grasp and faced forward. "Why are there mirrors?"

He snorted. "The designer wanted the office to appear bigger, but he failed to realize what you get when the midday sunlight hits those mirrors. Hence why those two shades are pulled."

Sophie rolled her eyes. "Yes, because the last thing this place needs is to 'appear bigger.'"

He raised his hands in surrender. "Don't shoot the messenger. Anyway, those papers I need are on my desk."

She grinned. "So, take them off."

Chuckling, he braced his hands on the arms of his chair and inched closer. He trailed his shallow breaths over her neck and along her ear, disrupting stray strands of her messy updo. Body heat radiated off him in waves, and her lungs stopped working.

Brown eyes met hers and he lifted two papers in the sliver between them.

"Got them," he murmured. "Question is, even though I'm not qualified, do you still want that private tour?"

Cushioning her teeth in her bottom lip, she nodded.

His pupils blew wide. "Then get on the desk."

His pinch on the papers dissolved and they fluttered to the floor beside him. Sweeping his gaze to his desk, he brushed everything aside except for his computer. They thumped unceremoniously to the carpet, pens scattering and bouncing.

"On the desk." He straightened and backed up.

Boosting herself onto the gleaming surface, her pulse thrummed and her blood transformed into a swarm of butterflies, fluttering in her veins.

Standing between her legs, he wound one of his hands into her hair and cupped the side of her neck.

Her heart sped up as he pulled her closer, tracing his free hand down her side to grip her thigh.

"Sophie," he mumbled. His gaze gouged deep marks in her as it swept across her face.

A symphony swelled in her ears as she closed the distance, crushing them into an elegant mess.

Her arms latched around his neck, and she sighed against his lips.

His hold on her thigh pushed her dress higher and higher, the pads of his fingers brushing her underwear. Playing with the lacy material, he slipped it aside and traced his fingers over her arousal.

Sparks shot up her spine, electrifying her limbs, and she groaned into his mouth. *I can't get enough of him.*

"Fuck, already so ready for me," he hissed. "Lie back."

Pressing a kiss against her shoulder, he sank to his knees and pulled her to the edge of the desk. Dragging her underwear off, he spread her legs wide and nipped her thigh again.

"If I remember correctly, you needed a stress reliever," he murmured.

"I didn't think you were listening," she admitted. Craning her neck up, she met his midnight gaze, and heat coiled in her belly.

His breath gusted over her in hot bursts, and he readjusted his hold on her calves. "Don't you know by now that I'll always listen to you? Now, tell me what you want. Beg for it."

Closing her eyes, she focused on his breath tickling her skin. *How can he be so endearing and demanding at the same time?*

"I'm waiting." His thumbs rubbed circles against her.

A dismayed whimper slipped past her lips and she bucked her hips. If he didn't hurry up and put his mouth on her ...

"Please," she murmured, looking at him.

Chuckling, he backed out of reach, and his voice turned silken. "Not good enough."

Bracing one of her ankles on his shoulder, he held onto her calf and mouthed her inner thigh. He sketched his hand back to the swell of her ass and dragged his touch down one cheek. "Fuck, that ass."

A shudder rattled down her spine, and her eyes widened as a crack rent the air, a sting zinging her skin. "Did you just—"

"Use your words." He smoothed his hand over her. "Or I do that again. Do you want to let me lick that sweet pussy of yours until you're screaming my name?"

Tremors of anticipation rocked through her, and she nodded frantically.

"I can't hear you." Another smack cleaved the air, and his fingers moved from her hip to skim headily over her clit. "Or are you just not able to use your words?"

Her legs quivered, and she managed to whisper out her answer. "Yes. God, please, yes."

A sharp smack broke the silence. "Louder."

Maybe I'll just stay quiet. Maybe I–

He pressed her clit. "Sophie."

She unleashed a sharp gasp and repeated the words with more force.

"Good girl," he praised. Moving forward, his cursed tongue danced over her, switching between swirls and flicks.

She moaned and her back arched, gasping as he sucked her clit into his mouth.

"Oh, God," she breathed as fingers dug into her skin, gripping her ass. "*Yes.*"

She was going to die. She was going to die, and she didn't even worry about it. Her fingers fisted his hair, bringing his head closer to her.

Losing herself in sensation, it wasn't long before his name flowed from her lips. Her limbs flopped against the wood, her legs drooping.

He rose to his feet, bending to kiss her with glistening lips.

Sitting up, she fumbled to undo his belt, dropping his pants and boxers to grip him.

He groaned and batted her hands away. "Don't."

Confusion rocked through her, and she tried to take him in her hands again. "I don't under–"

"Today is about you," he murmured. "Making *you* feel good."

She gasped as he pushed his thumb against her clit before sinking his middle and ring finger into her. Moaning, she canted her hips toward him. "Holy–*fuck.*"

A familiar building stacked at the base of her spine. Her staggered breaths came in hiccupping gasps, and all she could focus on was his lips hot on her neck.

His fingers curled and moved, his thumb rubbed her sensitized clit gently, and he had tugged her neckline and bra down to mouth at her nipple.

"*Fuck.*"

"That's it. Let it out, Sophie. Let this whole building know who's making you feel this way."

She poured herself over the cliff, and her hands latched

like a vise down onto his shoulders as she rode out her release on his fingers.

"Use me," he whispered. "Take everything."

She rested her forehead on his shoulder as she caught her breath. Scooching forward, her sandaled feet graced the floor.

He groaned softly as he helped her off his desk, brushing the pad of his thumb over her bottom lip.

"What?"

He grabbed her hips before she collapsed on wobbly legs. "I hate myself for not having a condom right now."

His thumbs scored twin streaks of heat as they swished back and forth across her skin, and she shuddered.

The pulsing between her legs grew. "It's fine. I'm on the pill, and I've been tested recently."

His gaze latched onto hers. "I've never ... the risk–"

"I said it was fine," she affirmed.

Would it be too intimate without anything between them? She wasn't sure and she didn't care.

After a moment, he spun her with a growl, bending her over the polished wood surface. "Me, too."

Her legs trembled with anticipation, and she was sure her knuckles whitened from the force with which she gripped the desk. She spread her legs, widening her stance, and gave her ass a slight wriggle.

The gloss of the desk was cool beneath her hands, but she barely processed it. All she knew was she was on Cloud Nine as he methodically rubbed her clit from behind, his mouth caressing the shell of her ear.

"Look in the mirror for me," he purred.

She let out a breathy moan as he rubbed her clit while teasing her entrance with his cock. Gasping as he pushed into her, she lifted her head, her gaze meeting her reflection.

His voice coiled in her ear. "Tell me, do you like what you see?"

The question caught her off guard, and she peered over her shoulder at him.

"Eyes on you." He gripped her jaw and turned her head forward. "I'll ask again. Do you like what you see?"

"I ... I ..."

"Let me tell you what I think," he murmured. He drove harder into her, and the desk creaked. "I think you do. I think you love seeing yourself take my cock like the good fucking girl you are."

She whimpered, gasping as his hand snaked around her hip to rub at her clit again.

His other hand gripped her throat, pressing her back against his chest, his hips slamming into her with every thrust.

She peered at the woman in the mirror. The one with cheeks colored a delightful shade of rose, frizzy hair, and a dress where the top had slid down, making her breasts spill over the collar. The skirt was a mess around her waist, and every movement he made as he fucked her reflected in the mirror.

Her stomach filled with delicious heat, fighting to burn its way out.

They spoke without words, their breaths twisting around one another, swirling into silence.

Crying out, she approached the edge inside her again, the brink shining like the end of a marathon.

"Fuck," she swore as his movements grew faster. "Ah, *fuck*."

"Such a dirty mouth." He pressed his lips to her neck. "God, look at you. You're doing so well." He groaned, fingers tightening at the base of her throat. "Let me hear who your pussy belongs to, Sophie, and come all over my cock like a good girl."

A few thrusts left her gasping and crying his name, clawing at his desk as her release hit her, her fingers hooking and sliding uselessly against the surface.

He didn't stop moving, and a moment later, he groaned, grunting as he came.

They lay there for a moment, him bracing his weight on

his arms.

Her breath came out staggered, and a shiver ran down her spine as he pressed a kiss to her shoulder.

After a moment, she asked, "Do you think your desk can take it if we go again?"

He pulled out of her and spun her to face him. A wolfish grin plastered his face. "Let's find out."

Sophie popped another bit of fried seaweed in her mouth.

Oliver grabbed a bag of crab chips and cradled it to his chest. "So? What was it like? He stayed at a hotel, but was the car ride awkward as fuck?"

Chloe shuddered. "Like a three-hour date against your will."

Sophie stopped short as she reached for another chip. *Right, I never told them what happened to the original plans.*

"Actually, things changed," she admitted, and explained what happened.

"Oh, God," Taylor whispered. "You are *so* fucked."

"Maybe it didn't mean anything to him," Chloe jumped in.

"What, so you're saying he's a player?" Oliver asked. "That's not better."

"No, I meant that maybe he was freaked out, but he got over it," she amended.

"Um ... there's more," Sophie launched into how they flirted the whole weekend, ending with what had happened at his office.

Chloe's mouth hung open. "I take it back. He's not over it."

"Okay ... so this guy's got it bad for you," Taylor said. "What are you going to do about it?"

Sophie sat back on the couch with the bag of seaweed chips. She could very well abandon James and whatever they had entirely. They danced into dangerous territory and she was the one who put them there. So, it only made sense for her to be the one to take them out.

Her mind raced. That was the easy way, but if she chose that, she would be no better than her exes.

She wouldn't put James in that position. She couldn't lead him on with a false string, hoping for something that wasn't possible.

"Let me rephrase this," Taylor said. "Do you *want* to?"

'Let me be there for you.'

But what was the point if she would only drag him down?

"Yes," she admitted. "I just ... need to think."

Sophie tugged Chloe toward the elevator and pressed the button for the top floor.

James had asked them if they wanted to watch the baseball game with him and his friends.

Sophie and Chloe felt the same way about sports, but ... they also weren't about to turn down a visit to Billionaire's Row.

"I forgot you said he had the penthouse," Chloe muttered.

"No, I said he had *a* penthouse," Sophie corrected. "This building has multiple."

"*Multiple*?!"

Sophie laughed. "That was my reaction when he told me, too."

The elevator slid open, and Luc stood there, smiling. "Hey."

Chloe made a choking noise.

Luc frowned. "Um ... are you okay?"

She waved away his concern. "You're seeing the same apartment I am, right?"

Realization glossed over his face, and he grinned. "Okay, well ... was the trip over okay? I can give you guys a ride back later."

Sophie wasn't sure if his apartment was in the direction they had to go, but from the way he was looking at Chloe, she didn't think it was.

"Yeah, it was." Sophie noticed the hearts populating Chloe's eyes. "Uh ... is someone in the bathroom?"

"Yeah, Pip. The one in James's room should be empty, though. He's on the phone, but tell mec to hurry up," Luc responded.

She chuckled. "Are you calling him a swear, too?"

Luc snorted. "No, though he deserves it. Mec means 'bro.'"

Sophie laughed as she approached James's room. Her hand froze on the knob as the frustrated hiss of his voice stopped her in her tracks.

"No, I don't actually want anything to happen to him." He paced the room. "But I don't care how much you have to give him, or what you have to say. Just make sure it gets done."

Quietly, she pushed open the door and padded into the bathroom, gripping the counter.

Who had he been talking to? Was this about Lotus and the problem he described yesterday?

She had half a mind to burst into the room proper and tell him to wait for them. Marilyn would come up with a solution soon enough.

But ... would he even listen to Sophie if she tried? Would he assume she was thinking about *her* company, not his?

Pushing the doubts away, she rushed out of the bathroom.

He spun to face her, eyes wide. "Oh, hey, I didn't know you got here already."

"Is everything okay?" she asked.

He blinked. "Did you overhear?"

She hesitated, then nodded. "You said it could lead nowhere yesterday. But that didn't sound like it was just a false hope."

"It ... became more than that," he admitted. "Look, don't

worry, okay? I told you, I have someone on it."

She arched a brow. *What* did he say?

Eleven

James

He wanted to shove the words back down his throat. Fuck, had he really said that to her? It was *literally her job to worry*, but he cared more about looking heroic. He wanted to smash his head against the wall.

She blinked and stepped back. "Excuse me?"

He winced, wishing more than anything he could take back the expression on her face.

"I know one client besides Fukada has found its way back to Lotus, and I know you don't think that's enough," she continued. "You hired us for a reason, so why aren't you letting us do our job? Why aren't you letting *me*?"

"Sophie, please. I hadn't counted on any of this happening."

"But it did! So explain to me right now how that changes anything."

He jammed his hands in his pockets and looked at the ceiling. Fuck, he hadn't expected to explain himself to her. He had never had to explain himself to *anyone*, now that he thought about it, not since he was young, at least.

"You don't ... no, you *do*, probably better than anyone. You *know* how important this is to me," he started, lowering his gaze back to her.

She tipped her chin in ascent.

"I'm pretty sure I've got the guy who tried to take my company down," he continued. "I can't wait around for the way things are done to catch up to him."

He left it at that and silently begged her to see his reasoning.

His mother's words from years ago echoed back.

'Remember, boys. Our last name holds meaning, but it doesn't define everything. There are more options in your future than just staying with the family.'

He was the only one who took her words to heart, with Adam choosing promised security.

But now, he was in danger of losing it all.

So really, if Sophie were in his position, she would be doing the same thing, too, wouldn't she?

Neither of them said anything, and she continued to fix him with that same frozen stare.

He was being splintered apart by it, sliver by sliver, but dammit, he couldn't tear himself away.

"Fine," she said. "Just ... don't do anything drastic."

It was like someone punctured a hole in his lungs to let all the pent-up air escape. He couldn't promise that, but he nodded along anyway. "Of course."

A wry smile tainted her lips, and she extended a hand to him.

He stared at her upturned palm before taking it. But his heart still beat rapidly.

The truth was, the call set him on edge more than he'd like to admit. Now, he doubted if Torrence really was their man at all.

But ... James needed someone to blame, at least until they found the actual perpetrator. With the correct wording, he could easily blow things out of proportion.

Growing up, he wasn't blind to the privilege his last name brought. And like any sixteen-year-old, he had plenty of things that'd pissed him off.

But unlike most teenagers, he had access to the money needed to solve them.

He learned that long ago with his dad, who harbored a plethora of things that could take him down. And like any good businessman, he had shoved it out of sight with money and power.

But if you knew where to look, that same money and power could unearth it again.

Angry and fed up, James had compiled a bundle of incriminating evidence against his dad and had been that close to releasing it. But then ... Philip had come.

He was the only friend he had who remembered a time when James's mom had been around. That being said, he was one of the only ones who had been able to talk James off the ledge, so to speak.

Maybe it was because Philip had just been kicked out and disinherited that made James scrap whatever he had on his dad. But he hadn't delved into that territory again until he started Lotus and found that he needed to in order to survive.

Now, the issue with Torrence was no different than any of the other hurdles that James had to overcome.

Torrence had hurt him and, involuntarily, hurt people he cared about.

For that, the bastard deserved a lesson.

"James Tian."

"Hey, James. It's Raymond Laveau."

James pressed his cell to his ear with his shoulder and typed away on his monitor. "Oh, hey. Find anything?"

"Uh ... nothing helpful," Raymond started. "I dug a little deeper and found a string of emails on Torrence's computer. It's funny, he thought, if he deleted them, they were gone forever. You think he'd know better, working at a secur–"

"Raymond." James played with a pen, rolling it between his thumb and index.

"Right, sorry." Raymond cleared his throat. "Long story short, someone planted Torrence as a red herring. The emails came from a random account asking Torrence to spread crap about Cross and Delacroix, which, after they laid him off, he was more than happy to do. The account's been discarded since, obviously, but I'm working on tracing the IP address. It's still taking me a minute, though."

James sighed and rubbed his temples. "Alright, so if I'm getting this right, what I'm hearing is that Torrence might not have been directly responsible, but he's still guilty by association, right?"

"Yup." Raymond popped the 'p'.

James clamped his phone between his ear and shoulder again and hummed.

Aside from the scrape with Cross and a brief stint in jail for a minor crime when Torrence was in his twenties, he was clean. But now ... now they had this.

James could play with this.

"Perfect, thank you so much, Raymond," James said.

"Of course, I'll let you know when I know more."

The beep signaling the end of the call slid into James's ear, along with someone clearing their throat. A chill worked down his spine as he glanced up.

Jackie darkened the entrance to his office, shock coating her features.

"Tell me you didn't," she said.

He broke out in a cold sweat. "I'm sorry?"

Did she overhear? Or did she somehow find out about him and Sophie? If so, he was sure to get an earful about ethics.

Jackie didn't seem to care that he was her boss, and it was within his power to fire her. She never had the entire time she worked for him.

His assistant narrowed her eyes and walked into the office, shutting the door. She took a seat in front of his desk. "You might be the big, scary CEO, but you're still younger than I am. Which means I get to worry about you, including what you do under the table."

He kept his hands above the desk, resting them on top of

his keyboard, though his leg bounced nervously.

Did she *actually* know about him and Sophie? Had Jackie somehow found out about yesterday?

"I seriously don't know what you're talking about," he said coolly.

He had done nothing wrong.

Besides, there was no telling if what Jackie was going to say was about Sophie, anyway.

"Did I just catch you on the phone with Raymond at Key Security?" Jackie asked. Her eyes widened, lashes fluttering as she blinked. "James, are you serious?"

James sighed. "Okay, I just–"

"No, absolutely not," she interrupted. "Honey, *you* went to Covey"–she shook her head–"you don't get to blackmail the guy."

"But–"

"*No*."

He swallowed whatever fight he had left and gave in. Resting his head back against his chair, he closed his eyes. "Fine. Sorry."

She clicked her tongue, and chair legs scraped. When he opened his eyes again, she was gone.

He hung his head. Well, so much for that lead.

The clacking of Jackie typing greeted him as he opened his office door. It was nearing ten p.m., and he had sent everyone else home earlier, including the other C-Suite members.

"Jackie, seriously, go home," he said.

She shook her chestnut locks away from her face and looked up from her computer. "I'm your assistant; I can leave when you leave. Besides, it's not like I'm dying to get home."

He smiled wryly. "I just have some emails to send. I'll be fine."

She studied him for a moment, fingers laced. "Okay.

They're not illegal emails, are they?"

He snorted, though his gut twisted. He knew she was joking about it, but it still put the fear of God into him.

Her hazel eyes twinkled. "Also, as long as I have you, do I want to know why that woman from Covey was in your office for so long today during lunch?"

"She came over to discuss some things on Marilyn's behalf," he blurted, faster than intended.

If Jackie hadn't suspected, she sure as hell did now.

His assistant hummed. "Of course. That explains why your door was locked."

"How do you know it was locked?"

"I tried to drop some papers off and couldn't turn the handle. I asked you if you were okay, remember?"

His jaw clenched. "Oh, right."

But honestly, he couldn't remember much. Sophie had his dick in her mouth, and everything else had been a bit ... foggy.

He laughed to throw Jackie off, but fear coursed through him again. There was no telling what she heard. "Night, Jackie."

Closing his office door behind him, he sank into his desk chair, groaning.

Aside from the Fukada deal, which he still had to follow up on, there were also a slew of other cases that needed his attention. Plus, he had been in and out of meetings all day. He was exhausted.

Clicking open his email, he took a deep breath and flexed his fingers over his keyboard. Maybe he would respond to one email and then go home.

When he sent it off, his phone buzzed, and he glanced at the message on the screen. His insides went cold as his eyes picked up on his dad's name.

We need to talk.

His dad never just wanted to talk. If he spoke to his son, he yelled. If he wasn't yelling, it was a barb wrapped in a thin layer of kindness.

Still, something in James made him swipe on the message and respond.

When?

He hoped his dad didn't want James to call him. James didn't think he had the mental energy for that.

Did you forget about dinner on Saturday? Bring that girl you've been seeing with you.

James went completely rigid.

How had his dad found out about Sophie? And if he knew, who else did?

He forced his fingers to move across the screen.

There's no girl

That's not what your brother said. Bring her. End of discussion.

He gritted his teeth as he put his phone down.

Of course, Adam had told their dad. But how...

Oh, fuck. Lina.

James rubbed a hand over his face. It was his fault; he had Adam go pick Lina up when she was drunk, and it had come to stab James in the back.

He leaned back in his chair. This wasn't good.

Charles Tian held credibility in the business world, and one word from him to the right person could end James's career. It could end Sophie's.

She worked for Marilyn, and that was enough to spark a scandal into existence.

They would be hounded and criticized for months, possibly years, and they would lose any credibility they had.

She could kiss the promotion she wanted so badly goodbye, and he ...

Hitting Sophie's contact, he put the phone on speaker as he opened up another email.

The last people he wanted to know about him and Sophie were his family, and from the way his dad phrased his sentence, it was apparent he thought she was some brazen gold digger.

"Hello?" she answered.

He cut straight to the chase. "Hey, so, my dad knows about us."

She was quiet for a moment. "How?"

"My brother. When he went to get Lina, I'm pretty sure she told him about us."

"I see," she murmured before fading into silence.

"I'm sorry."

"Why are you sorry?"

"Because it's my fault. Because I potentially just left us to drown."

"Stop that," she said. "It was going to get out sooner or later, and your dad just happened to find out first. At least it's not the public, right?"

James shook his head. "No, but it could be. You don't understand what my dad could do with this."

"I understand just fine." Steel cut into her tone. "But there's nothing we can do now except control it."

"So, tell me how we do that," he said. His gut twisted itself into abstract pieces of art.

She laid out their game plan.

It didn't matter if they arrived early or were dressed to impress. His dad already formed an opinion on them. They would need to be on their best behavior and tackle both perception and emotion.

Apprehension filled James as she talked. If this didn't work, both of them were done.

James kissed Sophie as soon as she exited the elevator on Saturday.

Clinging onto her, he breathed deep, her floral shampoo and perfume sweeping over him.

She laughed. "Well, hey. Good to see you, too."

He sighed. "You saw the news this morning, right?"

"It was hard not to," she said. "It was everywhere. But to be honest, Lina's been soft launching this on her Instagram for the past week."

"When I first saw them, I recognized the watch on my brother's wrist, along with the ring he wore," James admitted. "But I kept denying to myself that it was him. Our family hasn't gotten along with the Solano Castillos for over a decade."

"But you and Philip get along."

"That's different," James said. "I'm talking about our parents, and Adam hasn't talked to any of them since, either."

James's brows knit closer.

"Are you okay?" Sophie asked.

"Oh, uh ... yeah, just tired." He shrugged, mind reeling, recalling Lina once admitting she had a crush on Adam back when they were younger. *I guess she meant it.*

"I meant about the engagement," she clarified. "It's a big deal to your family, right? And you said Adam didn't mention it at all to anyone?"

James shook his head. "Yeah, I'm fine about it, just ... in shock. Lina told me that all those years ago, right after her dad told Philip to get out, she remembers seeing Adam watching everything with this strange look on his face. There wasn't anything he could do, obviously, but he didn't try to say something that might've helped a little. He just stood there and let it happen."

"I see." Sophie's forehead marred.

James hummed.

Complications always ran amok in wealthy families, but none so much as theirs. To tie the two together through marriage ...

The engagement seemed like a blessing in disguise. It would tame the bad blood running between the families. But that couldn't be further from the truth.

Not even their children joining together in holy matrimony could make Manuel Solano and Charles Tian amicable again. Not when Manuel viewed taking his son in as a direct blow after everything that happened.

Adam would be at dinner later, and James hoped to get some answers, since it was his fault that Adam and Lina met up again anyway.

James blinked as what Sophie wore finally clicked in his mind.

Her hair remained down, but it had been styled into loose waves that cascaded over her shoulders. A silky, navy cocktail dress clung to the curves of her body in a way that was sensual yet conservative at the same time.

"You look amazing," he blurted.

"Thanks. You do, too," she said. "Did you color coordinate with me?"

James himself was clad in a navy button-down tucked into a pair of dark pants. Silver cufflinks and the sparkling silver Cartier watch on his wrist complemented the delicate silver accessories she donned. If anyone asked, he'd deny spending as much time on his hair as he did.

If they wanted to make a good impression on his dad, play his game, and walk away with all the winnings, they hit the nail on the head.

He snorted. "Thanks."

"You're wearing a tie," she observed.

"It's not the first time you've seen me in a tie."

Tightness wound in his belly as she crossed the space between them, her eyes lighting up.

Taking the end of his tie in her hand, she wrapped it in her fingers. "I know, but I've never told you how good you look in them."

His breathing shallowed; anything more than that made him lightheaded.

"What if it was tied around your wrists?" His voice dipped, and he put his hand on her hip. "Or wrapped around your eyes?"

Her throat bobbed. "Tempting. But don't be the reason we're late."

The smile written across her lips said she wouldn't mind that one bit. But she let go of his tie.

He stepped back reluctantly and followed her toward the elevator. The sleek doors slid shut, and James's father yelled at him in his head.

All James's exes had come from prominent, conglomerate families who knew the Tians through some business or other. They offered deep connections and even deeper pockets. But Sophie ... what was James thinking, bringing some random woman from a simple PR firm into their world?

He shoved the thoughts aside.

Tonight was going to be different.

Twelve

Sophie

It took Sophie and James two hours to reach Montauk. They snaked down the long, gravel drive, and he killed the engine.

She cataloged the steel-gray Aston Martin they pulled up alongside.

Is his brother already here, or is that his dad's?

Dying evening sunshine cut across James's face as she took in his expression, and her lips tilted downward. She gritted her teeth and caught his wrist, the pads of her fingers burning where they touched.

"Do you know if there are carrots on the menu for dinner?" she asked. She wasn't sure where the question came from–it slipped past her lips uninhibited. All she knew was she couldn't let him leave the car looking like *that.*

He frowned. "What?"

"Carrots," she repeated. Shit, she was going to regret telling him this. "I can't do carrots. I get ... weird."

He raised a brow. "Define weird."

She let out a nervous laugh. "As in ... I get really gassy."

Laughter burst from him, the back of his head hitting the headrest. A smile creased his lips, showing off his smile lines and wrinkling his eyes.

She smiled. *Good.* She needed him to laugh before they walked in.

As they left the car and crossed the driveway, the gravel crunching under their shoes, she stared at the huge house.

Holy...

She'd done her best to ignore it before in the car, but now that it loomed head-on, it was impossible.

The mansion was overwhelming. Those were the most windows she'd ever seen on a residential building outside of Manhattan, and every step they took did nothing for the ball of nerves clanging around in her stomach.

What if his dad didn't like her? She knew he already didn't, but what if it got worse? What if ... no.

She hadn't come this far in her career because she worried about what others thought of her. She just needed to treat the Tians as another case. Even though she had a deeper connection with one of them, there was no reason to lose her head.

She took a deep breath and gazed upwards.

A figure stood in an upstairs window, their face obscured as they turned their head. They combed an elegant, manicured hand through their long, dark brown waves before walking away.

Sophie frowned. *Was that Lina*?

They reached the front door and James's grip tightened.

She bumped his hip with hers and squeezed his hand. "Hey, it's okay."

He blinked, and it was like an entire ocean melted off his shoulders; his tense posture relaxed, and his hand loosened.

But when he rang the bell, everything came roaring back, and he looked one breath away from tipping off the ledge.

She sighed but steeled her expression as the door opened.

Instead of James's dad, an elderly woman stood at the entrance. She dried her hands on the tea towel she held and beamed, stepping back to let them by.

"James! It's wonderful to see you again," she gushed. "How are you? Have you been eating enough? You look skinnier than the last time you came by. Are you sure you're taking care of yourself?"

In Sophie's mind, she knew the woman had to be Charles Tian's housekeeper. But for some reason, she kept thinking it was James's grandmother, given the way she fussed over him.

He smiled back. "Hi, Mrs. Le. I'm okay, and yes to everything." He removed his shoes and slipped into a pair of slippers. "This is Sophie Huang, my ..."

"Girlfriend?" Mrs. Le supplemented.

"Um ... yes," Sophie lied. She extended her hand. "It's nice to meet you!"

The housekeeper clasped her hand. "You, too. Lah, you're so pretty, honey!"

Sophie blushed. "Thanks. Uh, is Mr. Tian in the living room?"

"Yes, he's right down there." The housekeeper pointed toward a room at the end of the hall. "Go on in, I'll be back with drinks in a minute." She started to walk down another hall before pausing. "Oh, yes. James, your brother is here. I think he's upstairs?"

James went rigid. "Thanks for letting me know."

Sophie put a hand on the crook of his elbow, not missing Mrs. Le's gaze dip toward the contact.

"You're welcome, dear," the housekeeper said. "His fiancée is here, too. You know he's acted kinder toward you over the years, but I think that she's made him even better."

Sophie raised her brow.

Mrs. Le disappeared down an adjoining hall, humming to herself.

Sophie took James's hand and headed toward the living room.

"Girlfriend?" he murmured. "I thought we weren't doing that."

Sophie's back stiffened. "We're not, but why else would I be here with you? Besides, it's not like your family doesn't think we're seeing each other."

'Seeing each other' in the loosest sense of the term.

"And from what I could tell," she continued. "She seems like family.'

James hummed. "Yes ... Mrs. Le's been with my family

since Adam and I were kids, so she's practically another grandmother to us."

Sophie nodded. "It's nice to know you had someone."

Despite the soaring ceilings and cavernous rooms, without someone who made the place a home, you might as well be trapped underground.

They passed by pictures hanging on the wall, including a few of James sitting at a piano on a lit stage.

Her steps faltered. "I forgot you played piano."

"Yeah." He let out a hollow laugh. "My mom insisted I learn in the first place and after, I kept at it, even though I sucked. I don't know why my dad keeps those pictures up. Sentimentality, I guess?"

In the time since they had left the foyer, his grip had become a vise again.

She needed him to calm down if their plan was going to work, and she meant to distract him. But with his tone, she clearly just made everything worse.

"James, wait–"

"Oh. You're here."

Her head swiveled toward the entrance where a man stood with his hands in his pockets. Her insides went cold; she had seen plenty of pictures of Charles Tian, but seeing him in person was a different matter altogether.

James obviously inherited his towering frame from his father, and they bore the same defined cheekbones and jaw, as well as perfectly arched brows. But besides those, they looked like two completely different people.

She stepped forward, extending her hand. "Hello, I'm Sophie Huang, James's girlfriend. It's nice to meet you."

The tips of James's fingers lingered on the small of her back as she moved, providing a constant, reassuring warmth.

Charles looked at her hand for a second before taking it and shaking it briskly.

"James's girlfriend," Charles repeated. "Is that what you're calling it? Well. It's my pleasure."

Sophie had to applaud whatever force kept his lip from

curling, and she stiffened as the brunt of his words hit her. But she kept a smile on her face.

"I uh ... I heard from Mrs. Le that Adam's upstairs. Where's Lina?" James asked, breaking the tense silence.

"She's in the bathroom," Charles replied. "I haven't seen her in a long time. She's looking well."

He walked into the living room without another word, expecting to be followed without question.

Sophie kept her face schooled into a placid mask as James's words shot back to her.

'Our family hasn't gotten along with the Solano Castillos for over a decade.'

Given the animosity, why would Philip's sister willingly be engaged to James's brother?

She shook her questions away and focused on the task at hand.

Taking a seat beside James on the tufted, white couch, she crossed her ankles.

The slapping of slippers interrupted the silence, and Mrs. Le entered with a tray bearing a water pitcher and glasses. She set it down on the coffee table, not speaking a word the entire time. But she shot Sophie a reassuring smile and patted her shoulder before she left.

Sophie wished she wouldn't go. Discomfort wound tight in the air, threatening to snap.

Filling the glasses, she grabbed one and chugged the contents as the hairs on her arm prickled.

Charles scrutinized her. "So. How long have you known my son?"

The question was posed innocently enough, but its true meaning lay beneath the surface.

How long have you been sleeping with him?

She resisted the urge to wrinkle her nose and smiled sweetly. "A few weeks."

A piece of advice from years ago came floating back to her.

To sell a lie, you had to work in elements of truth along

the way.

It was a delicate process–you didn't want to put in too much–but if you did it right, the lie became more believable.

"We met at a coffee shop," she continued. "He accidentally took my drink."

Charles arched a brow but said nothing as he poured out a glass of alcohol. She wondered if he assumed she'd staged it. Handing it to his son, he turned to her. "Whisky, Sophie?"

It was a little early in the day to be drinking hard liquor, but she accepted anyway.

"My other son tells me you work at the PR firm James hired after his ... slip-up," Charles continued. Disdain curled his lip ever so slightly.

She curbed her frown even as James openly glared at his dad. Clenching her jaw, she tapped his ankle with her foot.

None of this was his fault and Charles had no right to imply it was, but if James didn't control himself, this wasn't going to work.

"I–" she started.

A man who was clearly James's brother slipped into the room, typing something on his phone. Like James, he was tall–close to six-five, if she had to guess. From the nose up, he strongly resembled his brother, but everything below that was like a younger copy of their father.

"Oh." Adam pocketed his phone. "Hello. You must be Sophie." He strode across the room and offered his hand. "Pleasure to meet you."

She hesitated before standing to shake it.

From what James had told her, Adam kept to himself in slimy silence. But his pleasant smile could've fooled her.

"Yes, nice to meet you," she said. "I hear congratulations are in order."

"Thank you," he said. "Have you met my–Ah."

A woman entered, shaking her dark waves from her face. Sophie smiled, introducing herself again.

"Catalina, right?" she asked.

"Just Lina is fine. It is so nice to meet you!" Lina said. Her accent mirrored her brother's and added a musical quality to her words.

Sophie smiled. "The pleasure's mine."

Lina's eyes matched her brother's, although the gleam in them was slightly sharper. Along with their eyes, they also bore identical jawlines and fair, bronze skin. But while Philip resembled pictures of his father, Lina must've been a mix of both their parents.

Both she and Adam had the distinct, sophisticated countenance that came with their lot in life. But whereas Adam held dark clouds, Lina harbored a blend of clouds and sunshine.

James cleared his throat and smiled. "Lina, how have you been?"

Lina beamed, embracing him and pressing her cheeks to his. "James, so good to see you again! How is my brother doing?"

"Pain in my ass, as always."

She laughed, placing a hand on the pronounced curve of her hip. A glittering engagement ring set with a halo of small diamonds around a massive, rounded diamond in the center, winked on her finger.

"I will come visit soon," she promised.

Sophie offered her congratulations again, not missing the briefest hint of strange gratification in Lina's gaze.

"Can I get a closer look at the ring?" Sophie pointed at Lina's hand.

Lina nodded, holding her hand out. Her free hand threaded through Adam's, clasping their fingers. "It is beautiful, no? He got it custom-made."

Sophie's brows lifted. *Interesting.*

James whistled and clapped his brother on the shoulder. "Nice job."

Adam offered his fiancé a small smile, his eyes shining with a warmth he couldn't quite hide. "I was serious when I said you deserve the best."

Lina glanced at him, her lips parted slightly. "Really?"

His gaze fastened to her lips and bounced back to her eyes. "Really."

James cleared his throat and Lina and Adam tore their gazes from each other.

"Pues, please." Lina gestured to the couches again. "Continue what you were talking about."

"Um ... right." Sophie shifted her attention back to Charles, who'd been doing something on his phone. "Well, I do work at that PR company, but we didn't plan for this to happen." Her hand drifted down to James's knee and rested there. "But since I'm not directly overseeing his case, we thought it'd be fine to date."

Charles pounced. "Yes, but you're not dating, are you?"

She smiled, giving James's knee a squeeze to tell him to keep quiet. "I'm sorry?"

"You're not dating," Charles repeated. "No society papers know, nor anyone of standing beside the people in this room. Why?"

She smiled woodenly and gathered her words. "I—"

"Sophie's on her way to becoming the account director for her PR company," James cut in.

"Uh ... he's exaggerating. I haven't been there long enough yet," she corrected.

Dammit, she hadn't wanted to let loose the fact that she was going for a promotion. It would give her a boost with Charles, but it also meant giving him the impression she solely wanted to use James for his power.

Adam took a sip of his whisky, intertwining the fingers of his free hand in his fiancée's atop her knee. "How long have you been there?"

"About five years," Sophie admitted. "I've got enough experience, too."

"Which is?" Charles asked.

"I don't think she has to answer that," James said. "If she says she's got enough, then she does."

Charles stared his son down, and if looks could kill, James would be dead and gone.

"Uh, well. It certainly seems like enough to me," Lina cut in. Her fingers had closed over Adam's, and her thumb absentmindedly stroked against his skin.

Sophie's lips curved up.

Not only did Lina own her family's company back in Spain, but she also did a damn good job running it.

If someone in such high standing in a male-dominated field thought her ambitions were warranted, that had to count for something, didn't it?

Charles flashed an icy smile. "Well. Let's hope she really does like you for you, then."

Sophie laughed awkwardly and cut James a look.

A murderous glint lay in his eyes, but a forced chuckle slipped from his lips a moment later.

After dinner, James's dad moved things over to the living room again, where whisky and dessert would be served.

Adam and Lina had left, given their drive to Stamford, where they'd stop before heading back to Boston. James's dad excused himself to the bathroom.

Sophie glanced toward the entry and figured she'd take advantage of her and James having the room while she could.

"We're winning." The cut of the cool glass in her hand was a heavy contrast to the alcohol pooling in her belly.

James stared at a painting on the wall and nodded. "Yes, we are."

Over the course of the night, Charles continued to prod at Sophie and James with questions that Sophie recognized as meant to catch them off guard. But she'd readily combatted each one.

Slowly, Charles's answers became less jaded, and his expression morphed from disdain into impressed.

Sophie blew a breath out of her lips.

Meeting Charles made her reflect on how much she loved

her job.

Carefully shifting the chess pieces across the board, never making too sudden a move. Then, watching everything come together into your ideal outcome.

When Sophie first entered the PR field, the adrenaline rush scared her. But now, she enjoyed the excitement.

James pushed his plate of cake over to her. "Here, take this."

"Thanks." She picked up the plate and pursed her lips as a dab of frosting smeared onto her finger. Setting it down again, she reached for a tissue. "I thought you had a massive sweet tooth?"

"I do." Taking her hand, he swooped forward and captured her finger in his mouth.

Heat poured into her belly and settled in her cheeks as his tongue moved.

He released her finger and leaned back, cutting her a wink.

Her jaw dropped and she fixated her gaze on the ceiling as a whirlwind blew through her, disrupting her organized thoughts. Maybe ... maybe they could make what they had official.

Oliver was right; feelings had gotten involved, and if Sophie was being honest with herself, they were present from the beginning.

Wasn't this whole thing based on feelings anyway? You couldn't let him go, and neither could he let you.

If that was the case and they were still able to hide what they really felt for each other, then why not just make it public?

You don't even work at the same company. You wouldn't be breaking any HR codes. And wouldn't it be nice not to have to duck in dark corners anymore? Wouldn't it–

No.

None of that mattered when the weight of the glass depended too much on gossip and hearsay, and if Sophie let it drop ...

She wasn't ready for it to shatter, or where the shards would fly.

She cleared her throat and turned toward him."James—"

She squinted in the dim light and frowned, all previous thoughts forgotten. "If you're not eating, maybe you should lay off the alcohol."

His cheeks boasted a red flush, and she didn't need him saying anything that would lead to him putting his foot in his mouth.

He cast her a lazy smile. "I'll be fine."

Someone cleared their throat, and her head whipped toward the entry where Charles stood.

"Can I talk to my son for a moment alone?" he asked.

She nodded, moving into the hall. The sour look gracing Charles's face, like he'd sucked on a lemon, swam before her eyes.

And we thought we were winning.

Charles's voice floated out of the room, bouncing in the airy hallway. "Well. It looks like she actually gives a damn about you. Congratulations."

"What's that supposed to mean?" James asked.

Sophie froze.

She should walk away. All she would do was hurt herself and give herself something new to worry over too late at night, but she couldn't help it. Her feet stayed rooted to the ground as the pop of a cork burst through the air, followed by liquid glugging.

"Don't think I don't see what you two are playing at," his dad continued. "But I have to hand it to you. She knows what she's doing. No wonder you went to her agency. But don't you think that there's some power imbalance here?"

"What?"

"You heard me," Charles said. "Unless you haven't thought of it?"

"You're one to talk."

"Excuse me?"

"You know who I'm talking about," James snapped.

The edge in his voice cut her and she winced. *Oh, God. It's his mom.*

Pressing herself to the wall, Sophie inched toward the living room.

Charles's eyes were wide. "Don't you dare bring her into this. Our situations are different."

Twin patches of red marred James's cheeks, and cold leeched into Sophie's own. Fuck, she had to get back in there.

"Are they?" James demanded. "I figured it out over the years. Mom only married you for your money and a green card. Do you think she would've gone for a hypocritical bastard otherwise?"

His dad's face contorted in rage. "You ungrateful piece of shit. After all I've done for you over the years, you think you can talk to me like that?"

But either James ignored the words being launched at him, or he chose not to hear them because he let out a laugh. "You're just proving my point."

His dad's eyes narrowed. "And you think that woman will stay with you forever? You think she won't leave when she realizes she can't get your money? Watch yourself, James."

Sophie bristled, fingers digging into the wall. Who the hell did Charles think he was?

James scoffed. "Or you'll what, cut me off? I don't take my money from you anymore."

His dad's jaw hardened and he opened his mouth before pausing. Tilting his head slightly, he sighed and shut his mouth. His spine somehow straightened even more, and he rested both his hands on the credenza.

"Enough. You're drunk, James," he said curtly. "I won't argue with you when you won't be able to see reason."

Sophie had a feeling no one would be able to see Charles's reasons even when they were stone-cold sober.

She stepped back into the room, not bothering to keep her approach muted. Her slippers slapped the hardwood.

"As you said, he's drunk," she said, calling both men's attention to her. "Thank you for dinner, but I think it's time we go. Seeing as I haven't driven for too long, I'm not comfortable being behind the wheel, especially this late at night. I can call a rideshare to take us back to Manhattan."

James's car would have to stay at his dad's, but James barely drove it, anyway. She doubted it would be a problem.

Charles scowled, the sole indication he was aware Sophie overheard everything. "No need, my driver can drive you back."

"Figures you'd only help to get us out of here, but we don't need it." James turned to Sophie. "I'm fine. Let's go."

She arched a brow. "Look at yourself, and say that again."

"We're not staying, Sophie," he said.

"Fine, but how are you going to get back?" Charles asked.

James fell silent, and Sophie rolled her eyes. She walked over to him and took his arm.

She forced herself to smile. "Thank you again. We'll wait outside. Good night."

She and James headed toward the foyer and bumped into Mrs. Le coming down a hall.

"Oh! Are you two leaving?" she asked. "Wait, wait. I have some things for you."

She turned back the way she came, disappearing through a swinging door.

"I bet you it's food," he said.

"She went into the kitchen, of course, it's food." Sophie shook her head. "You really are drunk, aren't you?"

He grinned and swapped his slippers for his shoes. Staying down on one knee, he grabbed one of Sophie's heels and gestured for her to step forward.

"What are you doing?" she asked.

"Helping," he explained. "Now, come on. Unless you want to wear those slippers back to Manhattan."

"Honestly, that's not the world's worst idea. They are comfy."

But she stepped out of them. Taking his hand, she lifted one foot into her shoe. She motioned for the other, but he shook his head.

"James–"

He ignored her and clasped the shoe's strap around her ankle. He muttered a swear as he shoved the small prong toward the little holes marking the strap and missed.

"This shouldn't be this hard," he muttered.

"Well, being drunk doesn't help," she said. "Leave it, I got it."

He ignored her as he finally got the prong through, then moved on to the other shoe.

Goosebumps pebbled her skin as his fingers brushed her ankle repeatedly. Raw desire cycled through her veins as she imagined his touch gracing her calves and moving higher.

Closing her eyes, she held back the sigh threatening to escape.

"All set."

She snapped out of her fantasy and opened her eyes. "Thanks."

He stood, still holding onto her hand. "You know, if you wanted to steal the slippers, you could. It's not a big deal."

She swallowed any lingering want and smiled. "Tempting, but I'm trying to make a positive impression on your family. I don't think stealing from them is going to do that."

He laughed as Mrs. Le came back out of the kitchen with two massive bags.

"I had the chef make some extras of what was served tonight, along with some other dishes." She thrust the bags towards them.

"Oh, thank you. This is too much," Sophie said even as she accepted the bags.

Mrs. Le waved it off and patted Sophie's arm. "Lah, it's nothing! Oh, I heard you loved the potatoes, so there's more of them in there."

Sophie didn't bother hiding her ear-splitting smile. "Thank you!"

Mrs. Le chuckled and turned toward James. "I like her. You better bring her again with you next time, you understand me?"

"Noted." He saluted.

Mrs. Le grinned and opened the door. "You have everything, yes? Alright, you should head out before it gets too late. Have a good night!"

After profusely thanking her, Sophie headed toward James's idling Mercedes. Boosting herself in, the top of her head smacked into something soft. She looked up and took in James's hand, which was covering the hard car frame.

"And that's why I covered it," he teased, getting in after her.

She rolled her eyes and smiled as the car pulled away.

In the darkness, she became that much more aware of James than ever. He had been beside her all night, but now, it was like someone turned the heat up to ten thousand.

The driver went over a pothole and mumbled a gruff apology as the car jostled.

She fell into James's side and cleared her throat as sparks snaked up her side. She tried to pull away, but his hand grabbed her arm and tugged her back.

"Okay?" he muttered.

She swallowed but nodded. "Thank God we're heading back. I didn't think I could stay in the same house as your dad any longer. No offense."

James laughed. "I think I wanted to jump out of a second-story window."

"Why do you come then?" she asked, her voice still lowered so the driver wouldn't overhear. She glanced at him, taking in the way the moonlight gilded his skin, making him seem ethereal.

He was quiet, staring out the window. "Honestly, for my mom."

Sophie's eyes flared. "Oh?"

"I can see her there," he continued, his hand around Sophie's shoulders drawing unconscious circles against her skin. "When I look at the pictures in the hall, I remember that she was the one who took them. When I go up to my room, I see her standing in the doorway, coming to tuck me in."

Sophie swallowed, fisting her hands. "I'm sorry you lost all that and got stuck with your dad instead."

"It's alright," James murmured. "And while we're on the topic, I'm sorry for what he said."

"It's fine," she said.

In the years she had been with Marilyn, and even before Covey, Sophie had heard and been called her fair share of derogatory terms. It came with the territory, and what Charles confessed when he thought she was out of earshot slid right off her skin like an inconvenient rain.

"No, it's not," James said. His breath brushed over her neck. "Just because it happens, doesn't mean you have to get used to it."

She sighed, sinking into him. "I know, but–"

"No buts."

"Alright," she murmured. His body heat seeped through her dress, eliciting shivers of desire.

They carried on in silence for some time before he spoke again. The words came sparingly, with too big a gap between them, like he wasn't sure if they were right.

"When we get back, just stay at mine," he said. "With the route we're taking, we'll pass my place first, anyway."

She stiffened. "I'm not sure if that's the best idea."

"Sophie, please?"

It was crazy how much one word could tear her apart and build her back up all at once.

Growing up, how many times had he been in this exact position, just asking for someone to stay with him? How many people refused and walked away to let him drown?

"Okay," she whispered.

They had already broken rules when he stayed with her that weekend in Connecticut, and they broke even more now. If they didn't want to cross any more boundaries, they had to end that before it went any further but even though there were rules to re-establish and lines to redraw, all that could wait.

Thirteen
James

A knock rang out into the silence and James glanced up from his phone, staring at Sophie in his bedroom doorway.

In lieu of her dress, one of his shirts covered her frame, tucked into a pair of his pants. Even though she'd asked for them so she wouldn't have to sleep in a cocktail dress, his brain still short circuited at her draped in his clothes.

"Hey," he managed. "It's late."

"I can't sleep," she admitted. "The mattress in your guest room is killing my back."

He nodded and set his phone down. Getting out of bed, he motioned for her to take his vacated spot. "Then we can switch rooms. You take my bed for the night."

A strange look crossed her face, but she quickly wiped her face of the expression. She crossed her arms, hugging herself as her toes scrunched. "Just stay."

"I'm sorry?"

"Look, it's not like we haven't shared a bed before," she said. "And it'll make me feel better, knowing I didn't kick you out."

He chuckled. "I really don't mind."

She shook her head. "Stay."

He nodded after a moment, retaking his spot.

She flipped back the covers on the other side. Scooching in, her foot brushed his calf.

Goosebumps rose and he shivered.

"Sorry." She shifted a little, moving away and threatening

to fall off the edge of the bed.

"It's fine. Come closer before you hurt yourself," he said.

She inched closer again before lying down, rolling onto her side, and turning her back toward him. "Thanks. Your bed's better, by the way. Softer."

He turned off the lamp on his nightstand, plunging the room into darkness. He mirrored her movements but faced her back instead. As his vision focused, he stared at her raven locks and resisted the urge to play with the ends of them.

"Sure thing." He smiled. *It's the same kind of mattress, but I'm not complaining.*

The next morning, James woke to Sophie lying on her stomach, half on top of him.

Her position mimicked the last time, with her head on his chest and one leg cast over his hips.

His hand rested on her back, beneath the soft fabric of his shirt. Reaching blindly for his phone, he held it above his face and tapped the screen for the time.

Groaning slightly, he set his phone back down and stared at the ceiling, doing his best to ignore Sophie's soft breaths sweeping his torso.

Outside, the honks of mid-morning traffic split the air. Bars of golden sunlight split the high ceilings. It was so much later than he was accustomed to, but he'd never slept better in his life.

Sophie shifted and, a moment later, boosted herself, yawning.

"Morning," he greeted.

She rubbed her eyes and bestowed a small smile. "Morning. Oh–"

She stared at their position, blinking rapidly. Climbing off him, she avoided eye contact. "Sorry."

"It's fine." He glanced at her again and all the oxygen left his body.

Her hair was messy and her makeup from the night before slightly ruined, but he couldn't care less.

"What?" she asked, tilting her head.

"Nothing," he managed.

She adopted a strange look. "Alright, then I'm going to use the bathroom."

She yawned again and swung out of bed, heading into the en-suite.

The breath whooshed back into him and he sighed, grabbing his phone from the wireless charger on his nightstand again. A new message from Marilyn lay in his inbox, and he clicked it open.

Since signing with them, Covey had released a flight of articles from reputable sources about Lotus, and while they had experienced a few new clients, it was hardly enough.

The Delacroix disaster had already become ingrained in Manhattan society, which meant whatever this was had to be some new tactic to gain Lotus good publicity.

He scanned the text inside, eyebrows flaring up.

> We got invited to this gala because we represent the publication. You need to come, too. This will be a good way to gain connections and make good impressions where it counts. It's only one night, but the publication blocked out rooms for the attendees at the hotel where the event is. So be prepared.

Below was an attachment for a fundraising gala on Friday being thrown by an online news publication.

Clicking his phone shut, he slipped it back onto the nightstand, a smile building on his lips.

The right conversations with the right people could ensure that only positive news about Lotus was circulating.

Excitement gathered and had a party in his stomach.

This could be it—this could be what finally fixed *everything*.

The ensuite door opened and Sophie came into view

again, a strange look on her face. But before he could ask, she wiped it away and tilted her head.

"You look happy," she noted. "What happened?"

He held his phone aloft. "Marilyn emailed about this event on Friday. She wants me to attend with you guys. We both think this could do wonders for Lotus's image."

"Oh, the fundraising gala?" Sophie asked, absentmindedly scratching her elbow. "I agree." A strange look came over her face, but she wiped it away. Clearing her throat, she jabbed her thumb over her shoulder. "Um ... I'm going to go change and head home. Thanks for letting me stay again."

The ends of her hair whirled as she turned, heading out his bedroom door.

He blinked before getting out of bed and rushing after her.

"Wait," he blurted.

She paused, glancing over her shoulder.

"That's it? You're just going like that?"

"Well, what did you expect?" She turned fully, not quite hiding that same strange glimmer in her eyes. "This isn't a relationship, James, and I realized in the bathroom that last night ... I shouldn't have done that."

Things clicked into place.

The gala might be a positive development, but it was also a step closer to them being done.

Of course, she didn't want the commitment.

"Okay, but just listen to me, for a moment." A lump formed in his throat, blocking his words. But he forced them out, anyway. "I know we don't like it, but we have to face the facts. If Friday turns out to be the last day I'm working with Covey, then why don't we start dating? We can announce it publicly after the gala."

Her brow furrowed, and something flickered into her eyes before it disappeared. "We can't do that. At least, not right away."

"What? Why not?" he demanded. "There wouldn't be a conflict of interest anymore. We'd be two people dating, like anyone else."

She looked at him incredulously. "No, we wouldn't. Please tell me you can see that."

A lump formed in his throat as the hidden reality hit him hard, the double-edged sword finally revealing itself.

With his status, it wouldn't make sense why he was dating her. People would wonder if something had happened when they worked together, which would ultimately lead them back to square one–speculation that Covey LLC. was committing the cardinal sin of PR and wasn't reputable at all.

How could he have lost sight of that?

"Fine," he gritted out. "So, what, this thing ends when I end things with Covey?"

She flinched. "I didn't say that."

"No, but you might as well have," he muttered.

"Look, the boundaries that we set when we started this thing ... faded," she said. "Like I said, me staying overnight and asking you to stay instead of taking the guest room just worsened that."

He fisted his hands and clenched his jaw.

Even if we didn't let them disappear, we would've still gotten here eventually.

His lips pressed together as he stalked toward her. "Alright, so we set the boundaries again. Starting now."

Winding her hair around his fist, he tugged her toward him and kissed her furiously. A moan slipped from her lips, getting lost in his mouth.

She was right; they had lived with obligations and commitments for too long, and now, if she wanted to go back to being no-strings-attached, he would give her that.

Breaking away from her mouth, he pushed her against the wall with his body and roughly planted kisses against her jaw. His hand pulled her hair again, tethering her to him.

"James–" she gasped.

"You want to leave?" He wouldn't stop her if she said yes.

"No."

He hummed, squeezing her breast over the shirt. "Okay,

and you wanted no caveats, right?"

"I ... yes."

"Well, *this* is what no caveats looks like."

Carrying her toward the kitchen counter, he set her on the edge.

"What are you doing?" she asked.

Sitting her down on the cool marble, he gripped her hips and tugged her toward him. Pushing the hem of her shirt up, he motioned for her to boost up so he could pull the shorts down. He sank to his knees and spread her thighs.

"Setting boundaries."

He was insanely glad Pip hadn't walked in.

Considering his friend lived so close, he tended to waltz into James's apartment whenever he wanted.

They'd known each other for twenty-six years, but there were still unspoken boundaries between them, and Pip seeing James going down on Sophie while she was spread out on the kitchen counter was one of them.

"So, let's talk about Friday." He was going to pretend she hadn't just ridden him so hard he saw stars.

She laughed. "You want to talk about business now?"

No.

What he wanted to talk about was where they were going. Sophie never gave him a definitive answer. Were they going to stay as ... whatever this was forever, or would they part ways when all was said and done?

But he knew if he brought that up, they'd get nowhere.

Sophie glanced over at him. "What about it?"

"Are you bringing anyone?"

She arched a brow. "Would it make a difference if I was?"

A heatwave rolled down his skin, turning it feverish and clammy as his stomach twisted with nausea at the sudden thought she had a date. Maybe that was why she hadn't said anything.

"No," he said. "I just want to know what to expect, that's all."

She eyed him and got up. Going into the guest room, she emerged a moment later with her dress, and slunk it on. "No. Are you?"

Shaking his head, he fished his pants from the floor, pulling them on over his boxers.

He shouldn't have cared if she had a plus one. It wasn't like they could show up together, anyway.

"Okay, well, I guess I'll see you then," she called as she headed for the foyer. Grabbing her purse from the hall table, she waved. "Thanks for the weekend."

"Sophie, I–"

She held up her hand, waved, and walked into the elevator.

She disappeared behind steel doors, and he buried his head in his hands.

Fuck, this was all too much.

What deity had he pissed off to make it so the woman he wanted was the one he couldn't have?

It proved impossible *not* to want something more with her. He constantly craved

it, and he couldn't bring himself to stop.

God, I'm an idiot for thinking that there might ever be something between us. Screwing his eyes tighter, he groaned.

He wouldn't be the reason she lost her chance at that promotion, or worse, her job–not after what he understood.

The elevator dinged and his head whipped up. Had she come back?

"Hey, cabrón." Philip traipsed into the room, tapping away on his phone. "Did you see Lina's Instagram? Or Adam's–oh, right, I told you he requested to follow me, right? Anyway, it's disgusting. They're not even trying to hide their PDA."

James chuckled, grimacing. "Well, they *are* engaged. And also, they're not doing anything crazy in public."

"Yeah, but Lina's my sister. I don't need to see your brother kissing her like his life depends on it."

Philip finally looked up, his gaze crawling over James, and he frowned, tilting his head.

"Did you–with Sophie–out here?" he asked.

James started to deny it, but seeing as the belt and tie she used to bind him were flung on the ground five feet away, the answer was pretty obvious.

"Damn, she was over here early, then." Philip looked at the counter. "Breakfast date?"

"No dates, remember?" James's jaw clenched. "But yeah. Something like that."

"Nice, ni– what do you mean 'something like that'?"

He ran a hand through his hair, ignoring the question. "She stayed overnight."

Philip's eyes widened. "What are you talking about? You just said you two aren't doing all that."

"No, I said no dates."

"Tomato-Tomahto." He went to sit at the kitchen island.

James stopped him. "I wouldn't do that."

Philip narrowed his eyes. "You didn't."

"I said we had a breakfast date." James smirked. "What do you think we ate?"

"Stop while you're ahead, *please.*" Philip sighed, wiping a hand over his face. "I'd be clapping for you, but for Christ's sake, your room is *right there.* You couldn't have taken the few extra steps?"

"Well, something was clapping, if you catch my drift." James held up his hand for a high-five.

Philip let out a long-suffering sigh and returned the high-five. "Jesus, how do I unhear the last few minutes? Ay, never mind. I'm assuming the couch, too? You have to get a new one now because I'm not sitting on that." He rubbed a hand through his hair. "Joder, please, *please* tell me nowhere else."

James got up and walked down the hall, chuckling. "Might want to disinfect

the counter before couch shopping."

"The–*where on the counter*?!"

Heading into his room, he shut the door, leaning against the cool wood.

On top of not being able to go where he wanted with Sophie, they had that party on Friday, where he had to be on his best behavior. The thought of both of them there in close proximity ...

He pulled out his phone and started a text thread with Marilyn, his fingers shaking as they poised over the keyboard.

Hi. When do you want me to meet you Friday?

She responded a moment later.

Hi James. We're taking a car there, and can get you on the way. It's better if we show up together, anyway. We can discuss further tomorrow afternoon.

Shit.

Getting lightheaded, he sat on the edge of his bed. Heat soared through him, and his pulse pounded in his ears. His grip hardened on the edges of his phone.

A car, *a* car.

Which meant sitting in close quarters with Sophie on the way to a party where he had to keep his goddamn hands off her.

Also, what did Marilyn mean by tomorrow afternoon?

Thumbing over to his email, he noted the new message from Jackie with his forwarded schedule for the week in his inbox.

He had a few meetings with clients scattered throughout, including the Fukada walkthrough on Friday.

He gritted his teeth. Great, just what he needed: a walkthrough right before he left to mingle and pretend not to stare at Sophie.

Scanning the list more closely, Covey's name jumped out at him not once, but a total of three times.

Jackie had scheduled meetings for him with Marilyn on three separate days.

He had to see Sophie on *three separate days* in the same room as her boss. Tossing his phone on his bed, he covered his eyes, a loud groan reverberating out of his mouth.

God, this was a nightmare.

He was walking a tightrope, trying desperately to reach her on the other side, and not noticing that the rope started to fray in the middle.

Giving in to his feelings wouldn't do him any good, not when admitting them would bring everything crashing down faster.

A knock curled off his door, and Philip called through the wood, "You're not making me do this alone, cabrón. This is your fault! So put on some clothes and go on the Ikea website or something."

James sighed, grabbing a T-shirt and shorts from his closet.

What was he even going to wear on Friday? He wanted to make a good impression, of course, not just on potential clients, but on Sophie, too.

Another knock sounded just as he donned a sweatshirt.

"Yeah, yeah, I'm coming, Pip!" he called.

Luc's voice cut across the space. "Damn, mec. You have this whole penthouse, and you chose the couch?"

James sighed and hopped into his shorts. Yanking open his door, he brushed past his friend. Fuck, of course Pip would tell Luc about it. Nothing was sacred between them.

James flinched as Philip tossed a bottle of disinfectant spray at him.

"Take care of the counter," his friend ordered.

Desperate to turn the spotlight on something other than him, James asked, "So how'd it go with Chloe, Luc?"

The two of them had gone out again on Saturday night, and his friend had been quiet about it since. It had been less than twenty-four hours, but it was extremely uncharacteristic of him.

"Oh, yeah," Philip chimed. He looked up from where he sat on the floor, laptop in front of him. "Spill it, cabrón."

Luc rubbed the back of his neck, melting into a lopsided grin. "It went well."

James arched a brow, finishing wiping the counter, and dumping the paper towels in the trash. "Why'd you wait to tell us?"

He'd expected a conference phone call the minute Luc got home.

"Because things are getting more serious, and Chloe asked me to keep it between us," Luc continued.

"Already doing what she wants?" Philip quipped.

Luc flipped him off. "Yeah, yeah, like we don't know you've crawled for Mariana. Literally."

"And I'd do it again." Philip shrugged. "The other night, she did this thing with her mouth, and ay Dios–"

"And you're done talking." James hopped onto a barstool. "Also, I don't think Chloe meant us. I'm pretty sure her friends know."

"Prudence est mère de sûreté," Luc muttered. "Anyway, get over here. I hear there's some nice couches at that furniture store in DUMBO."

James swore the stakes had never been higher.

Sitting across from Marilyn in her office while she leafed through some papers, he clenched his jaw and crossed his arms tightly across his chest.

Sophie hovered behind her like an angel on her shoulder, one he wished to touch, but lay just out of reach.

At least their interactions at Joseph's only lasted ten minutes or less, and he could control that. But here ... it was impossible to ignore her presence.

Was this a preview of what Friday would be like? Sneaking glances at her like he was some pathetic teenager in love?

Tension so thick you could drown?

Sophie blatantly ignored him, staring at a painting on the wall. Then her attention slid to him.

He flashed her a small smirk.

Her eyes narrowed, and she gave a near imperceptible shake of her head.

Blowing a breath through his lips, he clenched the arms of his chair, bouncing his leg.

Centuries ticked by in seconds.

In his peripheral vision, Marilyn set down the papers and laced her fingers together.

"The articles we've been putting out for the past few weeks are getting good responses," she said. "Plus, the emails we've been sending to past Lotus clients highlighting the positives of working with you are gaining you good attention. But neither of those things is enough. That's why the gala on Friday is so important."

She pushed back from her desk. "I'll let Sophie finish explaining to you while I run to the bathroom. Excuse me."

Walking out, she closed the door behind her, the click resounding in finality.

"So," he said into the silence. "The gala?"

Sophie leaned back against the wall. "Um. Right. Like Marilyn said, it's not enough to tell potential clients that you can be trusted. We need them actually to see you do something philanthropic. Not only will it boost your image, but hopefully bounce you back from the Delacroix mess." She nodded, crossing her arms. "Likewise, clients seeing you in a black-tie ensemble will give them an even more positive perception."

Oh. Of course.

In the six years since he started his own business, and in all the years he attended important parties, he learned that image was *everything.*

He cocked his head. "Just clients?"

They trod into dangerous territory, but dammit, he didn't care one bit.

"No," Sophie replied after a moment. She pushed off the wall and stopped right in front of his knees. Placing the folder she held on the edge of the desk, she leaned down until her face was level with his. Her monochromatic-tipped fingers curled around the arms of his seat, and one of her hands slinked down his blazer, gripping the lapel. "A black-tie ensemble will also make a positive perception on *me*."

Against his better judgment, he grabbed her wrist as she backed away, fettering her. One of his hands moved to grip her chin between his fingers. "How positive?"

Her eyes darted to the door, but she smiled. "You'll just have to wait and see, won't you?"

The door opened, and Sophie backed away, knocking the file off the desk in her haste.

"Sorry about that." Marilyn took a seat again. "Did Sophie explain?"

He cleared his throat, gaze running over Sophie as he shifted in his seat. "Perfectly."

Fourteen
Sophie

"Oh, come on." Sophie sighed, staring at the angry gray clouds unleashing slashing rain from beneath the awning of Covey's lit office building.

Pursing her lips, she glanced back through the doors into the lobby. *Maybe I should just forget it and wait for this to let up. How badly do I want to get home, anyway?*

Her stomach growled, silently goading her to step into the downpour. Sighing, she lifted her bag above her head.

"Don't tell me you don't have an umbrella," James called from down the block, a dark umbrella over his head.

She turned toward him, frowning. "What are you doing here?"

"I have another meeting with Marilyn," he explained and raked his gaze over Sophie's ensemble. "I'm assuming you're not going to be there?"

What looked like sadness flashed across his face, but it was gone before she could decipher it.

Sophie's breathing shallowed. "A new staff member is shadowing Marilyn. He'll be there instead. I was going to stay late, but she pretty much kicked me out of the office."

James's eyes flashed and he peered around. "In this weather?"

"It wasn't forecasted. It's a quick run to the subway station and besides, I have this." She patted her bag. "I'll be fine."

He hummed and stepped closer to her.

To the naked eye, he was simply ducking under the broad awning.

But to her, he might as well have stuck a thousand needles into her skin as tension prickled.

He passed the dripping umbrella between them. "Here."

She tilted her head. "What?"

"Take the umbrella," he clarified. "Hopefully, the rain stops by the time I get out."

She closed her hand over the handle. "Alright, thank you."

"Remind you of anything?" He grinned.

"Want me to buy you another muffin to make up for it?" She poked her tongue in her cheek and lowered her voice. "Or I can make up for it in ... other ways."

With the weather and the roar of traffic, no one would hear the words. But a thrill lit up her veins, anyway.

He closed his eyes and let out a long breath. "I'm about to go into a meeting with your boss, Sophie. Don't make this harder on me."

She laughed and angled the umbrella over her head. Stepping out into the rain, she glanced over her shoulder and grinned. "Thanks for the umbrella, James Tian."

The hairs on her neck prickled as she walked down the block, and her smile widened. Pulling out her phone, she tapped in a short message.

Now you'll have to come see me to get your umbrella back

A moment later, a reply swooped into the thread.

Or you could be waiting at my apartment when I get out in an hour. Give it to me then

Leaning against the door frame of Chloe's room, Sophie cleared her throat.

Her friend was curled on her bed, scrolling through her phone, and she popped an earbud out. "Yeah?"

"I'm assuming your date with Luc went well." Sophie perched on the edge of the mattress. "Three dates in two weeks ... damn, Chlo."

Last night, Chloe had texted Sophie updates throughout the dinner date, and instead of coming home, she sent a location to a townhouse.

She flushed. "I mean, yeah. Oh, hey, did you know he's got an entire room in the basement for wine bottles? Not for work, but just for the wine he likes. He'll pick up a bottle whenever h–"

"Chlo."

"Yeah, I know." She clicked off her phone. "But it's like I said. He's a good one, Soph."

"That's what I think, too," Sophie admitted. "I just really hope it's true."

If Chloe listened to her friends when they told her something wasn't right with the men or women she dated, that might not have been the case. But she always ignored them, preferring to see the person through rose-colored lenses.

It led to some fights until Chloe's last partner cheated on her, and she dumped them, refusing to date for the previous year or so.

"I know what you're trying to do," Chloe said. "And I love you for it. But you don't have to worry. Really."

Sophie smiled. "Okay."

"How are things with you and James?" Chloe asked. "Oh, right, sorry. I forgot you guys aren't doing the couple thing."

Sophie sighed. "Well, I mean, things are great physically between us–"

"But?" Chloe asked.

"But he asked the other day if we could really date after his campaign was over," Sophie continued. "Like publicly. And I ... I chickened out of giving him anything more than a business answer."

Admitting she was falling for him was downright terrifying.

Maybe it wasn't the best measurement, but the last few times she acknowledged the truth, things went down the drain.

James proved time and again that he wasn't leading her down the route Alex and Brian had.

But a small, cynical part of her held back regardless.

"Soph, y–"

Her phone vibrated in her hand, interrupting Chloe. Sophie glanced down at the caller ID, reading Philip's name.

Chloe nodded at the phone. "You should take that."

After a moment, Sophie nodded and left Chloe's room, answering her phone. "Hello?"

"Sophie, hi," Philip whispered. Strain ran through his tone, accompanied by panting.

She frowned. "Uh, are you okay?"

"Yeah. Are you free now?" he hissed. "I'm at James's because–you know, never mind. Listen, how fast can you–Mierda–can you come over here?"

"Should I be–"

"¡Ay, venga! Sophie, just get over here, okay? ¡Oye, mocosa malcriada, callate!"

The line ended and she yanked her cell from her ear, staring at it. *What the hell? Is he okay? Oh, God, is it James?*

Panic seared through her blood.

Collecting herself, she tugged on her shoes and shouted a hasty goodbye to Chloe.

"What? Where are you going?" She rushed out of her room after Sophie, using the wall for support.

Sophie threw open the front door. "Something's going on with Philip, and I'm worried James got pulled into it. Philip asked me to hurry over."

Chloe's eyes widened. "What? I should go with you, then."

Sophie shook her head. "I'll be fine. Just stay here, and I'll call you if I need help."

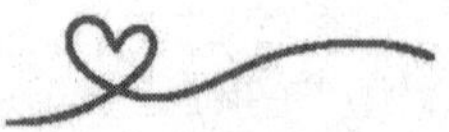

She had never been more grateful that James put her on the list of approved visitors.

After checking in, she got into an elevator, swiped the fob, and tried to keep her foot from tapping.

When the doors slid open, she breathed a sigh of relief.

James leaned against the doorframe to his living room, unscathed and rubbing the back of his neck.

"Hey," he said. "Security called to let me know you were coming up. What are you doing here?"

She resisted the urge to smother him in a bear hug. "Philip called me."

James frowned. "Why? It's only–"

They both winced as something crashed into a wall, followed by a bellow of rage.

"¡Ay! What the hell, you almost killed me!" Philip yelled.

"Good! Honestly, Felipe. I should cut off your balls and feed them to the dogs!" a woman shrieked.

Sophie peeked behind James's shoulder. "Lina's here?"

James nodded. "You know Philip's girlfriend, right?"

Sophie nodded. She'd never actually met Mariana, but Sophie heard the two had been going out for a few months after meeting at a party, and–she paled. "She's ... also from Spain, right? Two years younger?"

James's lips twitched.

Sophie closed her eyes. "Don't tell me–"

"My best friend?! Really?!" Lina screeched.

"Hey, you said before you forgave us!"

"Newsflash, I *lied*! Just like you two did."

"Oh, fuck, did he–I mean, he had to know, right?" Sophie asked.

"He knew," James confirmed. "He just didn't know that my brother had some business to take care of this weekend, so Lina decided to take a quick vacation to New York. She surprised us by walking into Pip's office where the three of us were having lunch, and–"

A high-pitched yelp that sounded suspiciously like Philip rang out, accompanied by angry shouts in Spanish.

"And?" Sophie prompted.

James grinned and cleared his throat. "And Lina saw her best friend kiss her brother."

Philip dashed out of the living room, hiding behind James.

"Please don't let her get me," Philip begged. "She's terrifying."

"I know." James stepped out of reach. "But you're currently destroying my apartment, and she's *your* sister."

Philip ran behind Sophie, cowering as Lina flew in, her wavy brown hair streaming.

"Get back here!" she seethed.

James walked over, pulling Sophie from Philip's grasp.

"Don't use her as a shield, dumbass," he muttered and leaned against the wall. "Lina, Sophie knows your brother messed up."

Lina spat hair out of her mouth and switched on a megawatt smile. Stepping forward, she pressed her cheeks to Sophie. "Hi! It is so good to see you again. I am sorry for my brother being so stupid."

"Ay, listen here, mocosa malcriada–"

Lina shut Philip up with a simple wave of her hand. "I hope he has not caused any trouble for you."

Sophie laughed, shaking her head. "No, he's been great. But I'm confused. Why are you mad at him?"

Shouldn't you be happy your best friend might become your sister-in-law?

Lina rolled her eyes. "He and Mari did not trust me enough. They decided that instead of telling me right when they got together, they would keep the truth from me for months because they did not know how I would react to the situation."

"But wasn't Mariana at fault, too?" Sophie asked. "I'm sorry if this is crossing a line, but why are you only mad at your brother?"

"It is not only my brother. I am not happy with her, either. Mari and I have been friends since we were young, and we have always known we could trust each other with our secrets. But her choosing to keep this from me ... it went against that."

Sophie's eyes widened. "I see why you're frustrated. I'm sorry."

Lina shook her head. "Ay, do not apologize, it is not your fault. When all is said and done, I think I am more hurt than angry. It is just going to take me some time to come to terms with it."

Sophie nodded, understanding completely. "Of course. Oh, I hear the wedding is happening soon."

Lina smiled. "Yes, in Granada, but as James must have told you, we are having our engagement party in Shanghai this weekend. Are you sure you cannot come?"

Sophie shook her head. "Thank you, but unfortunately, I have plans."

The white lie stung to get out, but at least it was better than the truth.

"Alright. I will have James take a party favor back for you, yes? Tell me, do you prefer Gucci or Dior?"

"Um ... Dior?" Sophie squeaked, trying her best to keep her jaw together.

Lina nodded and muttered to herself in Spanish before whipping out her phone. She tapped something out before putting the cell away.

James hummed. "Oh, right. Lina, I wanted to mention the posts on Instagram?"

"Yes?"

"I could do without them."

She frowned. "There has not been anything provocative."

"I know, but Adam and I don't have the level of brotherhood where I need to see my friend's lipstick stains on his neck." James shook his head. "Ignorance is bliss, after all."

Sophie cleared her throat and fussed with her scarf as she crossed into the park. The evergreen fabric was light enough for early autumn in New York, but it constantly loosened around her neck.

Marilyn had needed to discuss something with James regarding his campaign, but her busy afternoon sent Sophie in her stead.

Sophie wrapped her coat tighter around herself, sitting down on a bench. *I should've changed our meeting place to a café instead.*

But she'd been in the mood for fresh air.

"Sophie." James approached, his hands wrapped around two cups of coffee. He extended the iced one, his eyes crinkling as he smiled.

She stood and walked over, taking the drink. Her fingers brushed his, adding additional shockwaves to her bloodstream. "Thanks. But what if Marilyn had showed up instead? You were gambling a lot, buying this second coffee."

"You texted me saying she was busy, so I figured it'd be alright." He lifted a shoulder. "Besides, I was going to get you one anyway. And maybe a croissant."

"Stop trying to feed me all the time." She sipped the icy caffeine, withholding a groan. Motioning with the cup for him to follow her, she walked down the narrow path.

He fell into step beside her. "You know, I've seen that face on you before."

"What face?"

"The one you make when you pretend not to like something."

She slurped her coffee. "Oh? Where?"

"In a more ... private setting." He offered a ruinous grin. "If I remember correctly, the last time was two nights ago. With that plu– "

"*Shut up*," she hissed. Peeking around, she gauged if anyone had overheard.

But few people dotted the park's paths, the cloudy and chilly weather deterring most of the city from seeking the outdoors.

Laughter soared from his mouth. "Sorry, sorry. So ... Marilyn said she wanted to cover ... what was it, again?"

"Optical tactics." Sophie cleared her throat and fixed her scarf as she walked. "Again, she's sorry she couldn't be here. But like I said, a few things came up for her."

"And like I said, that's more than alr–"

A bicycle bell split the air.

She glanced behind her shoulder at the incoming cyclist right as her world jerked off-kilter.

James tugged her so she was in front of him, and she smacked into his body, the ice cubes in her coffee rattling.

His coat swirled as the cyclist whizzed on by without a care in the world.

"Are you okay?" James asked, relinquishing her bicep.

She nodded, gulping air down as she shook her hair out of her face. "Thanks."

"Hang on." He set his coffee down on the low stone wall bordering the park and reached for her scarf. Fixing it just so, his grasp lingered on the fabric as his gaze crept up to hers. "Better?"

"Yes." Heat radiated from her heart throughout her chest.

He smiled, releasing her. "Good."

She motioned to the next empty bench and sat, placing her coffee beside her. She pulled her laptop from her bag. "Alright, so these optics."

He hummed and shifted closer as his fingers found hers.

She stiffened, her breath freezing in her lungs. "James."

"It's fine." His cologne washed over her and dragged her into heady oblivion. "No one's around to see."

Protests found themselves on her tongue, but they died as she took in their empty surroundings. "Okay, well–"

He slipped his glasses on. "Go on."

Her mouth dried out and she sighed, squinting against a gust of wind. "You're really making it hard to concentrate today, you know that, right?"

"Am I?" He grinned.

She nodded, twisting slightly to face him. "What's gotten into you?"

He hummed and his thumb swished against the back of her hand, drawing addicting, slow circles. "Nothing."

She snorted. "James, please."

"Fine. It's been a week, that's all." He shrugged. "And I don't know, I just want to hold your hand."

Something shifted inside her chest and she closed her fingers a little tighter around his. "Alright, but we have to look at these too, okay?"

He reached over to her with his free hand and plucked a small leaf from her hair. Discarding the object onto the ground, he nodded. "Alright."

"Thank you." She smiled ruefully and snuck a quick peck onto the hinge of his jaw.

I know what I told him, but...

She needed this glowing kernel. A brief moment where she could pretend and gloss over the risk.

His eyes widened and he looked over at her. "Sophie?"

"Like you said," she said, "There's no one around to see."

Fifteen

James

Rifling through his closet, he blew a breath through his lips. He hadn't bothered to go shopping, thinking he had plenty of suit options to choose from at home, but, God, was he wrong.

Even though he left work right after the walkthrough with Fukada, he still only had three hours until he had to leave for the gala. It wasn't nearly enough time for him to stress.

Gem had offered to go in his place, but he shot her down. While tempting, from a humanistic standpoint, it was better for him to go himself.

His gaze bore down at the outfit options he had thrown on his bed, but the longer he stared, the more horrendous they looked. Muttering under his breath, he shoved them back in his closet.

God, he wished he had some help. But everyone he trusted enough with this was busy with work or something else.

Gnawing on the inside of his cheek, he ruminated for a minute before FaceTiming Philip and Luc anyway, hoping they weren't too busy.

After a few seconds, they answered.

Philip propped the phone against something, his fingers returning to his computer keyboard. "Hey, cabrón."

"What's up, mec?" Luc chimed. The camera moved with him as he walked.

James sat in defeat and explained the situation to them. Christ, there were only two-and-a-half hours left. But his stress dwindled that time down to nothing in his mind, and quick tasks like showering stretched into eternity.

"Okay, let's make it simple," Philip said, his attention now completely focused on the camera. "Choose three suits. You pick one of the three."

Luc nodded. "Pip's right. You've gotta limit your options."

James frowned and left his phone on his bed as he picked options off the rack.

Why was this so hard? It should've been a straightforward process.

But ... he cared more than he liked to admit what Sophie thought of him. He didn't want to give her the wrong impression.

What was she even wearing?

It would be a lot easier if he knew, but she hadn't mentioned anything in the past few days. Why hadn't he just asked her point-blank?

He balanced his phone against the lamp on his nightstand. "Okay, here's what I've got."

Backing away from the camera, he held up a pale pink jacket he bore no memory of buying, and a stark white shirt.

"This is kind of an unconventional option, I know," he started. "But hear me out, I think this would make me stand out in a crowd."

That was what Marilyn wanted, right?

A smile spread Luc's lips. "It works, but–"

"Tell me, cabrón, are you trying to kill someone?" Philip interrupted.

James scowled and put down the clothes. He grabbed the next set he'd put together, displaying the white shirt and matte black jacket.

"Better." Philip tilted his head. "But–"

"Foutu–is that velvet?" Luc demanded. "Tell me that's not–did I let you buy that?"

Philip typed something on his computer. "He's going to get mugged."

Luc got into an elevator. "I'm the one holding the gun."

"Fine, a 'no' would've sufficed," James grumbled. "Okay, the last one I have is just a regular suit. But are you sure I shouldn't–"

"No, cabrón," Philip cut in. "Look, don't overthink. Just act like you always would."

Luc strode down a hall. "Yeah, don't be an idiot, and remember, you're not actually her date. So, keep your hands to yourself."

All James's practiced self-control went out the window as the car Marilyn arranged rolled to a stop outside his building.

The driver took James's overnight bag and opened the door for him, and James's mouth ran dry.

The streetlights illuminated the dress Sophie wore, the deep green material sinuous.

He greedily drank up her frame, the extremely form-flattering dress outlining every well-defined curve.

Hands to yourself. Hands to your goddamn self.

But he couldn't stop his eyes.

In the light, his gaze easily picked out the top quality fabric that marked it as an Oscar de la Renta. He made a mental note to ask her later how she got her hands on the dress that looked like it was made specifically for her.

Sophie met his searing gaze and smiled, crossing one leg over the other. "James."

"Sophie," he greeted. "You look–"

Stunning, intoxicating, breathtaking.

"–beautiful," he settled.

Scarlet lips curved upwards. "Thank you."

"Ah, James," Marilyn greeted. "Good to see you. This is my husband, Tom."

She gestured to the portly man with a receding hairline

and bushy mustache beside her.

James greeted both of them before climbing into the car.

Marilyn and her husband took up the back row, leaving James no choice but to sit two seats down from Sophie.

He gritted his teeth as the material of her dress shifted to reveal silver stiletto pumps, the thin straps snaking around her ankles and mocking him.

"You cleaned up nice," Sophie said.

He grinned and lowered his voice. "As opposed to when I'm wearing nothing at all?"

She flushed magnificently and discreetly checked behind her shoulder before knocking her ankle into his.

In the middle of a turn, the driver was forced to make a hard stop, and James pitched sideways into her.

His hand shot out to grip the driver's seat headrest before he could completely land across her lap. His other hand automatically covered her head, the cool windowpane slapping into his knuckles.

She gasped as the driver called apologies before continuing forward.

James backed away, but his gaze feathered across her lashes and the part of her ruby lips.

"Sorry," he muttered. "Are you okay?"

"Yes. Thank you." She stared out the window, the glow of passing buildings highlighting her crimson cheeks.

"New York drivers," Tom huffed.

James grinned, a sting of pain flared across his knuckles, and he looked down at the reddened skin.

"Is your hand okay?" She frowned.

He shrugged. "I'll be fine. The important thing is that you are."

In his peripheral vision, the flush of her cheeks matched his knuckles.

The car slowed as the hotel where the gala was being held came into view, scattering bright lights onto traffic and gaggles of people. The driver tacked onto the row of cars, depositing new groups on the sidewalk.

The vehicle jolted, and his knee brushed hers. The motion was small enough to be construed as an accident, but neither of them shied away from the contact.

"James," Marilyn said. "When we get in, I want you to start talking to the gentleman at the table next to us. I have it on good authority that he heads a prominent news outlet."

"Of course." James cleared his throat. He couldn't forget the purpose of the party tonight, and yet ...

His gaze lingered on Sophie, whose knee still touched his.

Electricity played jump rope with his heart, arcing up and down his limbs.

Yeah, okay, he was doing this.

Fuck Luc.

James pulled out his phone and opened the thread he had with Sophie.

Save me a dance later

Marilyn mentioned there would be dancing after the silent auction, where she instructed him to bid on a few things. Nothing too drastic that he would regret in the morning, but enough to make people think he had more of a purpose to attend than just shoulder rubbing.

His phone pulsed.

Should we be texting when they're right there? They might catch on

James glanced over his shoulder and smiled.

I think they're too into each other to notice. Besides, your knee has been touching mine for the last few minutes and no one's said anything.

Will you have time to?

I'll make time

Sixteen
Sophie

The news publication's decision to block out rooms was a smart move. It would save them money in the long run, since most guests would be too drunk to make it home, even if they weren't driving themselves. The last thing the publication wanted was lawsuits.

"Tom and I will take care of the luggage," Marilyn said. "Just stop by our room later to get your bags. James, I want you in there and mingling by the time I get down. Sophie, you go with him."

Before either of them could protest, Marilyn shoved her husband in the direction of the front desk.

Sophie turned to James, who stared at her again.

She caught his gaze lingering five times since leaving the car, and fire lapped down her spine. She placed her hands on her hips. "What?"

He parted his lips, staring at her, entranced. "Beautiful doesn't cover it. You're perfect."

Her breath hitched. "Thanks."

She blinked as he offered his arm. Should she take it? Would it make them seem too much like a couple?

Oh, to hell with it.

She curled her hand around his bicep, fingers clenching the soft material of the classic suit, fitting perfectly to his body. The silver cufflinks and watch he'd chosen flashed in the light.

As a couple bustled past, he tugged her closer against

him. But once the space cleared, he kept her by his side.

She could step away; she *should* step away. But him in that suit, and his previous gestures, both big and small ...

Why would I want to?

"You have no idea what that dress is doing to me," he murmured.

Her lips quirked as she bent to examine the frosted glass seat map. "Whatever it is, you'd better hold the reins on it. I love that suit on you, but it won't be doing you any favors."

The tailored, inky material was far from revealing, yet James drew the calculated eye of more than a few individuals.

"Your dress ... that's an Oscar De La Renta original, isn't it? Did my card buy that?" he asked.

"No. We're at table three, by the way."

They stepped into the ballroom, her evergreen-tipped grasp tightening on his bicep.

"Then how–"

"Second-hand store that didn't know what they had." She flashed a wicked grin. "But your card *did* buy the accessories and shoes. Along with another five sets of both."

"Just five?" He guided them to the table.

"I would've bought the entire store. But I don't think I can fit it all in

my apartment."

He clucked his tongue. "How rude."

"Isn't it?" She smiled. "By the way, that's the man Marilyn wanted you to talk to."

James followed Sophie's finger to a wiry man already nursing a glass of liquor and nodded curtly.

She forced herself away from him, and the absence of his body heat was immediate. Raw desire to clutch James's arm seared through her, and she grasped the back of her chair.

No, stay here. He's got things to do.

But warmth coated her back, and a pair of hands rested beside hers.

She looked behind her shoulder and her breath stole away from her lungs as she took him in, standing much closer to her than he'd ever voluntarily dared to in a public setting.

"They're not back yet." James pulled out Sophie's chair. "I can stay a little longer."

"But–"

He sat in his own seat and shook his head. "It's fine. I'm pretty sure most people haven't even gotten here yet."

She sighed and crossed her arms. "It doesn't matter. You shouldn't stay with me."

"But what if I want to?"

She tilted her head. "Why?"

He smiled. "Because you're more interesting than anyone else in this room."

More people than she anticipated populated the room. As the night wore on, throngs of young influencers and VIPs crowded the bar and dance floor.

What was worse was the press bottlenecking foot traffic as they took pictures of guests, the decor on the tables and ceiling, and the live band playing instrumental versions of jazz-crooner songs.

With the crowd so potent, she lost sight of James in a flock of heirs and heiresses.

Not that she kept an eye on him for anything other than work. Or at least that was what she told herself.

Her phone buzzed in her hand.

Oliver: How's the party?

Chloe: And how's James?

Sophie let out a sigh and started walking as she tapped in her answer.

It's fine and idk i lost him. Chlo, don't you have a date with Luc tonight?

Chloe: He's in the bathroom

Taylor: Wdym you lost him?

Sophie didn't respond as she looked around. Even with her heels, she still strained her neck to see over the crowd of people.

Someone bumped into her shoulder, and she stumbled forward, catching herself before falling over.

Slipping her phone into her clutch, she continued to push through the crowd. Her head swiveled left and right before her gaze caught him, talking with someone at the bar.

She recognized the woman as she drew closer.

Selena was a popular lifestyle influencer on Instagram who recently launched her own brand of athleisure wear, and always garnered thousands of likes on her posts.

James's name died on Sophie's lips as she made her way up to them and glimpsed Selena's hand on his arm. Her eyes glimmered and she wore a massive smile on her face.

On the other hand, tension racked James's body. Contrary to his polite smile, tautness pulled at his shoulders and lined his stance.

Heat flared in Sophie's chest as she approached, terrifying her. The last time that happened, chaos reigned within weeks. She'd opened her heart, and it took years to patch the cracks.

But with James ... her heart always squeezed, and her stomach always flopped uselessly down onto the pavement.

And she didn't regret it one bit.

"Hi," she said. "Hope I'm not interrupting."

"Oh, hi," Selena said. "I don't believe we've met. You are?"

Sophie introduced herself, stepping closer to James, but still keeping a reasonable modicum of space between them.

A smile remained pasted on Selena's face as she nodded, but a sliver of doubt and alarm had crept into her eyes.

Sophie's gaze cut to James. He had visibly relaxed and looked at her as if she had created the universe itself.

Fuck, fuck, fuck, no.

He couldn't look at her like that. Not when there were too many cameras for comfort.

But ... Selena was going to keep flirting with him if Sophie didn't do anything, and she couldn't let that happen.

"James." Her hand rested against the small of his back—lightly, delicately, and so easily that it scared her. "Can I talk to you for a minute?"

Selena's gaze flicked toward the intimate contact, and her mouth tugged into a thin line.

Satisfaction bloomed in Sophie's stomach.

"We were in the middle of something," Selena supplied. Although her tone was friendly enough, nothing but venom coursed underneath.

Sophie smiled cooly and her hand curled a little more on James's suit, bunching the fabric. The heat pressed firmly into her skin, lighting it up.

"I'm sure, but my boss wants to speak to him." She shrugged. "Business calls."

"You heard her," James said, taking a step toward her. He subtly increased the contact, taking her wrist in his hand. Against her skin, his thumb moved up and down. "Let's go."

She glanced down subtly, but with the crowds, the touch appeared undetectable. And yet, it seared all the same.

Her blood roared as her body flashed hot and cold at the same time.

Desperation to keep her hand in James's tugged at her gut, combating with years of professional training and reminders.

No, this is too much.

She moved to step away, but before she could, Selena's head moved.

Her gaze dipped to where James and Sophie touched. "I thought you said you weren't seeing anyone."

Panic rent through Sophie, erasing all her jealous urges.

Her mom didn't know about Sophie's plan to make amends for all those years, but all of it would go down the drain in this one moment.

And James ...

He cleared his throat and released her, taking a step closer to Selena. He pulled out his phone and tapped around.

"I'm assuming you have Chase?" he asked Selena. "I can wire you one hundred thousand for starters, but the rest will come later. I imagine this total will be sufficient?"

Sophie craned her neck and blanched at the note scrawling across his screen.

Two million dollars.

It was a mere blip in his account, but ... the cavalier attitude was startling.

"Do we have an understanding?" he murmured.

A smile fanned out on Selena's rosy lips, and her sharp green eyes met his. "You're really willing to give me this much for my silence?"

"No." A strange expression clouded his eyes. "I'm willing to pay much more."

A landslide tumbled through Sophie's heart and she stumbled back a step.

Selena's perfect lips formed an 'O', and something gave way in her piercing gaze.

"You don't need to buy me off," she said. "I won't say anything. Enjoy the party."

Striding off, she left nothing but aching silence behind her, somehow louder than

the party sweeping back in.

Sophie cleared her throat. "There you go again."

He turned to face her, brow arched. "Excuse me?"

Opening her mouth to shoot him a response, she froze, thinking better of it.

It was no secret that Covey was in attendance. They had helped out enough people in the room that their name had begun to circulate.

It was also no secret that she was Marilyn's right-hand

woman, or that James was currently a client. The last thing they wanted was to get into a fight in the middle of a publicized party.

Grabbing his wrist, she dragged him toward the nearest exit and out onto the patio.

An unusually balmy night caressed her face, perforated by horns and car engines.

Closing the door, she shut out the noise of the party and sighed, stepping up to grip the cold stone of the rail.

She stared out at the city. "Thank you, but ... you're buying off problems again."

A cloying breeze brushed her face, and she turned, the rail digging into her back.

He scrutinized her, the flush of golden city lights gilded half his face while the other was thrown into shadow by a nearby building. "Are you telling me you'd rather I didn't do anything before?"

She shook her head, crossing her arms. That hadn't been what she wanted at all.

"Of course not. I understand why you did it. But you shouldn't–you *don't* just throw a check at whatever you want whenever you want," she said. "I know you've had money and power your entire life but imagine for a second if you didn't. What would you do then?"

He shoved his hands in his pockets. "My mom used to say that."

Sophie cocked her head. There had been minimal information on James's mother online, but from what Sophie did find, everything pointed to Rose Tian having come from money.

Taking a deep breath, he continued, "Mom's family had money, but back then, it wasn't much. They barely managed to break into the upper class. My dad was 'New Money,' but in comparison, he might as well have been swimming in cash for generations. It was a perfect match, in that regard, and they loved each other, so..." He swallowed hard. "The point is, she used to tell Adam and I something similar because she knew firsthand what it was like to potentially lose it all the very next day."

"I ... I see." Sophie sank back against the railing.

No wonder James wanted to keep his company afloat so desperately.

At the end of the day, he's trying to do the best for his mom. She hugged herself tight. *Just like me.*

"I'm sorry, Sophie." He surveyed her. "I should've known better."

She let out a sigh and smiled wryly. "Remember when you said you liked complicated? That still holding true?"

"Let's put it like this," he said. "If Selena had asked, I would've given her everything." A soft expression lingered in his eyes, and he grinned. "You're worth it, Sophie."

Her chest tightened astronomically, and all at once, she threw everything to the wind.

As she took the few steps between them, she hauled everything over the ledge of the balcony they stood on and pulled him behind the leaves of a large potted plant to kiss him roughly.

She wanted him, no matter how messy it got. All the strings and then some, unconditionally and forever.

'Let me be there for you.'

Desperation shoved her fingers into his hair and loosened his tie. Hunger pinned him against the wall, chasing any guise of sense from her mind.

"Sophie, wait." He pulled away, panting. He disentangled his fingers from her hair, dropping his touch from the sides of her face. "We can't ... not here."

Her fingers stilled from where they started to undo his shirt buttons, and logic struggled to float back into her body.

"Right," she gasped. "Right, I ... sorry."

Guilt rushed her. *After what he just told me, too? You idiot.*

He pulled his keycard from his inner jacket pocket. "Not here, but..."

She smiled, relief replacing the blood in her veins. "You go first and I'll follow."

The door numbers descended in order as she drifted past. How strange that things changed so much in such a short amount of time.

Just last month, she would never have dreamed of leaving a work event for a brief fling. But that was before she was consumed so wholeheartedly by someone; her heart ached. To see them as your endgame, and for them to see you as such.

She knocked on James's door, and a moment later, it swung open. A tattooed arm shot out, hand latching around her wrist.

"How long do we have?" He pushed the door shut.

She racked her brains for the itinerary she had memorized earlier that evening. "We have to be back for the auction in an hour."

He grinned devilishly. "That's more than enough time."

Heat pulsed low in her belly and she walked further into the room, steps muffled by the plush carpet.

"My hair and makeup have to stay intact, and we have to stay quiet," she said. "These walls are thin."

His lips landed on the shell of her ear while his arms wrapped around her waist. "That can be arranged, but that second part is on you."

She let out a breathless laugh, turning to glance at him. "Should I be worried?"

His chuckle sent arrows of desire soaring between her legs, and she shuddered with anticipation.

"Turn around for me, bǎobèi."

She froze, turning her back to him. "I think we found it."

Her dress loosened as he undid the zipper. Tugging it over her head, he draped the material on an armchair. He undid his tie and dropped it and his suit jacket alongside the dress.

He bent, his fingers working the clasps of her shoes. Each

sweep of his hand against her skin was like dancing in a deluge of flames.

"Your nickname?" he asked, sliding off her thong. He pressed a kiss to her ass as he straightened, making his way in front and snaking his arms around her again.

Gone was his suit jacket, and the sleeves of his white button-down were rolled up, exposing his forearms. The top few buttons were undone and the shirt itself threatened to untuck from his pants. His gaze dragged over her, setting her ablaze.

Her mouth dried out as she nodded.

The shift of his shirt against her sent shivers racking up and down her spine, and the rough grace of his watch against her bare skin was intoxicating.

"I think so, too," he murmured. Sitting on the edge of the mattress, he patted the space between his spread legs.

"James, we only have an hour."

"Then you better hurry up and do as I ask." Nothing but pure lust dripped from his words.

She breathed deeply as she perched before him, nestling in his lap. She'd be lying if she said she didn't move back against his cock in retaliation.

He grunted. "Ah, that's a good girl."

One of his arms clapped around her waist, holding her against him, and his lips captured hers while his other hand swept down her skin, feather-light.

She sighed, pushing into his touch.

He swallowed the sound, nudging her legs apart.

Breaking their kiss, her head dropped back against his shoulder as his fingers skimmed her clit.

"Fuck," she groaned.

Her head lolled, and she moved against his crotch, pushing her ass back against his hardening cock.

His motions stilled, and he took a fluttering breath. "I'm going to need you to stop that."

"And if I don't?" she teased. "What are you going to do about it?"

In her peripheral vision, she glimpsed the playful smirk adorning his mouth as a trying expression tightened his jaw, and his eyes met hers. The desire crashing there overwhelmed her, and she gasped as he slapped her pussy, pushing two fingers into her.

She groaned as he started moving them in and out, rubbing her clit with his thumb.

"Then we both don't make it to the auction," he murmured. "We stay here, and I show you just how good I can make this for you."

She let out sweeps of air and let him take complete control, writhing against him as he drove her wild.

He squeezed her bare breast as his hand continued to move between her legs, drawing her to the edge, and then withdrawing right before she tipped over.

"Do you see what I do to you?" he hummed. "Do you see what a mess you're making for me?"

She took a shuddering breath, her hips rocking towards his fingers.

"Such a good fucking girl." His fingers pumped faster and his voice could give crushed velvet a run for its money. "Keep riding my hand. Just like that."

His fingers twisted before curling, and she gasped, grabbing onto his forearm and pressing into the Ace of Spades.

Breathing heavily, she latched onto his wrist as he relinquished her breast and encircled her throat instead.

"About before with Selena," Sophie started. "I don't know why I—no, that's a lie. I knew perfectly what I was doing."

"And what was that?" he asked. His mouth placed kisses on her shoulder as his fingers flexed languorously.

Her gaze landed on them, and she groaned, writhing. So close, she was so close. If he just—

But his fingers stilled, and he repeated his words, his voice low in her ear.

She whimpered, letting her head loll on his shoulder. "I ... I wanted her away from you. Because you're mine."

Even though she couldn't have him, not properly, at least,

she didn't want anyone else's hands on him.

A few more pumps of his fingers sent her back arching and breath-stopping as she came so hard, stars floated behind her eyelids.

With some difficulty, she turned her head and glanced at him.

"You're mine," she repeated. "Understand?"

"Dāngrán, bǎobèi," he murmured. Smiling, he lifted his fingers to his mouth and closed his lips around them.

Seventeen

James

The next morning, they descended in the elevator, the slightly stale air curling on his neck.

Sophie shouldered her duffle, the strap catching on a few stray strands of her hair.

He gently pulled them out and simply because he couldn't help himself,

his fingers traced her ear.

She leaned into him. "You left marks last night."

He laughed as the floor numbers ticked down in his peripheral vision. "Sorry. But it's not like you're going to be wearing shorts right now."

She shot him a rueful smile.

His arm snaked around her waist, pressing a kiss to the top of her head.

Turning to face him, her face lit with a smile. "You know, ma–"

The elevator let out a merry 'ding,' and her eyes widened as she stepped away.

Two men who had been at the table to their left last night entered and immediately struck up a conversation with her.

James cleared his throat. Even though they stood apart, her touch lingered on his skin, and he flexed his hands.

The elevator emptied them into the lobby, and James hung back, shooting a cautious glance at Sophie.

She was still ensnared in a conversation with the two men, with no indication that it was going to end soon, and James made a beeline toward Marilyn.

She'd set up camp by the window and was peering out through the large panes as he took a seat across from her.

"Morning. Where's Tom?" James asked.

"He went to get coffee before the car gets here," Marilyn responded. Taking off her sunglasses, she tapped them with the tips of her polished fingers. "Let's talk about last night."

Alarm rang through him at her words.

Did she somehow see him and Sophie out on the patio? When they came back down for the auction, did Marilyn notice the fact that they'd both been gone? His crooked tie or Sophie's slightly frizzy hair?

"I'm sorry?" he asked.

"Good job. I think you'll get decent exposure from this." Marilyn's lips tipped upwards. "I know you've mentioned that Lotus has seen an increase in clients since you joined us. But a large reason for your attendance at the gala was that it wasn't up to the standards you wanted. And we're not in the business of denying that when possible. So, what's the verdict? Do you think the gala will help you experience even more?"

He nodded, relief flooding him. "Thankfully, and I can't thank you enough for that."

Without the publicity work from Covey, Lotus wouldn't have bounced back the way it did. It still hadn't, not completely, but they were doing better than he dreamed.

"Actually, I want to talk to you about something," he said. His gaze slid toward Sophie.

She was still talking to one of the men, the other nowhere in sight.

He cleared his throat and refocused on Marilyn. "Sophie did an amazing job last night."

Since Marilyn had been occupied with her own tasks, Sophie had reminded him to talk to someone, turn on the charm when needed, and ensure that there was only positive output. Without her, he wouldn't have made it through without blurting something stupid.

Marilyn inclined her head. "She did, didn't she?"

Something lingered in Marilyn's eyes, and James could practically see the gears chugging in her head.

He blew out a breath between his lips. His gut thrummed in warning, screaming that he was making a mistake. But ... was he?

Well, here goes nothing.

"She mentioned once you were looking for a new account director," he said, the words punching out of his mouth. "Have you thought about her?"

Not a second after a knock bounced off his office door, did Philip stroll in, hands in his pockets.

"Hey, cabrón." Sitting down in one of the chairs, he sighed and stretched his arms behind his head. "What are you doing?"

James leveled his friend with a glare. "Work. Like what you should be."

Philip rolled his eyes. "Yes, yes. Ay, did you see what Lina posted earlier?"

"No?"

"Oh. Maybe that's a good thing."

"What? You know I'm going to look now, right?" Dread flooded James's stomach. "Just show me."

Philip squirmed and pulled out his cell. Hitting a few options, he displayed an Instagram post of Lina's crossed ankles propped across a man's toned stomach.

"Oh, that's it?" Relief rushed James as his mind settled. "I thought something serious happened."

"Wh–this *is* serious!" Philip squawked. "My sister is *in bed* with your brother!"

"You *have* to get used to the fact they're engaged." James eyed Adam's dagger tattoo, scribbling down the side of his ribcage, and what was clearly a mattress under him.

James swallowed his gag.

Philip shook his head. "I know, I know. I'm happy for her, but it's just ... weird, you know?"

James sucked his teeth. "Yes, I know exactly what you mean."

At the engagement party over the weekend, it became evident that what started as a business deal between Adam and Lina had ricocheted into something more.

Philip blew a breath out of his mouth. "Anyway, has Sophie contacted you at all?"

James nodded and swiveled in his chair. "Every day since Saturday."

But he hadn't seen her in person since.

Once he got back, he and Philip had jetted off to Shanghai for the engagement party.

"Why?" James asked, curiosity getting the better of him.

Philip leaned forward, bracing his weight on his forearms. "I heard from Luc that she got the account director job. She didn't mention that to you?"

James's eyes popped, and an uncomfortable sensation gnawed away at his stomach.

Sophie was friends with Luc, but why was she telling him? Unless ... she was upset at James.

His lungs tied themselves in knots. "Pip, I need you to get out."

"What? Why?"

In a flash, James crossed the small distance between them and wrapped a hand around Philip's upper arm.

"¡Ay, cabrón!"

James pushed him out the door, shutting it and leaning back against the wood. Dialing Sophie's number, unease pulsed through him.

She couldn't know that he suggested the idea to Marilyn, could she?

But even if she did, why was he so worried about it? It wasn't like he forced Marilyn to come to a decision. But his heart still leaped when Sophie answered.

"Hello?"

Croaking leaked from his mouth in response, his words getting stuck and drying out on his tongue. Fuck, he had to calm down.

"H-hi," he managed. "So, I heard about you becoming an account director!"

Striding back to his desk, he collapsed in his chair. He reached for his water bottle and gulped down large mouthfuls as she talked.

"I did! Sorry, I haven't told anyone yet. Marilyn swore me to secrecy. Chloe saw my laptop screen and then blabbed to Luc, and ... yeah. I've been swamped lately. I have a lot more things to take care of now."

James laughed. "I can imagine."

As she carried on, happiness bogged down her words, and it switched something on inside him. A honeyed warmth replaced the icy dread flooding in his veins, assuaging his fears.

"Congratulations," he said. "You deserved it."

She really did.

It was a little terrifying, how much time she spent slogging away to get things done. And that was coming from him—someone who had given up more than he wanted of his life so that his business could thrive.

She never admitted to the real reason behind her work ethic, but she didn't have to. Every sharp gleam in her eye said enough.

"By the way, along with the bag from Lina and Adam, I got you something I thought you'd like from Shanghai," James said. "When can I give them to you?"

"Oh, um, thanks. You didn't have to get me anything," she said.

"Yes, I did," he interjected. "Just treat it as a congratulatory gift and promise me you'll come with me to the wedding."

She laughed. "James—"

"Sophie." His voice dropped. "I thought you'd learned by now that I like spoiling you."

She chuckled. “A reminder would be appreciated for just how much. And maybe that could be my gift instead.”

“I can be over in ten,” he said. His cock was already hardening at the thought, and he debated whether he would be able to slip out of the building unnoticed.

Another knock wrenched him from the haze, and Jackie poked her head in, her eyes wide.

“We need to talk,” she mouthed. “Now.”

He nodded and held up a finger. The last thing he wanted was to let Sophie go, but he had no choice. “Sorry, change of plans. Something came up, and I have to go.”

She clucked her tongue. “Dammit, you can’t tease me like that, James.”

He laughed. “I’ll send them over. Congrats again.”

Hanging up, he nodded at Jackie to enter and she hastened into the room, shutting the door behind her.

“I swear to God, that was her, wasn’t it?” she hissed. “Honestly, James, what were you thinking?”

He blinked. What was Jackie on about?

She tossed a few pages of paper on his desk and he grabbed them.

Two articles from different sources stared back at him, and his breathing grew labored as he scanned the headlines.

‘Bachelor Off The Market? James Tian Romantically Involved With His PR Company!’

‘Is Lotus’s CEO Relying On Bias To Regain Momentum After Delacroix Scandal?’

His gaze dipped, and he sucked in a breath. There was photographic evidence.

The photo headlining both articles was one of his and Sophie’s heads, bent toward each other at the table, with secret smiles frozen in time. Smiles that looked a little too happy.

There was also a picture of their dance, along with pictures of the two of them touching each other on the elbow or waist, captured at just the right time.

“Tell me this isn’t true,” Jackie hissed. “Tell me you’re not that stupid.”

He set the papers down with trembling hands and covered his mouth. "How many are there?"

She sank into a chair. "Only these two and a few others right now."

He sighed, mind racing. How had they gotten pictures of those moments? He had sworn they'd been safe.

Christ, had they gotten anything else? Had Selena said something, after all?

No, no, no, no.

Sophie had *just* been promoted. If this gained any substantial traction, she wouldn't only lose that, she'd lose everything else.

As for him ...

Back when he first started Lotus, and after it started gaining some traction, he tracked down his mother's contact information.

It was a shot in the dark, but he sent her the link to the company website, along with a few charts and the names of some clients.

He hadn't told anyone, and he sure as hell didn't expect her to reply ... but she called him.

"Yízhāo, you did this on your own?" she had asked.

"Yes." He fell on his couch. "For you, Mom."

Hours of spreadsheets, meetings with people he'd rather not deal with, far too much coffee, and becoming intimate with late hours.

It was a living hell. But it all came to fruition now.

"Um ... we're having a party to celebrate our opening next week. Do you think you could come?" It was blind hope wrapped up with a neat bow, but he needed to ask, anyway.

"Oh, I ... No, I don't think that's the best idea," she said. "But I'm so proud of you, Yízhāo. So, so proud."

That did it.

He broke into tears right there. Great, big, hiccupping sobs that bled into each other.

He didn't care if he was twenty-seven and it was unbecoming. Suddenly, he was seven again.

"Mom," he whispered. "I miss you."

He shut his eyes and she was beside him on the couch, patting his back just like she did when he was young and woke up from a nightmare.

"My sweet boy," she murmured. "I'm sorry. I'll still be cheering you on, just from a distance."

He opened his eyes again and his mom melted away, back to her new husband's house in California.

"Okay," James breathed. "Okay."

But after she hung up, he buried his face in the cushions and bawled.

Now, the admiration in his mother's voice, the respect, and high regard ... fissures rent up that perfect moment, threatening to shatter it into a million pieces.

His throat itched, threatening to crack his voice and bring tears to his eyes.

"James," Jackie said. "What are we–what are you going to do?"

Ignoring her, he typed his name in his browser's search bar and clicked the first article he saw.

Lotus Art Consultation has made a name for itself over the last six years, brokering deals with notable business figures such as Marco Russo and Joshua Thatcher.

Headed by James Tian, the young CEO already holds gravitas with his last name, but his talent for selecting art pieces is no doubt what drew lucrative businessman George Delacroix to Tian's doorstep.

But after the scandal that rocked the business world last month, Lotus shot into the spotlight for a very different reason than before.

In the aftermath, Tian decided to hire outside help, and it wasn't long before romance blossomed between Tian and Sophie Huang, the executive assistant to the CEO of this external PR firm.

After the two were captured in several suggestive positions, an inside source at Lotus provided further information regarding Tian's and Huang's relationship.

Their speculation? Sparks are indeed flying between them.

This raises a major concern: How much of what has been publi-

cized about Tian's image is accurate?

An inside source.

James's hand curled into a fist beneath the desk.

"James," Jackie prompted again. "It's not just a speculation, is it?"

He met Jackie's frantic gaze with what he had been told was an unearthly calm.

"No, it's not," he whispered. Sighing, he explained everything to his assistant.

She was silent, her face drawn.

"Okay." Her voice trembled. "Well. I suspected as much, but this is..."

He could practically see her trying to fix things in her mind.

They couldn't go to their own PR department, nor could they rely on Covey.

"Okay," she repeated. She shut her eyes. "We're lucky. Right now, they think this is just a rumor. So we need to keep it that way."

He nodded and stood. Turning and staring out the windows of his office, he shoved his hands deep in his pockets to hide the quiver. His mind cycled through options before landing on the most obvious.

Money was a universal language, and enough of it opened and closed doors you didn't even know existed. He'd relied on that time and again when things got too tough to handle, and now was one of them.

He kept Sophie's words on the patio in mind, but now ... he had no choice.

"I don't care what you have to do, just get them taken down," he said. "All of them. It's like you said. We keep a rumor, a rumor."

Eighteen
Sophie

Papers and campaigns hit her from all sides, but Sophie would never ask them to stop. She was Account Director at Covey LLC. She made it.

The moment she got the green light, she called her mom and all but screamed the news in her face.

As expected, Sophie's mom was ecstatic and planned a celebration the following weekend.

"And maybe you could bring James," her mom had suggested.

Sophie's eyes rounded. "You knew he wasn't just a friend?"

"Please, I'm your mother."

She had laughed. "Alright, maybe, then."

Her feet ached as she left the office on Friday, and she wanted nothing more than to collapse on her bed and sleep forever. But her friends wanted to go out and celebrate, and she was never one to deny free alcohol.

"Sophie!" Oliver stuck his head out the sunroof of the private town car idling by the curb. "Over here!"

Lina rolled down the back window and waved. "Surprise!"

Sophie blinked, delight zooming through her veins as the other woman hugged her and pressed her cheeks against hers.

"What are you doing here?" Sophie asked. She buckled her seatbelt as the car left the curb. "I didn't expect to see you until after the wedding."

"Chloe asked me to come, and besides," Lina shrugged, "I had time. Adam is handling a meeting with the decorators and planner tomorrow morning, but I will be back by the afternoon."

"Really? Is that a good idea?" Sophie asked. "From what James has said, Adam doesn't strike me as someone who'd do that well."

Lina laughed, scratching her arm. "Surprisingly, he is. He is addicted to HGTV and The Food Network."

Sophie snickered. "Okay, I did *not* see that coming."

Lina's hand winked in the passing streetlights, and Sophie lifted it, examining the flashing engagement ring. "My God. I've seen it before, but it always impresses me. Adam really didn't cut any corners, did he?"

"I know," Taylor said. "I'm surprised she can still walk around without getting robbed."

Sophie laughed, but queasiness whirled through her stomach. The caliber of money people in James's circles possessed was dizzying.

"Oh, I saw the pictures of the engagement party, and it looked amazing! How'd it go?" she asked.

Lina smiled. "It was beautiful, thanks for asking. Do you like the bag?"

"I love it, thank you!" Sophie exclaimed. When she wore it, the deep burgundy Dior bag accented her outfits just so.

"Are you alright with the color? I can exchange it for a different one," Lina said. "You like a dark green, yes? I think that color was a limited one, but I can pull some strings and–"

"No, it's fine," Sophie interrupted. "Getting me a designer bag was more than enough."

"Vale ... those earrings look great, by the way." Lina leaned in and examined the jade pendants. "I have to hand it to James, he really did know what he was doing."

"You didn't help him pick these out?" Sophie asked.

"He asked me what I thought about getting them, but

picking them out was all him," Lina confirmed. "He knows you well."

If you ran the numbers through any processing software, Oliver had a ninety-nine percent success rate of fainting.

That last bottle of wine was a mistake.

She readjusted her hold on Lina, who straddled a drink-induced blackout. The elevator slid open and her heels tapped against the marble tiling of James's apartment.

"Through there," Sophie said.

"Holy shit," Taylor muttered. He stared at the penthouse as he dragged Oliver toward the couch.

"Lose your mind later," Sophie coached. A strangled cry flew from her as Lina pitched forward, her arm tugging down on Sophie's collar.

Philip strode out of the hall, leading deeper into the penthouse. "Hey, cabrón, did the doorman say someone was coming–Sophie? What are–Lina?!"

Philip rushed to help Sophie and guided Lina toward the couch.

"What are you guys doing here?" he asked.

"I should be asking you that question," Sophie said. "Don't you only live a few floors away?"

Philip shrugged. "James and I were hanging out, and I overate at dinner. Didn't feel like going home."

Oliver yelled something in Korean and lurched dangerously, his cheeks far too flushed.

Taylor let out a shout of alarm as he was thrown off balance.

Philip caught Oliver around the middle and walked him to the couch, too.

"Sorry, you are?" Philip asked, looking at Taylor.

"Oliver's boyfriend," Taylor replied. "Philip, right? Nice to meet you, Sophie's told me a lot. All good things."

Lina babbled a question in Spanish as Sophie put her down on the other side of the couch. She nodded in content, giggling. "Because you are. My most favorite."

A smile stretched Philip's cheeks as he raised a brow. "I'm your only brother, Lina. Not that I'm not happy to see you, but why are you not in Boston?"

"We are celebrating Sophie!" Lina exclaimed. "Ay, how is Mari into you? You look like a potato and she is gorgeous."

Philip sighed, shaking his head. "Why do you ... ay. Sophie, sorry we couldn't go out with you guys before."

Sophie shrugged. "It's fine. James said you guys had that meeting you couldn't push again. Besides, Chloe and Luc already had other plans, so they weren't there, either."

"Still," Philip said. He blew a breath out of his lips. "Right, I'm assuming you guys are staying here tonight?"

Sophie nodded and gestured to Lina. "Is she going to be okay?"

The woman in question bent toward Oliver, quietly singing in Spanish, and giggling uncontrollably.

"She lied about having a high tolerance, didn't she?" Philip asked.

"Wow, it's that obvious?"

"Ay, well. She'll be fine in the morning. This isn't the worst she's ... never mind. She'll bounce back," Philip said. Grunting, he wrapped an arm around his sister and helped her to her feet. "I'll put her in the guest room, and I can drag some blankets on the floor."

"I can stay with her," Sophie said.

"No, it's fine," Philip said. "It'll make me feel better."

A slight sheen of panic slotted through his eyes, and Sophie nodded, mouth tugging into a line.

This isn't the worst she's been, but what if it becomes that?

Assuming Taylor was staying with Oliver, she glanced toward James's room, knowing what lay before her.

A hand closed around her wrist, and Oliver asked a question in Korean, his head swiveling between everyone else.

Taylor nodded. "Sure, babe."

Sophie grinned. In addition to English, Taylor only knew Thai.

"Go, you guys. I got him," he said.

Philip pointed out the bathroom as he and Sophie supported Lina between them.

Settling her into the blankets, Sophie tucked Lina in and turned her onto her side. The last thing they needed was her choking on her own vomit.

"You sure you don't want me to stay with her?" Sophie asked. She eyed the blankets in Philip's arms. "I'm sure the couch is a lot more comfortable than the floor."

"Yeah, it's fine." Philip smiled. "By the way, congratulations again on becoming account director."

Admiration hung in his eyes, but something else glittered in his gaze. In a flash, he blinked it away and shut the door to the guest room.

Sophie marched to the cracked door of James's room and froze as his voice floated out through the slim space.

French angled his words, beautiful yet dangerous, and his tone was rife with exhaustion.

Knocking hesitantly, she poked her head in.

His eyes widened behind his glasses as his gaze locked on her, but he motioned for her to enter. The menacing wave in his timbre disappeared, though a line of intent ran underneath it.

"Parfait. A lundi." Hanging up, he pocketed his phone and turned, a smile crossing his face. "Hi. What're you doing here?"

She pulled him into an embrace, sighing, and resting her cheek against him. "Lina and Oliver are really drunk, and your place was closer."

His chuckle rumbled through her, and a shudder rolled down her shoulder blades with it.

Sighing, he tightened his arms around her.

"James?" she asked. "Everything okay?"

He dropped a kiss atop her head. "Yes, but let's just–I want to hold you for a bit."

She laughed. "Okay, is there something I don't know about? Because you're being weird and before, so was Philip."

"Everything's fine," he reassured her. "I'm going to London for the week—business things to take care of. We have a client in France who would like to meet. He was being difficult with the details, but I talked some sense into him." Relinquishing her, he stepped back. "I'm assuming you're staying overnight?"

She nodded. "Did you let Marilyn know you're going to be gone for the week?"

Once the gala happened, James reported a significant spike in Lotus's case load—higher than ever.

Sophie was happy for him, but her innards bunched and tangled.

How many meetings with us does he have left? Are we close to done? Do I ... do I want us to be?

Stomach scrunching, she accepted the clothes he handed her, twisting the shirt in her hands.

"I did," he confirmed. "Anyway, do you want me to stay on the couch?"

She hesitated. "No, it's fine. I think we've moved beyond sleeping separately."

Nineteen

James

James *did* have business in London. But not for the entire week.

Meetings dotted Monday and Tuesday, but the rest of the time would be spent digging further into the mystery behind Delacroix.

Damien Torrence might've been a dead end, but James was far from the finish line.

Raymond had put James in touch with some connections he had in Europe who did a good job investigating security breaches for high-profile clients. Since Delacroix was a French citizen first and foremost, it would be slightly easier than looking in America.

As Raymond promised, it took some time, but they managed to trace the IP address of the person who emailed Torrence to a house in southern London.

James employed certain people who never failed to get answers, and they had been paying the man visits every few days.

James wasn't sure what they had told the man so far, or what progress had been made. But James was set to fly over and sweeten the deal even more.

Movement fluttered in his peripheral vision, and he fought to prevent his jaw from dropping.

Sophie came out of the bathroom, her clothes balled in her arms and hair free from her bun. His shirt graced the middle of her thighs and clung to her curves in a heady way that drove him insane.

He wanted to tear the clothes right off her and show her exactly how much he venerated her.

"Here." She tossed him the pajama pants he offered. "They're too long. I had this problem with the pants last time as well. It felt weird against my skin. The shirt covers everything, anyway. Have you ever thought about shrinking?"

Jesus, she's only in her underwear under there?! He cleared his throat and shifted to the side. "I'll get right on that."

Chuckling, she climbed in next to him. "Please tell me that's not work."

Don't drool, don't drool, don't drool. Dropping his phone, he shook his head. "You remembered where the toothbrushes are, right?"

He always kept extras under the sink for his friends–they stayed overnight often enough that it was easier than having them bring one every time.

"Is that your way of telling me my breath stinks?"

"I–No."

"I know, I'm teasing." She grinned. "You should see your face." Her gaze dropped to his lips, then lifted back to his eyes. "You're staring. Do I have toothpaste on my face or something?"

"Just a tiny bit." He grinned and leaned forward. Using his thumb, he swiped the corner of her mouth.

Her lashes fluttered rapidly as she smiled and caught his hand before he could pull it away. Turning her head, she pressed a kiss to his palm.

"Thanks for letting me stay here tonight," she murmured, staring at him.

He said nothing and tucked a lock of her hair behind her ear. His fingers lingered, cradling the side of her head.

His thumb stroked across her cheek ever so gently, and his gaze fell to her lips, slightly parted and blowing minty breath over his face.

"James?" she whispered, shuddering.

On the off chance she found out about the articles when

he was gone, would she even want to see him when he got back?

A swooping sensation filled his stomach. Fuck it, he needed her. Just once before he left and in case everything hit the fan while he was gone. This might be his last chance ever to touch her again or taste the honey soaking her lips.

Kissing her deeply, he drew her onto his lap. He ran his hands under her shirt, smoothing his fingers against her skin.

She laughed, arching her neck. "I don't see you for a few days and you get like this? Maybe I should leave you more often."

"Don't you dare." A pang of sadness ricocheted in his stomach and he yanked her shirt up and off.

He couldn't get enough. He wanted all of her before an ocean separated them, and if that meant passionate yet rough, he would give her that.

His lips traveled down to her chest and he sucked a nipple into his mouth. Tongue roving, he made tight circles over the pert tip as she canted her hips against him.

Gripping her shoulders, he stilled her and removed his boxers. Moving his hips up, he mouthed along her collarbone.

She hummed, pressing the sodden cloth of her underwear against him. "Fuck."

He groaned, tapping the band. "Get these off. Now."

"No, you get them off," she retorted, boosting herself up.

He hurried to slide them off and toss them aside. Swiping two fingers through the slickness between her legs, he examined the shine coating his skin. "Look at you, making such a mess."

He kissed her again, his hand twisting in her hair before letting go, and gliding his palm down the curve of her spine.

Reaching her ass, he reveled in her moan as he gave it a sharp smack.

"Again," she said.

It took all his self-control not to give in to her demand, but he grinned, smoothing his palm over the reddened skin.

"As much as we both know how much you like it when I do that, that's not what I have planned right now," he said.

"Oh?"

He ran the pad of his thumb across her bottom lip. "Sit on my face, bǎobèi."

Her eyes rounded and she cocked her head. "Are you sure? I'm not exactly–"

"Whatever you're thinking, stop it right now because I can tell you, you're wrong," he said. "Now, sit. Down."

Gingerly, she positioned herself.

"All the way," he murmured. Gripping her hips, he gently pulled her the rest of the way down.

"I'm going to kill you," she protested.

He hummed out his refusal, gloating in the way her body reacted, and licked her slowly.

Her hips jerked in his hands as his tongue swirled and flicked, and a tugging hit his body as she let out the most scintillating moans.

Christ am I going to miss you.

His mouth puckered, sucking at her clit, and her back arched.

Expletives fell in a whispered rush from her mouth. "That's–keep doing–oh, *God.*"

Digging his fingers into soft skin, he held her hips tight as she writhed. Peeking up at her, he glimpsed widened eyes and pink dusted cheeks.

Her teeth pulled at her bottom lip. "I'm going to–"

He withdrew his mouth and kissed her thigh. "I know. Which is why I want you to tell me how you want it."

She panted, trying futilely to lower her hips again.

"Not this again," she pleaded. "I swear–"

He didn't give her a chance to finish as he lowered her hips, and she groaned.

The taste of her, the warmth. Teasing her until she was right on the edge, then pulling away–he somehow booked a one-way ticket to heaven.

Puckering his lips, he drew the tip of his tongue in tight

circles over her clit, and she jerked, gasping.

"*Please.*"

Cupping her ass, he slid his fingers between her legs, snaking his touch to her clit, and stroking it. "Please what?"

Her thighs shook. "P-please, I ... *James.*"

"That doesn't answer my question," he said as he gripped her hips and lowered her, burying his head between her legs again.

"Oh—." Her body stiffened and goosebumps raised under his touch. "Oh, my God."

Lifting her, he rubbed his thumbs on her hips as she panted. "I know you're close. So tell me how much you need it. What you want me to do."

Staring down through hooded eyes, strands of her hair dusted her cheeks. "I .. "

"Either you tell me, or we keep doing this." He raised a brow. "Your choice, Sophie."

Whichever one she made, he would win. Fire would muddle with satisfaction under his skin, knowing he was the cause of the crimson splashing her skin, her mouth forming into a perfect 'O'.

"Fuck me," she finally eked out. "With your mouth, with your fingers, I don't care. Just. Do. It."

A smirk licked his lips. "There, that wasn't so hard, was it? Now. Let me hear exactly who that pussy belongs to."

She cried out his name as he sucked her clit, tongue-fucking her until she came apart.

Christ, the sounds she made ... they were enough to almost make him lunge over the cliff with her.

By some miracle, he managed to hang on, his tongue never slowing as she writhed over him.

Groaning, she slumped forward. "Fuck."

He helped her into a proper sitting position once she caught her breath.

As soon as she was able, she grabbed his wrists and he blinked as they were pinned on either side of his head. "Wha—?"

She shushed him with a kiss, chest rising and falling rapidly. “My turn.”

Twenty

Sophie

Sophie's sweet tooth perked up the moment Philip mentioned the churrería Downtown.

"Best hangover cure I know in this city." He put in their order on his phone and nudged James's ankle. "Hey, cabrón, you go pick it up."

"What? Why not you?"

Philip leaned into Lina. "I want to spend time with my little sister. And Sophie can't go because she's hungover."

Lina squirmed, elbowing her brother in his gut. "Why are you–get off."

Sophie frowned. "What? I'm not hun–"

Philip nudged Sophie's ankle.

"I'm hungover," she corrected.

Rolling his eyes, James boosted himself off the couch and waved, heading for the elevator.

"Are you sure your friends don't want any?" Philip asked. "I can still order more for you to take back later. These churros are really good."

Sophie shrugged. "Yeah, it's fine. Ol prefers savory hangover cures, anyway. Excuse me a minute."

She checked her phone as she darted into the bathroom.

Taylor had sent a photo of Oliver devouring a bowl of Hangover Soup.

> Number three. I think this restaurant is about to give us an award or something

She snorted. *At least he's got an appetite.*

Emerging a few moments later, she shook water from her hands as she re-entered an empty living room, and quiet bickering led her to the guest room.

Philip and Lina's hushed voices snaked out, arguing in rapid-fire Spanish.

Sophie tilted her head but turned around. This was clearly a private conversation.

But in her haste, her ankle rolled and she tripped forward, grabbing the doorframe for balance.

The siblings' voices hushed, and their attention flew to her, both blinking with the same startled expression. Lina jumped to her feet.

"Um. What's going on?" Sophie asked.

The siblings exchanged looks and Lina lifted her shoulders. "Nothing. Do not worry about it, querida."

Sophie chewed on her lip but nodded, crossing her arms.

Even though the women had become close in such a short time, if Lina was hiding the fact that something was wrong, Sophie didn't have the right to ask.

"No." Something flickered in Philip's eyes. "She should know if she is seeing James."

Lina's lips pressed together. "Vale."

She threw one last frown at Philip before walking out.

"Philip?" Sophie asked.

"My sister has never been the best liar." His tone tightened, and his words flared with more of an accent than ever. "Or so I thought. Maybe that is why she has been doing such a good job with the family business."

Glancing over his shoulder, he continued, "Did James ever tell you why it went to her instead of me?"

Sophie shook her head.

If she was correct, Philip was angry at his parents, and they were angry with him. Or had been, at one point. Enough so that he used an Anglicized version of his name and went to a different country.

"Just that you guys used to spend summers together, although he didn't say why it stopped," she said.

Philip's jaw was set, and a haunted expression hung in his eyes. "Lina said my parents would welcome me with open arms, but they will not."

He sat down in the armchair and twisted to face Sophie. "Pride has always been a big thing in my family. Lina gave my parents pride."

"But you didn't," Sophie finished. She leaned against the closet. "Why?"

"This kind of explains things." He tapped on his phone, and a moment later, showed her the screen.

An article from a Spanish tabloid dominated the screen.

"I can't read that," she said. "My Spanish isn't that good."

"Son of the CEO of Dawn Bank arrested by police." Philip translated without looking at the screen.

She frowned. "I recognize this tabloid. It isn't the most credible source."

He shook his head, pocketing the device. "I know, but at that point, it did not matter."

"What?"

"Papá ... he did not like that I did not want to take over the family business. One night, we had a fight. I went to a bar and I was about to leave when I overheard this sicko making comments about my sister. My sixteen year old sister." Disgust washed over Philip's face. "I lost it and left the bastard with a broken nose and a bruised up face, and I know I would have kept going if people had not pulled us apart. Of course, he pressed charges and my arrest making headlines was the last straw."

Sophie frowned. "But ... the only reason you got arrested was for defending *his* daughter. Did he not understand that?"

"He understood it, but he also understood that getting arrested so publicly like that was unacceptable." Pursing his lips, Philip sat on the bed and rubbed his neck. "Papá used his name to bury the shame deep, so much so that a Google search would not bring up my past. Then he wrote me a check and told me to get out. Since I wanted to leave the family so badly, I might as well do it now. He forbade anyone from helping me, and they listened to him."

"Even Lina?" Sophie asked quietly.

"Even her and Mamá. We had one rule when Lina and I were growing up. You didn't interfere with business, and with this ... everyone was too scared of Papá and what he could do. So, I came to America." Philip's lips twitched upward. "I found out the hard way that Papá froze all my accounts."

Sophie sat beside him. "But so much time has passed, it must not matter to them anymore, right? And Lina took the company to such new heights–"

Philip laughed. "You would think, but my parents did not talk to me at the engagement party. I think Mamá wanted to. But Papá ..."

Sophie's heart tore right down the middle and nausea filled the cracks. Being in that position, especially at such a young age ... she shifted to hug him. "I'm sorry."

He shrugged, getting up and smiling ruefully down at her. "It is fine, it is not your fault. If anything, the party was even more proof that I should not go home. Like you said, Lina really made our family company thrive, so maybe it was the universe telling me to go."

Sophie made a face. "That's not what I meant."

"I know what you meant." He shrugged again, trying to pass a grimace off as a smile. "Anyway, come on. James should be back soon with the food, and I am telling you, you have not lived until you have tried these churros."

She fought to keep her jaw up. *How does Philip do that? How does he just pretend so suddenly that everything's okay? And now, the chance for him to fix everything has practically seized him by the collar, and he's running away?*

She scoffed. "No."

He stopped in the doorway. "What?"

Shooting to her feet, she shook her head. "Seriously, what is wrong with you and James?" she demanded. "No wonder you're best friends! You both have a problem with dropping something huge and thinking it's okay to move on with your day. Look, listen to Lina. Go home to visit, at least. You're going to Spain for the wedding, right? So do it then."

"Sophie–"

"No, you're being stupid," she said. "And stubborn beyond belief. If I was in your shoes, I'd be jumping at the chance to make amends. But you're going to hide because you're scared things might not go the way you want?"

It was ridiculous.

How many times had she told herself the same thing? Except she didn't have the luxury of hiding.

He fell silent, jaw clenching and Adam's Apple bobbing. His gaze remained steadily on her, though it flickered with indecision.

"Philip. Please," she pleaded.

"I–" he began. "What if it is a repeat of the party, except this time, they refuse to see me? Do you know how stupid that would look to have your own parents turn you away on your own doorstep?"

She shook her head. "No, I don't know. Maybe the worst will happen, but then you walk away with your head high because that's all you *can* do. But what if it doesn't?"

He cracked a wry smile. "Hit me harder, why don't you?"

"I'm sorry, but I won't let you throw this chance to get your family back out the window." Her lips twisted. "Look, I'm not saying you need to make a choice right now. But just ... make the right one."

Darkness collected in pools of ink on the ceiling of her room that night, cut through only with beams of light thrown by passing cars outside.

The high she carried with her since the gala flickered out last night with overhearing James's phone call.

She hadn't had time to stop and mull it over before, but it served as a harrowing reminder that he was a client, and she might as well be the one representing him.

Tightness burrowed into her chest, and she rolled over, clutching her blankets.

'*Make the right one*,' she'd told Philip. But that was rich when she was sure she wasn't doing the same.

Pushing away the thought, she sat straight up and blew strands of her hair from her mouth. Grabbing her phone from her nightstand, the bright screen blinded her, and she squinted at the time.

James took off from the private airport soon and she shot him a text.

Hey. Did you board yet? Probably, right?

His reply came through instantly.

Sitting on the tarmac rn. What are you doing up?

Insomnia. Anyway have a safe flight and text me when you land

Of course

She loved the message, then clicked her phone off, letting it drop next to her. Sighing, she lay back, and–

Her door swung open and she jumped, bumping her head against her headboard.

"Holy–Chlo?"

Chloe rushed over to the bed and brandished her phone. Her cane, which she'd been leaning heavily against, clattered to the floor. "Have you seen these?"

Sophie took the device from her friend's shaking hand and scrolled down the screen.

There were only two pages of links available, but every single one bore a similar heading.

'Lotus CEO Uses Connections With PR Company To Set Up Biases'

Sophie's blood froze over. It was like she was in a car

swerving clean through the barrier of a bridge and plunging straight toward the water below.

"The oldest are from last week," Chloe explained. "But everything after the first five are dated last night."

Sophie shook her head. "Chlo, what is this?"

She tended neither to set up any news notifications for any of the clients they worked with nor to check Apple News. Despite everything, she still wanted some semblance of work-life balance.

Chloe's expression hardened. "It's not good, Sophie. They have everything: your name, where you work, your position."

Sophie's heart dropped and she lifted a shaking hand to her lips.

Was there really no way for her to get her cake and eat it, too?

Clicking on one of the links, she forced her gaze to remain on the screen, the bolded words searing in her eyes.

A picture of James took up the top of the page, followed by a paragraph of text.

The sentences lashed out, whipping across her skin and flaying her open.

James Tian is submerged in a pot of boiling water and has been for the past month. He only dipped his toes in after the scandal involving doing recent business with the disgraced George Delacroix, but Tian plunged himself even deeper this past week.

Let's back up a little. In light of the aforementioned scandal, Tian hired the hard-hitting Marilyn Covey to help build up his company's image.

But the external boutique PR firm isn't the problem here; it's the romantic scandal between the firm and Tian.

The media first caught wind of prospective sparks after the gala thrown by OnLine, when pictures first surfaced of Tian and Sophie Huang looking awfully cozy.

Given that Huang works as Marilyn Covey's executive assistant, it's no wonder rumors circulated regarding whether Tian's positive image was being presented truthfully.

Now, rumors turned to fact as an inside source at Tian's lucrative art consultation company confirmed the news the company has been putting out does not reflect Tian's true nature. Furthermore, while the photos from the gala didn't provide concrete proof of an intimate relationship, new images that have come to light do.

Drawing her knees to her chest, Sophie bit her nails and scrolled to the pictures at the bottom of the article with her free hand. Her spine stiffened as her gaze landed on a picture of the two of them on the patio.

Although the view was a bit obstructed, there was no denying the evidence. The photographer had captured the exact moment she kissed James, their arms locked around each other.

James displaying a keycard.

Sophie's answering smile.

Another kiss, not as hungry as the first, but just as charged.

Oh, God, she was going to be sick. Her mind ran wild as Chloe's words floated back to Sophie.

'The oldest are from a week ago.'

Sophie's innards iced over as she zoomed back up to the text in the article, skimming the lines.

There.

The media first caught wind ... after the gala thrown by OnLine ...

An entire week. Her head spun and she pressed her hand to her forehead.

How had this gone unnoticed by her and everyone else she knew for a week? No one had given her any looks at work, and none of–

Her breath caught as she remembered the way Philip had looked. The way Lina chugged her wine at dinner.

Was James responsible for keeping this from her radar?

Blind hope and faithless optimism struggled to poke their heads through the anger blooming in her chest, and heat formed into starbursts, crackling and sizzling into her vision.

"I mean, James had to have a reason for staying quiet about it, right?" The phone fell to her blankets, hitting her thigh as it bounced. "He wouldn't–he isn't the kind of person who would willingly hide it."

Two months of ducking in corners and dancing in the shadows taught her that.

Chloe sat on the bed and bit her lip, worrying it between her teeth. "Sophie, I'm going to tell you what you've told me. Look past the rose-colored glasses for a second and remember that James is a billionaire. And you know better than most the extent to which the rich are willing to go."

Sophie hung her head, squeezing her eyes shut. God, how was this happening to her right now? She knew the risks, but two months had flown by without incident, and she let her guard down.

Stupid. So stupid.

She *just* got the promotion she needed. She hadn't even celebrated with her mom yet, the one whom all this was for.

Sophie's bracelet flashed in the dark, the cold metal stark against her wrist. She clutched onto it, the thin circle cutting into her palm.

She doubted that when her mom gave it to her, she had intended Sophie to use it as a means to jog her spite. To remind herself, she needed to push herself as the result of the man who had broken his family's hearts.

And now, I'm going to lose it all.

Chloe's hand melted on her back, gentle and warm. "Soph, what can I do for you right now?"

Blowing a slow breath out her lips, Sophie glanced over at Chloe and offered a wan smile.

"I ... I think I need to be alone," she stammered. "Could you–"

Chloe hesitated, then nodded. Taking her cane and phone, she paused. "I'll be in my room if you need anything."

"Thanks."

Chloe hugged Sophie tightly and walked from the room, casting one last look back.

Once the door shut, Sophie fell back against her pillows, her heart thumping. A piercing white light floated behind her eyelids, and a high-pitched whistling filled her ears.

Pieces of the mess fluttered to the ground around her, and God, did she need James here. But ... that would make things even worse.

Marilyn probably knows already ... no, she definitely *knows.*

A million questions shot through Sophie's head, one outshining the rest.

Would Marilyn fire her and drop Lotus as a client?

Sophie's mind went haywire at that.

It wouldn't be the first time Marilyn had fired a client, but that had only ever been because they had done something themselves to make her remove Covey from harm's way.

In this mess, Sophie was every bit as culpable as James.

Oh, my God, oh, my God.

A tightening pain started up in her stomach as the names that jumped out at her as she scrolled swam behind her eyes.

The Wall Street Journal, The New York Times, USA Today.

It didn't surprise her. She had seen Lotus's roster, and James hadn't exactly been secretive about who they took on, either. It only made sense for a company that dealt with billionaires and business tycoons to make it into the *Financial Tribune.*

And plus, Chloe was right. He's a businessman and a billionaire himself, and those publications prove it. Do you really think that after you destroyed his reputation, he'll still want you? And who cares what you told him? That just shows how fucked up you are, of course, he's going to run now, a sickening voice in her head wheedled. *Additionally, consider* your *reputation. You've worked so hard to get here, and you're going to throw it away for a man?*

No. No, no, no, no, I need to fix this. Her breaths came in shocks and shudders as she unlocked her phone with trembling fingers.

Outside, the sky lightened, the first rays of weak sunshine puncturing through her blinds.

She typed in a short message in the thread between her and James, her heart leaping into her throat.

It's over

Twenty-One

James

As soon as the flight attendant told James they were readying to take off, he switched off his phone.

Time was money, and his jet was equipped with the latest communication technology, enabling him to keep on top of calls, emails, and texts while in the air.

But the past week had been exhausting, and he went straight for the bedroom in the back.

Once he landed in London and turned it back on, a slew of notifications racked up on the screen. Bypassing the useless popups from various apps, he stopped when he came to the mountain of missed calls and messages from Jackie, the C-Suite, his friends and family, and countless business colleagues.

Confusion lanced through him before his gaze landed on the news notifications, and he nearly tossed his phone across the terminal.

'Alert: Lotus CEO…'

'Breaking: James Tian In A Relationship With…'

No.

If these were the same articles he had Jackie take down last week, that meant that their hold on the media had ended.

His heart raced and he forced himself to clear the black creeping into his vision. Clearing his throat, he hit the top deck of messages from Luc.

WHY AREN'T YOU PICKING UP

DAMMIT CALL WHEN YOU LAND MEC

Ok you know what I'm just sending this to you

His following message contained a link.

Pressure shoved at the back of James's eyes, but he ignored the link and switched over to the Lotus group chat.

Gemma: James this is not good. I'm running damage control over here but there's only so much I can do

Gemma: ANSWER YOUR DAMN PHONE I KNOW YOU HAVE VOICE OVER WIFI ON YOUR PLANE

Cami: Gem maybe he's asleep you know he's been tired. But James seriously call one of us back. It's all anyone can talk about at the office

Gemma: Ok ok sorry

Pip: Maybe stay away for an extra week

Cami: When you see these take a look at this

She followed up with the same link as Luc, and James's lungs knotted as he gave in and clicked on it. He'd done his best to brace for the results, but the efforts proved futile as his eyes widened.

Things were so much worse than when Jackie had first

shown him, and instead of five articles, there were *five pages.*

Some of the sources he recognized as Manhattan society rags, but there was no denying that there were some big publications littering the scene.

Nausea worked up his throat as he parked himself on a bench, only one name spinning repeatedly in his head.

Sophie.

Fingers twitching, he hastened to make a call to her, but it went to voicemail. Trying again, his stomach climbed into his lungs as the dial tone spun into oblivion.

"Hey," she answered.

"Oh, my God, hi," he replied. "Are you okay? I'm so sorry—"

"Don't," she interrupted. "You saw my message, right?"

Lightning struck him dumb. "What? No, not yet. I slept the entire flight. Hang on—"

Panic clawed down his spine and burrowed under his skin as he yanked his cell from his ear and switched to the message thread with her.

A blue dot indicating a new message next to her name singed his eyes, and he clicked without looking at the preview.

Fuck, how had he missed the notification when he read his other messages?

Her simple, two-word message threatened to make him lose his breakfast all over his phone screen.

"Sophie, are you still there?" He pressed the phone back to his ear. "What do you mean it's over?"

Maybe she wasn't talking about them. Maybe she meant the ruse and the hiding.

Buzzing infiltrated his ears at her silence, threatening to obscure her words when she spoke.

"I mean, we're done," she clarified. "Look, this was a mistake. You and I knew that, and yet ... I'm sorry."

Distress battered him and stung his eyes. "Mist—Sophie, you're hardly a mistake!"

She sighed. "The point is, this thing between us isn't good

for either of us, so it's best if we just end it."

Her answer was straightforward, blunt, and a knife to his back because it made too much damn sense. A boulder blocked his airway as he shut his eyes tightly, and pretended he wasn't having a near breakdown in the middle of Luton.

"Sophie, please–"

"I need you to face the facts." She drew in a shaky breath, and her voice wobbled. "You know what people will say if you come back from Europe and see me. Hell, they're already saying it. So just ... make it easier for me. Please."

Keeping his eyes closed, the burn of tears stung his nose. "So, am I done with Covey, too?"

That was the million-dollar question, wasn't it? His campaign was on the up-and-up, and now ...

"I don't know, honestly," Sophie said. "I haven't heard anything from Marilyn yet, but regardless, I think I need to remove myself from your campaign."

Nerve wracking seconds ticked by, dominated by silence. Uncertainty and agitation jumbled together in his gut.

"So–"

"Look, James," she interrupted. "At the end of the day, I need to do what's best for Covey. For the promotion I worked my ass off for. And ... *who* that promotion was for."

His lips pressed into a thin line.

Protection. She was protecting herself and who she loved, and honestly, why shouldn't she?

Something I know all too well.

But ... this was *them* she was talking about.

How could she just toss this away so easily?

"I should go," she mumbled. "For what it's worth, I'm sorry again."

"No, wait. None of this is y–"

Three beeps slashed across the space between them, and he yanked the phone away from his ear.

Pressing the heels of his hands into his eyes, he dropped the cell in his lap like it burned. Unshed tears prickled his skin and a pained tightness scratched at his throat as he swallowed hard.

Fuck, fuck, *fuck*.

His phone buzzed in his lap, and he didn't even bother with the caller ID before picking up. "Hello?"

Maybe Sophie changed her mind. Maybe–

Luc yelled something incomprehensible in an explosion of French.

James's heart plunged back from false hope. "Luc–"

"You must be crazy!"

"I–"

"You're lucky there's an ocean between us right now because I swear to God–"

"Lucien, shut up!"

"Are you kidding me?!" Luc demanded in English.

James sighed, resting his head back against the seat. "You knew about this."

"I know, but I didn't think you were stupid enough to get caught," his friend hissed. "There are pictures of you and Sophie kissing, mec."

"There's *what*?!"

His heart hadn't slowed but now it threatened to pump right out of his chest.

"Don't you pay attention to your news alerts?" Luc demanded.

"I was sleeping!" James spluttered. His leg started bouncing up a storm. "Cami sent the same link you did and I looked at a few articles. They were relatively the same and I don't know, I assumed they'd all be like that."

Luc sighed. "Dear God. How did you qualify to open your own company again?"

"Alright, calm down, I'm looking now."

James quickly switched to the link Cami sent and clicked on an article from yesterday. The top picture was of him and Sophie, meeting in a fiery kiss on the patio.

Shit, things had gotten so much worse.

At least with the initial shots, they could deny everything and claim the tabloids were making a mountain out of a molehill. But this ...

His gaze hooked and lingered on the other pictures, and every muscle in his body clenched, burning.

This would be nearly impossible to conceal.

He lifted the phone back to his ear. "Oh."

"'Oh?!' That's all you have to say about this?" Luc demanded.

James rubbed his eye. "Of course, not, but what do you want me to say?"

This was overwhelming.

He was used to knowing his next two moves in advance—had trained to do just that his entire life. But with Sophie, this tipped the scales into a territory where he searched blindfolded.

Luc groaned. "What does this mean for you? For her?"

"I don't know," James admitted. "I don't even know if I'm still working with Covey, at this point, but she made clear that *we* weren't going to be working together."

"Wait, so you did talk to her?"

He detailed the conversation with Sophie, his anxiety flying anew at the repetition.

"Okay, so. Long story short, she wants you to stay away from her," Luc clarified.

James pinched the fabric of his pants between his fingers and rubbed the dark material. "Yes, but I'm going to get Carl to fly back here, and—"

"What? No!" Luc interrupted.

"Why? I can get Gemma here to meet with the clients this week," James said. There was also the matter regarding Delacroix to attend to, but he would simply wire his team.

"Christ, did you even listen to her? Even if you come back, she's not going to want to see you!" Luc pointed out.

Reality spiraled and crashed into James as he leaned back against his seat, hating that Luc was right. But ...

"What, I'm supposed to just leave her alone?" James demanded.

"Uh, yes. What good will it do you to push it?" Luc reasoned.

"Because after everything she's been through, I can't just let her go like that." James gritted his teeth.

She didn't deserve that, especially after her dad.

Luc quieted, then murmured, "Okay, but what if she wants you to let it go? What if she really wants nothing to do with you anymore?"

A crossbow shot phantom pain into James's chest, the bolt twisting sharply. Forcing the words past the block in his throat, he wrapped his hand into a fist. "Then ... I accept it."

If Sophie wanted him gone for good, he'd do it. It might run him into the ground and stomp him underfoot, but he'd let her go.

"But I need to try, at least," he continued.

Luc sighed. "Okay."

They spoke for a few more minutes before James hung up and stared out the window at the gray sky.

Before he could do anything else, his phone beeped, and he glanced at his dad's name on the screen.

James steeled himself and answered. "Hello?"

"When you and this girl came to dinner, I saw just how much I was wrong about your initial connection," his dad said, no greeting to be found.

Confusion funneled through James and he checked his watch. "Dad, I don't–What's your point?"

"You're lucky your company has done so well. Honestly, I'm surprised. But this news could undo all of that." His dad's tone was rife with finality.

"You don't think I know that?" James headed for the nearest exit, tugging his suitcase off a snag in the rug.

His dad hummed. "I'm not saying that. Just ... if you play your cards right, it won't."

James didn't pause in his steps as he exited into the gray sunshine and made a beeline for the private car he had confirmed earlier. He handed his suitcase to the driver and slid into the back seat. "What do you mean?"

The car pulled away from the curb a moment later, lurching along with James's stomach as his dad answered, "Say that Sophie blackmailed you into everything, and that you only looked happy in those pictures because you had to be."

Something rumbled and flipped in James's lungs, disbelief twining through them. Was his dad seriously asking him to throw Sophie under the bus?

"Like hell, I will," James snarled.

God, his dad was known for being a ruthless businessman, but dragging Sophie down to cover James's ass ...

"Listen to me," his dad barked. "I know you might have feelings for her, but she's just a woman with nothing to her name. At the end of the day, what matters more–your company that's already on thin ice, or her?"

"Her."

"Wrong," his dad said. "She doesn't matter in our world. You know, you're lucky I even let you keep seeing her."

"Since when do you care?" James snapped. The remark was immature, but he didn't care.

"Since she's made you the subject of a significant conflict of interest regarding your business practices," his dad continued, unfazed. "You need to protect yourself and watch where you step."

"I don't give a fuck," James growled. "And *she* didn't do anything, so don't you dare go blaming it on her."

"I'm only saying this for your own good," his dad asserted.

"No, you're not," James responded tightly. "And let's not pretend otherwise."

He hung up and stared out at England as it passed by. It had started drizzling slightly, and the ground darkened.

'You need to protect yourself.'

If Sophie understood that, why couldn't he?

I don't want *to.*

James could barely focus on what was being discussed at

the meeting, and his leg thumped incessantly as the head of the French company droned on.

All that clouded James's mind was how to fix things with Sophie.

"What are your thoughts?"

He blinked and stared at the CEO, who returned the look expectantly.

James searched for the right French words, stumbling as he spoke. "Uh ... I think ..."

The CEO's personal assistant caught his attention.

A smile tilted her lips as she stared at the pen he had picked up and started rolling between his fingers subconsciously. Meeting his eyes, she raised a brow suggestively.

A twinge racked his heart and he cleared his throat, focusing on the CEO.

"I believe we have what you are looking for, but I'll give my assistant a call to check. If we do, I'll have her email in the photos," he confirmed. "Excuse me."

Pushing back from the table, he walked into the hall, staring at his phone.

The ringer heralded into the silence once, twice, then connected. "Hello?"

The windowpane pressed against his back. "Hey, I hope it's not too early."

Keys clacking filled the air behind Jackie. "No, you're fine. Is everything okay?"

He blew a breath out of his mouth. "Yes. Do you know if we have this piece in our collection?"

He named the one the CEO described.

"Our database says we do, but I know we just sold some pieces last night," she said. "It might not have been updated yet. I'll have to get back to you on that. By the way, why are you calling me? Don't you normally email this sort of thing?"

The cool glass trailed icy fingers through his suit and he shivered. "Sure, but I guess I felt like calling for once."

"Uh-huh, right. Tell me, how worried *are* you about the state of things?"

Chuckling, he perched on the window ledge, bracing his free hand on it beside him. "Fine, you got me. How are things?"

"I'll be honest with you, it's not good," Jackie reported. "Half the company doesn't care about what you did, and half do. They don't want to work under a 'corrupt CEO.'

James sighed, crossing his ankles.

"Also," Jackie continued. "I checked again and there's more now."

James's heart dropped and he kneaded his temples with his fingers. "More articles? Fuck, I thought Gem and Cami were trying to control them."

"They're doing their best, but there are still two more pages."

He bit his knuckles. *Shit, shit, shit.*

"Right, well. Keep me updated," he said.

Hanging up, he ignored the ringing in his ears and moved toward the conference room again when his phone buzzed in his pocket. He drew it out and nearly dropped it.

His eyes fixed on the name he'd hoped to see since that day at the airport, staring at the option of answering the call.

Sophie ignored the messages he sent, so he backed off, convinced she really was permanently done with him. But here she was, calling.

Swiping the screen, he lifted the cell to his ear with a shaky hand.

"Sophie?" he said. "Listen, I–"

"I was going to hang up." Her voice was too quiet.

Panic flooded him, and he braced his hand against the nearest door frame.

"Are you okay? Are you still the account director?" he blurted. "Are you still at Covey? God, Marilyn knows, doesn't she? I am *so* sorry."

If she lost that because of him ... *I understand why she never wants to see me again.*

She was so quiet he thought she'd gone, but then she spoke. "Yes, I'm still at Covey, and I'm still account director.

And yes ... she knows."

"I'm so sorry," he said. He was more desperate than he had been his entire life.

"Why didn't you tell me about the articles?" she asked, ignoring him.

He sighed. He hated every second of the secrecy. Every time he looked at her after the initial rumors, it was like someone plunged a knife straight into his gut, then yanked it out and poured a blend of lemon juice and salt in the wound. But ...

"You'd just gotten your promotion," he explained. "If you knew, it'd have added more stress onto your shoulders and you would have lost the promotion on top of that. Hell, you might even have lost your whole job."

"Yes, I suppose," she mumbled. She cleared her throat. "What about the other part?"

Shaking his head, confusion zinged through him. "What?"

He glanced at his watch, then cast his gaze to the conference room. He had to get back. As it was, he already walked the tightrope with this company.

The CEO had read about the scandal and, with some reluctance, agreed to meet with James.

But right now ... he needed to stay here and hear Sophie's voice.

"I'm talking about me getting the promotion," she said. A strange anger gripped her words, making each one sting as they latched onto him. "Was any of it because of what I did? Because of my skills? Or was it all you?"

He clutched his phone, ears hollowing out. This was what she was mad about?

I knew I was making a mistake. I should've trusted my gut.

"Of course, it was you!" he spluttered. "You've been talking about this since we met. I know you've wanted this for longer than that, too."

"And I was proving it myself!"

He stepped back towards the window, shrinking into himself.

"I didn't want or need you to step in," she continued. "Now, every time I come into work, I have to face the fact that I didn't get here myself. Do you know what kind of feeling that is? Not to mention the looks I get." She scoffed. "I ... I was doing this for my mom. For *myself*."

"I know." He gripped the windowsill. "I figured it out."

"Then that makes this even *worse*," she snapped. "You stepping in made me seem incompetent!"

"Sophie, I'm sorry." He took off his glasses. "But–"

"If you say it's me again, I swear to God."

He shook his head. "I really had nothing to do with this."

"Right, so after you talked with Marilyn, she just *happened* to give me what I wanted? Excuse me if I don't believe that."

His argument died, shriveling to dust on his tongue. She had a point. What if her promotion *did* have something to do with him?

But, no, that wasn't possible. Not with everything she had told him about her hard work. All he'd done was give Marilyn another example of that.

"Sophie, wait. I–"

The beeping signaling the end of the call cut across the silence and he snatched the device away from his ear, staring at his home screen in shock. He swallowed and hit his messages icon in a frenzy, swiping into the thread with Sophie.

I'm sorry. Please call back?

He waited a few minutes and when she didn't reply, he called her. It rang endlessly before resulting in voicemail. Trying again, he got the same outcome.

Checking his watch, he swore. He had to get back to the meeting, but he couldn't help but feel like he was turning his back on her.

Twenty-Two

Sophie

In the few days since the scandal snaked its way to front pages, whispers invaded Covey, hounding Sophie at every turn.

In the breakroom, people spoke in muted tones around her. They danced on their toes, but the murmurs found their mark each time.

What she and James did fell outside the realm of professional, but the constant reminders hurt. Especially the accusations of not being good enough at her job by people who knew the opposite to be true.

At least Nico was on her side.

He'd gloated, of course, and had his "I was right" moment. But he soon sobered and was quick to snap at anyone who looked at Sophie too long.

It was only right for Sophie to speak to Marilyn about stepping down as account director, given that Sophie hadn't secured the job through her own efforts. But she hadn't yet, and if she was honest, it was because she was scared.

If she lost her job due to this scandal, she'd be blacklisted from every PR firm in the area. On top of her reputation, she'd lose her paycheck and the years she spent turning the city from a house to a home. Worst of all, she'd lose her mother's pride.

But ... days had passed, and Marilyn hadn't sought her out either. Hell, the only time she mentioned the scandal was when Sophie asked to be taken off Lotus's case. But other than that, it was business as usual.

Whether that was for the best or worst, Sophie had yet to decide. But until Marilyn came to a conclusion, what choice did Sophie have but to give it her all?

She sighed, settling into her office chair and glancing at her phone.

James had tried to call her back twice, and she declined the calls each time. Honestly, she shouldn't have called in the first place, but once she overheard George and Amelia in the breakroom ...

"Well, it is some weird way of showing that he likes her, I guess. Do you think she knew?"

"Of course, she knew. Why else would she date him when he's such a big client for us?"

"Yeah, you're right. I knew she wasn't as good as everyone claimed. Wow, Marilyn really fucked up promoting her, huh?"

Sophie gritted her teeth and rested her head in her hands.

A text from James rolled in on her phone screen in her peripheral vision, and against her better judgment, she opened it.

I'm sorry. Please call back?

She shut her eyes and clicked her phone off.

I'm sorry. She opened her eyes. *I really did try to let you in.*

But just like every other time she thought it would be fine, it came back to haunt her.

I guess it is better to deal with things on my own.

It was always worse for the woman than the man in a situation like this, and conveniently, he was out of the country.

If she didn't know him better, she'd have accused him of doing it on purpose.

But what if he is *doing it on purpose? Remember what Chloe said about the lengths the rich are willing to go to.*

But that was the thing. In the days since the news broke and in his frantic apologies, Sophie found no evidence that James harbored any intention to throw her to the wolves.

It doesn't matter.

She sighed again before opening her email and clicked on the first one in her inbox, going through it on autopilot. Then she repeated the process again and again until it was time for her to leave. Before she signed out of her computer, she ensured that she had fully booked herself in meetings for the entirety of the next day. If she just kept herself busy, maybe she could reverse the rumors. Maybe then people would see that *she* was working for her accomplishments.

She tossed on her coat and collected her bag. Tucking her chin, she read a file as she walked.

As she passed Marilyn's office, the other woman called out to her. "Sophie, can you come in here, please?"

Oh, God. Here it was–the inevitable conversation.

She took a deep breath, counted to three, then backtracked. Poking her head in, she pasted a smile onto her face before stepping fully into the office. "Yes?"

Marilyn motioned for her to sit as she leaned against the desk.

"I wanted to talk about this since Monday, but I just haven't found the time," she started. An apologetic look crossed her expression. "I know you've been going through a tough time at the office, and I'm sorry about that."

Sophie crossed her legs and smiled wanly. "That's ... one way to put it. But really, I'm the one who should be sorry."

Marilyn frowned. "What do you mean?"

Sophie looked past Marilyn's shoulder, waiting for the other shoe to drop.

"Marilyn, I was the one who made Covey look bad. So I understand why you're doing this." Her following words latched onto her throat like burrs, but she forced them out. "I'll have my office cleaned out by the morning."

Her stomach twisted into knots and pinched her skirt, rubbing the fabric so hard, she was convinced she'd dig a hole.

It's fine. It's fine, it's fine, it's fine. I'll just find a new job not in Manhattan. There'll be less growth opportunities and job outlook, and oh yeah, I'll lose the past five years of hard work, but I–

Marilyn held up a hand. "Sophie, I'm not firing you."

Sophie's spiral screeched to a halt. "You're not? Why?"

Marilyn snorted. "Don't get me wrong, I'm not happy with you *or* James. However, you're doing a remarkable job handling this problem while still working on your campaigns and excelling at them. I'd be an idiot to fire you."

Sophie's heart slammed against her ribcage. Was Marilyn being serious? "But I'm bringing the company bad–"

"Sophie," Marilyn interrupted. "Remember that no PR is bad PR. This situation is less than ideal, but it puts our boutique company out there. Rather than losing business, our waiting list is months long."

"But they're all looking to get you on their campaign, right?" Sophie asked. Her lips pressed thin and she gripped the handles of her chair. *And they want nothing to do with me.*

"I won't lie to you and say no," Marilyn acquiesced. She brushed a curl of honey-blonde hair from her face. "But the point is, you're doing well on the campaigns you *are* working on. So no, I'm not firing you, and instead, I want to talk to you about a joint solution."

Sophie's eyes widened as the gears in her mind chugged along. "What are you suggesting?"

Relief shuffled through her veins, melting her into the chair. But her palms still sweated up a storm.

Marilyn was proposing a solution, not firing her, like she suspected. Unless Marilyn's solution was to fire her *and* James–maybe that was what she meant by 'joint.'

"Articles." Marilyn shut the door and turned. "What we need is another leak."

Sophie blinked, her palms going clammy. "Tell me more."

"Once we're done here, I'm going to make a call," Marilyn started. "As you know, we have connections at several news outlets. So, we simply tell them that you and James attended the gala separately, as nothing more than business partners. You both had a bit too much to drink, and it led to poor decisions."

She took a seat at her desk, crossed her legs, and continued, "We make it look like you were targeted by the media—which you were. Our connections spread the word to other outlets, and we let it snowball from there."

Doubt crowded Sophie's veins, scampering straight toward her mind and bombarding her with worse-case scenarios.

What if this didn't work? What if this just made everything worse?

She pulled her bottom lip between her teeth. "Do you think that'll work?"

Marilyn shrugged and laced her fingers together in front of her chin. "You tell me. I made you account director for a reason, didn't I?"

Sophie took a deep breath and held it before releasing it slowly through her lips. *But that reason wasn't* me.

Scrunching her eyes shut, she pushed that aside and focused on the situation at hand.

Even though the circumstances were different, this was precisely what she went through with James's family. They needed to control the narrative by seizing the reins and never letting go.

It was simple when put like that, and much less nerve-wracking.

Her eyes locked on Marilyn's in the fluorescent lighting of the office, dark brown clashing with slashing hazel.

"We can make it work," Sophie replied.

Marilyn's lips tilted upwards into a smile, and she braced her elbows on her mahogany desk. "That's what I like to hear."

Sophie walked into her office, hand closed around her cold cup of coffee. Looking around the cramped space, she closed her eyes and breathed in whatever product the cleaning crew had sprayed the night before.

Eight-forty-five. Fifteen minutes till the article broke.

"Hang on!" The mail courier ran up to her with a package. "Got this for you!"

She frowned, taking the scratchy rectangular box. She hadn't ordered anything, especially from ... Hong Kong.

Wait, is it from...

Taking it to her desk, she opened up the package and froze.

Under the layers of wrapping was a simple, lacquered box. Flowering branches scrolled across the otherwise unmarked surface, carved into the dark wood.

Gingerly, she removed the top to reveal six golden, round mooncakes, nestled in swaths of deep red packaging. Intricate designs shone atop their glossed surfaces, gleaming in invitation.

Her eyes slid to the box they came in and a quick Google search of the return address showed the mooncakes came from an upscale bakery. The chef who made them had three Michelin stars and only made ten sets a year.

There was only one person who would have sent them.

Sure enough, familiar handwriting unraveled over a creamy notecard taped to the cover.

Sophie, since the Mid-Autumn Festival is coming up, I thought you'd like these. What you choose to do with them is up to you, just know I'm sorry, 宝贝 *bǎobèi. -J*

Jumping at the knock on her door, she dropped the note as her door opened.

Marilyn strode in, checking her iPad. She nodded at the box sitting on the desk. "What's that?"

Sophie blinked.

Would Marilyn be happy if there was still the inkling of something happening between Sophie and James? That something might rekindle?

But even so, what was the use of spinning a story?

"It's from James," Sophie said.

Marilyn raked her eyes over the box, her expression unreadable.

"I see." She walked briskly over. "Is it an apology?"

Sophie nodded, sitting behind her desk. "But I don't know if I should forgive him."

Marilyn sighed. "I'm so sorry. You never deserved to be accused like this."

"But didn't I?" Sophie shrugged, scratching her nose. "We knew this would be the potential consequence, but we did it anyway."

She clenched her jaw. *And we both had too much to lose.*

"Sophie, look at me."

Meeting Marilyn's frown, Sophie's eyes searched for any sign of exasperation, but there was none.

"*No one* deserves these accusations; do you understand me?" she said. "You and James did nothing wrong, and if strangers choose to believe you did, that speaks more about them than you."

"We vi–"

"No, you didn't," Marilyn interrupted, pressing down on Sophie's shoulders. "I hate that you had to go through this, but I'm *so* proud of you, Sophie. And, as I said the other night, the fact that you're not letting this affect your work is ... well. I wish I had your courage when I was your age."

Sophie quieted as she opened her email, mind spinning. An icy river coursed through her body, and something seized her lungs in its fist.

"And yet, I still didn't get it on my own." The words tipped off her tongue, far too stiff.

"What?"

She looked over her shoulder and swallowed, not quite meeting Marilyn's eyes. "I know James talked to you."

Marilyn took a few steps back. "Yes, he did. He told me what a good job you did in my absence at the gala and–wait, do you think he had some kind of sway over my decision?"

Sophie turned her chair and stood. "Didn't he? He suggested it last week, and then I suddenly got the promotion I've wanted for years."

The one she had sacrificed weekend plans, trips home, and nights out with friends for. The one she had spent hours diligently preparing for, and yet, Marilyn never noticed until now.

It didn't make sense unless James had tipped the scale in her favor.

"Sophie." Marilyn's tone condensed into something impenetrable. "I can assure you, James had very little influence on me. I meant what I said after the Shasta case–I couldn't spare you enough to promote you then. But now, I can."

"Then–"

"Yes, he brought my attention to your effort that night, but don't think that I hadn't seen it before." A smile hung on her lips. "Do you think anyone else here would willingly add campaigns to their roster, or stay overtime?" She shook her head. "You worked for every bit of this promotion. *You* proved it to me, not James."

By the next morning, the click rate on the leaked articles Covey put out skyrocketed, and Sophie had more than a handful of apologies directed at her around the office.

"It's about time," Chloe grumbled when she called on her lunch break. "Anyway, did you hear from James yet? Those mooncakes were *amazing*."

"No," Sophie said, poking at her sandwich. "Listen, Chlo, I've gotta go. I'll talk to you later."

"Okay. Hang in there."

She hung up and stared at her phone.

Irritation was a burr under her skin as she pressed a shaking hand to her forehead.

God, she had to call him and apologize for blowing up.

Digging her nails into her palms, she took a few shaky

breaths and picked up her phone. Swiping open the thread with him, she paused.

What if he doesn't want to hear from me? After all, I essentially accused him of ruining my life.

Her phone pulsed and she glanced down at the new message from him.

A ruined church touched her screen, walls crawling with tangled vines. Trees brushed their branches over empty arches that once housed windows, their green leaves already turning golden, dangling over the edges.

St. Dunstan in the East. Wish you were here with me

Her heart ached as her gaze lingered on the message. There was no use torturing herself by staring at it, but it was impossible to press the back button.

She lurched her head up at a knock on her door. "Come in."

Nico opened the door, smiling like a kid on Christmas morning. Behind him stood a deliveryman bearing a large bouquet of yellow carnations.

"These just came for you," Nico said.

Sophie strode over and took the flowers. There was no question about who sent them, but she rustled through the petals for a card anyway.

"It was a scheduled delivery," the deliveryman explained. "We would've started yesterday, but it took a minute to set up. It's interesting they chose this bouquet, though."

Sophie tilted her head. "It is?"

"Sure. We usually get requests for rose bouquets when it's an overseas delivery, but yellow carnations?" The deliveryman shrugged and shook his head. "Whoever sent you those must really want you to know they're sorry. Anyhow, see you tomorrow."

Her eyes widened. "Wait, tomo—"

The door shut and Nico raised a brow. "So it's a recurring delivery. Interesting."

Chuckling to himself, he slipped out.

Sophie finally dug out the manila card from the flowers, and glanced at the message inside.

Hope you like the flowers. I don't know if you'll see this, but I hope you understand that I really am sorry. I can't say that enough -J

Maybe it was the conversation with Marilyn, or something else entirely. But Sophie's feet slid out from under her as her heart started to crumble.

Right as Sophie opened up her email after lunch the next day, her phone buzzed.

James, again.

Guilt flooded Sophie as she glanced at his contact name. She hadn't called him after the news broke, or when she found out she was wrong. She couldn't bring herself to.

Yet here he was, no doubt texting an attachment of a beautiful place.

Opening the message, she glanced at the picture of a water canal, golden bobs of lamplight skittering across the river.

Little Venice. Also, I'm going to be staying in London for a few more days. Things are taking longer than I expected. Marilyn mentioned you took yourself off Lotus's case and I'm assuming since I haven't heard from you, that answers the question on whether or not I can see you when I get back

Settling back in her seat, she placed her phone beside her keyboard and sighed, covering her mouth with her hand.

'A few more days.'

What did that mean? One more day or week?

Turning the rose-gold bracelet on her wrist, she worried

her lip.

As to whether or not he can see me...

The false anger surrounding her thoughts a few days prior had left, and only pure apprehension remained.

The person who hacked Delacroix and stabbed James in the back was still out there, and it was likely the same person who leaked James and Sophie's relationship. With someone like that lurking around, doubt poisoned Sophie's blood.

What if whoever the leak was watching them, waiting for them to find each other again before striking?

No, that's just paranoia talking.

She bit her lip and picked up her phone. Reclining in her chair, she opened the text thread with her mother.

> Sorry I had to cancel our celebration but I was thinking we could reschedule for a few weeks from now?

One of the hardest parts was hiding the truth from her mom.

She tended not to read pay attention to the news, and it was a miracle no one had sent her anything. Getting Noah to keep quiet was easy enough, but lying to her mom's face ...

Sophie's phone pulsed and she read the message from her mom.

> Aiyah, you're scheduling your own mother now? But yes, a few weeks sounds wonderful

Sophie smiled and set her phone down.

I'll tell her at some point that this was all for her. But for now...

A knock rang out on her door frame and Nico entered with the same delivery man in tow, this time holding a bouquet of white orchids.

Thanking him, she glanced at Nico's coy smile. "What?"

"My sister is obsessed with flowers, and last night, I asked her what flowers symbolized apology." Nico's grin doubled in size as he eyed the orchids. "Guess he really wants you to know he's sorry."

Twenty-Three

James

It turned out the man James and Raymond found was another red herring. He was only part of a network of people hiding the real felon. Which meant James's team offered a hefty compensation in exchange for staying quiet, as well as the real culprit's name, before leaving the man alone.

It left James no choice but to extend his trip by a week; however, given what was at stake, it was worth it.

Strolling into the café, his steps echoed as he wound through the main room and into the back.

The café was closed indefinitely for renovations, and nearly all the chairs and tables were pushed up against the back wall. Alongside them sat a surly security guard, keeping a sharp eye on the man in front of him.

He sat behind the lone table, his fingers laced as he twiddled his thumbs. The mousy-looking blond man crossed a leg over the other as he stared at a sign advertising a menu from two years ago.

He glanced at the entryway and smiled. "Someone actually came. I feel like a celebrity."

James dusted his gaze over the man and ran his tongue over his teeth, cycling through what his people gave him.

Albert Davenport was the ringleader of a network of hackers operating on the dark web. His specialty was unearthing nasty secrets and using them to blackmail the rich and powerful to the point of ruin.

If he hadn't indirectly come after Lotus, James might've hired Davenport for future problems. But alas ...

"I have to say, you're not what I expected you to look like," James said, taking a seat across from Davenport.

He cocked his head. "Neither are you. When I was hired, I didn't bother looking you up. Money is money, after all. But you're younger than I thought. Especially for such a successful company." He barked a harsh laugh. "But I guess that's what happens when Mummy and Daddy have money."

"Shut up," James snapped.

"Oh, touched a nerve there, didn't I?" Davenport sneered. "Well, I hate to break it to you. But you're a prime example of how the rich only trust the rich to handle their dirty work. Still, I am a little disappointed your boss didn't show himself. But I guess he doesn't want to bother."

James blinked. *Does he think I'm from Cross? Well, alright, then.*

James wasn't going to pass up an advantage.

"Why do you look like that? Unless"– Davenport frowned and tilted his head–"you're not from Cross."

His face remained a blank slate for a moment before his eyes widened, and a smile spread across his lips. "You're from the company that hired me, aren't you? Oh, this is rich. Credit where credit's due, I was *not* expecting this." He fell into laughter, his shoulders shaking as he bent toward the table, his merriment ringing in the silence.

James said nothing as his mom's voice floated through his head.

'Yízhāo, look at you. Look at what you've done.'

He gritted his teeth.

Davenport had threatened everything, and judging by his demeanor, that meant nothing.

James looked at the guard and jerked his head toward the door.

The guard nodded and shuffled out without a word.

"This isn't funny," James said and leaned forward, bracing his forearms on the table. "Tell me. Do you think Interpol would pay me more than what I lost to hand you over? What about MI5?"

At that, Davenport sobered quickly. "Excuse me?"

"When you decided to hack into George Delacroix's bank accounts, you also decided to tear my company apart," James said. "You decided to hurt good people with families who depend on them."

"But all of them, including you, are still a bunch of greedy, rich bastards." Davenport's placid face contorted into a sneer.

"I'd read this before you keep running your mouth." James reached into his pocket and pulled out a folded paper, sliding it between them.

Davenport clucked his tongue but took the paper, examining the contents. A bored expression coated his features before he tossed it down on the table. "A list of jobs I've done? Well, it's nice to have a record of my accomplishments, but what's your point?"

"I thought you might like to physically be able to see what's at stake here," James said. "Look, I have better things to do at home. The only reason I bothered to show up was because my people told me they've been trying to get information out of you for days, and nothing."

"Yes, well, I wasn't going to talk for ten-thousand quid, now was I?" Davenport rolled his eyes. "That's what I've been telling them, but clearly, they didn't listen."

"No, I guess not." James sucked his teeth. "Well, then, maybe I can make it worth your while. Twenty-five thousand for the name of whoever hired you, or I hand that list over. And I doubt you want that to happen."

"So, this isn't just a bribe, but blackmail?" Davenport's eyes sparked. "Your men didn't try that."

"Would it have made a difference if they did?"

Davenport cocked a shoulder and returned his attention to the menu he'd stared at before. "Not for twenty-five thousand."

James stayed the twitch of his lips. *Now, who's the greedy bastard?* "Fifty thousand."

Davenport shook his head, rapping his fingers on the paper. "I'm not going to give up so easily. You know that, right?"

James pursed his lips. "Not even to protect yourself? Alright. Seventy-five."

Davenport laughed. "What is this, an auction? And I am protecting myself. I've got people who will gladly take the fall for me. Dumb fucks who won't know what's wrong until it's too late."

James froze. If that was how Davenport felt about his men, then James harbored absolutely no remorse.

He pushed back from the table, his chair legs scraping noisily into the quiet. Reaching into his inner jacket pocket again, he pulled out another folded paper.

"What's that?" Davenport asked,

"The same thing as before." James nodded toward the paper. "Since you never confirmed whether you'd take the seventy-five thousand, then there's no harm in handing this over, is there?"

Davenport's throat bobbed, and he kept his gaze pinned on the paper. "You won't. You can't do anything without incriminating yourself."

"Except I have contacts at both those agencies I mentioned," James said. "And who do you think they'll believe?"

The air between them stretched like a violin string close to snapping, and for the first time, Davenport looked scared. He cleared his throat, tugging at the collar of his shirt as his eyes shifted back and forth.

James checked his watch and sighed. He turned toward the door. "My team will drop you home, but don't get too comfortable. The authorities will be there later today."

"Wait ... I want a hundred thousand."

James smirked and turned around. He lifted a brow. "Bold move to make requests right now."

"A hundred thousand," Davenport repeated more assuredly. "I'll give you the name, but alongside the money, you promise to tear up these lists."

There was never a question of whether Davenport would take the offer. As such, James had walked into the café before with an envelope of cash in his inner jacket pocket.

He withdrew it now before taking the list and folding it with the other one. "I'll do you one better."

Taking out a lighter, he flicked his thumb against the spark wheel and held the resulting flame against the corner of the papers. Extinguishing the lighter, he repocketed it before dropping the papers in the metal trash can.

He tossed the envelope on the table, trying not to wrinkle his nose as Davenport lunged for the packet.

"A hundred thousand, even," James said and glanced at the trash can.

The small fire had almost entirely extinguished, but a few licks of flames remained.

"You knew," Davenport surmised and scowled. "Once a rich bastard, always a rich bastard, eh?"

"Money talks." James shrugged and crossed his arms before raising his voice and calling the guard back in. He turned toward him. "Return Mr. Davenport home, please."

"Understood," the guard said. "Will we be expecting anyone to drop by his residence later?"

James shook his head. "Someone was smart and finally took the deal."

"So, he gave you a name?"

James narrowed his eyes and examined Davenport. The man's head was bowed as his lips moved in a silent tally of the bills.

"Not yet," James said. He raised his voice. "But I trust you'll give it to us, won't you?"

Davenport stilled and lifted his head. "Excuse me?"

"The name of whoever hired you," James repeated. "I paid for it, after all. So, you'll give it to my colleagues later."

"Or what?"

"Do you think I don't have another copy of that list at the ready? Also, I don't like wasting money, and I don't like when people lie to me." He gestured to the gun resting in the guard's holster. "So, I highly suggest you cooperate."

Davenport swallowed hard. "Then why don't you get it before you go?"

"Like I said, I have better things to do," James said.

Turning on his heel, he reentered the front room and sniffed as he descended the crumbling steps outside the café.

Back when he'd first dealt with something like this, he found the whole thing a bit nauseating. To be honest, he still did.

Threatening to reveal incriminating information about someone unless they did what he wanted ... it left an unsavory taste in his mouth. But what choice did he have?

Without his investigative team, there wasn't a doubt he would've floundered early.

You didn't run a successful business without smoothing out a few bumps in the road.

A lightness ballooned his chest. The night air surrounded him in its brisk embrace, the lilt of soothing music from nearby restaurants assaulting his ears.

Pulling his phone out, he glanced at the time. *Dammit.*

Navigating to the message thread with Sophie, he sent a picture of the rows of flowers he had taken that morning.

> Sorry for the late message. I don't know if you're still awake, but here's Columbia Road Flower Market. I also wanted to let you know that my business in London finished, so I'll be back tomorrow night

Slipping his phone in his pocket, his feet carried him on autopilot toward the main street.

He had no idea if she liked the recurring flower deliveries he started a few days after leaving, but he hoped so. Hell, the only reason he knew she saw them at all was because she still hung out with Pip, Luc, and Lina.

Once he had finished with the list of flowers representing apologies, he moved on: pink roses, white tulips, and blue hyacinths.

From the very start, each bouquet had been accompanied by a lengthy text message, apologizing profusely and explaining all the ways he'd make it up to her if only she'd let him.

But every message went unanswered, and she still hadn't called him, not that she was obligated to.

Flagging down a taxi, he got in and gave the driver the address of the hotel.

The hotel was so close that James could've walked. But he was exhausted and the last thing on his mind was a ten-minute trek.

His phone pulsed, and he glanced at the screen, doing a double-take.

Sophie had responded. After a week of one-sided messages, *she had responded.*

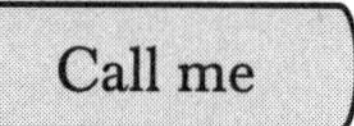

With shaking fingers, he hit the appropriate option and sat back in his seat as the phone rang.

"Hello?" Desperation and emptiness swirled in his tone.

"Hi," she said after a moment. "I'm sorry about not calling you sooner."

"It's okay," he said. "You ... didn't need to."

Relief flooded him, but how could he tell her the truth without spilling just how much she drove him out of his mind?

"Yes, I did. I should've," she murmured. "Thank you for the flowers. And the pictures, and I'm sorry."

He frowned. "Sorry for what?"

She drew a deep breath. "I—"

"Sorry, hold that thought for a minute," he said as the cab stopped. Paying, he clambered out and headed into the bright fluorescents of the lobby. "Go on?"

She sighed. "I'm sorry because Marilyn told me you had nothing to do with my promotion, and I should've believed you when you told me instead of getting mad. But I—I don't know. There was so much other stuff happening and–I'm sorry. I found out days ago, but didn't call because I wasn't sure if it was a good idea."

His footsteps faltered, squelching on the marble tile as he exited the elevator. "What? Why wouldn't it be a good idea?"

Something rustled on her end. "Well, I mean, think about it. The person who leaked the news is still out there and most likely still has eyes on us. If I called you and you decided to come see me when you get back tomorrow, that undoes this new leak Marilyn just put out trying to save our asses."

"Sophie, we'll be fine," he assured as he pulled his keycard from his pocket. The past two weeks had been like fighting his way through a blizzard, and he never wanted to repeat it.

"But how do you know?" she demanded. "That's what we thought the first time, and–"

"I *don't* know,' he admitted. "But we risk it, just like you told me."

She heaved a sigh. "Alright. So ... how've you been?"

"I could be better." He somehow found it in himself to chuckle. "What about you?"

"Same here."

He grinned. "Did you get the other things I sent?"

"What others?"

"I guess they haven't gotten there, then." Dropping into the armchair, he put the phone on speaker and slipped it on the coffee table. "It's only three items, so hopefully they get there soon."

"Be honest, how much did they cost?"

"Not enough," he admitted.

"James–"

"I told you, I like to spoil you," he teased. "Anyway, tell me about your week."

Even if he'd been in New York, he'd want to know, for no reason other than it was Sophie.

Her rich laugh rolled over him. "I mean, if you insist."

The information started as a slow trickle, but it quickly turned into a waterfall. Her voice twisted around him, filling him in on details both insignificant and noteworthy.

"Really, that's all that happened?" he asked. "Nothing else interesting?"

"Is this a trick question?"

He crossed his ankles, eyes gleaming. "No, but I guess both my financial advisor *and* accountant called me by mistake. Apparently, I've been spending a lot of money in the past two weeks, and they worried my card got stolen since I don't tend to frequent The Bergdorf Goodman Women's Store quite so much."

"You were the one who said to use your card," she protested

"Yes, but a hundred thousand's worth? What did you even buy with that much money?"

"Hey, do you know how much clothes are at that store? Things add up. Plus, I spoiled my friends and family a bit. But if it's such a big deal, I'll–"

"Don't you dare say you'll pay me back," he warned. "I told you–that's your card, now. Do whatever you want with it."

She scoffed. "Then why were you making a fuss?"

"I wasn't," he said. "I was just upset you didn't spend more."

"I would've, but I got busy."

He let out a laugh, pride blooming. "Listen, can I call you back? I need to take a shower."

Her breaths shook. "Or ... you could stay on the line."

He blinked. "What?"

"Don't hang up," she said. "Just put me on speaker and pretend like I'm there."

A door clicked shut behind her words, followed by the rustle of fabric and the creak of her bedsprings.

Oh.

Swallowing, his cock hardened as he stripped and stepped into the shower. He rested his phone on one of the built-in shelves, far from the water's reach.

"If I were there with you, tell me what'd you do." Her

voice fluttered,

brushing over his skin like the water streaming down his back. "What'd you do to me."

He stared at the ceiling, his eyes searching out a crack and following it.

"I'd undress you." His voice dropped to a fraction of his standard octave. "And then I'd lay you down on the bed and brush my fingers across your skin."

Her breathing hollowed out as she put the phone on speaker. "That's it?"

"Patience, Sophie," he coached. Closing his eyes, his fingers transformed into hers, gliding over his cock.

Bracing a hand on the wall, he bowed his head, breathing deep.

"Patience is for losers," she moaned. "Now be a good boy for me and keep going."

His legs almost gave out as his cock swelled in his hand. "Jesus, say it again."

"Keep going, and maybe I will."

He grinned and obliged, telling her in a midnight voice how his hands would play with her nipples, trace down her torso, and dip between her legs. How he'd do it so slowly, she'd wonder if she was going insane from the pleasure.

Electricity built at the base of his spine, but he pushed it away as he explained how he'd fuck her with his fingers until she begged him to replace them with his cock.

Small moans and gasps floated from the receiver and he groaned as his fingers inched up and down his cock.

"Tell me, are you fucking your fingers and pretending they're mine?" His voice lowered, barely audible over the rush of the water. "Do you like knowing you're soaked for me?"

Whispered obscenities escaped her, and his lips kicked up. "What was that?"

"Check your texts."

Reaching for his phone, he swiped over to his message thread with her. A second later, an image popped into existence.

It was slightly blurry and darkness coated the room in the background, but there was no mistaking what it was.

There was the curve of her calf, the swell of her thigh, and right above that–

Jesus Christ.

"You're drenched," he breathed.

"It's better in person," she panted.

"I know." He chuckled. "But let's settle for the next best thing."

"Which is?"

"Telling you how I'd lick every inch of you, and drive you crazy until the only thing you can remember is my name." He closed his eyes, nothing but her behind them.

"Fuck," she whispered.

He smirked. "Would you like that?"

A vibrating broke up her sharp gasps and shaky breaths, and satisfaction bloomed in his stomach.

"A vibrator?" he mused. "Dirty girl. That's an unfair advantage."

She hummed. "I'd say you're the one with the unfair advantage." She moaned. "All the way over in London, and making me see stars. How is that fair?"

"Remind me to use it on you when I get back," he said.

The buzzing increased, and he fisted his cock, tightness gathering in his lower belly.

"James," she gasped. "I'm going to–"

Her moans carried through the receiver, her orgasm hitting hard, and he gave in to the tension bracketing his own body.

His body stiffened, and grunts worked up his throat as he came, doubling over.

Beats of water drummed on his back as he straightened. "Look at you. Over three thousand miles away and still bringing me to my knees."

She laughed. "Yeah? What else can you do while you're

down there?"

He grinned brazenly at the shower tiles. "I've got a few ideas."

Twenty-Four

James

Early morning sunshine pierced his eyes as he grasped his phone on his nightstand, hitting the button to answer the call.

"Hello?" he rasped.

"Morning, Mr. Tian." The crisp voice of the head of his investigative team broke through his haze. "Sorry to wake you, but we got a name from Mr. Davenport."

James yawned, pushing away the remnants of last night.

"It's fine. Go ahead." His eyes fell shut, sleep still bearing down heavily on the lids, and threatening to pull him back.

"Jacqueline Harris."

His eyes flew open and he sat straight up, nausea shooting up his throat. "Th–that's the name Davenport gave?"

"Yes, and like you said, he wouldn't lie about it."

"Yes, of course," James said. *But that doesn't matter right now.* A bright light invaded his vision.

"Mr. Tian?"

James blinked. "Sorry, did you say something?"

"I asked if that name means anything to you?" His head of security paused. "I'm sorry if this is out of line, but you don't sound too good."

"Unfortunately, yes, the name means something." The blankets pooled around James's hips and he wrung the duvet cover. "I've got it from here. Thank you. I'll send over a check later today."

He hung up and buried his face in his pillow, groaning. This had to be a mistake, but there was a nudge in his gut screaming that it wasn't.

He forced himself to sleep the entire flight back to New York. *Maybe then, I'll wake up ... in some strange way.*

That's all this was–a twisted dream.

But somehow, the information hurt *more* after he woke, and the only thing burrowing on his phone when he landed was a message from Sophie, and a slew of messages from Philip and Luc.

Sophie: Hope you land safely! See you later :)

A bemused smile touched his lips. *Did she think I forgot I promised to see her first thing?*

Although he did need to make a pitstop at a florist.

He switched threads and read the texts from his friends.

Luc: Hey mec. Help us settle something: what pie would you be?

Pip: You better not be sleeping on the plane again. Why did you buy a jet with a bed in the

Luc: We're horrible friends for letting him make that decision

Pip: We really are. Anyway, tell us when you wake up

Luc: Or you could wake up now and give us a goddamn answer

Luc: Seriously. I'm losing money

James's lips twitched as he scanned through the messages, each more ridiculous than the last. The chaos of it all was welcome after the morning.

Blueberry

He texted Luc privately.

A second later, Luc sent a slew of celebratory messages in the group chat.

Philip responded with a middle finger emoji and an Apple Pay notification for fifty thousand dollars.

Stepping out of the terminal and onto the sidewalk, James hit a contact on his phone.

Storm clouds lingered on the horizon, and the sky was already darkening.

The call connected, showcasing low laughter and a cocktail of soft Spanish and English on the other end.

James raised a brow.

That was the first time he'd heard Adam genuinely laugh in years.

"Hello?" James prompted.

"Oh, hi, Jamie," Adam greeted, coughing the remainder of his laugh away.

"Glad things are working out with you and your fiancé," James said. "Just keep things PG, alright? She's still my best friend's sister."

"Fuck off. What do you want?"

"When I was looking for an assistant, you suggested Jackie to me, right?"

A sleek town car dawdled by the curb, the driver leaning against the hood bearing a sign with James's name.

Handing his suitcase to the driver, James slipped into the back.

"I did," his brother said. "You know she worked for Dad for years and was great at it. I thought she'd be good for you. Why? Did something happen?"

James withheld his snort. “Sort of.”

Adam sighed. “Care to clarify that?”

“Not particularly.”

“Fine,” Adam grumbled. “Good luck, then. I’ll see you next Saturday at the wedding.”

Twenty-Five

Sophie

Three Hours Earlier

Philip leaned against the wall of Sophie's office. "James texted the C-Suite group chat this morning."

"About?" Sophie shoved the last bite of her pasta in her mouth.

"The leak," Philip clarified around his sandwich. "It's Jackie."

A pasta noodle slithered down the wrong pipe and Sophie pounded her chest as her mind raced. "Excuse me?!"

He nodded and passed her water bottle. "Unfortunately."

"How are you not more upset about this?" She chugged her water.

"Oh, I am," he clarified. "You should've seen the self-control the C-Suite and I had to use this morning when we saw Jackie. But James wants us to pretend like nothing's wrong for now until he figures out what to do."

Sophie leaned back in her chair. "Well, you know I'm off your case, so I haven't heard anything. Has he talked to Marilyn yet?"

Philip shrugged and took a bite of his sandwich. "I think so?"

Sophie steepled her fingers, her mind spinning. *Why the hell did Jackie do this?*

Jackie treated James like another son, and it didn't make sense that she would do something so drastic to his company.

"Is Jackie not happy there?" Sophie asked.

Philip polished off his sandwich and shrugged. "Not that I'm aware of, and none of the others have ever noticed anything, either."

Sophie's eyes narrowed. *No, but maybe Jackie said something to James–something he brushed over.*

She had three kids. Was there a financial reason behind her betrayal?

Sophie sighed and dragged open her bottom desk drawer, snagging a box of chocolate. "God, this is a mess."

"Tell me about it." Philip's eyes rounded at the box. "No way, I love these. You can only get them in Barcelona, so it's been a minute. Can I have one?"

She nudged the box toward him. "Knock yourself out."

"They're so much better than American chocolate." He stuffed one in his mouth and groaned. "Did James send them?"

"Yes. Oh, right. We made up, by the way." She popped one in her mouth.

A smile adorned Philip's mouth. "He mentioned earlier. Luc and I have a running bet on what he does first when he lands."

Sophie's brows rose. "I don't know if I should be offended."

Philip chuckled and snagged another chocolate. "If he's just coming to see you, or if he brings a gift with him."

She laughed, glancing at the bouquet that arrived that morning. "I have a feeling he's going to bring something."

But nausea gripped her.

Of course, she wanted James to knock at her office door when he landed, but with the revelation about Jackie, would Sophie still be James's top priority once he got back on American soil?

"That's what I said, but *someone* thinks the opposite." Philip rolled his eyes and dropped into one of her chairs. "Right.

If you were a pie, what pie?"

She laughed. "What?"

He grinned. "Luc and I made a bet last night. We're trying to see who can get fewer people to say 'Apple.'"

"You two make a lot of bets."

"What can I say? We get bored."

And I'm sure James's absence isn't helping.

Drawing herself up, she placed her hands on her hips. "Well, lucky for you, I'd be boysenberry."

He snorted. "That was fast. You think about what pie you are often?"

"I'm sorry, did you want typical?" She sniffed.

"Well, no, but–"

"Then you're welcome. What's the score now?"

"You just tied me with Luc," Philip said. "We need James to be a tiebreaker, but cabrón won't answer the phone. He's probably sleeping or something."

Sophie snorted. That was mainly her fault, but Philip didn't need to know that.

She laced her fingers together. "So, what kind of pie would you be?"

"Pecan," he replied without hesitation.

"Okay, you had that *ready*."

He smiled. "We spent way too long talking about this."

"How bored were you guys?"

"Bored enough that James got some interesting text messages last night."

Present

Thunder cracked outside and rain pelted the windows, dragging icy fingers against the glass.

Sophie's phone buzzed and she glanced down.

Oliver: If you get a cat can I have joint custody?

Sophie grinned.

Fuck no.

Whyyy

Bc then the cat is going to have to have you as a parent. And as far as I'm concerned that's

Oliver sent a middle finger emoji.

That's what Chlo said too WHY IS EVERYONE AGAINST ME

A knock bounced off Sophie's office door and she pulled it open, blinking at the figure blocking the opening.

James. There, in the flesh.

He held an umbrella in one hand, but water still somehow managed to darken the shoulders of his shirt.

He smiled. "Hello, bǎobèi."

"You came." Her lip trembled as a smile cycled on her face. *You didn't run.*

"I promised I would, didn't I?" He brandished the bouquet of flowers he clutched. "Also, I got you these."

She gasped softly and eyed the violets before a sense of dread crashed down onto her shoulders. She grabbed his bicep, dragging him into her office.

Technically, it didn't matter anymore if anyone at Covey saw them alone together, not now that Marilyn spun the lie.

But James showing up at her door with flowers would send her colleagues' tongues wagging again. And what if Jackie somehow had eyes inside Covey?

You're overthinking again ... but better safe than sorry, right?

Shutting the door, she plucked the bouquet from him. "More flowers, huh?"

He grinned, leaning against the wall. "You didn't like the deliveries?"

"No, I did." Warmth enveloped her at the memory.

"Then take one more," he said. "And know I'm sorry."

Her fingers wrapped around the pale stems of the flowers, and she stared at the deep purple petals. The bouquet shook in her grip, the starchy brown paper wrapping sliding against her fingers. "James, you have nothing to be sorry for."

Why did he blame himself when it was her fault?

Her fault for not believing him, or that he would ever try pulling one over on her.

"Yes, I do." He cupped her cheek. "I have too much to apologize for. And I know these flowers can't even begin to cover it, but I just ... God. I'm so sorry."

Drawing away, she set the bouquet on her desk and braced clenched fists on worn wood.

Sucking in breath after breath, she cast her gaze out her window.

Fine, he wasn't devoid of fault, but he also couldn't take the entirety of the blame. He was neither the one who made the news leak nor the one who had willingly left her to deal with it alone.

And now, he was here, acknowledging his mistakes instead of running when it would've been easy to.

Brian would've run. Alex would've run. Dad *would've run.*

Her mind's tiny reminder was enough to unfurl her fingers and turn to face James.

He hadn't dared move from the spot he stood.

She stepped toward him, her gaze traveling to his lips. "I wanted to kill you, you know that?"

"I know." He shifted from one foot to the other. "Tell me how to make it up to you. Please."

Want clawed at the lining of her stomach, desperate to escape. Taking the end of his tie between her fingers, she toyed with the silky material.

“Kiss me,” she whispered, sliding her hands over his shoulders. “Touch me.”

His hands cupped her face and he leaned down so his forehead rested on hers. His eyes shuttered, transforming into hooded half-moons, as he twisted his fingers into the ends of her hair. “Sophie.”

“Please,” she whispered. Her gaze darted to his lips, then back to his eyes. “Don’t leave me again.”

“Never,” he breathed and crushed his mouth to hers.

Twenty-Six

James

He hadn't figured out what to tell Marilyn if she asked how he found out Jackie was the leak. He figured he'd cross that bridge when he came to it.

But as Sophie knocked on Marilyn's office door and they waited to enter, he found himself already standing smack dab in the middle.

Only his close friends knew how he got through challenging obstacles, and his family had inklings. But no one had ever said anything.

Would Marilyn see him differently when she found out?

Would Sophie?

His heart rate soared and his head spun as he struggled to breathe. He just got her back; he couldn't bear to watch her leave again.

Can she tell how nervous I am? He reached out for her. "Sophie–"

She pushed the door open. "Look who's back."

Marilyn's blue eyes crinkled at the edges. "Ah, James. Good to see you in person, but," she fished a tissue from the box on her desk, "you might want to wipe your face."

She tapped her jawline.

He blinked, heat creeping into his cheeks as he took the tissue. Wiping his face, he glanced down and drew his eyes across the light pink lipstick, stark against the white surface.

"Thanks," he mumbled.

"He knows who the leak is," Sophie said, seemingly unfazed.

Marilyn raised a brow. "And how did you get your hands on that information?"

He hesitated long enough that Sophie looked at him.

She frowned. "You do know, right? Philip said you texted the group chat."

"Yes," James said. He looked at the ground like a kid who had been caught somewhere they weren't supposed to be. "This isn't the first time I've run into issues with Lotus. So I ... have people who help me when I need answers."

He swallowed hard, the words slicing through the air. It was the first time he came close to admitting it aloud to someone whose opinion he cared too much about.

"You mean your PR team?" Sophie crossed her arms. "I thought you couldn't use them. Isn't that why you came to us?"

He shook his head. "Not them. Other people."

"Wait, I'm confused."

Chills racked his body as he tried figuring out another way to shuffle the words together.

Marilyn cleared her throat. "What he means," she narrowed her eyes, "is that he used an unsanctioned route, isn't that right?"

That works. He sighed and nodded, staring out the window.

The weather had cleared, and rays of sunlight threatened to poke out from behind tall buildings and streaks of clouds.

Pulling his attention back, he made eye contact with Sophie.

She gaped at him. "How often have you used this method before?"

He dug his hands into his pockets. "Only when I have to."

"I see ... and are you a participant in these methods?"

"Sometimes," he mumbled.

She fell silent, save for the tapping of her foot. Indecision flickered in her eyes and her jaw jumped, like she was fighting the urge to scream at him.

He gulped and further explanation poised on the tip of his tongue, ready to fall at any moment.

But Sophie did the impossible. She *shrugged.* "You do what you have to."

"Yes," Marilyn agreed after a moment. "While I certainly don't condone those methods, and I'm sure there were other ways, what's done is done."

James's jaw threatened to drop. Swallowing, his ears popped as he tried to make sense of it.

Was he in a parallel dimension? Of course, he was glad the women hadn't gotten too mad at him, but their reactions seemed so ... neutral.

His gaze switched between Sophie and Marilyn for a moment longer before he blinked.

The answer stared him in the face the entire day.

Covey wasn't above pulling whatever strings necessary, and what Marilyn did with the articles was a prime example of that.

"At least tell me no one has ... left because of these methods," she continued.

"Of course, no one has."

He didn't think he could live with himself otherwise.

"Thank God for that," Sophie muttered.

Marilyn sighed and rested her elbows on her desk. "So, who's the leak?"

Nausea slammed down on James again. "It's my assistant."

God, saying the words aloud instead of just thinking them was salt in the wound.

Each breath was futile, and his throat seared like he was underwater. "I don't know why. I thought she was happy, I—"

Was the room always spinning?

"Sit down. You don't look too good." Sophie took his hand and guided him to an open chair. Her hand squeezed his, then rested on his shoulder.

"Don't panic." Marilyn sat behind her desk again, bracing her forearms on the surface. "I don't want you or anyone else to confront her, at least not yet."

"You're joking, right?" James laughed, his chest clenching. "This situation ... I really think I–"

"No," Sophie interrupted. "Don't do anything."

He stared at her. "What?"

What the hell else am I supposed to do? Sit around while Jackie figures out her lie dissolved?

"You have the upper hand right now," Sophie continued. "I don't know what Jackie will do when she finds out you know, but we can't risk you undoing everything we've helped you do the past two months."

He wanted to protest. This was ridiculous, but at the same time ... he heaved a sigh.

Begrudgingly, he nodded, grasping Sophie's hand.

Marilyn tracked the movement with keen eyes. "Good, and until we get her to talk, I don't want any word of *this* to get out." She gestured between the two of them. "Jackie used this information to her advantage before, and we don't want her to expose us for covering up the truth."

"There's only one problem with that," James said. "She knows the truth. I told her before I knew about her, so she knows the articles were fake."

Marilyn's mouth tugged into a firm line, and she blew a long breath through her nose.

Next to him, Sophie sighed and tightened her grip on his shoulder. "Are you kidding me right now?"

He winced. "Sorry."

He risked a peek at her and swallowed hard. *If looks could kill...*

Marilyn crossed her arms. "Okay, here's what you'll do, and *only* do this if she asks. You tell her you and Sophie broke up at the gala, and as long as Jackie doesn't see you with her, she'll believe it."

James didn't know about that. If they looked closely enough, anyone could see how he felt about Sophie.

But for the sake of their plan working, he nodded.

Twenty-Seven

James

"I'll fight you for it!"

James held the donut above his head. "Stay away!"

Philip grabbed onto him, reaching one arm up, his fingers wiggling for the treat.

James stepped back, his lower back hitting the counter in the break room. He tried to lift the pastry even higher, but it didn't matter.

Philip was six-four, same as him, and the attempt was futile.

James grunted. "Go to the cafe down the street!"

"I want this one!" Philip whined. "You know, you're being a terrible CEO, right now. Talk about not caring about employee satisfaction!"

He grunted, waving his arm. "Didn't you just get the thing with Sophie cleared up, too? You don't want people talking shit about you again!"

"I don't think they'll care if I don't give you a donut," James growled. "And don't bring her into this!"

"I was going to see if you two wanted to get lunch, but never mind."

Luc leaned in the doorframe, his arms crossed. He sauntered into the room, stopping in front of Philip. "By the way, here."

Philip relinquished James and dusted himself off before

taking the stack of one-hundred-dollar bills Luc brandished.

James eyed the money. "Do I want to know?"

"This idiot bet you would only see Sophie when you got back without bringing her something." Philip shook his head, muttering under his breath as he counted the bills. "Ay, you're two hundred short."

"In my defense, I was drunk when I made that bet," Luc said as he pulled out his phone.

"Whatever." Philip waved his hand. His phone dinged and he glanced at the screen. "Thanks."

"Yeah, yeah," Luc grumbled. "Enjoy your exploitation."

James rolled his eyes.

Luc was doomed to lose from the start.

"Anyway, lunch?" Luc gestured toward the door. "Pip, you're treating, okay? Now that you're richer, it'd be the right thing to do."

James nodded and pulled out his phone. "He's right, you know. Let me look up places."

"Make sure it's expensive," Luc said.

"I like how you think." James lowered his other arm, alleviating the slight ache that had started up.

Philip stole the donut and crammed half into his mouth.

"Hey!"

"That's what you get." Philip flipped him off and ate the rest of the pastry.

James grumbled and walked out of the breakroom. He turned the corner and nearly crashed into Jackie.

She wobbled and tightened her grip on her armful of files, but she dropped a few anyway. "Sorry!"

"It's fine," he said, and looked at his friends. "Go, I'll meet you two downstairs."

Philip and Luc hesitated for a moment, then headed toward the elevators.

James stooped to get the files and schooled his face into a neutral mask. Keeping a hold of the files, he took half the stack from Jackie.

"You look like you've got your hands full," he said. "I'm

assuming you want these on your desk?"

When the news broke about him and Sophie, Lotus lost almost all the clients they gained since Delacroix. But with Marilyn's fix the other day, they experienced a significant rise in cases again.

And to think we could've lost it all thanks to Jackie.

Red clouded his vision, but he kept his expression cool as he headed for the elevators.

He had to let Covey take care of things, but that didn't mean he couldn't speed things up a little.

Swiping open his message thread with Jackie, he tapped a simple message in and sent it off.

"Thanks for dinner again." Jackie cut into her steak, looking around. "This place is nice. Why are we here if it's just for a standard work dinner?"

"You're right, it is a bit upscale for business." He shrugged, lifting his wineglass to his lips. "But you know I like this place, and I thought you'd like the food."

Truth be told, he wanted to put her at ease and turn her mind off the inkling that anything was wrong.

She snorted, narrowing her eyes. "James Tian, are you using your negotiation voice on me?"

"No ..."

She laughed. "Nice try. I'm a mother, James. I worked for your father while you were growing up, *and* I'm your assistant. I know when someone wants something."

He sighed and set down his wine, tracking a bead of red rolling down the side. It hit the tablecloth, a brilliant bud blooming against the white.

He should wait for Covey. He had gotten a message from Marilyn that she would give him a solution in the next few days, but so far, there was nothing.

He couldn't wait that long, couldn't keep on pretending.

Jackie raised a brow. “Well?”

He tugged at his tie, loosening it slightly. Here went nothing.

“Why’d you do it?”

Twenty-Eight

Sophie

She squinted at the selection in front of her and picked up one of the plastic forks, sinking it into the mousse cake at the end of the row.

Licking the frosting from the tines, she moaned. "James has competition."

"So does Taylor," Oliver agreed.

Taylor tucked another bite of cake in his mouth and closed his eyes. "Yeah, I give you full permission to leave me for this strawberry chiffon."

"Already done," Oliver said. "We have a secret child."

Luc gasped. "The *drama*!"

Chloe swatted his shoulder. "This is your fault; you brought us here!"

He reclined in his cracked seat. "To be fair, I gave you a heads-up that they had amazing desserts."

The hole-in-the-wall bakery he brought them to downtown looked sketchy at best from the outside. Crumbling bricks and cracked steps led up to the worn door, and a flickering neon sign declared they were open until one a.m. every day aside from Sunday.

Worn linoleum floors decorated the small space, along with a hodge-podge of sticky tables. Humming pastry cases displayed their wares under fluorescent lighting, and a tired menu with an even more tired cashier stood behind a run-down counter.

Sophie fell in love the moment they stepped in.

Chloe shook her head in exasperation. "What did I get into when I agreed to a date?"

"A blessing in disguise." He grinned.

Sophie laughed, forking a portion of cheesecake into her mouth. "Luc, does this mean you'll chip in for child support?"

"Of course," he said. "Since it's partially my fault."

"Oh, right, I've been meaning to ask, how is James?" Chloe wiped her mouth. "How's he doing with the news?"

Sophie hadn't been able to keep quiet about that to her best friends. Sue her.

"He's good, and he's handling it well." Sophie ate some more of the cheesecake. *Well, I'm not sure if that's true.*

Wisps of memory from hours earlier snaked into her brain, rattling their tails in warning.

"I've got a meeting tonight I can't push." He had brushed his lips over her forehead. "I'll see you tomorrow."

He ambled out of her office, his fists clenched and his shoulders tugged back.

Iciness seeped into her cheeks and she braced her fists on her desk. I hope he's not going to do anything rash.

Panic never preceded good decisions.

Now, the bell over the door jingled and Sophie blinked, knocking her elbow into the napkin dispenser.

Chloe frowned. "You good?"

Sophie nodded, rubbing her elbow. "Like I said, he's handling it as well as anyone would if they were in his shoes."

"I hate that this is happening," Chloe said.

Sophie shrugged, pursing her lips. "You and me both."

She crossed her arms, rapping her nails against her biceps.

"Well, onto happier topics. Please tell me the apology sex was good." Chloe asked. "You guys did have apology sex, right?"

Sophie laughed and lowered her voice. "You know that vibrator you told me about? He held it against—"

"*No.*" Chloe gasped. "Down–"

"*Yes.*" Sophie said. "And it was unreal, I tell you. I could barely–"

Luc cleared his throat loudly. "We're in public. *Please* don't finish that sentence."

She snorted. "That's why I'm whispering."

"And he's one of my best friends. I don't need to know what you guys get up to in your own time."

"You know I know about the Crème Caramel, right?"

His eyes widened. "What?! Chloe, mon soleil, you told her?"

"She's my best friend," Chloe said. "And we're oversharers with each other."

Sophie laughed as her phone buzzed.

James's contact lit up the screen, and she hit the option to answer. "Hey, what's up?"

"Hey, how fast can you get to Lotus?"

Luc pulled to a stop outside of Lotus's headquarters, hitting the brakes a little too hard.

Sophie stepped out onto the curb, worry fluttering in her veins. God, she could only hope she wasn't too late.

"You sure you don't want me to come with you?" Luc called out the window.

She shook her head. "It's fine, just go meet the others!"

She had detected the mild panic underlying James's words, but after hanging up, she played things cool. The last thing she needed was to upset her friends.

It was no use, though. Chloe had already been suspicious and she demanded the truth from Sophie.

Once she came clean, they piled into Luc's BMW and sped for the office. The ride took half as much time as usual since he broke every traffic law there was.

Now, the rest of Sophie's friends camped out at an Ethiopian place around the corner, and Sophie was pretty sure Chloe tracked her location.

Turning, Sophie hurried into the building, jamming her thumb on the elevator button.

Her mind ran to unwarranted conclusions as she ascended.

Was James incapacitated in some way, or lying hurt somewhere, or tied up?

Wait, that's ridiculous. He called *me, remember?*

The elevator let her out into darkened corridors, and she glanced around for a moment before spotting the sliver of light peeking from beneath his closed office door.

She pushed it open, her heartbeat thudding, and expelled a sigh of relief.

James sat behind his desk, looking incredibly serene, though his eyes stretched wide.

Oh, thank God he's oka–oh, shit.

Jackie parked in one of the chairs before his desk, her arms and legs crossed. Her face looked like she sucked on something sour, and her fingernails tapped on her biceps.

"Hey," Sophie said, shutting the door behind her.

"Oh, good, you're here." James didn't look at her as he linked his fingers. "I was just talking to Jackie, and I thought you might want to be present."

His lip curled, and the muscles in his shoulders bunched. He looked every bit the domineering, intimidating CEO she had imagined him to be before she got to know him.

I guess he turns it on when he has to.

Being such a young CEO was like being stuck in a constant chessboard, and the way he looked at Jackie ... it was like a player calling checkmate.

Sophie took a few steps forward and stopped at his desk. Bracing her fingertips on the surface, she was torn between who to look at. But she swallowed her indecision and tipped her chin toward him.

"Marilyn and I both told you not to do anything yet," she admonished.

He shrugged.

She rolled her eyes.

He was so impulsive that the fallout often became bigger than the problem.

She peered down at the desk, drumming her fingers. Then she turned her attention to Jackie.

The other woman sulked, narrowing her normally warm hazel eyes at the wall.

"I'll keep it simple," Sophie said. "Why?"

"Why do *you* need to know?" Jackie snipped. "Why are you even here?"

"Because this concerns me as much as James," Sophie said. "And on top of that, I'll be the one to decide with Marilyn when we call the cops. Whether they come right now or after you finish explaining is up to you."

"The cops?" Jackie scoffed. "And what are *they* going to do when they show up? It's not like you can charge me with anything."

"No," James said after a moment. "But when the commissioner owes you a ... big favor, I don't think coming up with something and planting the evidence to make it appear real is out of his wheelhouse."

Sophie's eyes widened and she cut a glance at James. *I was bluffing ... what exactly does he have on him?!*

Jackie's gaze flickered between him and Sophie before something in it gave out.

"I only did it out of loyalty," she began.

Sophie smirked. *Wise choice.*

She crossed her arms and cocked her hip. "Go on."

Jackie expelled a long, suffering breath through her nose. "When I worked for Charles, I learned that company loyalty got you a long way. I saw that long-time shareholders and benefactors were rewarded."

"You were unhappy," James cut in. "You wanted those for yourself."

Sophie glanced at him. She pursed her lips–this wouldn't do at all.

She couldn't have him cutting in and letting his emotions dominate. They would get nowhere productive like that.

"James, do you mind stepping out?" she asked.

He blinked. "Excuse me?"

She leaned toward him, lowering her voice. "You can't be here right now."

He raised his brows. "Why not? This is my office, and she's my assistant."

Sophie huffed. "That's the point, she's your assistant. She's never going to talk freely if you're in the room."

Especially since she just gave that spiel about loyalty.

A muscle ticked in his jaw and he tilted his head, sucking his lips between his teeth. "I don't know..."

Sophie rested her hand on his shoulder. "Please."

Tense muscles relaxed and he dipped his chin. "Alright."

Clenching his fists, he rose, moving to the door.

"Where are you going?" Jackie called after him.

He ignored her and walked out, dragging the door shut behind him.

Sophie cleared her throat and drew the vacant chair from next to Jackie. Sitting, she crossed her legs and rested her laced hands on her knees. "Right. The one thing I learned from meeting James's dad was that he won't give you anything if he doesn't think *you* can give him something in return."

"I know that," Jackie snapped. "That's why I did what he wanted when he wanted. There were never any mistakes, and that should've counted for something. But it didn't, and it wasn't fair."

"It never is fair," Sophie forced herself to say.

"Exactly." Jackie's tone was intrepid. "But I kept waiting because I knew that one day, my talent would be recognized."

Sophie nodded. "But it didn't, and you stayed an assistant. I see."

Jackie chuckled and crossed her ankles, a maniacal smile balanced on her lips. "If Charles couldn't see my potential, that's his problem."

A cold disk slipped into Sophie's stomach, and she swallowed down her nausea. Her nails dug into her upper arms. *If I'd let my anger at Marilyn overwhelm me when she didn't promote me after the Shasta campaign, would I have done what Jackie did?*

Relaxing her jaw, she gestured for Jackie to continue.

"I was going to say something, but then Charles's oldest son came to me and told me that his little brother wanted to go off and start his own business."

Sophie's eyes widened and she sat straight up in her seat. Ice sluiced through her veins, numbing her limbs. "James always planned to leave Tian Corporation."

And I'd bet everything Adam knew that for years.

Jackie nodded. "Yes, and Adam proposed that I leave with James. He said that if James was leaving, then he wanted him to get a good head start. I saw this as my chance to finally get my recognition, so I agreed."

Sophie's mouth set into a grim line. "But then why become his assistant? Why not ask for a higher position?"

"Because I just wanted James to get out," Jackie declared. "I saw the way his father treated him since his mother left, and I ...well. I figured it would be better to start at the bottom and work my way up. James told me the team would be small, so I figured it'd be easy. But..."

Goosebumps prickled Sophie's skin, and she hugged herself tight, worrying her bottom lip. "So let me get this straight. You abandoned years of security for the hope that James would see the potential his father didn't. But when that never happened, you somehow decided taking it all down would be better?"

Jackie unfurled a saccharine smile and tossed a lock of chestnut hair away from her face. Her voice rumbled like that of a person fragmenting into trillions of shards. "Of course."

Twenty-Nine

James

"James, can you come back in here now?"

He blinked, squinting at the jagged cut of moonlight slashing across Sophie's face. "Everything okay?"

Her eyes were a bit too wide, but her body relaxed. "Yes, I just think you need to hear this."

His brows rose, but he slipped into the room, taking a seat behind his desk.

Glancing at his assistant, he ignored the heat swirling in his veins and cleared his throat.

She stared at a bookshelf, lips pursed and hissed a breath out her nose. "I thought you were different than your father, James, but he really did pass his penchant for figuring things out for yourself down to you, didn't he?"

James lifted a brow, confusion lancing through him. "I'm sorry?"

Jackie laughed. Her hazel eyes, once so warm, iced over. "Don't act like you weren't the one who made me do this. Better yet, don't act like you didn't *want* me to."

James stared at her, eyes wide and hands suffocating the arms of his chair.

Was Jackie delusional? How could she possibly think that the entire time, he was silently goading her to take control of the situation?

A ball of nausea skipped into his stomach, rolling to a stop.

"No PR is bad PR, isn't that right, Sophie?" Jackie bit out. "I overheard Philip talking to James in his office. Philip was concerned that the past quarterly projections had not been as high as he would've liked. He wanted to bring in a client with a higher profile, not only to raise our profits, but also to draw in potential clients."

Dread flooded James's system as he laced his fingers together.

Jackie's words from months ago floated in his ears.

'Sorry to interrupt, but I couldn't help but overhear ... what about George Delacroix? I remember you said he was looking to decorate the new branch of Cross Law.'

James blanched, heart kicking into overdrive.

"Initially, I hired Davenport to make sure that Delacroix was squeaky clean, and I was going to tell you what I did, but then ... he found a few things that didn't add up." She clenched her fists in her lap. "I knew that if I told you after that, there was a high chance I'd be fired. So, I told Davenport to use the things he found against Delacroix. It was either do business with us and spend a certain amount, or have his crimes leaked."

James sucked in a breath. "He didn't try to reach the amount because he thought you were bluffing."

Jackie let out a maniacal laugh. "His mistake. I thought you would be proud of me for doing what I did. After all, I learned it from watching you. You weren't as quiet about it as you thought."

James gritted his teeth and laced his fingers beneath his chin.

But she ignored his expression and continued with a glimmer in her eye. "I put Lotus in the public eye, even though it was the result of something negative. I knew it would result in us getting attention. We'd start drawing in clients and money as soon as everything blew over, and I would take over Gemma's position because I brought in such a big account in the first place."

James stared at a point on the wall just beyond Jackie's

shoulder, his jaw clenched to the point of pain.

What started as a small lie had snowballed, and instead of confessing, she let it fester.

Jackie's expression fixated between glee and disgust, and the effect was terrifying. "When I overheard you talking to Cami and Gemma about how you had found Davenport, I panicked. But luckily, you said you weren't going to do anything until after Adam's engagement party." She sneered. "Still, I couldn't risk you tracing it back to me. That's why I went to the press when I did, and told them what I knew, making sure they kept me anonymous."

James's fists trembled on the arms of his chair. His throat grated with each swallow.

Jackie had to know that he never would've given her the job, didn't she? With her position as his assistant and her previous experience, it wouldn't have made sense to give her the role of COO.

"Jackie, do you know what you cost me?" James's voice trembled with anger, and he shook his head. "Cost Sophie?"

Years of work, just trying to escape from the shadow of his family. It almost swirled down the drain.

Jackie lifted her chin. "From where I'm standing, all I see is that what I did brought you more publicity, more clients, and more money."

It took all his power to keep his jaw from unhinging as his eyes bugged. Ringing began in his ears, and his leg started bouncing under his desk.

Jackie was too far gone to be reasoned with.

"You know I have to fire you, don't you?" he asked even though they all knew the question was only a courtesy. "You'll get a considerable severance, of course, and I'll make sure you and your family are looked after."

Jackie gaped at him, too shocked at the obvious answer. "You ungrateful–"

"Careful, Jacqueline."

Scorn filled her face, but she nodded once and stood. "All I wanted to do was help you," she got out quickly. She walked toward the door, lip trembling even as she threw daggers with her eyes. "That was all I wanted. James–"

"Jacqueline," he snapped.

She stared at him before she left, shutting the door behind her.

With the click, he slumped forward, squeezing his eyes shut, and sucking in rattling breath after rattling breath. God, he wanted to punch something.

"James."

Gentle hands rested on his shoulders, and he lifted his head, glancing at a wide-eyed Sophie.

God, I must look terrible.

In one swift motion, he pulled her down onto his lap and crushed her into a tight hug.

The light seeping in through the window gilded her hair in glimmering bronze. The Jasmine flowers in her shampoo mixed with the autumn smoke from outside, snaking up his nose.

"I'm sorry," he murmured into her hair. "You shouldn't have been dragged into this."

God, he was so fortunate to have her by his side. Even though everything was crumbling around him, at least she was there amongst the wreckage.

"It's okay," she whispered. She clung to him, everything laid out in her touch.

And yet, he still wanted to whisper a thousand and one apologies.

He didn't know how he had managed to get through the week.

The days passed in a haze of meetings and paperwork, and on top of that, he had interviews for a new assistant to oversee. By the time Friday rolled around, he was dead tired.

Collapsing into the Uber, he directed the driver to Sophie's apartment.

Sighing, he tucked his chin back and crossed his arms. He could shut his eyes for a few seconds.

"Hey. *Hey*!"

He blinked and looked out the window, squinting against the sharp lights of nighttime traffic zipping by.

The car had stopped outside the noodle shop that stood below Sophie's, and the driver stared at him.

Apologizing, James quickly paid and got out, wiping drool from his mouth. He shook his head and rang the buzzer for her apartment, rubbing his eyes as he waited.

The door opened a few moments later, and Sophie beamed at him.

All his exhaustion promptly faded away, and his lips crashed onto hers, his arms looping around her body.

"Hey," he murmured against her mouth, and she laughed.

"Hi to you, too," she whispered. "As much as I'd love to stay here, we're attracting attention, so let's go inside."

He tramped up the threadbare carpet lining the stairs, hiking over the creaky step at the top.

"I did want to talk to you about something," he said as they entered her apartment. "Now that Jackie is gone, what does it mean for me and Covey?"

He assumed they were done, since what he had originally sought them out for was over.

"Technically, you don't need us anymore," she confirmed. "But there's the bit with Marilyn lying to cover our relationship."

He frowned, sitting on the couch and hugging a throw pillow. "So, she just leaks another story, right? She says she was wrong, and we actually have something going on."

Sophie shook her head. "It's not that simple. If Marilyn leaks another story, people will start to wonder why she's the one going to the press. I'm the account director now, so I should be the one to say something, and since you're not our client anymore, we're not stopping you from saying anything, either."

He nodded, his brow furrowed. Focusing on a knot on the coffee table, he clutched the pillow in his lap tightly.

She smiled and grasped his hands. “But don’t worry. We’ll figure it out.”

“I think we should figure it out now,” he protested.

She shook her head. “Believe me, I know how important this is. But truthfully? *I* need some time to think of what to do.”

Thirty
Sophie

Staring at her phone, the keypad burned a rift into Sophie's eyes.

This is crazy. There's no telling if this will even work.

Behind her, James mumbled something in his sleep, then resumed softly snoring.

Fishing his shirt from the floor, she pulled it on and slunk out of bed, padding to the kitchen.

The dial tone spiraled heavily into silence as Sophie leaned against the counter, worrying her lip.

"Hello?" Curiosity flowed through Jackie's voice, completely at odds with the desperate contempt that ruled it last week.

"I'll cut to the chase." Sophie refused to let any doubt flood her for even a second. If there was so much as a flicker, she would fall to her knees. "I need your help."

She laid out her plan, then turned around, tapping her nails against the countertop. "If you don't agree, it'd be a shame to tell Marilyn that we found you after you got away."

Jackie chuckled. "Are you blackmailing me?"

"Yes." Sophie examined her nails. "Either you go to the press, officially confirming James and my relationship so Covey can release an official statement. Or ..."

"Or you call that commissioner he has in his pocket," Jackie finished.

Sophie played with a cabinet door, opening and shutting

it quietly. "Exactly."

Jackie laughed. "Was this your idea or James's?"

"Mine."

"I've got to hand it to you–I didn't think you had this in you. But who's to say I won't double-cross you?"

Sophie's brows rose. "I'm sure we can come to an arrangement. But it really is better to take door number one, Jackie."

Life was only bad if you let it be, and Sophie had spent her entire life trying to turn a self-fulfilling prophecy into a self-defeating one.

Jackie nearly knocked it all over in one, selfish swoop.

Sophie would be damned if she let that happen.

Not just for her sake, but for Marilyn's, Covey's, and James's.

Jackie's tone lightened, like her lips formed a coy smile. "I understand. You've got yourself a deal."

"Excellent."

A blip sounded, ending the call.

Sophie slipped the device into her pocket and took a deep breath before pouring herself a glass of water.

Sophie strode into the lobby of Covey's building, her heels clicking against the marble flooring. In one hand, she held her coffee from Joseph's and in her other arm, she cradled a stack of files.

James's hand pressed into her lower back, her purse swinging from his shoulder.

Her spine stiffened as they waited for the elevator, the significant stares they garnered sinking into the nape of her neck.

She and James had yet to release a statement, and until they did, rumors about them being seen in an intimate position that morning were sure to circulate.

The hushed shouts and whispered screams had been terrifying, and she couldn't take a repeat of that.

But the difference between then and now is that you have the upper hand. You don't have anything to worry about. This won't *fail.*

"Relax," he murmured.

She stepped into the waiting cart and sucked down some coffee. "Right, you're right."

Steeling herself, she swallowed and took a few deep breaths. "Do you remember those men in the elevator after the gala? I arranged for Jackie to talk to one of them."

James raised a brow. "A journalist?"

Sophie nodded. "And one that believed the worst about us until Marilyn's 'fix.'"

James's jaw clenched and she leaned into his side.

"It's fine," she said. "It's better for someone who knew he was wrong to do this. He wants to get the right story out now."

The elevator doors slid open, and she stepped out into Covey's lobby, waving to Nico. Walking into her office, she set her things on her desk and sighed.

She curled her hand into a fist and gripped her bracelet. *You got this.*

James offered her his hand, smiling. "Don't worry, bǎobèi."

She stared at his upturned palm for a moment before taking it, interlocking their fingers.

She barely registered leading him down the hall until she stared at Marilyn's shut door.

But even though Sophie's spine was stick straight, and her chin held high, her nerves still twitched, and her pulse was a war drum.

James squeezed her hand as she knocked, simultaneously pushing into Marilyn's office.

Marilyn looked over from her computer, her brows rising as she took in James's hand in Sophie's.

"You decided to go public with it now that Jackie's gone?" Marilyn asked. "That's gutsy, especially so soon."

Sophie smiled wryly and let go of James's hand. Taking a

seat, she crossed her ankles. "About that ... Jackie isn't gone."

Footsteps muffled behind her, and James's hand settled on her shoulder as she started explaining.

Marilyn's brows climbed and she laced her fingers together, resting her chin atop her hands. "What I'm hearing is you blackmailed Jackie into making an official statement."

A proud smile tilted Sophie's lips. "I did."

She hadn't done anything when Alex and Brian broke her heart, and she'd been too scared to. But those days were long gone.

She wasn't letting James go, and if she had to, it wasn't without a fight.

"Well." Marilyn sighed. "I'm not exactly happy with what you chose to do, but I can see why you did it, and it would work."

"I'm sorry, Sophie explained it to me, but I'm still confused," James sat down in the other chair. "Aren't you still going to be under fire?"

Marilyn nodded, shrugging. "It's unavoidable. But this way, we control the entire situation much better."

"And it's like I said earlier." Sophie cast her gaze toward him. "If we went to the press without Jackie telling her story first, this whole thing would be messier than it needs to be."

Outside, a car honked and an engine sputtered, the revving drawing farther away.

James was quiet, his gaze faraway. His jaw clenched, a muscle feathering in his temple.

Sophie's palms broke into a cold sweat. *I don't like that look.*

He screwed his eyes shut for a moment, then looked at her. "Then ... what if we broke up?"

Her world cracked and shattered, and black crept in at the edges of her vision. A tunnel of rushing wind took up residency in her ears. "W-what?"

Intent glittered in his eyes, dilating his pupils. "If I went away, then there would be nothing to worry about. We wouldn't need Jackie, and you and Marilyn would get away scot-free."

Protests and disgust threatened to erupt from her. Maybe she and Marilyn would be in the clear, but she would lose him in the process.

They had fought tooth and nail to get to where they were. Finally, *finally*, all the pieces had entered the playing board and assumed their rightful positions, and he wanted to throw it all away?!

"No."

She jumped as Marilyn broke into the moment, and Sophie's attention whirled on her.

"No," Marilyn repeated. "We didn't go through everything–*Sophie* didn't go through everything–for you to play the hero now."

She stood, crossing her arms. "You might not be our client anymore, but your actions still matter."

Pride and admiration welled up, spilling over the sides of Sophie's heart.

Glancing at James, her gaze traced the flush of embarrassment brushing his cheeks. "You're right. Sorry."

Sophie's phone pinged in her pocket, and she drew it out, glancing at the text notification from Jackie.

"I hope you know what you're doing." Jackie's tense voice came over the receiver.

Sophie's fingers flew across her keyboard as she drafted up the email to one of the reporters from the publication they'd attended the gala for. "Just like you knew what you were doing the entire time you played James?"

Silence oozed and James's grip tightened subtly on the pen he was holding. He had folded himself into one of the chairs across from her and was scrawling things down on papers Gemma dropped off.

"And how is this any better than what I did?" Jackie asked.

Sophie tilted her head, drumming her fingers on the surface of her desk. "Because I'm actually trying to help others here. And don't tell me that's what you were trying to do, too."

Jackie was quiet before harrumphing. "Fine. Anyway, let me know if this works."

The call ended.

Sophie cleared her throat and resumed typing, putting the finishing touches on the email. "Okay, what do you think?"

James came behind her desk and bent to read the email they workshopped. He nodded, fixing his glasses that had slid down his nose.

"It looks good," he said. "But I hate that we have to do this."

She blew a breath out of her nose. *You and me both.*

They shouldn't have to jump through hoops. They shouldn't have to seek approval from news sources or wait for anyone else's say-so. They should just be allowed to *be.*

But there were procedures to follow, and rules too rigid and fragile to break. The cards had to be played right if they valued their reputations.

Hitting the send button, she received a reply from the journalist a few minutes later, promising to get it released that afternoon.

Glancing at James, the burning nausea creeping up Sophie's throat increased.

This was it. In a matter of hours, they either sank or swam, and James ...

James had spent the entire day at Covey, helping when he could, and getting the stuff he had to do dropped off. As he'd explained it, he wanted to be there if something happened.

She pressed her lips tight.

If this were any of her exes, or hell, even her father, there would've been complaints. There would've been significant objections.

But James hadn't put up a fuss once.

God, he must be so worried right now. Swallowing hard, she moved toward the door. Shrugging into her coat, she clutched the soft, black woolen material. "I'm going to get us some lunch, but I just wanted to say I'm sorry."

He blinked. "What?

"Um ... lunch. Salad good?"

"Salad's fine, but I was talking about that last part." Crossing the room, his hands lay on her shoulders. "Why are you apologizing?"

She shrugged, letting her head fall. For a minute, she debated running anyway. All she had to do was rip herself from his touch and make a break for it. But her feet stayed planted on the carpet.

'*You tried to fix things. It's not your fault that this is what you have to do to make that happen,'* her therapist said in her head.

She knew that, and yet ...

"You've been stuck here all day," she murmured. "You got dragged into this, and you didn't need to be."

"If I got dragged into this, it's because I *wanted* to be," he said. "I'm not going to let you take all this shit by yourself," his fingers tightened slightly, "and for the record, I meant what I said before. I'll go, if that makes things easier for you. I'll leave."

She grimaced. *I don't doubt it.*

It would kill both of them, but if she asked, he wouldn't hesitate to go to the other side of the world.

The fact he was *asking* instead of just *doing* didn't escape her. But...

"That's not what I meant. You know what they'll say if you leave, right?" she asked. "They'll say I *told* you to do it. It doesn't matter if it's not true, I'll be framed as the bad guy."

He frowned and cocked his head. "What are you–why?"

She scoffed, shaking her head. *Does he still not understand this?*

"James, you have money and power," she explained. "You're a good-looking man who's barely older, but they'll take those five years and blow them into fifty."

"So what?" he demanded.

Hot, thick air filled her lungs, choking her, and she pulled away, sitting down in one of the chairs by her desk.

She shut her eyes. "So, everything."

Ever since she offered their arrangement to him, she knew it would be a dangerous, deadly dance.

They risked it all to love in secret—their individual positions and reputations, their companies' prestige and notoriety, their hearts.

But she did it anyway, and now, it might come back to bite her in the ass.

Headlines that called her a golddigger, a lifesucking leech, and a shameless, exploitative parasite who ruined a promising young man's career swam before her eyes.

She buried her head in her hands.

Everything started because she couldn't let James go, hadn't it? If she had just let him be the One Who Got Away, then maybe ...

God, her therapist was going to have a field day at their next session.

Quick footsteps were her only warning before a crushing warmth enveloped her, stealing her breath.

"I'm sorry." James hugged her tight. "I'm so sorry. I should've—no, I *can* do more."

She closed her eyes, breathing him in. "James—"

"I can make it go away," he continued. "I can—"

Sickness twisted her stomach. "No."

He'd use his name and connections to strong-arm everything away from the media and brush things under the rug.

As much as this was driving her up the wall, she didn't want to hide behind a check. She couldn't handle people always whispering behind their backs about a relationship they only pretended to accept.

Besides, what can he really do that won't also tear himself down in the process?

A shuddering breath ghosted past her lips, and she swiped at her cheeks, grimacing at the wetness that littered her fingers as they came away from her face.

Her jaw clenched. She had never cried over this whole

damn thing once, so why was she doing so now?

Nothing even happened, for God's sake.

She sniffled. *No, but it might have.*

And at the end of the day, that was what she was so terrified of. That 'might.'

If her dad hadn't abandoned his family, returned for his own desires, then ran again after a few hours, Sophie *might* have had a different upbringing.

If her exes hadn't subjected her to hit and runs, then she *might* have been in a different place with her love life.

The last thing she wanted was for James to become another 'might.'

Her therapist always said it was healthy to let your emotions through, but they probably didn't mean the sudden urge Sophie got to punch something.

Settling for the next best thing, she clenched her hands around her chair and squeezed. She didn't know what she hoped to accomplish by strangling an inanimate object, but did she need to?

"This isn't your fault," James murmured, and swiped away tears with his thumb. "None of this is on you."

"I know, but–"

"No buts," he interjected. "Cry over them and they win. Get mad over them, and they win."

She glanced at him to see that his jaw was set, eyes glistening.

Ice replaced her cheeks. *How long has he felt like this*? *Did it start with Lotus, or much earlier*?

His arms trembled around her. "I'm not saying don't cry, or don't get mad. But don't let them see. Never give them the satisfaction."

The journalist did it, and it wasn't just him. Somehow, he circulated the story to other news publications and got them to post it on short notice, too.

But that wasn't all.

Since Lotus possessed such a renowned repertoire, the story once again graced the front pages of primary news sources.

It was a shocking déjà vu, except this time, it was welcomed with open arms.

Sophie sat behind her desk, Marilyn and James crouched behind her as she scrolled down the list.

She covered her mouth with a hand. "This is..."

Oh, God, she was going to start crying again.

The article was *exactly* what she wanted and needed. It didn't even come close to putting her or James into a negative spotlight.

The journalist somehow wound their quotes and Jackie's into beautiful paragraphs that explained the situation perfectly.

There were no twists or turns, no darkened corners for misunderstandings to happen.

Beaming, she turned to kiss James deeply.

"We did it," she murmured against his lips.

He pulled back to kiss her forehead and beamed. "No, *you* did it."

Sophie chuckled and glanced at Marilyn.

A satisfied smile glinted on her boss's face, and she crossed her arms. "I'm so glad this worked out. You really handled this with grace, Sophie, and I'm proud of you. But what about Jackie? Are we just going to let her get away?"

James cleared his throat and fiddled with the dazzling watch on his wrist. "Don't worry about her. I've got it under control."

"Right, you mentioned that friend of yours." Marilyn sighed.

"I wouldn't call the commissioner a friend, but yes," James said. "If Jackie doesn't want trouble, then we shouldn't be hearing from her again."

"I see. Well, there's something to be said about that,"

Marilyn began. "But ... since you aren't Covey's client anymore, I can't stop you."

Weights tied themselves to Sophie's heart, dragging it down into her stomach to drown.

That's right, he's done with Covey.

But ... what about them?

She put off giving him a definitive answer because the thought gave her a headache, and it still did. But if she was being honest with herself, the obvious answer had stared her in the face for too long.

She curled her fists in her lap, using the pain of her nails digging into her palm to ground herself.

"Marilyn, can we have the room for a minute?" Sophie asked. "I need to talk to James."

He stared at her, brows knitted.

Marilyn's gaze flicked between them, but she nodded and grasped Sophie's shoulder for a moment before stepping out.

The minute the door closed, Sophie slowly pushed herself up from her chair and faced him. "We're done."

Thirty-One

James

If freeze frames could happen in real life, he was damn well engulfed in one.

Seconds ticked by, and words balanced on his tongue but stayed there instead of tumbling out. He blinked. "Excuse me?"

"I said we're done." Her voice wobbled, and she clenched her jaw, gesturing to her office door. "Well. You know the way out, don't you? Keep in touch, Mr. Tian."

His feet grew roots. "What?"

"If you are ever in need of our services again, please don't hesitate to reach out," she said thickly. "And we would appreciate it if you could recommend us to any associates you have."

She can't be serious, can she?

She turned away from him, staring out the window, but he caught the tremble in her lips.

"Sophie," he murmured. His feet finally deigned to move, dragging over the worn carpet lining her office floor. And even though he wanted to take her in his arms, his hands remained at his sides.

She shifted a little to reveal lips pressed so tight, they were practically nonexistent.

"Look at me, bǎobèi."

After a moment, she met his gaze. Tears rimmed her eyes, threatening to fall with each blink, and she crossed her arms as she perched on her desk. "Don't call me that. Not anymore."

A sickening feeling crawled into his belly and died there. "Why not?"

"Because it's inappropriate to do so. " She sniffed and dabbed at her eyes with a tissue. "So please, stop and show yourself out."

An arrow launched itself into his chest. No, a fucking sledgehammer, and her flat tone worsened the blow.

"When did we decide it was over?" he demanded. His voice rose slightly, and black crept into his vision. "After everything we went through, when–why would we decide that?!"

She shook her head. "*We* didn't decide anything, James."

"What?!"

"*I* did. You asked me to, remember?" She stopped in front of him. "I think I always had this answer, and I just never wanted to face it. The article changed that, and I understand why you would want to walk out. I get why you want to dust your hands of everything."

His eyes rounded, and his pulse raced. "What?! What are you talking about?"

Chest heaving, she hugged herself tight. "Did you forget already? What I said about you, the money, and power?" She lifted her chin slightly. "It is *always* the woman's fault, even when it's not. I'm only going to drag you down, and you don't deserve that."

He rested a hand on her desk, mind reeling. "Sophie–"

She held up a hand. "Like I said, the article made me think about what's on the line for *you*. Everything you've done so far has been to finally prove to your family that you don't need them to be successful. I can't just let you throw all that away over me. Over a nobody when there are so many better women out there that could help lift you, and–"

"Is that what you think?" he cut in. "That you don't matter?"

"Yes," she admitted after a moment. "I mean, look at you

in conjunction with me. Don't tell me that hasn't crossed your mind before."

He frowned as her voice hissed in his head. *'James, you have money and power ... you're a good-looking man who's barely older, but they'll take those five years and blow them into fifty.'*

His dad's voice joined hers, swirling in the muck. *'She's just a woman with nothing to her name. She doesn't matter in our world.'*

On top of it all, she'd been left one too many times and told she was better in retrospect.

And he unintentionally added to that.

N*o wonder she's reacting like this.* He gritted his teeth.

The smooth wood under his palm grounded him, and he curled his fingers into a fist, fixating on the tiny succulent she kept next to her computer.

"I don't care," James whispered. "I'm not leaving you."

"What?"

"I don't care," he repeated. "I'm not leaving you, or us. I'm not leaving, period."

Yes, he would have no problem finding someone to date him.

But the problem was they wouldn't be with him like Sophie was. They wouldn't share her smile or dry humor. They wouldn't love him for *his* accomplishments, but rather his father's.

Her lip quivered as she stared at him. "But–"

"No." He strode to her, stilling his hands before they could reach for her. "Sophie, why would I want to leave when *you're* all I want?"

She stared up at him before curling her arms around his waist. "What if–what if we run, and they catch up?"

Tension melted from his shoulders, and he pulled her close. Cradling the back of her neck, he dropped a quick kiss to the top of her head. "Then we let them."

Her cheek pressed into his shoulder. "And what if you get tired of me?"

He shook his head. *I understand why she believes that, but...*

He'd gladly walk through Hell and back if it meant he could spend forever with her. She was his alluring obsession, his sweetest infatuation.

She might've gotten used to being a simple recollection, but it was far past time he changed that.

His hold tightened. "Like I could."

A smile painted her lips and she kissed him like she was about to take her dying breath.

He melted into her, a brightness bubbling in his chest and buoying there.

Thirty-Two

Sophie

One Month Later

Stopping outside the Guggenheim, they posed as camera flashes went off, and a crowd of journalists and paparazzi roared.

Sophie dusted off the skirts of the ruby red dress she wore and wrapped an arm around James's waist. Her fingers curled around the silky material of his dashing Tom Ford suit.

For the past month, they'd been present at every charity, gala, and fundraising event that crossed either Lotus or Covey's inboxes. A week after their fix, they attended Lina and Adam's wedding in Granada.

As with the other events, pictures had been taken and posted in various media outlets. Although no unsavory headlines graced the front pages, it didn't mean they didn't exist.

What she and James had gone through would give chase the rest of their lives. But it was a crux they'd learned to accept.

"This is giving me flashbacks," she remarked. Her skirts swished around her legs, and she blinked away the bright pops that lingered behind her eyelids.

He hummed, stopping in front of the sign bearing the table numbers. "To the last event we went to?"

She nodded. "That, and that first gala when you were still working with Covey."

"That makes sense," he said. "But I liked the dress from last time more on you."

A flush crept across her cheeks as she remembered exactly *how* much he liked that dress.

Her heels clacked against the terrazzo floors as they crossed the room. "Yes, but it would look bad to wear the same thing twice in a row to something like this."

Elegant lighting lit the surroundings, and classical music flowed from hidden speakers.

Sophie nodded to a few people she recognized before glancing at James, cocking her head. "Why are you looking at me like that?"

"This is much better than that first gala," he said.

Her lips quirked. "Oh? Enlighten me, Mr. Tian."

"For starters, I get to do this," he said. He pulled her closer to his side.

Even though they had stopped, she still tripped over her own feet. Slamming into his chest, she hastily pushed off of him. "Sorry."

"Don't be," he murmured. "We don't have to hide it anymore."

She smiled, tilting her head toward his. "No, we don't."

Epilogue
Sophie

Ten Years Later

"Hey, why did Sammy just say my cock is like her dad's?" Philip demanded, his voice echoing on speakerphone. "And now she keeps saying it to Mari."

Sophie burst into laughter, clutching onto the lip of one of her shelves for stability. "Oh, my God, I forgot to tell you about that."

"Tell me about what?!" His panic was evident. "Stop laughing, and *help me*. Seriously, you know my heart's fragile."

"She's saying your watch is like her dad's. The clock." Sophie grinned as she finished packing her bag. She shrugged on her coat and shook her hair out. "Do your kids not do this?"

"*No*. They just started talking, remember?"

"Well, savor the moment." She chuckled. "Next thing you know, they'll be two-years-old and saying it for the first time to their grandfather at a family dinner. Adam almost choked to death on a meatball, and James and I had to leave the room because we were laughing so badly."

Philip huffed a laugh. "I'd have paid good money to be a fly on the wall."

"I think your sister got part of it on video. Actually, I'm

surprised no one's mentioned it to you before," Sophie remarked.

He hummed. "James probably did and I forgot. I'm forgetting more things these days with how busy I am."

"Yeah, I just think you're getting old."

"I'm going to pretend you didn't just say that to me." He sniffed. "Anyway, hang on."

He called something to Mari in Spanish.

"Okay, I'm back," he said. "Why did James's face look like a tattoo session gone wrong?"

"That would be because while he was asleep, Jack and Violet took advantage of the markers my mom got him for his birthday." Sophie winced, remembering the fiasco. "In their defense, they *are* supposed to be washable. We just didn't think it'd take so long to fade. Thanks for watching the kids tonight, by the way. You and Mari have your work cut out."

Sophie's kids could be wild enough on their own. But when you tossed them in a room with their cousins, it was worse.

"It's fine, just enjoy yourselves tonight." Philip gasped and raised his voice. "Xavi, Sierra, put those down! Do you want your mother to yell at you?! Sorry, Sophie, I gotta go."

Sophie laughed. "Alright, thanks."

She hung up and stepped into an empty elevator, jabbing the button for the lobby. Her phone buzzed, and she swiped into the message from Marilyn.

> Happy anniversary!

Sophie thanked her former boss and stared at Marilyn's small contact photo.

It'd been taken on Sophie's last day at Covey, the women's twin smiles immortalizing a golden afternoon.

Six years after the scandal, Sophie had left and struck out on her own. It'd been a significant risk, but she shouldn't have worried as much. She was skilled at what she did, and the few clients she brought along with her spread the word about how great she was. Soon, Focus PR Management boomed with success and became one of the top PR firms in the city.

The elevator slid open into the lobby, and she strode across the lobby, her heels clicking against the tile.

"A one-on-one with the CEO? Wow, what did I do to deserve this honor?"

She glanced at James's tall frame crossing the lobby, a bouquet of violets in one hand. A slight smile tilted his mouth before he leaned down and kissed her.

"You'll be getting more than a typical one-on-one if you play your cards right." She winked and took the flowers.

He grinned and intertwined their fingers, tugging her outside and toward the private car waiting by the curb. He helped her before heading for the other side.

Her phone pinged, and she hummed as an email rolled into her inbox. She clicked in and read it, chewing on the inside of her cheek.

"Stop that," he said as the car pulled away.

"I know, sorry. I'm just going to read this and–"

"No, you're not." Leaning over, he clicked her phone off.

"Hey!"

"Sophie, we both know where this is going," he said. "Reading it is just going to lead to answering it, which is going to lead to you working on it right now. This is your personal time, and I want my wife, not the CEO."

She sighed and slid her phone into her pocket. "Alright, alright. Where are we going?"

He smoothed the pad of his thumb in circles over the back of her hand. "We have a reservation at La Lanterna, and I booked a room at this hotel downtown for the night. Adam suggested it, actually. He and Lina stayed there for their fifth anniversary."

"I still can't believe you listen to your brother now." Sophie smiled. "Also, La Lanterna? Aren't they booked solid for months?"

"Yes, well. Parker's a friend."

"Oh, right, right." She shook her head and leaned against James's arm.

It didn't matter that she'd been a part of the one percent for ten years, she would never get used to the strings they were able to pull because of it.

Her phone buzzed again, and she pulled it back out, frowning as she read the contact name.

"Mari? What's wrong?" Sophie asked the moment she slid to answer.

"Nothing, don't worry," Mariana said. "Your kids just want a bedtime story."

"You got them in bed already?" Sophie asked. "Which God did you have to pray to for that miracle?"

"It was surprisingly easy."

She sighed. "Of course it was."

She loved the little rascals, but her patience was regularly tested. But, unsurprisingly, they were little angels for their aunt.

"Okay, put the phone on speaker?" Sophie motioned for James to put up the privacy divider between them and the driver as she hit the speaker button.

"Mommy, Daddy, we miss you," Violet said.

"I know, xiǎo bāo, but we'll see you and your siblings tomorrow morning," Sophie soothed. "Your aunt already told me you guys got in bed easy-peasy tonight. Can you keep up that good behavior?"

"If you do, I'll tell your uncle to make those waffles you guys like so much for breakfast," James added.

"He already is," Mari said. "Talked my ear off about them before."

Sophie laughed. "Alright, which story do you guys want?"

"The princess and dragon one!" Samantha piped.

"Yeah, the princess one!" Jack agreed with his twin in the background.

"I'm sure your aunt already told you guys a nice story," James said.

"Yeah, but it's different," Violet explained.

"Fair point." He grinned. "Okay. Once upon a time, there was a big, scary dragon named Adam–"

"*James*," Sophie cut in.

"Alright, sorry, sorry," he apologized, laughing. He rolled out the story, nudging Sophie at points to chime in with little details.

"And they lived happily ever after," Sophie finished. "Go to sleep, guys. Your father and I love you so much, and we'll see you in the morning. Mari, kiss them for us."

"Absolutely," Mariana promised.

After hanging up, Sophie sighed in contentment and leaned back against the seats. She was a firm believer in the fact that you didn't experience the highs of Life without first going through the lows. It took some time, but now, she soared.

"Are you alright?" James asked, settling his hand on her knee.

"Yes," Sophie confirmed, holding onto his arm with both hands and snuggling into him. "I'm just happy, is all."

He blinked, then smiled, and pressed a kiss to her temple. "We did good, Sophie."

"Yes, we did," she murmured, her lips curving upward.

Acknowledgments

To me, acknowledgements were always like an unattainable dream. They were something you admired from afar, but knew there was a minuscule chance that you yourself would ever get to touch them.

Until it came time to write my *own* acknowledgements and I had an 'Oh, my God, this is *real*' moment. (To be honest, I'm still having that moment).

There are *so* many people to thank and not enough words in the universe to do it, but I'll try my best.

To my family, thank you for being the best support system, and for giving me the time and space to work. There were so many opportunities for you to complain as I typed away, but you never once did. I love you so much.

To Alex, Tina, and the whole team at Rising Action Publishing–thank you from the bottom of my heart. Thank you for all the hard work and for taking a chance on me. Your support and what you have done for this book are unparalleled. Without you, I would not have made it this far, and I will never be able to convey just how grateful I am to you for everything you've done.

To Amy, we've seen Taylor Swift, Cinderella Castle, and so much more together. It was fitting, then, that you were one of the first people to hear this idea (and the one before it). You didn't understand what I was rambling on about, but you were always supportive and my biggest cheerleader since the start. Thank you so much!

To Sara and Kyra, the three of us were coming up with unhinged fantasy stories in third grade, and here we are over a decade later, still doing it in our own ways. Thank you so much for being there over the years and for hearing my insane ideas out.

To Adam and Lauren, thank you two for always listening with a smile and offering to help in any way you could. It means everything to me.

To Alex M., thank you so much for all your support and for entertaining my late-night ramblings and unhinged fun facts. You're always there with a smile and a shouted encouragement when things get heavy, and your unwavering belief and support in Sophie and James's story mean the world to me. And thank you for introducing me to the Goblin: The Lonely and Great God OST to make me emotional just as I was preparing to make things 10,000 times sadder.

To the train–Aleshka, Allissa, Brenna, Cara, Elizabeth, Emily, Haley, Isabelle, Katie G., Katie J., Kelsey, Lex, Lindsay, Makayla, and Megan–I love you all so much. Thank you for your endless support and kindness and for changing my life for the better.

To Lex, you know what this is. A BILLIONAIRE ROMANCE.

To Makayla, may you always receive unlimited sofas, candy canes, and unhinged Bibble memes.

To Megan, you will always be my little soda pop.

To Lindsay, I live for your unhinged commentary, and you ghosting after dropping something huge. Never change.

To Goldfish Flavor Blasted Xtra Cheddar (not sponsored), thank you for always having my back during late-night editing sessions. You're a real one.

To Destinee and Ola, thank you for being early, early readers. The first five chapters are so different from what you read, but I know things wouldn't have turned out the way they did without you guys.

To Audrey Goldberg Ruoff, thank you so much for your kindness and support. Your feedback on Wrong Order helped shape it so much and find its home. I genuinely don't think I would've made it this far on this story otherwise.

To Rebecca, thank you for supporting me indefinitely and for sharing my love of books. When I rediscovered my love for reading during the pandemic (as so many of us did), you were there to lend an ear and ramble just as enthusiastically about fictional worlds (and you still are, which I love!)

To Elizabeth, for whom this book is partially dedicated, thank you so, so much. I remember you being among the first I told about this wild idea, and you loved it from the start. Thank you for giving this piece a title that's fitting in more ways than one. And thank you for always showing up despite our hectic class schedules and for helping me brainstorm as we gossiped and emptied a bottle of wine.

To Nilda, the other person for whom this book is dedicated, thank you for more than you know. When I seriously got into writing, you encouraged it instead of dismissing it, and I will always appreciate that. You were the first to tell me about the publishing industry and the person who jump-started my querying journey, and I will forever be grateful.

To Michelle and Christina, thank you for encouraging me and my writing. Your support means so much, and I'll always be appreciative.

And finally, to little Alice, who started out writing short stories in elementary school. People are going to tell you they're silly and to stop. They're going to tease you for always having your nose in a book. But it's very important that you don't listen, and do it anyway, because you would never be here otherwise.

About the Author

Alice Li is an Asian-American author who writes romantic comedies featuring BIPOC leads. She loves incorporating a perfect mix of humor, heat, and sweetness in her stories. She graduated from the University of Connecticut where she obtained her Bachelor's Degree in Psychology. When she's not writing, she can be found drinking way too much coffee, listening to Taylor Swift, and baking up a storm. *Wrong Order* is her debut novel.